THE PROFESSIONAL IDEAL
IN THE VICTORIAN NOVEL

THE PROFESSIONAL IDEAL IN THE VICTORIAN NOVEL

THE WORKS OF DISRAELI, TROLLOPE, GASKELL, AND ELIOT

Susan E. Colón

palgrave
macmillan

THE PROFESSIONAL IDEAL IN THE VICTORIAN NOVEL
© Susan E. Colón, 2007.

First published in 2007 by
PALGRAVE MACMILLAN™
175 Fifth Avenue, New York, N.Y. 10010 and
Houndmills, Basingstoke, Hampshire, England RG21 6XS
Companies and representatives throughout the world.

PALGRAVE MACMILLAN is the global academic imprint of the Palgrave Macmillan division of St. Martin's Press, LLC and of Palgrave Macmillan Ltd. Macmillan® is a registered trademark in the United States, United Kingdom and other countries. Palgrave is a registered trademark in the European Union and other countries.

ISBN-13: 978–1–4039–7613–0
ISBN-10: 1–4039–7613–9

Library of Congress Cataloging-in-Publication Data is available from the Library of Congress.

A catalogue record for this book is available from the British Library.

Design by Newgen Imaging Systems (P) Ltd., Chennai, India.

First edition: May 2007

10 9 8 7 6 5 4 3 2 1

Printed in the United States of America.

For Carlos

CONTENTS

ACKNOWLEDGMENTS

If, as Elizabeth Blackwell said, hope is "the realization of the unseen, which foresees the adult in the infant, the future in the present," this book is the product of many hopeful colleagues, friends, and family. I have been surrounded by people who insisted on seeing, and making me see, a completed book in the half-formed ideas and fragments of text with which it began.

My foremost professional debt is to Barry J. Faulk, my graduate mentor, whose generosity, insight, and patience I cannot possibly do justice to. In true Socratic fashion Barry has midwived this project, reading countless drafts and providing judicious and discriminating feedback. Fred Standley and Eric Walker also contributed to the genesis of this book in their guidance of and responses to my dissertation. I completed much of the research for this project while supported by a Florida State University Graduate Fellowship.

I have been fortunate to be nurtured in an academic environment that enacts the best of professional ideals. Baylor University's Honors College has provided me with mentoring, autonomy, material support, and a richly collegial context in which to work, take risks, and develop as a scholar, teacher, and person. The Honors College has provided both the high expectations to spur achievement and the tangible and intangible support to make success possible. I especially thank my faculty mentors David Jeffrey, Alden Smith, Thomas Hibbs, and Stephen Prickett for their wise and timely counsel respecting all aspects of the scholarly life. I am grateful to Elizabeth Vardaman for her endless encouragement and for her responses to individual chapters, and to Peaches Henry for her reading of a portion of the draft. The staff of the Armstrong Browning Library, especially Cynthia Burgess, was unfailingly helpful and cheerful. The students in my two first-year seminars on professionalism helped me with their lively discussions—and disputations—on the subjects and texts here discussed.

Palgrave's contracted reviewer also exhibited hope in his or her thorough reading, showing me both what the book was and what it could become. The audiences of various conference presentations, including at VISAWUS 2003 and NAVSA 2005 and 2006, contributed important questions and ideas to earlier stages of this material. The anonymous reviewers of *Studies in the Novel* and *Women's Writing* helped me hone my ideas and the expression thereof.

Of course, it is my parents Larry and Becky Burrow who literally saw the adult in the infant and accordingly sacrificed for my education while teaching me, by example and precept, to pursue both excellence and service in my vocation. This book is a testament to their hopefulness. My beautiful twin girls, Elise and Monica, were born with this book and are by now writing "books" of their own (often on the backs of pages generated from drafts of this one). Finally, this book would not have been written apart from my dear husband Carlos Colón. He never lost hope that this book would be realized, though on more than one occasion he had to talk me out of abandoning it. He has always urged me and enabled me to make my passion my vocation, and so this book is dedicated to him.

*   *   *

Portions of chapter 5 are republished from *Studies in the Novel*, v. 37, no. 3, Fall 2005, pp. 292–307. Copyright © 2005 by the University of North Texas. Reprinted by permission of the publisher. Portions of chapter 3 are republished from *Women's Writing*, v. 13, no. 3, October 2006, pp. 475–494. Copyright © 2006 by Taylor & Francis. Reprinted by permission of the publisher.

INTRODUCTION: COOL HEADS
AND WARM HEARTS

It will be my most cherished ambition, my highest endeavor, . . . to increase the numbers of those, whom Cambridge, the great mother of strong men, sends out into the world with cool heads but warm hearts, willing to give at least some of their best powers to grappling with the social suffering around them.

Alfred Marshall, "The Present Position of Economics" (1885)

In his inaugural lecture for the chair of Economics at Cambridge, Alfred Marshall announced in ringing terms that his "most cherished ambition" was the preparation of future professionals who would bring their specialized expertise to bear on the social problems of the nation and empire.[1] Marshall spoke at a historical moment when the growing hegemony of professionals had become readily observable in most if not all areas of social leadership. Among the complex factors that made the professional class ideal persuasive and successful was the very passion articulated by Marshall: a zeal to combine rational expertise with sympathetic service in order to make the world a better place. The products of Marshall's ideal Cambridge education will be not only equipped with the specialized training to advance the nation's economic, social, scientific, and military interests, but they will also be formed in an ethic that assumes that the holder of specialized skills has an obligation to use those skills for the wider public good and not only for private benefit. Marshall wants for Cambridge to inculcate both professional skills and the professional ethos.

Marshall's lecture opens with a genial critique of the previous generation of economists, led by David Ricardo, for their exclusively materialist approach to their subject: they came to "regard labour simply as a commodity . . . without allowing for [the workman's] human passions, his instincts and habits, his sympathies and antipathies," and so on. The economists required the corrective influence of the early socialists, whose exaggerated rhapsodies never-theless addressed "the hidden springs of human action of which the economists took no account."[2] In other words, modern or enlight-ened economic study such as Marshall declares himself to undertake consists of a dialectic between the market and the "human passions" that are irreducible to market data.

This dialectic is later in the lecture folded into the very definition of the university-trained professional. With the assertion that the task of Cambridge is to foster men who combine "cool heads" with "warm hearts," Marshall assumes the complementarity of expertise and sympathy in the context of professional work. The close relation-ship between materialist analysis and idealist aims is conveyed again in a later essay, "Social Possibilities of Economic Chivalry" (1907).[3] Here Marshall asks his audience to consider what "careful, thorough, persistent study . . . can do towards helping the world to turn its growing resources to the best account for social well-being."[4] The title phrase "economic chivalry," a sort of reincarnation of John Ruskin's honorable merchant from "Roots of Honor," is another symbolic attempt to unite the seemingly disparate domains of head and heart.

Marshall's assumptions will seem counterintuitive to those who regard the category of the professional as the inheritance exclusively of secular modernity. They are, however, congruent with the view of professionalism that emerges from the fictional scene in the mid-Victorian decades. This study will argue for the need to understand Victorian professionalism in the light of its persistent relationship to ideals shaped by premodern and nonmarket sensibilities in tension with modern, market-driven notions of the division of labor.

The Professional Ideal in the Victorian Novel is not another social history of Victorian professionalism, nor is it a comprehensive survey of literary representations of the same.[5] Rather, it is an in-depth treat-ment of one particular aspect of the professional project, the profes-sional ideal, at a crucial moment in the history of that ideal and of professionalism in general. Hence I have selected figures whose engagements with the problems of the professional ideal illuminate complications within that ideal. Of course, this investigation will have implications for a social history of the professions. Previous social histories of professionalism have treated the mid-Victorian decades of the 1850s, 1860s, and 1870s as the heyday of the entrepreneur and have consequently all but ignored the discursive activity in service of the professional ideal during this time. I will argue that these mid-Victorian novels reveal not only a preoccupation with the

professional ideal but also an impulse to supply imaginative solutions
to problems that inhere in this ideal.

Since Harold Perkin's influential histories of professional society,
literary scholars have filled out the mid-Victorian decades with attention to the implicit and explicit theorizing about professionalism that
occurred in realist fiction.[6] Though they have not always directly
drawn the point, their studies collectively reveal that the professional
class did not wait until the last two decades of the nineteenth century
to develop self-understanding as differentiated from the entrepreneurial class. Rather, as Daniel Duman has argued, emergent
professional ideology "evolve[d] contemporaneously with the
[Benthamite] drive for efficiency and reform" in mid-century.[7] In
spite of Duman's sociological approach and tools, his evidence for
this early and sometimes self-conscious development of the professional ideal is primarily literary.[8] This is not coincidental: the working
out of the professional ideal and its implications was a preeminently
literary endeavor.

The visibility of the professional class and its ideals is attested in a
number of nineteenth-century novels, beginning at least as early
as Jane Austen (*Mansfield Park* and *Persuasion*, in particular) and
continuing through the mid-century realist novels of Charles Dickens,
William Thackeray, the Brontës, and Wilkie Collins, among others.
Since visibility is not the same thing as self-reflexivity, however, I have
chosen to focus on a handful of figures and texts whose contributions
to the Victorian discourse about professionalism can be seen in their
readiness not only to represent but also to problematize the
professional project, recording and commenting on its complex
relationship to idealist and materialist rationalities.

The novel therefore has an important and under-recognized role to
play in the development of the professional ideal, which must be seen
as an important constitutive element of the Victorian middle class.
The novels of Benjamin Disraeli, Anthony Trollope, Elizabeth
Gaskell, and George Eliot can be seen as occasions for examination
and definition of their class by authors concerned to work out problems that pertain to the emergent professional ideal. Their fictions
raise, and seek to answer, such questions as follows: How does professionalism relate to the materialist and idealist rationalities that impinge
on it and its aims? What effect does the formation of professional associations have on the autonomy of the individual practitioner with
respect to the association, and on the autonomy of the association
itself with respect to the state? What is the status of women with
respect to the ideal? How are the expertise and ethos of professional

culture to be transmitted to each new generation of practitioners, and what are the pitfalls inherent to that process? What are the contours of the famed service ethic of professionals: what are its legitimate claims and its legitimate limitations?

These novels attest that the professional ideal itself was under meaningful scrutiny concurrently with its formation. Drawing on Amanda Anderson's claims in *Powers of Distance* for a greater level of self-critical reflection among the Victorians than has usually been ascribed to them, I will uncover a nascent culture of professional self-critique in these fictional representations, a culture that hinges upon a robust idealist view of professional life. Such scrutiny was of course not confined to fiction, however. Hence I will also attend to nonliterary primary sources that illuminate contemporaneous ways of thinking about the same problems central to the novels' representation of professionalism. It is for this reason that I conclude with an in-depth analysis of the life and writings of Octavia Hill, who, I will show, exemplifies the very tensions under investigation in the earlier chapters.

I

In the effort to understand the discursive activity pertaining to the professional ideal, we must begin by recognizing that the ideal defined itself in relation to the ideals of the aristocracy, the working class, and the entrepreneurial class. Still the best description of these phenomena is available from Harold Perkin. *The Origins of Modern English Society* describes how, out of the social cataclysm that was the Industrial Revolution, the modern idea of class was born. As classes engaged in the struggle to appropriate for themselves a larger share of scarce resources, they developed characteristic modes of explaining their position within and contribution to the social order, and concurrently, of justifying their own claim to a position of leadership and privilege. Perkin therefore finds that in the 1830s and 1840s, there were three conflicting versions of the social good: the aristocratic ideal, the entrepreneurial ideal, and the working-class ideal. The ideal of each class "sublimated the crude material self-interest of the competition for income, sanctified the role of class members by the contribution they made to society and its well-being, and so justified the class and its claim to a special place and special treatment within the social framework."[9] Nothing less than societal hegemony was at stake in this contest of ideals.

The aristocratic ideal, rooted in feudalism, militarism, and chivalry, argued that the aristocracy's traditional chivalric virtues made it the nation's best safeguard of Britain's historical values and economic interests. Landed aristocrats, free from the acquisitive mania of the commercial classes, had the leisure, the intellectual capacity, and the honor to best represent and protect the interests of the country at large. Moreover, the noblesse oblige of the aristocracy was the best guarantor of the rights and privileges of the poor. The aristocratic ideal experienced a revival in the 1810s and 1820s, which eventually and briefly coalesced in Disraeli's Young England movement of the 1840s. The entrepreneurial ideal, grounded in Benthamite utilitarianism and classical political economy, derided hereditary privilege and instead propagated the myth of the self-made man. It held that capitalistic competition would result in the natural selection of the most meritorious contenders. The entrepreneurial ideal viewed laborers as debased and landowners as criminally idle, and celebrated instead the active owner-manager of capital resources, whose enterprising spirit created both wealth and goods for the nation. In Perkin's reading, the New Poor Law of 1834, with its undermining of traditional entitlements owed by the aristocracy to the poor and its ruthless insistence on efficiency, represented a triumph of Benthamite rationality.[10] The working-class ideal was less coherent, in that various elements within this class argued for different ends and sought different allies from among the other two classes, but on the whole its proponents emphasized the nobility and importance of the laborers' contribution and insisted on the worker's right to enjoy the produce of his labor.

A fourth group, which Perkin labels "the forgotten middle class," consisted of the "non-capitalist or professional middle class."[11] Perkin draws attention to the irony that this group was generally ignored by social theorists, yet it supplied the personnel who argued the merits of the other three ideals. In other words, the discourse in which the conflict of the ideals was debated was supplied largely by "social cranks"—professionals who aligned themselves with one of the other three classes.[12] Perkin finds, not surprisingly, that the arguments made by professionals on behalf of another class gradually amalgamated toward a fourth ideal, the professional ideal:

> [P]rofessional men had a separate, if sometimes subconscious, social ideal which underlay their versions of the other class ideals. Their ideal society was a functional one based on expertise and selection by merit. For them trained and qualified expertise rather than property, capital or labor, should be the chief determinant and justification of status and power in society.[13]

Eventually, the professional ideal displaced the other three ideals that the professionals had previously adopted and defended.

Perkin's account of the ideals and the competition among them is compelling, and it is quite useful in situating the literary and social analysis I am undertaking. I will show, for example, that Disraeli and Trollope are both, in different ways, social cranks whose versions of the aristocratic ideal are significantly infused with the professional ideal. However, Perkin's approach and priorities lead him to neglect important aspects of the experience, self-definition, and self-perception of the professional middle class during the mid-Victorian decades. He tends to conflate the professional middle class generally with the subset of active advocates of one of the other three ideals. Alternatively, as seen above, he effectively subsumes ordinary professional practitioners into the entrepreneurial class, claiming that the professional middle class "could be readily accommodated under the entrepreneurial ideal" because it "left itself out of its own versions of the class structure" and because its members "lived and worked amongst urban business men who differed very little from themselves in basic outlook and way of life."[14]

When describing the working-class ideal, Perkin notes that it "was ambiguous in itself and led to diverse and conflicting means of pursuing it."[15] His genealogy of the aristocratic ideal similarly observes at least two major strains of thought: the politico-economic justifications of Thomas Robert Malthus and the paternalist ethos of Michael Thomas Sadler. Perkin describes no such conflict within the mid-Victorian professional ideal, but I find that the professional ideal is similarly, though perhaps less obviously, internally contested. This study will therefore regard "the professional ideal" as in fact a cluster of ideals, especially including esoteric expertise, specialized training, autonomous work, meritocratic selection and promotion, and public service. This approach will allow us to consider how professional ideals were constituted not only in opposition to the other ideals but also with respect to their own contradictions. My reading of *Barchester Towers*, for example, emphasizes the imaginative distance Trollope creates between the entrepreneurial/Benthamite Evangelicals and their professional/aristocratic High Church opponents. My reading of *Daniel Deronda*, on the other hand, examines the internal contradictions of the professional service ethic.

More importantly, Perkin's materialist tools of analysis limit his ability to theorize the class ideals as anything other than sublimated self-interest, defined economically. Ironically, given that Perkin's formulation of the class ideals is so influential, Perkin's flattened understanding of idealism as false consciousness leads him to shortchange the centrality and persistence of idealism to the professional project. Hence in *The Rise of Professional Society: England Since 1880*, Perkin describes the professional project as the effort to "raise [professionals'] status and through it their income, authority and psychic rewards (deference and self-respect). With luck and persistence they may turn the human capital they acquire into material wealth." The means to this end are "persuasion and propaganda, . . . claiming that their particular service is indispensable to the client or employer and to society and the state."[16] Magali Sarfatti Larson lodges a similar critique, explaining how professional ideals were mystified so as to allow the functional linkage between education and the marketplace to justify "inequality of status and closure of access in the occupational order."[17] Larson therefore sees the service ethic of professionalism as a strategy to increase demand and secure market control.[18] Burton Bledstein finds that "codes of ethics" were designed to protect fellow practitioners rather than the public.[19] The professionals he describes used their detachment and expertise to manipulate the anxieties of their clients as a way of securing their own prestige.

This class- and market-based reading of professionalism is an important part of the story of Victorian professionalization. However, as is well-known, professionalism has long been something of an enigma to Marxist analysis. I suggest that this difficulty arises not only because the professional class is hard to situate in terms of labor and capital but also because of its investments in premodern sensibilities that resist market-based analysis. As Barbara and John Ehrenreich show, professionals understood as occupational groups cannot be simply aligned with either the laboring class or the capitalist class. The Ehrenreichs' revision of class theory distinguishes the professional-managerial class (PMC) by its function in relation to the capitalist class (reproducing the social division of labor) rather than by occupational group. As they define it, the PMC cannot "be considered to be a 'residual' class like the petty bourgeoisie; it is a formulation specific to the monopoly stage of capitalism."[20] At the same time, they treat the petty bourgeoisie of self-employed professionals as a throwaway, rendered irrelevant in the modern era because of its premodern origins. Yet the persistence of what the Ehrenreichs call the petty bourgeoisie and its obvious close ties to the PMC problematize their analysis.

The Ehrenreichs also make the assumption, since vigorously challenged by Bruce Robbins, that the formation and growth of the PMC equates to the co-optation of professional functions by the capitalist class.

The Ehrenreichs are of course keenly aware of pockets of resistance to capitalist ends in the PMC, but they do not really account for it except by assuming a remnant of right-thinking (or rather left-thinking) political activists in the professions. By the late 1980s, the fading numbers and significance of that remnant had left Barbara Ehrenreich even more pessimistic of the progressive, not to mention revolutionary, potential of the PMC.[21] Their schemata also excludes any attempt to explain the existence of practicing professionals identifying with the political right who pursue socially progressive ends in their profession.

These gaps point us to the principal inadequacy in Marxist professional theory: its reduction of class ideals to sublimated economic interest is an insufficiently historicized explanation for the centrality of idealism to the nineteenth-century professional project. Though professionalism participates in the modern division of labor that Marxism analyzes, it remains deeply invested in premodern idealist notions that are not reducible to class self-interest, as Samuel Haber's painstaking historicization of professional identity in the United States has shown. For Haber, professions "bring into the modern world ideals and standards that are premodern—both precapitalistic and predemocratic" and, I might add, presecularist.[22] As Rosemary O'Day puts it, "Rather than being characteristic of industrialization, then, the professions can be viewed more usefully as anachronistic phenomena existing in industrial, urban society, adapting to it and to some extent being modified by it."[23] A rigorously accurate picture of professionalization cannot, therefore, follow Marxism in "efforts to dissolve history into theory" (to return to Haber); rather, it must describe "mixed motives, composite conditions, as well as persons and parties acting upon contradictory explanatory schemes."[24] I will return shortly to the importance of "contradictory explanatory schemes," or what Lauren M. E. Goodlad calls "dueling worldviews," for understanding early British professionalism.

Materialist analysis cannot adequately account for such phenomena as the "culture of altruism" described by Stefan Collini in *Public Moralists.* Collini seems to be talking about readings of professionalism such as Larson's when he remarks that

> [h]istorians of the professions in this period have remarked on the implausibility of these bodies' claims to represent "altruistic" motives or an ethic of "service," and have often treated these claims as merely cynical. But a more complex intelligibility is restored to these claims when they are seen as a part of the [culture of altruism] I have been describing.[25]

Collini's formulation of the culture of altruism persuasively demonstrates that the Victorian moral vocabulary often required morally exemplary actions to be counter to economic self-interest. Collini, like some Victorians, is fully aware of how egoism can be justified in altruistic terms; nevertheless, he compellingly argues that acting against one's economic interest for the sake of a larger social good was regarded as an imperative duty by Victorians of all political and religious persuasions. The Marxist insistence on seeing all idealist formulations as smokescreens for self-interest simply does not do justice to Victorian realities.

Even where economic class interest and idealist notions of "duty" clearly coincide, however, we need not therefore automatically dismiss the idealism as disguised self-interest. Robbins's *Secular Vocations* energetically defends a view of modern labor in which professionalization is at least potentially compatible with a leftist social agenda. Deconstructing multiple narratives of a "fall" into professionalization from an imagined uncommodified practice of intellectual labor represented by the postwar "New York intellectual," Robbins explicates an array of "allegories of vocation" that diversely attest to the possibility of uniting social and political activism with professional careers.[26] Robbins scolds the left for having accepted the right's reflexive suspicion of all public work that results in private gain. Instead he maintains a position seemingly more natural to the left: that the vigorous self-critique within professions is evidence of the possibility that professions can serve progressive ends. Teachers' unions' support for free compulsory education is a case in point: such support was obviously in the teachers' economic interests, but it also met a working-class demand.[27]

The Professional Ideal in the Victorian Novel projects Robbins's critique of the critics of professionalism backward into the Victorian period. In doing so we find that Robbins's claims of the unity of professional critique and professional practice are anticipated by some Victorian formulations of professionalism. It is no accident that, as Robbins himself observes, "[i]n describing the force of these images, it is hard not to import the vocabulary of religion." His accounts of the "fall" into professionalism, the professional "jeremiad," and the relationship of "sin" to "vocation" reveal the need for a religious/transcendent conceptual vocabulary to explain aspects of professional theory and experience even in the modern expression of professionalism.[28] In fact, they make visible the reliance of professional structures of feeling on premodern, idealist notions that are not readily acknowledged by Marxist analysis.

Max Weber sees the Protestant theology leading to the development of "worldly asceticism" as relevant only to the early formation of the capitalist spirit, but irrelevant after the full institutionalization of capitalism from the eighteenth century forward.[29] However, the novels and other discourses of the mid-Victorians show clearly that ideals, even transcendent referents, remained important to the formulation of professionalism into the modern period. A more nuanced picture of this influence will improve our understanding of not only Victorian professionalism, but also of professionalism and its discontents today.

II

Haber's articulation of the mix of modern and premodern rationalities in American professionalism has no British counterpart. However, recent work on the importance of idealism to Victorian British sensibilities does something toward paving the way for the present investigation of literary treatments of the professional ideal.

Lauren Goodlad has uncovered not only that the meaningful distinction between the entrepreneurial and professional classes is necessary to an accurate understanding of the middle class itself and of its chief artistic contribution, the novel.[30] In *Victorian Literature and the Victorian State*, she has also explicated the valences of materiality and ideality that ideologically undergirded the bifurcated middle class, often in contradictory ways. In Goodlad's analysis, the progress toward the bureaucratization of English society, despite the momentum gained early in the century by Jeremy Bentham and his followers, was hindered by British idealist conceptions of local autonomy and personal character. She shows that the Benthamite materialist assumptions of political economy—particularly the anthropology of the *homo economicus*—were successfully resisted during the mid-Victorian decades by discourses of English "character," a powerful cluster of ideologies privileging local autonomy and positive, paternal, and interpersonal interventions to solve social problems. Goodlad's highly textured picture of Victorian "literature and society" is rendered in terms of "two antithetical, or 'dueling,' worldviews: one moral and idealist and the other materialist."[31] She further emphasizes that "all Victorians were, to some extent, syncretic thinkers drawing from two alternative worldviews, each of which made powerful claims to modern authenticity," and her description "demonstrate[s] much blurring both within and between each set of oppositions."[32]

For Goodlad's purposes in studying Foucauldian governmentality, this conception of the divided middle class explains much about the uneven and interrupted process of government expansion. Continental-style centralized bureaucratic apparatus was relatively slow arriving in Britain, where the impulse toward efficiency was checked by the impulse toward local control and intersubjective interventions. What has not yet been closely studied is the complex relationship of professionalism to both Benthamite and idealist sensibilities.

Goodlad's investigation is grounded in a critique of the reliance, exhibited by many leading Victorianists, on a paradigm based too prominently on Michel Foucault's *Discipline and Punish*, with Bentham's panopticon as its central symbol. She proposes instead a reconsideration of Foucault's later work on governmentality, with pastorship—voluntary social relations between classes conceived as a solution to social problems—as its central trope. Goodlad convincingly argues that Foucault's fundamental misunderstanding of Bentham's panopticon led him wrongly to ascribe to English governmental practice (or at least ambition) a set of governmental predilections normative on the Continent but still alien to English sensibility in the Victorian period. Foucault's later model of pastorship, more attuned to Britain's idiosyncratic prejudice against statist models of government, allows for a more nuanced reading of Victorian British discourses, fictional and nonfictional, about government.

For example, Goodlad's chapter on Thomas Chalmers and James Phillips Kay shows that a Foucauldian emphasis on the middle-class discipline and surveillance of the working class has the effect of flattening important distinctions between various mechanisms that formed the project of working-class embourgeoisement. Foucauldian critics have tended to conflate under the single rubric of "discipline" both the negative, deterrent tactics of Benthamites, such as Edwin Chadwick, and the positive, interventionist tactics of philanthropists, such as Chalmers. Instead, Goodlad distinguishes the "intersubjective ideal" of pastorship, whereby deeply personal relations between individuals of different classes were held to have a transformative effect by means of charisma, from the coercive modalities of Benthamite and Chadwickian deterrent methods. While the aim of both is "to make the working man like me," the difference in method and mentality undoubtedly remains significant.[33] The idealist rationality persisted as a powerful brake on statist solutions to social problems—and therefore on bureaucratic expansion—until late in the century.

This enriched understanding of the middle-class worldviews with respect to pauperism suggests what can be learned by a methodology more synchronic than genealogical. Crucially for my purposes, Goodlad notes that what Foucault almost dismissively describes as the

" 'residual themes of a religious or moral nature' " are in fact "far from residual" to the Victorians, actually comprising the central preoccupations of Victorian sages and novelists.[34] Moreover, Foucault's genealogical methodology, with its emphasis on disciplinary coercion of the subject by both hegemonic and putatively counterhegemonic forces, leaves no space to historicize relatively autonomous decisions and sensibilities.[35] As a result, the kind of self-reflexive scrutiny of professionalism that I argue occurs in these novels is elided in accounts of professionalism's history.

Tellingly, historical and literary treatments of professionalism dominated by paradigms drawn from *Discipline and Punish* tend to subsume all the cultural effects of professionalism into the expansion of disciplinary power over the subject. For example, Mary Poovey's discussion of the medical profession in *Uneven Developments* takes for granted that the debates about the essential nature of woman that swirled around the chloroform controversy were efforts to impose disciplinary power over women. The debates come off as a series of power grabs by various factions of the medical and clerical professions. D. A. Miller's well-known reading of *Barchester Towers* sees institutional conflict as a policing mechanism. The partisan struggles of the characters serve "not to resolve once for all the issues at hand, but to bind the combatants to the capacious institution that sponsors their disputes."[36] Professional relations discipline or regulate the professionals themselves and the city as a whole. The extent to which the key figures in the novel exhibit "character," or relatively autonomous moral agency, in their actions is elided in favor of Miller's notion of immanent, coercive power.

Jennifer Ruth is incisive in her critique of Foucauldian-influenced deconstructions of professional ideals, particularly disinterest. As she puts it, "Denouncing the professional, Victorianists fail to see that this figure's paradoxical position inside and outside the market—at once complicit and transcendent—is not a counterfeit but a dialectic—that is, a position that works both ways, enabling but also destabilizing the system within which it functions."[37] Ruth ably shows that there was no Victorian conspiracy to disguise the market basis of professional labor. Rather, an awareness of a tension between the market and the aesthetic economies was built into the Victorian professional self-conception. Once we quit playing gotcha with Victorian interestedness, thinking we discredit them every time we "discover" evidence of their interestedness, we can see the real work going on in the period to theorize a kind of labor that was both economic and transcendent, that both acquiesced to and resisted market logic.

However, the dialectic Ruth endeavors to elucidate strangely disappears from her analysis when she begins, in her final chapter, to fault Anderson for her failure to consider the material conditions that surround and characterize her instances of critical distance.[38] Essentially, Ruth returns to a one-sided theoretical model that sees economics as the basis, the real, on which all else is ideological superstructure. Having criticized Poovey for failing to regard the purported difference of aesthetic labor from economic labor as anything but "mere ideology,"[39] Ruth then criticizes Anderson for disguising materiality in idealist illusions. In short, the idealist or nonmarket side of the dialectic is again flattened into a vain reflection of the "real" market side of the dialectic. *The Professional Ideal in the Victorian Novel* keeps open the dialectic in professionalism between materialist and idealist rationalities in order to prevent flattening the existential tension between them that the Victorians experienced.

III

At this juncture it will be helpful to clarify the cluster of rationalities suggested by the terms "ideality" and "materiality." As I use it, materiality or materialism is aligned with Benthamism specifically and with the politico-economic rationality generally. In addition to a belief in a meritocratic system of rewards, the professional ideal shares with Benthamism a penchant for efficiency, including institutional assurances of competence. The economic rationality led Victorian practitioners to think of their occupations in terms of the commodification of expertise, the protection of markets, and the material rewards of their intellectual labor. There are good reasons why professionalism, with its emphasis on merit, expertise, and efficiency, has been seen as an inheritance of Benthamism, sharing Benthamite/Chadwickian methods and priorities. However, historians of professions have often elided important differences between Benthamite and professional values. For example, Perkin says that by accepting the doctrine of efficiency, reformers as diverse as Chadwick and Matthew Arnold "were, willy-nilly, Benthamites, conscious or unconscious."[40] In regarding these figures as more or less mystified materialists, Perkin shows again his inability to regard as important any other category beyond the economic. The bifurcated picture of the Victorian middle class, and the complexity of professionalism's various debts to diverse rationalities, is therefore neglected.

When I speak of "ideality" I refer to the overlapping religious, ethical, and transcendentalist convictions that structured much of Victorian life, including a belief in "character" or personal moral agency. Victorian professionalism retained important roots in traditional Christian notions of vocation: that is, of human obedience to a divine call to a particular mode of service to others. This rationality favored paternal pastorship of the public and made the service ethic central to the motivation and conduct of the practitioner. Goodlad's description of the idealist model of pastorship—locally directed and largely autonomous interpersonal interventions to cure social ills—bears strong resemblance to this important aspect of the professional project. For those to whom bureaucratic technocracy is coterminous with professionalism, the powerful check of ideality on bureaucratic expansion can be seen as an anti-professional development.[41] However, professionalism cannot be simply equated with bureaucracy. Rather, mid-Victorian professionalism could readily accommodate idealist notions of service and character that were at odds with Benthamite rationality. Gaskell's Margaret Hale, for example, the daughter of a shabby genteel former clergyman in *North and South*, quite naturally reverts to the language of aristocratic paternalism when disputing Mr. Thornton's defense of the entrepreneurial ideal. Similarly, in the Young England trilogy of Disraeli, the professional ethos of his aristocratic characters is imaginatively opposed to Benthamite assumptions and measures.

Moreover, a simple alignment with market rationality would hardly suit professional dignity, which retained powerful, if partially fictional, associations with gentility and its concomitant social obligations. To maintain a gentlemanly distance from trade, doctors and lawyers charged "honoraria" rather than fees; their incomes could therefore be thought of as independent of market forces. Jonathan Freedman therefore notes the importance to British professionalism of "differentiat[ing] themselves from what they saw as the acquisitive ethos of the mercantile classes or orders, and . . . conforming to the codes of behavior appropriate to the 'gentleman.' "[42] Geoffrey Searle shares Freedman's one-sided view of professionalism's disaggregation, in that he misleadingly describes the professional class's gradual separation from the "commercial world."[43]

In fact the disaggregation of professionalism occurred uneasily and simultaneously on two fronts: gradual separation from a religious rationality of vocation on one hand and from the commercial rationality of the market on the other.[44] As Duman puts it, "Collegiate institutions and the ideal of gentility and service co-existed with specialization, competition, and achievement orientation" in Victorian professionalism.[45] Goodlad has therefore rightly shown that the challenge facing the Victorian professional class was how to be "rational but unbureaucratic, omnipresent but personal, authoritative but liberatory, efficient but English."[46] The professional quandary was precisely how to marry these two powerful and convincing, but contradictory, rationalities of materialism and idealism. In other words, the essential problem of professionalism was how to maintain both a materialist's cool head and an idealist's warm heart.

Professionalism is an apposite subject to illuminate precisely the mix of rationalities that Goodlad painstakingly identifies, in that professionalism inhabits a unique space of tension between them. Fictional representations of professionalism from the time evince a sometimes uneasy collusion between materialist and idealist rationalities. Trollope's *The Warden*, for example, naturalizes resistance to statist intervention in the professional life of the Church precisely on the grounds that local and individual autonomy conduces to a higher standard of service to the public than could be attained by statist supervision. At the same time, the novel accepts the Benthamite assumption that the Church bears an ethical obligation to utilize its resources efficiently. To offer another example, we will see in chapter 6 that Octavia Hill believed ardently in the necessity of idealist interventions such as cross-class friendships to remediate the working class. However, she enthusiastically embraced the use of politico-economic mechanisms such as for-profit tenement management to create a context for those friendships to develop.

The result of this collision of rationalities was a palpable culture of self-critique arising even within the early formulations of professional discourse, a culture that modern critics of professionalism have largely underrated. As we have seen, critics of Victorian professionalism generally emphasize how professional ideals work in self-justifying ways, for the benefit of the professionals themselves.[47] Such readings of professional culture helpfully make us aware of the inevitably self-justifying tendencies that professional ideology shares with all ideologies. For that I remain indebted to these critics even while I shift the focus of study away from a suspicious reading of Victorian ideals toward a consciousness of the Victorians' own critical negotiation of the tensions between the ideal and the material.

What Anderson has said about critical reconstructions of Victorian modernity is equally applicable here: "By constructing a tradition of negative critique, Victorian studies imagines an external vantage point from which a society is criticized rather than acknowledging that such critique was already a part of the society, voiced from within."[48] Anderson's *Powers of Distance* demonstrates that professionalism was one of many Victorian social domains in which writers closely interrogated an ideal of detachment or critical distance even while using and defending it. *The Professional Ideal in the Victorian Novel* similarly explores the Victorians' complex and subtle handling of the ideals of professionalism.

IV

Historical and sociological studies of professionalism like those I have mentioned generally do little to pick apart the practical and philosophical contradictions that professionalism itself engenders. In the mid-Victorian novel, however, the representation of professionals and their dilemmas allows for an engagement with problems inherent to professional ideals. The novels and figures I have selected reveal, in their treatments of professional life, the faultlines of professional ideals in their relationship to materialist and idealist rationalities. These competing rationalities come to the surface in such matters as governmentality, autonomy, the woman question, mentoring, and the service ethic. The chapters of this book are arranged so as to draw attention to these individual problems as treated by individual authors without losing sight of the larger picture of the mid-Victorian formulation of professional ideals. Each chapter focuses on a different figure whose work illuminates a response to a particular professional problem. Consequently, the chapter on Disraeli examines the tensions of idealism and materialism with respect to governmentality; the chapter on Trollope explores professional autonomy; my reading of Gaskell's *My Lady Ludlow* takes up the relationship of gender to professional ideals; the chapter on Eliot's *Romola* considers problems of professional mentoring; and the chapter on "Janet's Repentance" and *Daniel Deronda* investigates the role of specialization in qualifying the demands of the service ethic.

While each chapter centrally features one problem or set of related problems, some of these issues arc across multiple chapters. *Romola* shares with "Janet's Repentance" and *Daniel Deronda* a deep engagement with the tension between self-interest and public service. *Romola*'s negotiation of the mentor's role—and when it comes to an end—recurs to the issue of professional autonomy explored in Trollope's early Barcetshire novels. *My Lady Ludlow* and Disraeli's Young England novels all consider, though in different ways, the validity of the aristocratic rationality of heredity as against professional meritocracy. The relationship of women to professional ideals is an issue—whether oblique or direct—for all the authors (though perhaps Disraeli least of all). And of course all five of the special problems under consideration here shaped the life and work of Hill. The novels have been chosen in part to facilitate this sort of cross-referencing, and the chronological sequencing of these chapters allows for insights into the development of Victorian thought on these recurring subjects.

Disraeli's Young England novels display the problems that the tension between idealism and materialism poses to governmentality. Disraeli is at one level a textbook case of the social crank: a professional who argued for the aristocratic ideal in his Young England trilogy of the mid-1840s. That early date precedes my principal area of interest by a few years, but Disraeli's transparent engagement with idealist and materialist contradictions make him well worth attention. For although Disraeli posed as an advocate of the aristocratic ideal, his own position as an outsider not only to the aristocracy but also to the English nation required him to theorize that ideal with a twist toward meritocratic professionalism. Young England can be seen as an effort to professionalize the aristocracy by importing into aristocratic thought the professional norms of efficiency, accountability, training, and disinterestedness. Thus Disraeli's imaginative answer to the question of who should lead the nation relies heavily on formulations of talent, merit, and trained expertise. In both *Coningsby* (1844) and *Sybil* (1845), the quasi-aristocratic heroes are given professional training and rise by their merits. In *Tancred* (1847), the hero of unquestionable aristocratic standing is distanced from the professional values of the previous two novels, but in such a way as to emphasize religious rationality at the expense of the material rationality of professional politics. Disraeli conflates this religious rationality with a racial logic resembling aristocratic norms. Ultimately, however, the idealist rationality is not sustainable for Disraeli, who reverts to materialist pragmatic politics to supply his hero's credentials. Although the trilogy sends mixed messages about the centrality of professional values to governmental functions, all three novels exhibit discomfort with the question of the relationship of political mechanisms to idealist social intervention.

Trollope's political novels, like Disraeli's, are more concerned with character than policy, a trait that is evident as well in his treatment of the "clerico-political world" of Barcetshire.[49] In *The Warden* (1855) and *Barchester Towers* (1857), the politics of Church life become the context for Trollope's treatment of the tension between professional autonomy and collectivity. Trollope's characters and their conflicts are construed around their relationships to other professionals and to the institutions that house them. In *The Warden* the Church is pressured to accept the oversight of the press and Parliament, whereas in the second novel Benthamite technocracy within the Church itself must be resisted by traditional elements of the clergy. The contested preferments that comprise most of the second book's plot—namely, the bishopric, the wardenship, and the deanery—allow Trollope to interrogate how professional institutions should be managed and how officeholders should be selected. The Whig-orchestrated Church reform of the 1830s and 1840s is a backdrop to the novel, allowing Trollope to comment on the problems of both intrusive and tyrannical management and of the absence of external accountability. Reading this aspect of the novel in light of Trollope's public statements about the professional standing of the Civil Service illuminates Trollope's attempt to imagine a professional body that does not compromise the autonomy of its practitioner-members and that serves the public best when allowed to function without state oversight.

While the professional worlds of Trollope's experience and interest—including the Church, Parliament, and the Post Office before his 1867 retirement—are exclusively male, Gaskell's ostensibly conservative provincial fictions embody a more progressive view of women's relationship to professional ideals. This view is particularly evident in the novella *My Lady Ludlow* (1858), later republished as the lead story in the collection *Round the Sofa* (1859). Both in the novel itself and in the neglected frame that introduces it in *Round the Sofa*, Gaskell shows the potentialities that a professional economic system offers for women and other marginalized groups. As an economy based on expertise gradually replaces one based on land ownership, barriers to women, the illegitimately born, and the working class gently give way to an inclusive meritocracy that gestures toward Gaskell's own position as a professional woman.

The issue of women's relationship to professional ideals is investigated throughout this study. Whereas the phrases "cool heads" and "warm hearts" might be expected to evoke gender stereotypes, in fact, as we have seen, the attributes of both cool heads and warm hearts are ascribed to male practitioners. Nevertheless, the professional values themselves are not inherently or even principally masculine.[50] In fact, feminine ideals of self-sacrifice and propriety overlap with professional ideals in ways that early feminists were not slow to exploit. Victorian feminism, like all other social concerns of the time, had a strong idealist component, as Barbara Caine has shown in *Victorian Feminists*.[51] The example of Gaskell provides a corrective nuance to reductive accounts of professionalism as a monolithic instrument of male domination.[52]

The gender question, as well as the professional self-critique generally, crystallizes in Eliot's fiction. My choice of *Romola* (1863) allows for an examination of not only gender and the service ethic in professionalism, but also of the problem of mentoring, or the transmission of professional values and expertise. For professional culture to perpetuate itself, a training mechanism that enculturates as well as educates aspiring professionals is essential. Like the other processes of professionalism under investigation here, however, mentoring has its characteristic pitfalls and problems, particularly how the service ethic can be responsibly transmitted. Despite its temporal and geographic remove from nineteenth-century England, *Romola* is preoccupied with the question of how ethical norms may be cultivated and transmitted by and to professionals. *Romola*'s central characters are all professionals in that they possess a store of human capital in the form of esoteric expertise, and each is judged on the basis of how he or she uses that expertise with respect to the public good. The trajectory of the novel's plot concerns Romola's successive relationships to each male mentor-figure, each of whom tries to imbue her with his understanding of the ethical use of expertise. From their disparate failures, Romola herself emerges as the idealized mentor, whose instruction of her adopted son Lillo epitomizes the appropriate balance between relativism and didacticism. Since mentorship of the individual novitiate (Romola) and pastorship of the social body generally (Florence) work as analogues for each other throughout the novel, it is possible to see in *Romola* a reflection of Eliot's beliefs about the obligation of the writer to be a pastor to the reading public.

Eliot is again my subject for my investigation of the complexities of the professional service ethic. Eliot's famous insistence on duty and fellow-feeling led her to take quite seriously the ideal of the service ethic; for her conscientious heroes the problem is rather the appropriate limit to the impulse of self-renunciation. High-minded vocational idealism, though a laudable corrective to the corruption of self-serving professionals, is nevertheless a problem that needs to be balanced with some degree of material pragmatism. In "Janet's Repentance" (1857) and *Daniel Deronda* (1876), Eliot investigates the meaning and the necessary limitations of professional disinterestedness by means of her representations of the altruistic heroes Edgar Tryan and Daniel Deronda. The tension between religious and market rationalities is prominent, indeed definitive, in Eliot's working out of the ethical norms of public service. In the early novella, Eliot juxtaposes a conventional satire of rapacious and irresponsible professionals to the otherworldly altruistic perfection of Tryan, an Evangelical curate.

Tryan's moral purity arises from his ascetic disregard for material reward for his labor, yet his renunciation of comforts is so extreme as to imperil his health and life. Tryan's early death of consumption is the inevitable, but unsatisfactory, result of the narrative logic that makes asceticism the only alternative to professionals' exploitation of the laity. In Eliot's final completed novel, she revisits the problem of excessive disinterestedness in another altruistic hero. Although Deronda is not in danger of destroying himself by physical deprivation, his excessive disinterest does paralyze his potential for active ameliorative service in the world. The resolution to his dilemma comes through the formulation of professional specialization: his vocation of Zionism, clearly partaking of both ideal and material rationalities, enables him to achieve the balance of self-interest and public service that a productive and sustainable career requires.

These authors all embed in their representations of professionalism an implied or explicit commentary on the structures of professionalism in which their characters—and they—simultaneously participate. Disraeli alternately shifts the locus of value from outside to inside the hereditary aristocracy, thereby destabilizing professional claims to political power at almost the same time that he legitimizes them. Trollope's fiction shows the resistance of professional ideology to Benthamite bureaucratic modalities (such as active supervision) while accepting some Benthamite principles (such as efficiency and productivity) as ethically normative. Gaskell uses professional ideals to nudge the professions toward a more inclusive self-definition, which she seems to assume is implicit in the ideals themselves. Eliot uses Savonarola to problematize the authority wielded by experts over both novice professionals and the lay public. Then in "Janet's Repentance" and *Daniel Deronda*, Eliot's minute dissection of the imperatives and limitations of the service ethic poses a remarkable response to Collini's "culture of altruism," even while she participates in that culture.

I will conclude by looking at an example of these problems as mediated in a historical personality. I have chosen Hill, best known for her work in housing philanthropy, for this analysis because of her remarkable determination to reconcile idealist and materialist worldviews (which she often troped as "heart" and "head") in her professional career. Born into the professional middle class, and mentored in the Christian Socialism of F. D. Maurice and the social aestheticism of Ruskin, Hill combined a passionate Christian commitment to helping the poor with a pragmatic sense that partook of political economy without wholly embracing it. She therefore negotiated the tension between materiality and ideality in virtually all of her many undertakings. Hill struggled imperfectly to resolve the questions of the limits of disinterest, of the relative autonomy of practitioners, of the optimal mentoring mechanism for reproducing "trained workers for the poor," of women's relationship to professional ideals, and of relating professional to aristocratic values. My reading of Hill focuses the concerns of this study by unpacking her troubled engagement with the conflicting rationalities to which she syncretically subscribed; further, it allows us to complicate the narrative of professionalization by seeing the materialist and idealist aspects of professionalism as distinct yet related phenomena.

Taken together, these figures and texts indicate the texture and complexity of Victorian critical engagement with professional ideals. The power of idealist notions of what it means to be professional is attested by the pressure those ideals come under from within as well as without. The Victorians' diverse negotiations of such pressures represent a yet untold story in the history of professionalism—a story that illustrates the early and abiding presence of professional self-critique.

CHAPTER 1

BRAINS MORE PRECIOUS THAN BLOOD, OR THE PROFESSIONAL LOGIC OF THE YOUNG ENGLAND TRILOGY

[O]f necessity [the oligarchy] isn't one city but two—one of the poor and one of the rich—living in the same place and always plotting against one another.

Plato, *Republic*, 551d

As far as I can tell, no one has traced Benjamin Disraeli's famous subtitle to Plato's critique of the oligarchic constitution found in book 8 of the *Republic*. It is, in any case, unlikely that Disraeli read the *Republic*, at least not in Greek: Disraeli did not ever reach the highest form in the school in Epping Forest kept by Reverend Eli Cogan, and Plato was read only in that form.[1] It is likely true, as Paul Smith has suggested, that Disraeli picked up the "two nations" idea as it circulated in "dinner-table talk" derived from Hegel and his disciples.[2] Nevertheless, Disraeli's frequent denigration of the "vulgar and ignoble oligarchy" of the Whigs has a Platonic ring, particularly when seen alongside Plato's ideal of the aristocratic constitution.[3] Rule by *arête*, to Plato, meant the purposeful selection of future rulers according to intrinsic and proven merit, and the extended esoteric training of those individuals both in virtue and in various branches of expert knowledge. Plato explicitly theorized political leadership as a disinterested service to the populace by prohibiting the ruling class from owning any private property. Among his more progressive ideas was the stipulation that promising future rulers would be chosen from any rank of society, and from either gender, in which they could be found. Understood this way, aristocracy or "rule by the most excellent/virtuous" corresponds closely to the professional ideal.

Disraeli's apology for aristocracy operated in a similar fashion. Young England, and the larger aristocratic revival of which it was the last gasp, imagined repairing the damage of the previous two generations of ineffective and blandly self-interested Toryism by restoring genuinely paternalistic relations between rich and poor.[4] However, the apparent revival of a feudal sensibility in the aristocratic class actually resembles the professional ideal more than anything. Young England's evocations of a romanticized medieval past by no means exclude, though they may mystify, the absorption of emergent rationalities. Young England aimed to transform the aristocracy to make it worthy and capable of the leadership of the nation, and that transformation involved selecting able and knowledgeable leaders, training them to discharge their responsibilities effectively, and cultivating in them a public service ethic.

Disraeli's affinity for an aristocratic form of government is axiomatic but far from absolute.[5] Smith is right to observe that Disraeli viewed "the reality of aristocracy as a faculty of command rather than a quality of blood."[6] In his *Vindication of the English Constitution in a Letter to a Noble and Learned Lord* (1835), Disraeli represents the English aristocracy as the nation's bulwark of constitutional liberty against the tyrannical incursions of Whig oligarchs, whose supposed electoral representation of the "people" is a self-serving fiction. The best legislative body, he urges, consists of "men refined, serene, and courteous, learned, brave, traveled, charitable, and magnificent, especially when . . . the supreme power in the State has the capacity of adding to their numbers at his will, any individuals, however humble and plebian their origins, whose wisdom will in his opinion swell the aggregate capacity of their assembly."[7] It is impossible not to note the self-referential quality of the final clause, but neither should we fail to note the blend of the professional and aristocratic ideals among the qualifications he prescribes for national leaders. Throughout *Vindication*, Disraeli defends aristocracy, however implausibly, as both democratic and meritocratic: the House of Lords is a "free and democratic Peerage" precisely because "[t]he ranks of our second estate have been periodically strengthened by an accession of some of the best blood, the greatest wealth, and the most distinguished talent of the community."[8]

This assertion is later revised in *Coningsby, or the New Generation* (1844), when the disinherited aristocrat exuberantly discerns that "[b]rains every day become more precious than blood. You must give men new ideas. . . . Greatness no longer depends on rentals; the world is too rich; nor on pedigrees, the world is too knowing."[9] Thus Disraeli deletes the first two of the three qualities he identified in *Vindication* as constituting the needed infusion of new personnel into the peerage. After eliminating "the best blood" and "the greatest wealth," Disraeli remains unequivocally committed to the needed accession of "the most distinguished talent." In other words, Disraeli's praise of aristocratic government is rendered in terms that evoke the professional ideal and in so doing make space for himself in the centers of power.

In the case of Disraeli, Harold Perkin's formulation of the social crank generally holds: Disraeli's infusion of the professional ideal into the aristocratic ideal in these novels took the form of "coaxing, goading, or shaming their members [of the adopted class] into living up to" professional mores, which over time differentiated more and more sharply from those normative to their adopted class.[10] Yet Perkin too readily dismisses the idealist rationality exhibited by figures such as Disraeli as an irrelevant aberration from the Benthamite norm. Young England's enthusiasm for the professionalization of Members of Parliament was accompanied by an emphatic rejection of Benthamism. The utilitarian "schoolmen" who reduce human social relations to economic competition are Disraeli's particular bugbear in the *Vindication* as well as in the Young England novels. Disraeli's ideological resistance to statist measures is widely recognized: Disraeli's "Toryism was typical in its approach to reform on the social side rather than on its political side; here he was naturally the enemy of the Whigs and Liberals, who, with the Benthamites, placed their trust in political measures."[11] I contend that Disraeli's rejection of Benthamism is a key element in his articulation of a professional identity that is open to self-critique.

The Young England novels' critique of Benthamism involves not only a recuperation of paternalist aristocracy but also a specific twist toward the emergent professional. The emphasis on idealist rather than statist or materialist solutions makes it possible for Disraeli's political novels to say next to nothing about public policy. But however much Disraeli may want to distance himself from those who place "their trust in political measures," as a politician himself Disraeli has little else to work with. Disraeli's critique of reigning political paradigms depends upon values that he cannot very well harness to any political program, including his own.

The trilogy provides an apt context for examining the configuration of the professional ideal particularly with respect to governmentality: what sort of relationship does Disraeli imagine between professionalism and Benthamite bureaucracy, or between professionalism and aristocratic paternalism? We will find that the professional ethos with which he equips his characters goes hand-in-hand with an idealism that problematizes their relationship to political mechanisms. Even as Disraeli's allegiance to ideality leads him to underrate political solutions to problems, his practical allegiances and contexts as an ambitious MP disallow him to escape such resolutions. Therefore the first two books end in an awkward compromise between the previous failure of political solutions and the present and future potentiality of political solutions as shaped by appropriate personnel. Disraeli's apparent attempt in the third volume to transcend politics altogether, substituting religious values that are actually racial values, only results in the auto-deconstruction of his narrative. Disraeli cannot divorce politics and ideality; he cannot keep Benthamism out of Young England, but neither can he reconcile himself to its presence. In short, the insistence on idealist conceptualizations of political leadership involves Disraeli in a difficult and finally destabilizing negotiation of idealist and materialist rationalities.

I

Coningsby, or the New Generation, begun in the autumn of 1843, was written to espouse the principles of Young England, which formed in the latter half of 1842. Tellingly, the eponymous hero must be temporarily deprived of privilege and subjected to professional discipline before ascending to his destined political role. Coningsby's preparation for his role of national leadership includes the usual stints at Eton and Oxbridge, but it is not limited to those conventional credentials. His frank conversations with Millbank, the manufacturer whose son he has befriended at Eton, instruct him in the fallacy of so-called noble birth, which is understood as chimerical and comparatively modern. Millbank voices the theme, familiar to readers of *Sybil*, that "we owe the English peerage to three sources: the spoliation of the Church; the open and flagrant sale of its honours by the elder Stuarts; and the boroughmongering of our own times."[12] Instead, Millbank schools Coningsby in the doctrine of Burkean "natural aristocracy," which he defines as "those men whom a nation recognizes as the most eminent for virtue, talents, and property, and, if you please, birth and standing in the land."[13] Disraeli's diminishment of "birth and standing" in comparison with the more meaningful distinctions of "virtue, talents, and property" is notable. Millbank himself is propertied, having bought an estate with his immense wealth earned by his "talents" in business. The logic is clear: virtue and talents yield property, which in turn yields "standing in the land" and which is, within a few generations, taken for noble birth. This formulation is a reversal of the traditional aristocratic understanding that birth and standing are coterminous with property and are productive of virtue and talent in the families that hold them.

That Disraeli would make an entrepreneurial manufacturer the spokesman of professional values ought not to surprise us. A very similar maneuver occurs in *Sybil* with Mr. Trafford. In Disraeli's mystification the ideal is unmoored from any specific class, thereby making it appear that all right-thinking men will hold these opinions derived from the professional rationality. Such a move is after all required by Disraeli's project of instilling professional values into the aristocratic rationality: these values can only be adopted as aristocratic if they are not specifically associated with any other class.

The sentiments and outlook acquired from his contact with the Millbanks inform in more than one way Coningsby's refusal to accommodate his grandfather Lord Monmouth's demand that he enter Parliament as a Conservative. It is unthinkable for Coningsby to campaign against Millbank: "the fierce passions, the gross insults, the hot blood and the cool lies, the ruffianism and the ribaldry" the campaign would necessitate are unimaginable in the context of his established friendship with the family, not to mention his love for Millbank's daughter Edith (357). But more importantly (for Coningsby professes himself willing to disregard his "interests" and "affections" to please his grandfather [361]), the principles of government Coningsby has developed under the tutelage of Millbank and Sidonia make it impossible for him to accept office on the condition that he "vote with [his] party," that is, Peelite Conservatives (359). Coningsby rejects Lord Monmouth's position that "the end of all parties and all politics" is "to gain your object," that object being personal aggrandizement (360). Rather, Coningsby asserts that "the essence of all tenure is the performance of duty" (362). This favorite mantra of Young England clearly partakes of aristocratic and professional rationalities simultaneously.

The professional tenor of Disraeli's ideal becomes clearer toward the end of the novel. Outraged at his grandson's refusal to serve as his political toady in the project of gaining a dukedom, and even more appalled at rumors of Coningsby's intimacy with the Millbanks, Lord Monmouth disinherits Coningsby. The young hero's principles—that is, his "virtue," one of the primary constituent parts of Millbank's "natural aristocracy"— therefore appear to exclude him permanently from the privileges of property, including serving in Parliament. However, Coningsby's despondency on learning of his disinheritance is soon dissipated by Sidonia's admonition to aim for professional distinction either in the diplomatic corps or the Bar. The disenfranchised aristocrat is redirected to professional activity. In reminding Coningsby that he has not lost "everything" in losing his expected inheritance, Sidonia emphasizes the human capital Coningsby still commands: "You have health, youth, good looks, great abilities, considerable knowledge, a fine courage, a lofty spirit, and no contemptible experience" (398). What he lacks, however, is specialized training. Coningsby realizes that now "he must, after all his studies, commence a new novitiate, and before he could enter the arena must pass years of silent and obscure preparation" (400). It is at this juncture that he discovers for himself that "[b]rains every day become more precious than blood" (401).

Coningsby's subsequent study of law, with the ambition of becoming Lord Chancellor, is undertaken with exceptional diligence: "He entirely devoted himself to his new pursuit. His being was completely absorbed by it" (407). Coningsby's steady application to his legal studies is in fact represented as the ground for the happy resolution of the novel. Even after Millbank resolves to rescue Coningsby from his poverty and allow him to marry Edith, Millbank "felt some interest in the present conduct of Coningsby. A Coningsby working for his bread was a novel incident to him. He wished to be assured of its authenticity" (415). While the principal motivation for Millbank's change of heart is Coningsby's earlier rectitude in resisting his grandfather, this passage makes clear that Coningsby's good conduct in his pre-professional role is a significant factor in Millbank's actions as well. The sudden dissolution of Parliament provides the occasion for Millbank to give Coningsby his seat and to permit the union of Coningsby and Edith. Coningsby soon inherits his grandfather's estate on the convenient death of Monmouth's heiress Flora, who is also moved by Coningsby's rectitude to leave the fortune to him. Thus for Coningsby, property and standing do not follow by default from birth, as the aristocratic norm would have it. Rather, the professional norm prevails for Coningsby as for Millbank, though in much shorter time: Coningsby's virtue and talent equal property and standing.

With Coningsby newly elected to Parliament along with his schoolfellows, Disraeli ends the novel with a series of questions about whether the young men will in fact live up to the potential they have hitherto exhibited. "Will they maintain in august assemblies and high places the great truths which, in study and in solitude, they have embraced? Or will their courage exhaust itself in the struggle, their enthusiasm evaporate before hollow-hearted ridicule, their generous impulses yield with a vulgar catastrophe to the tawdry temptations of a low ambition?" and so on (420). The outlook is hopeful—these new MPs at least have the human capital they will need to change the Parliamentary status quo for the better—but the results remain unknown. The question of whether and how Parliamentary means can be wrested for idealist ends is left untouched by the novel.

II

In *Sybil, or the Two Nations* (1845), a very similar logic is at work. Despite Disraeli's penchant for portraying Gerard in native aristocratic splendor, it is Gerard's class disinterest that Egremont and the narrator find most attractive, and in fact Gerard's specifically aristocratic qualities are eventually destructive. Egremont's own leadership is based not on his "noble" birth, which Disraeli takes pains to deconstruct, but on his proven qualities as a professional, as we shall see.

Stephen Morley articulates the problem that Disraeli broaches on the title page when he rebuffs Egremont's complacent patriotism with the assertion that the queen reigns over two nations, not one:

> Two nations, between whom there is no intercourse and no sympathy; who are as ignorant of each other's habits, thoughts, and feelings, as if they were dwellers in different zones, or inhabitants of different planets; who are formed by a different breeding, are fed by a different food, are ordered by different manners, and are not governed by the same laws. . . . The Rich and the Poor.[14]

The problem in England, according to Morley, is not poverty itself but the dissociation that is reflected in the socioeconomic disparity. Although he can "spare no pang for the past," Morley laments that the loss of the monasteries has left "no community in England; there is aggregation, but aggregation under circumstances which make it rather a dissociating than a uniting principle. . . . In great cities men are brought together by the desire of gain. They are not in a state of cooperation, but of isolation, as to the making of fortunes" (64–65). The overlapping causes of this dissociation are legion: the competition for wealth antagonizes social groups and overpowers normal human attachments; the lifestyles that pertain to the different socioeconomic levels function to prohibit intercourse and therefore prevent understanding between groups; and the lack of "community of purpose," which alone can unify, dooms people to a state of isolated contiguity (65).

The extent to which Morley's ideas on this subject reflect those of Disraeli is a complicated question.[15] Notwithstanding Morley's inadequacies, his observations here chime with Disraeli's social criticism in his *Vindication of the English Constitution*. In that treatise, Disraeli excoriates utilitarianism as the cause of a rampant individualism, which, by enshrining a purely materialistic notion of self-interest, alienates people and classes from each other.[16] The problem of the novel is to imagine a solution to this divide, a principle of unification that will restore the social cohesion of the medieval monastics and their tenants. As we will see, Gerard's own praise of the monastics implies that the present solution will be found in the professional model that forms the latent basis of Disraeli's imaginative politics. To understand how this solution takes shape, we need to trace both Disraeli's positive account of Egremont's preparation for and performance in his professional-political role as well as the author's ambivalent treatment of professionalism itself in the novel.

That some sort of unification is imaged in the concluding marriage of Egremont and Sybil is widely agreed, but what is being unified? There are almost as many answers to that question as there are critical readings of the novel. Earlier readings, such as that of Richard A. Levine, describe the marriage as the union of Tories and "the people."[17] Some subsequent readers have faulted the novel for failing to achieve this very union, still assuming Disraeli's intention to be a union of rich and poor, titled and common. These readings imply that because Sybil "turns out" to be a wealthy aristocrat, Disraeli's unification project is derailed.[18]

Most careful studies of the novel, however, take for granted that Disraeli never meant for Sybil to be taken as a working-class woman, pointing out that Sybil's and Gerard's essential nobility and even their claim to a title and land are presented unmistakably early in the novel. Raymond Williams, for example, observes that *Sybil's* ending showcases a wedding of agricultural and industrial interests, since Egremont, on inheriting his older brother's estate and taking possession of Sybil's urban fiefdom, becomes a major holder of both rural and urban property.[19] The problem with this reading is that Sybil is much more than a placeholder for the industrial complex, though she is certainly closely associated with it through her Chartist father, her missions of mercy among the industrial population, and eventually her inheritance of the property on which that complex is built. Rather, Sybil is a multifaceted signifier, pointing not only to the working-class population but also to the Catholic faith, medieval feudalism, the monarchy, and "true" Saxon aristocracy. Hence Jennifer Sampson, in her analysis of the parallels between Sybil and Queen Victoria, asserts that Sybil's marriage represents an ideal unification of the queen, whose female body is a positive symbol for the nation, and her ministers, whose legal power and dominance Disraeli wanted to instruct Victoria to accept.[20] Robert O'Kell, after unpacking the elements of religious allegory in the novel, concludes that the wedding signifies the marriage of "sensitive but secular leadership to a spirit of piety and devotion."[21] Ruth Yeazell more simply proposes that the wedding is a union of "old families and great estates."[22] To Daniel Schwartz, the concluding marriage is something of an artistic failure: it is "not the apocalypse that Disraeli seems to have intended," because the exposé of social dysfunction throughout the novel overshadows the happy ending.[23] Rosemarie Bodenheimer identifies the marriage as uniting Egremont's "real talent"—as opposed to the superficiality of the other MPs—and Sybil's "real aristocracy"—as opposed to the pretensions of the nouveau riche Whig oligarchy.[24] John Ulrich argues that Sybil's correction by and subordination to Egremont "symbolically mirror[s]" the political leadership of New Toryism over the people.[25]

I see the marriage that ends the novel not primarily as a unification of disparate interests or a fictionalized collapse of class. While I agree with Bodenheimer that Egremont's metonymic quality is his Disraelian "talent coming from nowhere,"[26] I cannot simply equate Sybil with the aristocracy any more than with piety and charity, or industrial interests, or Chartism, or the monarchy. She points in some way to all of these things; as Catherine Gallagher convincingly argues, she "represent[s], in as transparent a manner as possible, ahistorical values."[27] Therefore her marriage to Egremont simultaneously ratifies his worthiness to husband these national values and endows him personally, as she does the aristocracy generally, with timeless and absolute values. Gallagher proposes the concluding wedding as the "Coleridgean union of the sacred with its rightful representative, the state. . . . Through Egremont's union with the symbolic, politics is detached from social facts and political factions and fastened to the realm of values."[28] While this assessment is accurate, it does not attempt to specify how this value-added politics constitutes and preserves itself. In fact, the professional ethos both undergirds and provides the model for the politics-cum-values that Disraeli advocates.

In Sybil's marriage, the many positive values she represents—religious, social, historical, and monarchical—all come to rest imaginatively on Egremont. This fact functions to catapult Egremont from the status of a young and marginal MP to that of major political leader, just as his inheritance and hers translate him from a younger son living off his stepfather to one of the wealthiest peers of the realm. To be loved by Sybil is the ambition of all the professional men in the novel—Morley, Hatton, and Egremont—and Sybil's choice of Egremont serves (among other things) to validate his particular brand of professional service through politics by attaching to it the ahistorical values she represents.

The professional/aristocratic hybrid is embodied both in Egremont and in Gerard, but in Gerard the aristocratic ideal predominates over the professional, whereas the opposite is true for Egremont. Tellingly, it is Egremont who is positioned to lead at the novel's close, and Gerard who does not survive the novel's final cataclysm. The warm adulation poured over the quintessentially aristocratic Gerard for most of the novel does not negate the fact that he remains a residual figure, however admirable. Disraeli frequently reminds the reader of Gerard's innate nobility: his natural leadership at Trafford's mill, his eloquence at Chartist meetings, his ability to inspire loyalty among the commoners, his impressive physique, and his deference—neither sullen nor sycophantic—toward his superiors. His triumphal parade into Mowbray after his arrest in London, when all the people from miles around congregate in solemn and orderly procession to escort him from the train station, is of course calculated to reinforce the impression that he is nature's king, inherently suited to rule the people.

But Gerard remains one of Disraeli's nostalgic fantasies. He has no more place in modern English political life than the Catholic Church has in its religious life. Gerard is a relic, like the Abbey ruins where he first appears. He serves only to remind the leaders of the present and future, like Egremont, of the glories of the past, and thereby to inspire them to new and greater glories.[29] The traditional aristocratic ideal is fundamentally military, and Disraeli is not embarrassed by that fact, although it causes him some difficulty in representing Gerard and his fate.[30] One of the markers of Gerard as a true aristocrat, unlike the nouveau riche nobles of Egremont's world, is his masculine pugilism, as opposed to their vapid effeminacy. Gerard wishes for an opportunity to wield a pikestaff in defense of the people's rights, and laments that he was not there to fight with Harold against the Normans.

Disraeli can only celebrate this inclination to armed struggle when it appears as a nostalgic fancy: as a proud memory of Gerard's ancestor at Agincourt, or as a musing comment that the armor of Simon de Mortfort would fit Gerard better than the lord who plans to wear it to the queen's costume ball (228). When a violent uprising against the government is an imminent reality, Gerard's military instincts must be chastised. Gerard's readiness to resort to force when the Chartists' diplomatic efforts fail sends him to prison in an abrupt curtailment of his efforts at the height of his powers. When he emerges from prison he has learned to repudiate violence, seek peace, and avoid leadership. He is also a much less vivid character. Our closing impression of Gerard is therefore that of a man born in the wrong time, a hero whose noble character is too far out of synch with the age to continue as part of it. His death is lamentable, Disraeli indicates, but necessary, for the residual military order Gerard represents has no place in the political leadership of the future.

III

The leader of the future, then, for all Disraeli's distracting nostalgia, is not the Saxon aristocrat, but the professional politician. Egremont is of noble birth, but his political proficiency is based more on his energy and ability than on his heredity. The Marney title is of highly questionable legitimacy anyway, as Disraeli takes pains to indicate by tracing the history by which an enterprising royal steward plundered the Abbey at Dissolution in order to gain an estate, and how the family thereafter finagled a peerage by its calculated services to the Crown. This is not to deny that Egremont's access to Parliament is a function of his family's standing and especially of his mother's political connections and financial resources. His mother's money pays for his campaign and provides his livelihood while he serves in Parliament. By itself, however, this fact can readily be seen to suggest a critique of the system that requires financial independence for MPs, since only his mother's deus-ex-machina marriage to a rich man provides for Egremont's campaign debts and allows him to take his seat in Parliament. Apart from such miraculous provision, the circumstance implies, men of ability and promise could be prevented from serving their country.

Heredity, therefore, is not a significant qualification for Egremont's position of national leadership. Egremont ends the novel as Lord Marney, wealthy and titled, but like Coningsby he must earn that position before he is granted it. He first must prove his mettle and merit as an MP, as a righteous champion of the "people" (not "the working class," which is too divisive a nomination for Disraeli's taste), and as a worthy lover of Sybil. The path to his achievement is professional, not hereditary. He begins his career as the younger brother of a noble family; cadets had been the chief source of professional manpower since feudal times. When Gerard refers to aristocratic younger sons as "the natural friend of the people," he is referring primarily to an expectation that their marginalized status would prepare them to sympathize with other marginalized social groups (136). Because the marginalization of younger sons entails the necessity of entering a profession rather than the privilege of being supported in idleness, this moment also suggests Disraeli's own negotiation of his position as a social crank in Perkin's terms. As we saw in *Coningsby*, Disraeli redefines the proper aristocratic ruler as a professional, who proves his worth by earning his bread by expert labor. A man born to privilege and indulgence, Gerard and Disraeli suggest, is not likely to support the general welfare of the people. Significantly, not only Egremont but also Mr. Trafford and Mr. St. Lys are younger sons. Trafford, the benevolent mill owner who is an entrepreneur cast in the professional mold, comes closest to fulfilling the "baronial principle" in his paternal care for his employees (182). St. Lys, Mowbray's vicar, epitomizes the professional ideal by his combination of material charity and spiritual exhortation for the sake of humanizing the local workers.

Contrary to Gerard's theory, as Gerard himself is well aware, most younger sons do not intuitively align themselves with "the people." To be the right kind of politician, therefore, Egremont requires an education such as his privileged background did not afford; this is the role played by Walter Gerard and, to a lesser extent, Stephen Morley. Egremont's education begins the evening he visits the Abbey ruins and finds Gerard and Morley there. This scene is crucial to Disraeli's development of his political ideas and to his treatment of the professional ideal. The characteristics Gerard stresses about the monastics coincide with the professional ideal: managerial work in the service of the community, personal disinterest, egalitarian and meritocratic selection, and well-trained expertise.

According to Gerard, the monastics were "easy landlords," charging low rents, offering generous leases, and spending their revenue locally (61). Since the monastics were forbidden to accumulate individual wealth, their simple lifestyle fueled the local economy rather than draining it. Their interest was communal: taking a long-term view of land stewardship, they managed resources for the benefit of all who lived there rather than for their own short-term enrichment. Although he acknowledges that younger sons of the aristocracy often found a home in abbeys (his own noble ancestor, also called Walter Gerard, was apparently one of these), Gerard persists in contrasting that practice favorably with the Victorian practice of providing for younger sons in the pension list or with government posts. Without specifically averring that merit governed the selection of monastic leaders, he casts aspersion on contemporary disasters of patronage. Because of the existence of the monasteries, Gerard maintains, a medieval sovereign "need not, like a minister in these days, entrust the conduct of public affairs to individuals notoriously incompetent, appoint to the command of expeditions generals who never saw a field, make governors of colonies out of men who could never govern themselves, or find an ambassador in a broken dandy or a blasted favorite" (62). To Gerard, the travesty of patronage is explicitly the incompetence of individuals for the jobs they are given, with the result that important government work is neglected. Disraeli's method here of negative contrast does not require him to specify an alternative, but his outrage at government mismanagement clearly partakes of the professional ideal. Gerard goes on, "[T]he list of the mitred abbots . . . shows that the great majority of the heads of houses were of the people" (62), selected, Gerard implies, for their merit in an egalitarian process that recognized virtue and ability wherever it was found.

Egremont changes the subject to the safer topic of the monks' expertise: "[T]here is one [point] on which there can be no controversy: the monks were great architects" (62). Egremont's banal commonplace becomes the point of departure for another elaborate paean on Gerard's part, celebrating the monks' use of their expertise in service of the community: "These holy men, too, built and planted . . . for posterity: . . . they made the country beautiful, and the people proud of their country" (63).[31] His speech concludes by warmly reiterating that Abbey property, "under their administration, so mainly contributed to the welfare of the community" (64).

In effect, Gerard rewrites the culture of monasticism as a culture of professionalism. He summarizes, "The monks were . . . a body of individuals having no cares of their own, with wisdom to guide the inexperienced, with wealth to relieve the suffering, and often with power to protect the oppressed" (62).[32] The monks' combination of personal disinterest ("no cares of their own") and esoteric expertise at the service of others ("wisdom to guide the inexperienced") gives them the social position and cultural capital ("wealth" and "power") to effect real good in their communities. The monks' architectural and managerial expertise, their selection by merit, and their disinterested service to the public together make them function like a "true" aristocracy— under their leadership the community both prospered and maintained justice for citizens of all ranks—but it is an aristocracy that looks and operates like a professional meritocracy. Gerard does not rebuke the present aristocracy for its wealth but for its irresponsibility, that is, its selfish and inexpert management of physical and human resources. In contrast, he celebrates an ideal that reinscribes the landholding class principally according to the professional ethos, not the aristocratic one. Even the Chartist leader and natural aristocrat, then, hews more closely to the professional ideal than to the working-class or aristocratic ideals.[33]

IV

The scene at the Abbey inaugurates Egremont's "real" education, an education that continues during his stay near Mowbray at the hands of Gerard, St. Lys, and Trafford, who perform the functions of Sidonia and Millbank in *Coningsby*. This training culminates in Egremont's taking his seat in Parliament. Before we consider Egremont's performance in his professional role, we should first note Disraeli's cautionary treatment of professionalism in Egremont's foils, Stephen Morley and Baptist Hatton. Initially, Morley's error is only ideological, but this error and its corollaries come to involve him in moral failures that predetermine his downfall. Disraeli makes Hatton into a type of the insidious power, unscrupulous conduct, and dangerous knowledge that undergirded the aristocrats' anxiety concerning professional men.

Morley's ideological error, which is related to his irreligiousness, is his well-intentioned but flawed pet scheme of uniting workers in a socialist utopia. He believes that the solution to the problem of the two nations is to be found by an intentional practice of "the principle of association" through communal living. In effect, Morley proposes a Benthamite sort of solution to manage domestic resources more centrally and therefore more efficiently. The wrong-headedness of Morley's ideas emerges somewhat gradually. In the early scene described above, his assessment of the problem of disaggregation is allowed to stand uncontested, and it poses a salutary challenge to Egremont's complacency. Some of the problems with his notions come to the surface, however, when Morley's ideas are further expounded in a pub with a group of miners. The miner Mr. Nixon's accurate assessment of the alternative to strikes makes reference to the dissociation at the heart of the two-nations problem: "I never knew the people play [strike] yet, but if a word had passed atween them and the main-masters aforehand, it might not have been settled; but you can't get at them any way. Atween the poor man and the gentleman there never was no connection, and that's the wital mischief of this country" (144). Whether the phrase "this country" refers to England at large or the mining district in particular is left ambiguous, and to good effect. The real villain of the mining district is not the owners or lessees, who could set all to rights if they would only listen to the workers, but the butties, the middlemen who supervise the miners and pay them in overpriced goods rather than in cash. At one strike in particular, "the masters said they would meet us; but what did they do but walk about the ground and speak to the butties. The butties has their ear" (145). These butties, who represent in the worst possible caricature the mercantile middle class, interfere to prevent irenic mutual understanding between rich and poor.[34]

Morley brushes aside Nixon's diagnoses to propose a socialistic solution to the miner's complaints. "Suppose," he says, "fifty of your families were to live under one roof" (145). The result of such combination, he tells them, would be that they could all live better for less money, could save money and invest it in their own mines, and return a better profit with less labor than presently. Morley's hearers are skeptical and unimpressed. The novel implicitly endorses Mr. Nixon's assessment and solution, which invokes voluntarist, interpersonal involvement across class lines, exactly the sort of thing Sybil and St. Lys are seen to do on their mission of mercy to the Warners. Gerard later remarks cryptically that his only experience of "community"—the jail where he served a sentence for sedition—has hardly disposed him to greater sympathy for Morley's communitarian ideals (369). Morley's idea of community is more closely associated with the prison or the workhouse than the monastery. The novel rejects systematic social engineering in favor of individuated and domestic social relations.

Morley's fall is made complete by his association with Disraeli's other cautionary professional, Baptist Hatton. An antiquarian whose vast and esoteric knowledge has given him an extensive clientele among the nation's peers and would-be peers, Hatton places his expertise at the service of the highest bidder without regard for the moral claims of truth or right. Though he attempts to pass as a worker with the Gerards, he cannot persuade Sybil that his highly paid intellectual employment entitles him to claim the prerogatives of the champions of labor (248). Hatton even justifies his sale of the writ of right establishing Gerard's claim to Lord Mowbray's estate: it was, after all, a legitimate transaction, in which he sold the produce of his specialized labor for the highest price it could command. In other words, Hatton regards his esoteric expertise in mercantile, rather than professional, terms. It is Hatton who coolly suggests to Morley that a preconcerted riot attacking Mowbray Castle could put them in possession of the document. In the face of Morley's initial shock, Hatton offhandedly refers to his own suggestion as "a practical view of the case" (342). Morley is at first "disturbed," but after reflection he begins to calculate in the same vein, telling Hatton, "You have a clear brain and a bold spirit; you have no scruples, which indeed are rather the creatures of perplexity than of principle. You ought to succeed" (342–343).

This picture of the professional class conforms to popular stereotype, particularly that perpetuated by adherents of the aristocratic ideal. Pretending to serve society in the form of specific clients, Hatton serves only himself. Adopting the view that the end justifies the means, he vends his skills without regard for social consequences or moral right. Possessed of an insidious intimacy with his clients' private lives, he can say he knows his clients "better than anyone," and that he has "knowledge that can make the proudest tremble" (342, 253). Though Hatton is not really the cause of Morley's moral downfall, Morley's fatal loss of moral principle is associated with his tacit acceptance of Hatton's "practical view of the case." Morley then uses his own expertise as a journalist to collaborate with Hatton in determining the best time and manner for effecting the riot and robbery. How much Morley is persuaded to cooperate by Hatton's promise of ten thousand pounds, and how much by the crushed remains of his love for Sybil, is left unexamined by the novel. What is clear is that Morley abandons his socialist agenda after the disappointment in London, and that he speaks approvingly of Hatton's esoteric contribution: "We have not hitherto had the advantage of your worldly knowledge; in future we shall be wiser" (343). The "wisdom" of this sort of professional, Disraeli indicates, is worldly knowledge dangerously unmoored from otherworldly principle.

It would be a mistake, however, to overlook Disraeli's ambivalence toward these fallen professionals. A number of critics have persuasively argued that either or both of these men comprise ironic authorial self-portraits.[35] Sybil's restoration to her title and lands, after all, depends on their expertise and labor: Hatton's earlier researches validate Sybil's title; Hatton's "worldly knowledge" is needed to arrange the riot; and Morley's unscrupulousness is required to accomplish the theft of the writ. Hatton puts his lucrative career and his "respectability" on the line for this escapade, and Morley undertakes the burglary at the risk—and indeed the cost—of his life and reputation.

However ambivalent Disraeli's handling of these professionals may be, Egremont unequivocally emerges as Disraeli's idealized figure of the leader of the people, a type marked by the professional ethos.

By means of his extended education in the condition of England, Egremont is readied to assume his place in national leadership. As Disraeli takes pains to establish, Egremont is a good worker, a diligent public servant. After Gerard and Morley, in their role as Chartist lobbyists, are turned away from several doors of MPs who are not yet out of bed, they find Egremont "seated in his library, at a round table covered with writing materials, books, and letters. On another table were arranged his parliamentary papers, and piles of blue books" (229). Egremont is busy with esoteric texts: gathering, processing, and disseminating information about national affairs. Not only is he hard at work, but he has also given "particular orders" to receive the expected delegation cordially (229). Egremont's attention to and sympathy for the Chartist petition, as well as his diligent application to affairs at state, distinguish him from his Parliamentary colleagues. Disraeli satirizes the sentiment of the MP who reminisces, "Those were the good old gentleman-like times . . . when members of Parliament had nobody to please and ministers of State nothing to do" (283). Egremont's professionalism thus poses an implicit critique of Parliamentary norms from within the institution.

How Egremont is to achieve the ends to which his training, talents, and virtue direct him is not specified. The novel makes clear that the problem of national disaggregation is not to be solved by socialist communes, by trade unionism, or by party politics in Parliament. Morley's scheme of working-class communal living is a logical but colossal mistake: greater unity among the degraded working class could only, in Disraeli's view, exacerbate the class tensions that already pose the greatest barrier to national unity. The trade union of Mowbray requires its members to suspend moral judgment and to silence the conscience before the demands of the group. Disraeli's presentation of the initiation of Mick Radley is calculated to emphasize the surrender of individuality required by such institutions. The preliminary business the union transacts makes reference to the supposed mediocrity of democracy (they vote to expel any member who boasts of superior work) and to the arbitrary, totalitarian control of the lives of others (they vote to close down a mill on the basis of a single, uninvestigated denunciation). Mick must swear to perform any act, specifically any violent act, that "the majority of your brethren, testified by the mandate of this grand committee, shall impose upon you, in furtherance of our common welfare, of which they are the sole judges" (221).

The Parliamentary language of the trade union oath—"majority," "testified," "mandate," "committee," and "common welfare"— invites the reader to connect the activity of the trade union with that of Parliament.[36] Indeed, the presentation of Parliament in *Sybil* is of an institution in which the small-scale aggregation of parties is antithetical to the aim of national aggregation. Parliament itself, rife with factional discord, systematic misrepresentation, and petty selfishness, exemplifies the worst of national disunity. Members' loyalty is directly proportional to their gullibility, and everyone hopes eventually to sell his vote for a title. The "crotchety" Egremont, who resists party classification, is the conspicuous exception (281).

In other words, the associations and aggregations with which Disraeli and his audience are familiar are, far from being solutions, actually contributors to the problem of the two nations. Disraeli implicitly rejects statist, bureaucratic, and Benthamite measures in favor of vaguely conceived interpersonal relations between the higher and lower classes. The wish of the miners simply to meet with the masters as a way of preventing or ending strikes is briefly realized during the sacking of Mowbray Castle, when a segment of the destructive mob is instantly transformed into a squad of stout protectors by the mere fact of Sybil's calling their names. The personal addresses of St. Lys have similar catalytic power. The workers can be humanized and elevated only when they are known and individuated by their social superiors who are also their moral superiors. Presumably, something like this is what Egremont has in mind when he talks about "ensur[ing] equality, not by leveling the Few, but by elevating the Many" (294).[37]

At the conclusion to *Sybil*, like the conclusion to *Coningsby*, an awkward compromise is achieved between a stinging critiquing of Parliamentary norms and a ringing assertion that the nation's salvation will be achieved through Parliament. Disraeli manages this compromise by having Egremont tell Sybil that a new generation of Parliamentarians is on the verge of a concerted and irresistible effort to correct the evils of the recent past. As is the case with *Coningsby*, however, the novel does not look beyond the preparation of the needed personnel and the positioning of those individuals in seats of power. Is the reader to be hopeful, finally, because the new Lord Marney will be inordinately wealthy, sit in the House of Lords, and exercise considerable political influence? Or are we primarily to anticipate that Egremont's tenure as Lord Marney will redress the multitudinous grievances of his rural tenants, and that as mistress of Mowbray Castle Sybil will bring the "baronial principle" to bear on the urban catastrophe that is Mowbray and its factories? One could say that both outcomes are foreshadowed by the novel's trajectory. However, the nonstatist, interpersonal interventions valorized in the actions of Sybil, St. Lys, and Trafford do not go far to explain what Egremont will do with political power, or how the machinery of government can be turned to the idealist ends of Young England. This omission on the part of Disraeli allows him to insist on the one hand that the condition of the people can only be improved by idealist means and on the other hand that those idealist means will somehow find expression in the materialist mechanisms of Parliament. In *Tancred*, as we will see, this tension is not sidelined, and as a result it destabilizes the whole narrative.

V

In *Coningsby* and *Sybil*, Disraeli is on fairly firm ground: the quasi-aristocratic heroes who ascend to political leadership by virtue of professional talents and values make for a functional formula. In *Tancred, or the New Crusade* (1847), he abandons this formula to rehabilitate the aristocracy qua aristocracy by narrating the adventures of a young man of unquestionable aristocratic pedigree who pointedly rejects the political calling of Disraeli's earlier portraits of his Young England colleagues. The result is a startlingly different sort of book. In *Tancred* the militarism of the aristocratic ideal is favorably revived, a move made slightly more plausible by the exotic setting, and the professional values of virtue and talent are firmly attached to "race" or heredity. Although the formulation of race is in general compatible with English aristocratic values, Disraeli's use of it emphasizes Jewish/"Arabian" superiority instead.

By the time Disraeli approached this last novel in the trilogy, the Young England movement was defunct. Both Disraeli's putative subject (the Church's role in renovating society) and his political circumstances (the demise of Young England) work against his earlier formula of the development of a professional politician as the nation's savior. Disraeli now conceives that the only means of restoring the aristocracy and the nation to their proper grandeur is spiritual. However, Disraeli is out of his depth in treating spiritual subjects. As Robert Blake observes dryly, "To make the discovery of religious faith the central theme of a novel or of any book it is necessary to have had some inkling of that sentiment oneself. Disraeli lacked it."[38] The result is that the spiritual renovation that Tancred seeks and that Disraeli purportedly undertook to illuminate collapses into petty politics, Disraeli's truer element. After discarding the formulation of the professional politician, Disraeli has nothing to offer his readers but a hackneyed romantic resolution embellished by titillating inconclusiveness.

Professionals figure in *Tancred* as little more than buffoon-figures, and race is instead made the solid center of value.[39] Only "pure" races like the Sephardic Jews and, secondarily, the most authentic English aristocracy possess the *je ne sais quoi* which is the wherewithal for national or imperial leadership. A shift in Disraeli's strategy of self-promotion can be seen. His largely defensive stance of *Coningsby* and *Sybil*, in which birth is held firmly secondary to virtue and talent, works to validate his legitimacy as a political leader in spite of his non-English origins. This later offensive stance seeks to legitimate his power *because of* his belonging to the superior Jewish race.[40]

Disraeli's ambivalence toward explicitly professional characters has been noted in *Sybil*, but in *Tancred* his tone toward professionals becomes pointedly derisive. The young hero's overanxious but ingenuous parents consent to his voyage to Jerusalem only on the condition that he be attended by professional men, even at extravagant cost. The local doctor Mr. Roby is lavishly paid to suspend his practice in Bellamont and to accompany Tancred because of the duke of Bellamont's conviction of the necessity of Tancred's being attended by someone who "knows his constitution."[41] The duke and duchess similarly dispatch their chaplain and Tancred's former tutor, Mr. Bernard, to safeguard Tancred against falling victim to papist or other heresy. Colonel Brace, an old-fashioned retainer and veteran of the Peninsular war, is deemed an indispensable companion for his traveling experience and fighting capabilities.

Yet each of these figures proves to be comically ineffective on the "crusade" itself. In Jerusalem, their activities are described by Tancred's dragoman Baroni, a secret agent on loan from Sidonia:

> [T]he colonel never quits the consulate, dines there every day, and tells stories about the Peninsular war and the Bellamont cavalry, just as he did on board. Mr. Bernard is always with the English bishop, who is delighted to have such an addition to his congregation, which is not too much, consisting of his own family, the English and Prussian consuls, and five Jews, whom they have converted at twenty piastres a-week; but I know they are going to strike for wages. As for the doctor, he has not a minute to himself. The governor's wife has already sent for him; he has been admitted to the harem; has felt all their pulses without seeing any of their faces, and his medicine chest is in danger of being exhausted before your lordship requires its aid. (181)

This narrative pattern, in which the activities or inadequacies of the three professionals are catalogued together, is repeated multiple times in the novel. Each repetition reinforces the message that the professionals of

England are collectively not up to the functions they putatively profess. Indeed, these characters only figure in the novel as comic foils of inept and banal tourism compared with Tancred's exciting and, for a time, imperially significant adventures.

A sober instance of such a catalogue occurs after Tancred, having been disappointed in his vigil at the Holy Sepulchre, resolves on an excursion to Sinai and leaves without even informing his attendants. On the journey Tancred is ambushed and held for ransom and then, following a mystical vision at Sinai, becomes gravely ill:

> Notwithstanding all the prescient care of the Duke and Duchess of Bellamont, it was destined that the stout arm of Colonel Brace should not wave by the side of their son when he was first attacked by the enemy, and now that he was afflicted by a most severe, if not fatal, illness, the practiced skill of the Doctor Roby was also absent. . . . Tancred had been wounded without a single sabre of the Bellamont yeomanry being brandished in his defense; was now lying dangerously ill in an Arabian tent, without the slightest medical assistance; and perhaps was destined to quit this world, not only without the consolation of a priest of his holy church, but surrounded by heretics and infidels. (280–281)

When Tancred finally returns to Jerusalem after a six-month absence and many fantastic adventures among those "heretics and infidels," the tone shifts to the comic once again to relate the doings of his putative attendants. Not only were his friends not available in his hour of dire need, as seen above, but even "when Tancred at length did evince some disposition to settle down quietly under his own roof, and avail himself of the services and society of his friends, not one of them was present to receive and greet him" (480–481). Colonel Brace is energetically but futilely trying to educate the Syrian cook at the consul in the mysteries of plum pudding: "It was supposed to be the first time that a Christmas plum pudding had been concocted in Jerusalem, and the excitement in the circle was considerable" (480). Bernard is catechizing some converts, but the narrator knowingly remarks that the converts "had passed themselves off as true children of Israel, but . . . were, in fact, older Christians than either of their examinants; being descendants of some Nestorian families" (480). On leaving, Bernard is pursued by a band of "vagabonds" coincidentally led by "his principal catechumen" who is trying to rob him of his "very splendid copy of the Holy Writings, . . . which he always . . . displayed on any eminent instance of conversion" (482). Roby is busy collecting valuable medicinal herbs and roots, which are zestfully but ignominiously consumed by his guide as Roby sleeps in a tomb outside the gates of Jerusalem after being locked out of the city for the night. In such passages, Disraeli seems to share the locals' juvenile delight in pranking the earnest clergyman, the naïve medical attendant, and the absurdly self-important militiaman.

A similar infantilization of specialized expertise is seen in the portrayal of the chef Leander, summoned to Bellamont for Tancred's grand coming-of-age festivities. A cosmopolitan figure of unquestioned supremacy in his field, Leander at first seems a stand-in for the novel's missing positive portrayal of professionalism. But when Leander is disappointed by a lack of recognition for his culinary art on the part of the duke and duchess, an appeal to his "artistic" vanity by the worldly wise Lord Eskdale successfully raises him to even greater genius. Eskdale inspires Leander with the notion that "Leander, then, like other eminent men, had duties to perform as well as rights to enjoy; he had a right to fame, but it was also his duty to form and direct public taste" (38).[42] Eskdale thus ironically plays on Leander's professional sensibility—his ethic of service to the public—to secure Eskdale's own end of keeping the temperamental chef performing for his noble, but tasteless, employers.

And what of Coningsby and Egremont themselves? Tancred dines with them and a few other political leaders at Sidonia's house before his departure, an encounter that seems calculated to illustrate the gap between the ideals of the first two books and the final installment of the trilogy. Coningsby and Egremont are hardly the romantic heroes of the earlier books. They now figure as little more than job-men: well-intentioned but overly fixated on small ends. In effect, they concede Tancred's claim that politics is no savior, even as they try to persuade him to join the political battle with them. In the case of Lord Henry Sidney, one of Coningsby's boyhood friends, "what had been a picturesque emotion had now become a statistical argument" (135). Indeed the character of Sidney displays all the novelistic excitement a statistical argument can muster. Egremont himself is rather a dolt: "A man of fine mind rather than of brilliant talents, Lord Marney found, in the more vivid and impassioned intelligence of Coningsby, the directing sympathy he required" (139).

For his part, Coningsby is vivacious and spirited as the conversation glances from the day's activity in the House of Commons to the primal principle of race, but he attempts no response to Tancred's assertions about the futility of politics. Coningsby is piquantly mischievous, backing Sidonia's solemn observations about race but with a careless breeziness that borders on raillery. The sober steadiness that characterized him during his student days, part of the "virtue" that won Millbank's goodwill and his own change in fortune, has given way to juvenile antics that are nourished by his position of privilege: "[P]rosperity had developed in Coningsby a native vein of sauciness. . . . [E]ven there, upon the benches, with a grave face, he often indulged in quips and cranks, that convulsed his neighboring audience" (147). Edith and Sybil are similarly diminished. The group's savor for gossip about an upcoming masquerade ball contrasts unfavorably with Tancred's stoic disdain for society. In this scene Disraeli seems to ironize his own Young England colleagues, some of whom were represented in *Coningsby*.

The novel's positive figures, including Tancred and his parents, Sidonia, Eva and her father Besso, and Baroni, are either Jews or English aristocrats. Baroni is the closest thing to an effective professional in the book, but as the detailed history of his family embedded in book 3, chapter 11 makes clear, it is their Jewishness that engenders the genius of the various famous offspring of the "[p]ure Sephardim" patriarch Francis Baroni (336). The children's talent—in art, singing, acting, and dancing—is attributable to their superior Jewish blood, as is their physical perfection, seen in their amazing feats of strength, agility, and balance. "These arts are traditionary in our family," says the father (328). The children's virtue, including their industrious application to the cultivation of their talents, is the direct result of their traditional Jewish upbringing. The senior Baroni tells Sidonia, "when they wake, my children say their prayers, and then they come to embrace me and their mother. This they have never omitted during their lives. I have taught them from their birth to obey God and to honour their parents. These two principles have made them a religious and a moral family" (328). In short, the family members possess the human capital of talent and virtue *because* they are Jewish.

VI

Like the various members of the Baroni family, Tancred is preternaturally endowed with virtue and talent. Tancred's determination to make a "new crusade" to the Holy Land arises from his conviction that national and indeed continental regeneration is both desperately needed and locally unavailable. Europe is in a state of spiritual distress; its economic prosperity only masks a fundamental and pernicious malaise. Lacking any sure ground of faith and therefore of duty, Europe is powerless to determine its course by any transcendent principle. Tancred quixotically looks to "Arabia," by which he denominates all of Palestine, Syria, Lebanon, and the Arabian Desert, for divine inspiration, for "the Creator . . . has deigned to reveal himself to His creature only in one land" (54). Early on Sidonia gives Tancred the pretentious motto for his journey: "[W]hat you want is to penetrate the great Asian mystery" (124). After his vigil at the Holy Sepulchre yields no celestial vision, Tancred has already been prepared by his conversations with Sidonia and Eva to look deeper into the origins of the Church and "trace [his] steps from Calvary to Sinai" (225).

Tancred's journey into the Arabian Desert does yield the angelic visitation he craves, in an overwrought scene universally deplored by critics. But the doctrine of "theocratic equality" that is vouchsafed to him by the Angel of Arabia on Sinai is in no wise explained, and the adventures that precede and follow this vision belie its claim to sublimity. It was well said by Leslie Stephen that a reading of *Tancred* requires "accepting the theory of double consciousness, and resolving to pray with the mystic, and sneer with the politician, as the fit takes us."[43] The rollicking tale of Tancred's abduction and release, his travel in Lebanon in the company of a scheming young emir, and his visit to the remote and mysterious Ansarey tribe, has nothing in common with the mysticism of his vision or the idealism of his original crusade. Even the vision of the angel "is in the final analysis not religious at all. It is instead a worldly vision of imperial power and glory."[44] Rather, the slogan of theocratic equality serves merely as an excuse, or perhaps more grandly as an ennobling ideal, for old-fashioned imperial conquest of the Middle East, with a view to once again conquering Europe with an "idea." Why or how Europe is to be converted by persuasion to the doctrine of theocratic equality after "Asia" is converted at gunpoint is never explained, but Tancred assumes the one will follow the other as a matter of course: "Work out a great religious truth on the Persian and Mesopotamian plains, the most exuberant soils in the world with the scantiest population, it would revivify Asia. It must spread. . . . Asia revivified would act upon Europe" (303). After all, it has happened before, in the case of Christianity transforming the Western world. As Tancred subsequently says to Eva, "Send forth a great thought, as you have done before, from Mount Sinai, from the villages of Galilee, from the deserts of Arabia, and you may again remodel all [Europe's] institutions, change their principles of action, and breathe a new spirit into the whole scope of their existence" (309).

Yet quickly and even smoothly the prayer of the mystic becomes the sneer of the politician, as Tancred begins, little more than halfway through the book, to consider how his plan of conquering Asia for theocratic equality is to be accomplished. Fakredeen, the impulsive emir whose hapless political machinations are responsible for both Tancred's abduction and release, persuades Tancred to use Fakredeen's Lebanese forces as his initial army of conquest. "[F]ind a ready instrument in every human being," the angel had told the crusader; Tancred obediently repeats to Fakredeen, "The instruments [of conquest] will be found . . . for it is decreed that the deed should be done. But the favour of Providence does not exempt man from the exercise of human prudence" (368). In other words, theocratic equality, if it is to be achieved at all, must be achieved by Machiavellian politics and Alexandrian warfare. The materialist method of making people into instruments is adopted, and politico-military machinery is to bring about the world transformation.

From this point Disraeli's "exercise in astute political management of actual forces on actual territories" overruns the mystical quest entirely.[45] Tancred tells Baroni, "[T]here is not a soldier worth firing at in Asia except the Sepoys. The Persian, Assyrian, and Babylonian monarchies might be gained in a morning with faith and the flourish of a sabre" (303). At these moments Tancred comes under his creator's irony: such coolness is incongruous in this twenty-one-year-old who left England only months before and whose sole military experience is a failed frantic charge under ambush during which he got off two shots. By "faith" Tancred does not at all mean faith on his part that God will personally and supernaturally intervene on their behalf. Rather, he means that faith in a divine idea will so energize the army and galvanize the leaders as to make them invincible: "To conquer the world depends on men not only being good soldiers, but being animated by some sovereign principle that nothing can resist" (367). The world-animating power of Asian sublimity becomes indistinguishable from the calculated manipulation of the footsoldier by recourse to empty slogans (124). Tancred wants his "instruments" to do exactly what the narrator of *Coningsby* hopes the heroes of that book will *not* do—"[B]ow before shadows and worship phrases."[46] At this juncture Tancred's contemplated course is not unlike Lord Eskdale's playing on the sensibilities of Leander. The man of ideals operates like the materialist "man of the world."[47] The materialist bent of Tancred's project does not appear Benthamite in that it is explicitly military and only implicitly bureaucratic; nevertheless, the language of instrumentality and prudential utility suggests a slippage toward a materialist rationality that is out of synch with the resistance to the same in the first two novels. As Michael Flavin observes, *Tancred* reveals "the unavoidable contamination of the spiritual by the physical."[48]

Tancred introduces the question of the material means of reform—the very question kept at a distance in the first two books—into the heart of the narrative, and the tension thereby engendered between Tancred's idealism and his own and others' materialism leads to the defeat of the former. The rest of the book races through further adventures in which Tancred and Fakredeen attempt to strengthen their support base. This effort takes them to the Ansarey, a mysterious and secretive clan in the northern passes of Syria. Further embroilments lead to Fakredeen's betrayal and desertion of his friend, who is left to defend the Ansarey against an attack of Ottoman Turks. Here for the second time Tancred briefly displays his military mettle, leading a contingent of Ansarey cavalry in a thrilling charge. When their return path is cut off, however, Tancred readily yields to Baroni's advice to make their escape into the desert, leaving the Ansarey behind. Disraeli seems to relish giving his hero these military vignettes, the very thing that he repressed in the earlier novels. However, even the aristocratic grandeur of a cavalry charge is short-lived and remote, utterly alien to civilized life, even the liminal civilization of Jerusalem.

The return to Jerusalem brings the reader back to the ordinary pragmatic world from which all these adventures are an aberrant departure. Here we find the Jewish merchant Barizy, who resigns himself to the prospect of selling crucifixes to tourists with the sigh that "[c]ommerce civilizes man" (479). Immediately following Tancred's return from the desert, the conquest of the world by means of a great idea already appears quaint and quixotic even to Tancred. Tancred tells Baroni listlessly, "I wish the battle of the Gindarics had never ceased, but that, like some hero of enchantment, I had gone on for ever fighting" (481). The glorious "religious-politico-military adventure," as it is derisively termed by the disloyal Fakredeen, is finally nothing but the remembered fantasy of an overeager English traveler (439). Eva has this commentary on Tancred's adventures: "Your feelings cannot be what they were before all this happened; when you thought only of a divine cause, of stars, of angels, and of our peculiar and gifted land. No, no; now it is all mixed up with intrigue, and politics, and management, and baffled schemes, and cunning arts of men" (485). Indeed, petty politics have swallowed up Tancred's dreams of world renovation. It may be true that Disraeli "wants the reader to come away from *Tancred* with" the lesson that "world-conquest depends on 'faith' rather than 'intrigue,' " as Patrick Brantlinger has said;[49] however, the narrative itself teaches otherwise. Intrigue and faith are not so clearly distinguished in the final analysis, since faith becomes simply a means to make people into "instruments" of conquest. Tancred's own materialist intrigue is finally victorious over his prior idealist faith, just as the logic of material "blood" or race in this novel decisively prevails over the idealist logic of "talent" privileged in the first two novels.

Instead Tancred turns with his customary ardor to the pursuit of Eva's hand. When she tells him, "You no longer believe in Arabia," he fervently responds, "Why, thou to me art Arabia. . . . Talk not to me of leaving a divine cause: why, thou art my cause, and thou art most divine!" (485). The "great Asian mystery" that he set out to "penetrate" is after all nothing other than a beautiful and rich Jewish woman (124). This maudlin substitution of romantic love, Tancred's third sexual fascination in the novel, for the spiritual ideals of his original quest, can be satisfying to only the shallowest of readers. Even this resolution is undermined by the indeterminate ending, in which Tancred's proposal to Eva is interrupted by the news, brought by a crowd of attendants led by the officious Brace, Roby, and Bernard, that his parents have arrived in Jerusalem. The union of East and West, Jew and Christian, which appears to be Disraeli's telos may or may not be realized. In any case, whether the unlikely marriage takes place or not, Eva's analysis stands: Arabia is no pristine realm of continental spiritual renovation; the mystical is prey to the political, and the only recourse from the stain of politics is romantic withdrawal.

The novel that Disraeli described retrospectively as examining the function of the Church in national renovation demonstrates in its conclusion that in fact religion has no power to resist the prevalent malaise. On the contrary, the corruption and world-weariness of politics defeats Tancred's considerable ebullience; Tancred himself embraces the logic of materialist instrumentality to the demise of his own spiritual ideals. The message of this conclusion therefore goes directly against not only Disraeli's stated intention but also the message of the first half or so of the book itself: the Church, divine ideas, even race, all finally have no functional role to play in restoring England or Europe. Even all Sidonia's wisdom and wealth are finally efficacious only to prepare Tancred to love Eva. Notwithstanding Disraeli's palpable irony at his hero, the point remains that the ideals that receive the narrator's approbation early on prove unsustainable.

Reading Disraeli's intimations about the primacy of race in the first two books, and his unabashed declaration in *Tancred*—"All is race; there is no other truth"—it is easy to see why the novels can be taken as unambivalent, if fantastical, fictional expressions of Disraeli's penchant for an aristocratic polity (149). After all, "[t]his doctrine of race is akin to the belief in aristocracy," as William Flavelle Monypenny and George Earle Buckle observe, perhaps punningly.[50] However, as is apparent from the foregoing, the Young England trilogy contains mixed messages about the relationship of the professional values of virtue and talent to the aristocratic values of heredity or race. Disraeli's critique of the aristocracy on the professional grounds of expertise and training coexists with his critique of the professions on aristocratic grounds of honor and courage.

Moreover, the trilogy is just as incoherent about the work to be done by these virtuous and talented leaders. How are they to reinvent political parties *(Coningsby)* and elevate the condition of the people *(Sybil)*? What is the relationship of these leaders to transcendence *(Tancred)*? In the first two novels Disraeli negotiates these tensions by focusing on the preparation of personnel for positions of power and eliding the question of how exactly they are to use their power. When Disraeli tries to address himself to method in *Tancred*, his materialist rationality collides with his idealist loyalties. In concept Young England makes bedfellows of ideality and materiality, but the trilogy shows that for Disraeli at least, the troubled relationship between these rationalities proves irreconcilable.

CHAPTER 2

---◆◆◆---

"MANLY INDEPENDENCE": AUTONOMY IN *THE WARDEN* AND *BARCHESTER TOWERS*

> *What the Church of England wanted was increased liberty to adapt themselves to the present necessities of the people.*
>
> Samuel Wilberforce (1854)

In writing his comic early novels about Church life, Anthony Trollope is participating obliquely in the literary discourse about professionalism that it is the object of the present study to unpack. The clerical context furnishes him a readymade set of institutions and practitioners to represent the professional problems that inhere in that context. The novels treat such questions as follows: On what basis should clerical appointments be made? What sort of supervision of workers is appropriate? How should institutions be managed and governed? These issues are tinctured by the ongoing effects of the Parliamentary Church reform of the 1830s and by the inverse impulses of Puseyism and Evangelicalism as they affect the rural diocese.

Trollope's treatment of his subject is therefore essentially political. His reputation as a political novelist naturally rests on the Palliser novels; his ability to describe both the social and institutional dimensions of political life is frequently remarked upon. Trollope is aware, in fact, that politics does not equal Parliament—that social and professional contexts, provincial as well as metropolitan, are politically charged. It is arguable that Trollope's later Palliser novels dealt so successfully with politics as a profession because of his early experience, examined in this chapter, in treating the clerical profession as politics.[1]

For my purposes of studying professionalism and professional institutions, Trollope's representation of the politics of the clerical profession is especially revealing. Although the center of power under contest is a diocese and the actors clergymen, both *The Warden* (1855) and *Barchester Towers* (1857) are dominated by the story of a power struggle among professionals.[2] The "internecine war" for control of the diocese is frankly waged between representatives of old power on the one hand and usurping interlopers on the other.[3] Trollope is even more willing than Disraeli to represent the nuts and bolts of that contest: the councils where decisions are made, the conversations that determine outcomes, and the complex interactions between principle and personality that control events. Trollope has been faulted in the Palliser novels (not always justly) for reducing grand political ideas to petty social or domestic issues, but in *Barchester Towers* the opposite is true: even the domestic representations in the novel are often political.[4] Dr. and Mrs. Proudie are represented as political opponents, and Mr. Slope's romantic aspirations fit into the story only in terms of their political consequences. In short, *Barchester Towers* is a thorough demystification of what Trollope calls "the clerico-political world."[5]

In chapter 1 we examined the social-crank quality of Disraeli's politics: in advocating for the aristocratic ideal of Young England, he actually infused it with the professional ideal so as to imagine a hybrid aristocratic-professional class capable of leading the nation's affairs, too weighty to be left to amateur Parliamentarians. Trollope, in spite of the facts that he was a lifelong Whig and nursed a bigoted hatred of Disraeli, also exhibits some of the recognizable traits of a social crank.[6] Trollope's well-known penchant for rule by old, landed families is undergirded by his belief that gentlemen alone have the training, the service ethic, and the personal disinterest needed for running the nation's affairs. In other words, Trollope wants gentlemen to rule, but he understands that those gentlemen have to be professional gentlemen in order to rule well. Although Trollope wrote in *The New Zealander*, "The aristocrat is . . . of all men the best able to rule,"[7] he clearly defined "aristocrat" by function and expertise rather than by birth: "This aristocracy, these foremen in the great workshop of the world, are chosen from among the people, from out of the ordinary labourers, and should be so chosen on account of their special worth and value in regulating the allotted tasks of those beneath them."[8] The same is true of Trollope's views on the leadership of the Church: like good politicians, good clergymen are gentlemen cast in a professional mold—able, diligent, and conscientious besides being well mannered and well spoken.

Jill Felicity Durey, in *Trollope and the Church of England*, sees a progression in Trollope's ecclesiastical fiction that increasingly privileges merit, service, and skill in comparison with "the older-style gentleman clergyman." I do not share Durey's view of a gradual shift in Trollope's mentality from a gentlemanly to a professional standard for clergymen; rather, as this chapter will make evident, I see clear sympathy for the Church's need for "new vigour, new skills, and new blood" at least as early as *Barchester Towers*.[9] By the same token, Trollope's preoccupation with the gentlemanliness of clergy (or lack thereof) remains very strong even in *The Last Chronicle of Barset* (1867). Nevertheless, I concur with Durey that Trollope by no means simply reifies traditional myths of gentlemanliness but rather negotiates the interaction of such myths with rising professional ideology.

Trollope also brings some pressure to bear on professional ideals in that his novels explore, for example, how fictions of merit are used to legitimate entirely political appointments. In particular, however, my readings of *The Warden* and *Barchester Towers* will examine the tension between autonomy and collectivism in the professional ideal. By autonomy I mean not radically isolated, untrammeled personal choices as the literal roots of the word indicate; rather, I use the word to refer to a relative freedom from hierarchical regimentation, or the privilege to exercise one's trained judgment to make decisions about how to apply received general principles to particular circumstances.[10]

This chapter will first establish how autonomy poses a problem of self-contradiction within the professional ideal, in that the autonomy desired by the professional association is in conflict with the autonomy of the individual practitioner. Trollope's own positions on collective and individual autonomy in the Civil Service show his unwillingness to sacrifice either side of the autonomy equation, and his representations of professional disputes in his first Barsetshire novels evince his desire to imagine a way of preserving both forms of professional autonomy. Harding's most valorized actions are taken in defiance of the norms of his profession, yet for that very reason he obviates the need for supervisory intrusion by either internal or external managers.

I

Autonomy is an issue for professionalism in two respects: the autonomy of the individual practitioner and the autonomy of the professional group. In terms of the individual practitioner, it is self-evident that professionals, in dealing with their clients, must be capable of independently applying their theoretical knowledge to specific circumstances. This autonomy is enabled and bolstered by the service ethic: the professional's high ethical standard imbues him with the trustworthiness that makes possible his freedom from supervision. Burton J. Bledstein remarks,

> In the service of mankind—the highest ideal—the professional resisted all corporate encroachments and regulations upon his independence, whether from government bureaucrats, university trustees, business administrators, public laymen, or even his own professional associations. The culture of professionalism released the creative energies of the free person who was usually accountable only to himself and his personal interpretation of the ethical standards of his profession.[11]

As a fully trained practitioner, actuated by a service ethic to protect his client's welfare, a professional is by definition his own supervisor.[12]

Victorian professionals themselves undoubtedly held their autonomy dear. Byerley H. Thomson wrote in 1857 that among the benefits of the "professional classes" to "the great English middle class" is that they "maintain its tone of independence."[13] In an 1864 *Cornhill* article titled "The Church as a Profession," one of the chief attractions of a clerical career was held to be that "on the whole a clergyman regulates his duties to a very great degree by his own notion of their importance, and he has to act for the most part on his own sense of duty, with little, if any, interference or superintendence on the part of any official superior."[14]

However, autonomy, as we know, is always relative, and professional autonomy poses something of a paradox to itself. A few chapters after Thomson's assertion about the "tone of independence" maintained by the professional classes, he writes that "[i]n a profession a man must follow the trammels of a system, and any system of education that does not early train the mind and wishes to yield to the pressure of the harness is defective for professional education."[15] The "trammels" referred to are the protocols of professional associations, which, in order to maintain *their* autonomy from lay oversight, must in turn impinge upon the autonomy of their members.

The proliferation of new professional associations in the second half of the nineteenth century is often cited as the key index of the advance of the professional project.[16] The professional's resistance to accountability and oversight is necessarily complicated by this simultaneous imperative to institutionalize. The public trust that forms much of the professional's cultural capital can only be achieved by some degree of standardization of knowledge, and it is the task of the professional association to set and maintain that standardization or uniformity.[17] In the words of the barrister Alfred V. Dicey in 1867,

"[I]n the case of a profession its members sacrifice a certain amount of individual liberty in order to insure certain professional objects."[18] Indeed, when Dicey undertakes to explain to the public the nature and extent of the Bar's function as restrictive of free trade, he devotes considerable space to the question of whether and how the Bar's code of etiquette is binding upon its members.

The function of the professional association is therefore to guarantee the practitioner's autonomy precisely by compromising it in the interests of the autonomy of the profession as a whole. A professional association's power hinges upon the association's ability to convince the state and/or public that it has the exclusive ability to regulate the standard of competency and probity of its members. Partly by the persuasive effects of enculturation into the field, and partly by potentially coercive mechanisms such as licensing and censure, associations police their members (or pretend to do so) to ensure conformity to the high standard of service that is the basis of the profession's autonomy in the first place.[19] Convinced that the expertise they control is vital to society and that they are the only ones qualified to wield that expertise, professions paint their freedom from lay control as a victory for the public welfare.[20]

Critics, on the other hand, view professional autonomy as pernicious. According to Eliot Freidson, the professions' "autonomy has created their narrow perspective and their self-deceiving views of themselves and their work, their conviction that they know best what humanity needs."[21] Similarly, Magali Sarfatti Larson's critique of the production of professionals according to a standardized rubric of knowledge implies that the autonomy of the profession from lay oversight is problematic not least because of the way it infringes on the autonomy of the practitioner.[22] Where professions themselves are ascendant, Larson suggests, the individual autonomy of the practitioner is little more than a fiction.

Trollope explores a similar irony in his portrayal of the *Jupiter*. Tom Towers, the mysterious yet virtually omnipotent editor, sanctimoniously trumpets the public value of the "free press" and the necessity of the paper's being uninfluenced by interested parties. As Towers sermonizes, "Look at the recognized worth of different newspapers, and see if it does not mainly depend on the assurance which the public feel that such a paper is, or is not, independent."[23] Bold can only fume at this hypocrisy, knowing that Towers was eager for Bold's intervention as long as his information, accurate or not, coincided with the *Jupiter*'s predetermined agenda. The autonomy of the paper, secured by the anonymity of the writers and editors, becomes a smokescreen for highly interested partisanship. Anonymity gives Towers himself a radical autonomy that Trollope presents as dangerous: "Each of [the politicians] was responsible to his country, each of them must answer if inquired into. . . . But to whom was he, Tom Towers, responsible?"[24] However, as Slope learns when the paper turns against him, "a man who aspires to be on the staff of the *Jupiter* must surrender all individuality."[25] The so-called free press is based on totalitarian control of the opinions of its workers.

Trollope himself cherished both kinds of autonomy, as his record in the Post Office indicates. Edmund Yates recalled that Trollope "would savagely rap the knuckles of any hand meddling in his affairs."[26] It is well-known that Trollope's Post Office career—not to mention his fiction writing—first began to look promising when he was transferred from the London office, where his mechanical tasks were under continual supervision, to a post as surveyor's clerk in Ireland, where he enjoyed much more freedom of action.[27] His 1861 lecture on "The Civil Service as a Profession" addresses the necessity for both individual and corporate autonomy in the Civil Service. Trollope devotes more than a third of the lecture to the subject of the autonomy of the state worker, or in his words, the "manly independence without which no profession can be pleasant."[28] Unlike Crown offices in the old days, when patronage to sinecures entailed obligations other than the work to be done, the Civil Service of his time could properly require only the contracted labor of the worker, not his servility of opinion or conduct. Though Trollope acknowledges that young practitioners in all professions are subject to supervision and rebuke by their seniors, he denies that the Civil Service needs to be more coercive than any other profession as long as the workers themselves refuse to be so treated. Trollope defends the ability and the industry of the majority of the Crown's employees, implying that they are as worthy of public trust in the execution of their duties as the members of more prestigious professions.

Trollope was equally committed to the autonomy of the Civil Service as a profession in its own right. To that end he vehemently opposed Benthamite incursions into the operation of the Civil Service. Trollope particularly insisted that the leading offices of the Civil Service must be reserved for civil servants themselves rather than awarded as political offices, thereby insuring that the profession would be led by its own and not by outsiders.[29] In the same lecture he described Civil Service reform as the work of "certain government pundits who were selected to remodel our profession, and who thereupon proceeded to chop it up mince-meat fashion, and boil it in a Medea's cauldron so that the ugly old body might come out young and lovely."[30] Trollope was persistently outspoken on the subject of competitive examinations, which he deplored.[31] The competitive examination epitomized the Benthamite rationality in personnel decisions: it presumed that the best candidate could be ascertained by a mechanical procedure of determining the quantity of knowledge he possessed. Such measures, Trollope felt, were unreliable indicators of a person's ability to perform a given task. When used to make promotions, the examinations were grossly unfair because they privileged the young, with their superior and more recent educations, at the expense of senior workers, who might have served diligently for many years.[32] Thus Trollope was committed to the autonomy of the Civil Service as a profession in terms of its freedom from micromanagement by government figures.

Given Trollope's affection for "manly independence" in civil servants in particular and the Civil Service in general, we may expect Trollope's novels to conceptualize a way to cut the Gordian knot of the apparently irreconcilable claims of the autonomy of the profession and the autonomy of the practitioner. Indeed, Trollope has recourse to professional ideals to imagine how the autonomy of the individual clergyman can in fact reinforce rather than problematize the autonomy of the clerical profession. The fiction also makes apparent that "manly independence" is emphatically a privilege and responsibility exercised by men. Excluded de facto from the clerical profession, women in the novels are castigated for assertions of autonomy.

II

The Warden and *Barchester Towers* present both aspects of the problem of professional autonomy. *The Warden* is concerned with the general level of the Church's relationship to lay control, and *Barchester Towers* is primarily concerned with the particular level of the mechanisms for personnel management within the Church.[33] In both novels, the crass aspects of the dominant entrepreneurial or Benthamite ideal are unfavorably juxtaposed to professional ideals, which are presented as both vestigial (with roots in traditional gentility) and emergent (partaking of what is choiceworthy in the entrepreneurial order) at the same time. Thus Trollope aims for a "balance or synthesis between two mid-Victorian popular ideals: the upper-class myth of the born-and-bred gentleman, and the entrepreneurial myth of the self-made man."[34]

Harold Perkin astutely describes Evangelicalism and the Oxford Movement, the two poles of the clerical dispute in *Barchester Towers*, as twin efforts to "professionalize the clergy."[35] Whereas the Oxford Movement "emphasiz[ed] the sacerdotal character of the clerical office which segregated them from the laity and freed them from lay control," Evangelicalism "demand[ed] a more sober standard of conduct, morality, speech and dress than the average gentlemanly cleric of the eighteenth century."[36] These descriptions are apt characterizations of the positions of Dr. Grantly and Mr. Arabin on the one side and Mrs. Proudie and Mr. Slope on the other.

There is, however, a distinct affinity between Slope's and Arabin's sentiments about the responsibility of the Church hierarchy to the lower orders of clergymen: both seek to professionalize the backward rural clergy. In his letter to Tom Towers, Slope rhapsodizes about the need to make cathedrals "lead the way and show an example for all our parochial clergy!" (2:60). For his part, Arabin's early ambition is "to assist in infusing energy and faith into the hearts of Christian ministers, who were, as he thought, too often satisfied to go through life without much show of either" (1:190). Both movements seek what amounts to a contradiction in terms: to professionalize the clergy while taking away some of their autonomy—indeed *by* doing so. As Trollope sees it, professionalization cannot occur without "manly independence" or autonomy; therefore interference with clerical autonomy is the evil on all sides. As Trollope's resolution will show, the clergy do not need to be managed in order to be made professional; on the contrary, when allowed to practice with autonomy they will conduct themselves in accordance with professional ideals. Nevertheless, the insight that both Evangelicalism and the Oxford Movement participate in the same project of professionalization highlights the subtext of Church reform that runs throughout both books.

The Church reform movement of the 1830s and 1840s arose from the clash between traditional notions of Church prerogatives and Benthamite ideas about political utility. The traditional notion of the clerical freehold was challenged by Benthamism and the entrepreneurial ideal, which valued accountability and supervision. Since "churches . . . have functions which the principle of utility cannot easily test," these clashing ideals inevitably led to tension in the church-state relationship, as became visible in the Whig campaign for Church reform in the 1830s and 1840s.[37] Indeed, as Kenneth A. Thompson's useful and thorough account in *Bureaucracy and Church Reform* shows, the Ecclesiastical Commission itself was characterized by constant tensions between bureaucratic centralization (with its values of "speed, efficiency, economy, regularity, and uniformity") and the locally driven "principle of collegiality."[38]

The urban population explosion that accompanied industrialization created a need to shift Church resources from well-heeled rural dioceses to overcrowded slums in which Church presence was minimal. The Ecclesiastical Commission, begun by Sir Robert Peel in 1835 and reorganized and made permanent by the Ecclesiastical Commissioners Act of 1836 under the Whig administration, worked out compromises designed to reform the Church gradually under state auspices while avoiding heavy-handed infringements of Church privilege by the state. Not without difficulty, the Church accepted limitations to its autonomy as a means of warding off radical measures such as disestablishment or disendowment. Moreover, bishops on the Ecclesiastical Commission recognized that the principle of utility had to be observed in the allocation of existing Church funds before the state would be willing to put taxpayer money into Church coffers for badly needed construction.[39] In a series of three acts between 1836 and 1840, episcopal incomes were reduced and equalized while pluralities, cathedral sinecures, and nonresident prebendaries were suppressed. Most of these reforms were designed to take effect only with the death of the incumbents, so actual changes in the number and income of officeholders were phased in over the course of the next generation.[40]

The 1854 statement of Samuel Wilberforce, son of the antislavery reformer, expresses one Church response to these developments: "What the Church of England wanted was increased liberty to adapt themselves to the present necessities of the people."[41] Wilberforce thus represents institutional autonomy as necessary to the Church's efficient functioning and implies that state oversight is a hindrance, not a help, to institutional efficiency. One can imagine Archdeacon Grantly solemnly assenting. Yet Wilberforce, as the bishop of Oxford, was a very active diocesan reformer, using a variety of means to persuade or pressure the clergy in his diocese to take their spiritual and temporal duties more seriously. Wilberforce, then, was perhaps not unlike what Arabin aspired to be. He defended the Church against lay management by imposing a more managerial approach on his clergy.[42]

These developments form the backdrop for *The Warden* and *Barchester Towers*. Trollope's representation of the reform mentality of John Bold and Obadiah Slope finely captures the public mood. In *The Warden*, John Bold applies the Benthamite ideals of efficiency, accountability, and egalitarianism to the administration of Hiram's will (though of course Trollope ironizes these ideals in Bold himself).

Bold seeks to use legal processes and public opinion, represented by the *Jupiter*, to hold the Church accountable to the laity for its allocation of its revenues, while the representatives of the "church militant" aggressively defend their institutional autonomy. In *Barchester Towers*, the focus shifts to the working of Benthamite rationality from *within* the Church institutions. In this novel, oversight of the Church by civic authorities is regarded as a regrettable, but established, evil, whereas the presence of Benthamite overseers (literally, in the form of Bishop Proudie and his cohorts) within the Church hierarchy is an evil not to be endured. As Archdeacon Grantly puts it, the danger to the Church is not from outside but from "the set of canting, low-bred hypocrites who are wriggling their way in among us; men who . . . take up some popular cry" (1:44). The threat in the second novel is not that external forces may infringe on the Church's privileges but that the "popular" influences of the day will find their way into the ranks of the clergy.

III

John Bold, a nonpracticing surgeon and marginal professional, insists on the efficient (that is, utilitarian) distribution of Church revenues under public scrutiny, while Archdeacon Grantly is chiefly animated by his belief in the immunity of the Church to lay oversight, principally in financial matters. Grantly "would consign to darkness and perdition, not only every individual reformer, but every committee and every commission that would even dare to ask a question respecting the appropriation of church revenues."[43] His ecclesiastical loyalty is frankly an essentially pecuniary matter: "When Dr. Grantly talks of unbelieving enemies, he does not mean to imply want of belief in the doctrines of the church, but an equally dangerous skepticism as to its purity in money matters."[44] Traditional professional privilege and autonomy clashes with utilitarian logic, and Trollope highlights the inability of both to find a just resolution to the problem of the hospital.

The scandal over the hospital exposes both the vacuum that the passing of time-honored tradition has created and the poverty of the Benthamite efforts to fill that vacuum. Now that demands for managed, modern efficiency in the use of resources attach themselves even to obscure episcopal appointments, demands that carry a certain inarguable justice, Harding's simple equanimity in his fortunate situation can never be recovered. Trollope means for the reader to share Harding's disquiet. As he told his colleagues in his lecture on

"The Civil Service as a Profession," "[A] sinecurist is a contemptible fellow," and in his *Autobiography* Trollope applies the label "dishonest" to "[t]he clergyman who is content to live on a sinecure."[45]

Harding, literally unable to understand Hiram's will or to conceive how its stipulations ought to be applied in the modern day, believes he requires professional guidance to know what to do about the qualms of conscience thus awakened. However, his search for a "true" professional, one who combines expert knowledge of the case with sympathy with Harding's scruples, is ultimately futile. The bishop offers sympathy but neither the expert knowledge nor the active energy to settle Harding's doubts. Harding's other advisors, Archdeacon Grantly and the Attorney General Sir Abraham Haphazard, confidently tell him what to do but have no understanding of Harding's pained conscience. Since Grantly lacks this sympathy, his militant asseverations of the absolute rights and rightness of the Church carry no more moral authority than the mystifications of Sir Abraham Haphazard, whose refutation of Bold's case rests on a legal quibble rather than a principle of justice.

Harding is therefore required to act independently of all of them, guided by his conscience despite his imperfect understanding of the legal and ecclesiastical issues at stake. The heroism of the novel, understated as it is, is an act of professional autonomy. Harding is guided by his internal ethical code to resist the judgments of experts, including those of his superiors in the Church hierarchy. Thus he participates in the paradox of autonomy that I elucidated above: Harding's autonomous act both ratifies and defies the state oversight that was the hallmark of early Victorian Church reform. By resigning, Harding implicitly demonstrates his discomfort with the Church's logic of absolute property. This is, in fact, why Archdeacon Grantly tells him it would be "cowardice" to resign: Harding's resignation has the appearance of acquiescence to the reform agenda.[46] At the same time, however, Harding's act also obviates the reform process, since he voluntarily acts according to the very ideal that the reform ineffectively attempts to normalize. In being apparently disloyal to the Church in this way, Harding is actually loyal to a higher ideal that itself legitimizes the Church's claim to autonomy from state oversight. Trollope's solution, then, disallows a clear victory for either the Benthamite reformers or the traditional professionals; instead, it involves a traditional professional adjusting himself to utilitarian logic to the extent his conscience requires. This blending of old and new attitudes about professional work will be even more prominent in *Barchester Towers*.

IV

The effects of Benthamite reform on the clerical profession are more complex and insidious in *Barchester Towers*, in which the Benthamite ideal finds a foothold within the Church and excites the animosity of Archdeacon Grantly and his colleagues. In this novel, more because of a difference in Trollope's emphasis than because of a historical change occurring in the five years intervening between the novels, Parliamentary reform seems to be taken for granted by the clergymen as an established evil. The comments about the reduced income of Barchester's bishop and dean, the suppression of prebendary sinecures, and (newly enforced) prohibitions against absenteeism are generally made with a tone more of resignation than outrage.[47] On the other hand, the introduction of Benthamite rationality and activity into Barchester close by the Proudies and Slope arouses all the bellicosity the sleepy town can muster. The main matter of the book centers on whether a man of the new or old order will get each contested appointment: the bishopric, the hospital wardenship, and the deanship. The questions of institutional management, grounds for promotion, and individual and institutional autonomy are therefore in the foreground of the political machinations that fill the book.

To identify the players in the conflict as "old" and "new" is, however, insufficiently precise. Although Benthamism is new to the ranks of Barchester clergy, the novel represents the entrepreneurial ideal as being already dominant in society at large. The figures of Bishop Grantly and Dean Trefoil, both of whom die in the novel, are vestiges of an age already gone by. Whiggery may be newly in power on Downing Street, but it is hardly an emergent order. On the contrary, it is represented as a late arrival in Barchester; Barchester is being newly affected by trends that have already swept the nation. Trollope's ideal, as we will see, is a professional ideal that he manages to cast as both emergent and residual, a revision of traditional ideals that is newer than Benthamism because it is older.

The contest between these orders disputes nothing less than the nature of clerical work—in effect, the predominant ideal of the clerical profession. The novel's Evangelicals, spouting Benthamite or entrepreneurial ideals with their heavily predetermined distaste to the reader, seek to import into clerical life an ethic that insists upon real work, and accountability thereof, in exchange for a stipend, and to make personal merit the sole basis for professional advancement. The inherent congeniality of Benthamism and Evangelicalism, as Perkin demonstrates, made Benthamites and Dissenters reliable cobelligerents: "The Benthamites were in fact 'secular Evangelicals,' burning with a passion for moral reform."[48]

It is principally as a representative of the entrepreneurial order that Slope comes before the reader's notice. That is, his Whiggery, his lower-middle-class status (he was a sizar at Cambridge), and his Evangelicalism are all characteristics that position him as the spokesman of the "new" in the clerical profession. Therefore Mr. Harding's "antipathies . . . were directed against those new, busy, uncharitable, self-lauding men, of whom Mr. Slope was so good an example" (1:112). Slope's enthusiasm for the entrepreneurial ideal is not surprising considering that the traditional mechanisms of career advancement are all but closed to him; he aims to be the Samuel Smiles of the Church of England.

In announcing to the aged Mr. Harding that the hospital appointment will now be contingent upon an onerous set of new responsibilities, Slope delivers the following sermon on the new professional order:

> It is not only in Barchester that a new man is carrying out new measures and casting away the useless rubbish of past centuries. The same thing is going on throughout the country. Work is now required from every man who receives wages; and they who have to superintend the doing of work, and the paying of wages, are bound to see that this rule is carried out. New men, Mr. Harding, are now needed, and are now forthcoming in the Church, as well as in other professions. (1:111–112)

In this speech Slope puts the clerical profession on an entrepreneurial footing. He elaborates on the ways that the entrepreneurial ideal is changing professional activity in the country at large: the elimination of sinecures, the institutionalization of the work ethic, and the loss of autonomy occasioned by supervision and accountability.

Slope particularly covets and relishes supervisory power. The supremacy that is the ambition of Slope is the power "to assume the tyrant. . . . His looks and tones are extremely severe" (1:28). Slope "conceives it to be his duty to know all the private doings and desires of the flock entrusted to his care. . . . [H]e exacts an unconditional obedience to set rules of conduct" (1:31). When combined with his Evangelical and especially his Sabbatarian obsessions, this will to power is pernicious to Barchester and devastating to Mr. Harding. By representing Slope in this way, Trollope makes Benthamite supervision, as opposed to gentlemanly autonomy, the enemy of professional performance as well as of community goodwill.

Although Archdeacon Grantly is portrayed hyperbolically in *The Warden* as a "merciless tyrant" to his father and father-in-law,[49] in *Barchester Towers* Grantly's tyranny is greatly moderated to form a more conspicuous contrast to that of Slope. Grantly characteristically puts institutional loyalty above doctrine or conduct: "[A]s long as those around him were tainted with no heretical leaning towards dissent, as long as they fully and freely admitted the efficacy of Mother Church, he was willing that that mother should be merciful and affectionate, prone to indulgence, and unwilling to chastise" (1:31).[50] For example, both the archdeacon and his father the bishop had been "too lenient" to absentees such as Dr. Stanhope, who is summoned home by a letter from Mr. Slope within a few months of Dr. Proudie's installation (1:69). Slope threatens Stanhope with exposure to public outrage and to political sanctions: "[I]t behooved Dr. Vesey Stanhope not to allow his name to stand among those which would probably in a few months be submitted to the councils of the nation" (1:70). Slope's intrusive disciplinary method therefore involves utilizing the climate of reform as a stick with which to beat refractory churchmen. To gain personal supremacy, Slope is willing to compromise even the Church's jurisdiction over its own personnel.[51]

Slope's discourse to Harding on the character of clerical work also raises the question of how decisions about preferments should be made. Both the entrepreneurial and the professional ideals call for selection by demonstrated merit. Although merit was always in some way considered under the patronage system, the entrepreneurial ideal sought to make merit, as determined by competitive examinations, the only basis for promotion. Since the Church operates on a patronage basis, the question is how seriously merit is considered when those high in the Church hierarchy use their power to award desirable positions. Slope asserts (hypocritically, as we will see) personal merit as the only reasonable ground for promotion decisions; however, even he cannot resist the powerful public opinion that Mr. Harding has an indisputable claim to the wardenship. After Parliament's intervention, when no further scandal could possibly be raised, all assume Mr. Harding will be invited to resume his former place. For this reason Mr. Quiverful, in a heroic display of professional etiquette, is careful to ascertain Mr. Harding's voluntary renunciation of the post before accepting it himself. When the deanship later becomes vacant, Dr. Gwynne manages to secure the nomination of Mr. Harding by urging "the claims which Mr. Harding had on the Government" (2:259). Thus in the case of the deanship, Mr. Harding initially receives the preferment because of a prior claim represented to the authorities by an interested friend.

In cases where neither seniority nor a prior claim is involved, however, promotion decisions revolve around both interest and merit, or more usually, interest disguised as merit. That is, for a degree of legitimacy to be maintained in the public eye, personal interest must be represented publicly as merit-based. This phenomenon operates in Dr. Grantly's choice of Mr. Arabin to hold the living at St. Ewold's. When Dr. Grantly preaches the Sunday evening service on the day of Mr. Arabin's installation, "[h]e told them that it had become his duty to look about for a pastor for them. . . . Then he took a little merit to himself for having so studiously provided the best man he could without reference to patronage or favor; but he did not say that the best man according to his views was he who was best able to subdue Mr. Slope" (2:234). The narrative logic at work in the novel allows this appointment to be felicitous to all concerned: Arabin *is* worthy of Church leadership, and his position in Barchester allows for his eventual accession to the deanship. However, the fact that Grantly feels it incumbent on him to explain his disinterestedness and Arabin's merit is evidence of the operation and ascendancy of the ideal of merit-based preferment, a notion central to both the entrepreneurial and professional ideals.[52]

Slope, as the embodiment of the entrepreneurial ideal within the novel, has an even more convoluted relationship to fictions of merit. While acknowledging that his "merit," in the form of his ability to manipulate people, is the basis of his hope for success, he deploys his personal skills, particularly writing, to attain the interest that will further his success. That is, he endorses a system of meritorious advancement, but his merit (as acknowledged by the narrator) consists mainly of cultivating the support of all types of patrons. Thus when he aspires to the deanship, Slope artfully enlists the bishop, a Member of Parliament, and the editor of the *Jupiter* to act on his interest. Of the three, he puts the most confidence in the *Jupiter*, that self-appointed watchdog on ecclesiastical breaches of Benthamite rationality. Accordingly, Slope's letter to Tom Towers blends careful flattery and abundant appeals to the entrepreneurial ideal. He dwells on the importance of realizing the powerful contribution to be made by "cathedral establishments" without attempting to specify what that contribution might be; he only asserts that for cathedrals to make such a contribution they must be "managed" (2:60). As we have already seen, "management" for Slope is tyranny. Slope's letter to Tom Towers goes on:

The time has, in fact, come, in which no government can venture to fill up the high places of the Church in defiance of the public press. The age of honorable bishops and noble deans has gone by; and any clergyman however humbly born can now hope for success, if his industry, talent, and character be sufficient to call forth the manifest opinion of the public in his favor. (2:60)

Slope thus opposes hereditary interest to individual merit and the will of the people, guided or reflected by the periodical press. His putative celebration of the merit-based preferment of the emergent ideal appears in the context of a request for old-fashioned interested intervention.

When the *Jupiter* does print an enthusiastic endorsement of Slope, it does so in terms that further discredit the order of merit. The *Jupiter*'s stated preference for "a man of forty [rather] than . . . a man of sixty" is founded on its purported commitment to the entrepreneurial ideal that Slope has already expounded: "If we are to pay deans at all, we are to pay them for some sort of work. That work, be it what it may, will be best performed by a workman in the prime of life" (2:185). The *Jupiter*'s ignorance of the work of a dean is matched by its ignorance of the candidate it endorses. The *Jupiter*'s recommendation of Slope for the post is based on meritorious qualifications that are uninvestigated and counterfactual. Moreover, as the narrator points out, the *Jupiter*'s endorsement of Slope is nothing more than a gimmick for filling pages: "Those caterers for our morning repast, the staff of the *Jupiter*, had been sorely put to it for the last month to find a sufficiency of proper pabulum . . . and a dead dean with the necessity for a live one was a godsend. Had Dr. Trefoil died in June, Mr. Towers would probably not have *known so much about the piety* of Mr. Slope" (2:186, my emphasis). That is, the *Jupiter*'s "knowledge" about the merit of its candidate is based on nothing other than the self-interest of the paper's editor, who is hard-pressed for periodical content. The press's privileged expertise is only a self-interested sham.

The narrator cannot resist direct unfavorable comment on the ideals of Slope and his ilk. Immediately after Slope's confrontation with Mr. Harding, while Mr. Harding is sadly reproaching himself with what he imagines to be true in Slope's rebuke, the narrator is clear to exonerate Mr. Harding by discrediting the tone and ideology of Slope:

> What cruel words these had been; and how often they are now used with all the heartless cruelty of a Slope! A man is sufficiently condemned if it can only be shown that either in politics or religion he does not belong to some new school established within the last score of years. He may then regard himself as rubbish and expect to be carted away. A man is nothing now unless he has within him a full appreciation of the new era; an era in which it would seem that neither honesty nor truth is very desirable, but in which success is the only touchstone of merit. (1:116)

The narrator thus exposes and reproaches the faddism he sees as endemic to Benthamism, and his remarks are not specific to the Church although they include it. The order of merit theorized by the emergent professional order is discredited here directly as it is indirectly in the description of Slope's efforts to get the deanship; "merit" has become a smokescreen for faddism and celebrity worship. As Trollope sees it, the touting of "merit" has ironically become an excuse to ignore a person's real or intrinsic merit ("honesty and truth") and focus only on extrinsic "success," a measure of worth almost sure to reward those, like Slope, who are unscrupulous in using people and circumstances to their advantage.

Slope's outrageous ambition is one of two models in this novel for the inappropriate assumption of professional standing. The other model is expressed in different ways by the two principal women characters in the novel, Mrs. Proudie and Eleanor Bold. These characters show that autonomous action on the part of women is consistently regarded as disruptive and counterproductive, which is to say that Trollope excludes women from the status of the professional.[53] Mrs. Proudie seeks to dominate diocesan affairs in a manner that frankly astonishes Grantly and Harding. Finding her in the bishop's company when they come to call, they are forced to "make the best of her"; nevertheless, "[c]ome what come might, Dr. Grantly was not to be forced into a dissertation on a point of doctrine with Mrs. Proudie" (1:34, 38). By turning his back on her in the middle of her Sabbatarian diatribe and addressing a perfunctory question to the bishop, Grantly enacts the exclusion of women from professional activity that the novel as a whole performs. Mrs. Proudie's professional ambitions are set alongside those of Slope and Grantly only to be mocked: the narrator refers to the contest among Grantly, Slope, Mrs. Proudie, and Bishop Proudie for control of the bishop's seat as a "competitive examination of considerable severity" in which Mrs. Proudie is victorious (2:253). A more damning indictment of the examination system can hardly be imagined.

Mrs. Proudie's public and boastful display of dominance over her husband is contrasted to Susan Grantly's more subtle method of having her way. Susan is frequently successful in turning her husband's course of action because she exercises "the tact and talent of women" by reducing him to silence in private but comporting herself "meekly" in public. She exercises only the limited degree of autonomy she knows he will tolerate: "[T]hat wise and talented lady too well knew the man to whom her lot for life was bound, to stretch her authority beyond the point at which it would be borne."[54] Talent or expertise for women becomes the invisible manipulation of men; a woman like Mrs. Proudie, presuming to intrude upon the expert realm of the "business of bishoping" is not to be recognized by a gentleman like Grantly (1:35).

Professional status, and the autonomy that accompanies it, is therefore denied to the female characters in Trollope's work. Many of the missed cues that jeopardize the progress of Arabin's courtship of Eleanor originate in Eleanor's insistence on her independence from the Grantlys' managerial jurisdiction. First by telling her sister, "I do not choose to be cross-examined as to my letters by any one," and then by responding to her brother-in-law's questions with "sheer opposition and determination not to succumb," Eleanor effectively confirms their unfounded suspicions that she is encouraging advances from Slope (2:11; 2:19). Although Grantly's compulsion to micromanage is partly to blame for this episode, Eleanor's spirit of autonomy is held principally responsible. Her impulse to oppose Grantly is explicitly a refusal to fall into a faction: "I hate a religion that teaches one to be so onesided in one's charity" (2:11). Moreover, Harding's extreme reticence about exercising his paternal authority, even so far as to ask his daughter about her feelings, prevents the misconstruals from being easily cleared away. Caught between Grantly's excessive managerial impulse and her father's insufficiently active management, Eleanor flounders in her independent determinations. The same resistance to blind factionalism for which Harding is valorized is nearly fatal to Eleanor's happiness and indeed to the whole comic resolution of the novel.

V

While Trollope's negative ideal is transparent in the novel's hearty condemnation of Slope and of the Benthamite entrepreneurial ideal he represents, Trollope's positive ideal of professionalism is found in the pair that, arguably, serve as the novel's coheroes: Mr. Harding and Mr. Arabin. The novel concludes with these two men announced as "co-deans" (2:263), and their familial as well as professional union signals Trollope's effort to reconcile the best of the available ideals into an idiosyncratic professional ideal. Where the entrepreneurial and professional ideals coincide, as in the principle of selection by merit, Trollope has his heroes adopt the entrepreneurial ideal into their "gentlemanly" conduct. As we saw in *The Warden*, Trollope makes his own ideal partake of aspects of the entrepreneurial ideal he has discredited for being hypocritical when practiced by their most vocal adherents. Whereas in the first novel Harding comes to accept the imperative for responsible use of Church and charitable funds, in the second one Harding embraces the ideal of selection by merit. Both Harding and Arabin are loyal to the institution of the Church; both are conscientious in their service to the Church and the public; and both believe in the importance of "true" merit in selecting office-holders. Trollope therefore manages to cast the emergent professional ideals as something traditional and time-honored, yet capable of renewal in the contemporary milieu. Such renewal, moreover, is made possible by the *autonomy* that Trollope makes central to his imagined professional realm. Arabin's vocational crisis leads him to conclusions about professional autonomy that are a direct contrast to the tyrannical "management" of Slope, and Harding's most valorized actions are those taken in defiance of the norms, yet in compliance with the ideals, of his profession.

In Arabin Trollope offers an embodiment of professional ideals purged of Benthamite associations, and Arabin's professional ideal develops explicitly in reference to clerical autonomy. Arabin's early managerial ambition is to revitalize the rural clergy with elements of the Benthamite ideal. As we have seen, he wants to "do somewhat toward redeeming and rectifying [the rural clergy's] inferiority," and "to assist in infusing energy and faith into the hearts of Christian ministers, who were, as he thought, too often satisfied to go through life without much show of either" (1:190). Not unlike Slope with his obnoxious Sabbatarianism, Arabin believes himself ideally suited to improve others by regulating their conduct and attitudes. He imagines himself serving the public by subjecting other clergymen, whom he regards as inferior, to supervision by Oxford men and therefore depriving them of some of their freedom to exercise autonomous judgment.

Trollope's disapproval of this sort of compromise of professional autonomy, already apparent in his portrayal of Slope, is made more explicit in his account of Arabin's repudiation of this Benthamite rationality. Arabin's definitive crisis of faith takes the form of a vocational crisis in which he is taught the necessity of autonomy. Strongly influenced by Newman's conversion to Catholicism, Arabin takes a retreat from Oxford to meditate his own future allegiances. Arabin is drawn to Catholicism by his craving for the security of an absolute code of conduct: "[H]ow great an aid would it be to a poor, weak, wavering man to be constrained to high moral duties, self-denial, obedience, and chastity by laws which were certain in their enactments, and not to be broken without loud, palpable, unmistakable sin!" (1:189). In other words, Arabin desires to be under the same sort of mastery that he contemplated imposing on others.

Eventually Arabin decides to remain in the Church of England because of the influence of a humble, remote curate whom he meets on his retreat. "The poor curate of a small Cornish parish" somehow infuses Arabin with a sense of the duty of autonomy that Christianity lays on its clergy. From him Arabin

> first learnt to know that the highest laws for the governance of a Christian's duty must act from within and not from without; that no man can become a serviceable servant solely by obedience to written edicts; and that the safety which he was about to seek within the gates of Rome was no other than the selfish freedom from personal danger which the bad soldier attempts to gain who counterfeits illness on the eve of battle. (1:190)

The curate reverses the terms of Arabin's desired renunciation: the truly unselfish thing to do is not to escape temptations of the world and the flesh in a security that denies individual freedom but to combat and overcome those temptations by remaining vulnerable to them. The professionalism required of a good clergyman includes the duty to regulate his conduct autonomously, without external coercion. A "serviceable servant" of the public or Church is not a slave to "written edicts" but one who exercises his judgment independently under the guidance of his own conscience. For Arabin, the surprise of finding such a wise counselor among the group he desired to reform prompts a reevaluation of his previous supervisory impulse. As he learns the spiritual duty of preserving his own autonomy, he also learns as well the importance of respecting that of fellow clergymen.

Once convinced that autonomy is a religious and professional duty, Arabin is willing to remain in the Church of England. Autonomy remains central to his professional conduct: "He was content to be a High Churchman, *if he could be so on principles of his own*, and could strike out a course showing a marked difference from those with whom he consorted. He was ready to be a partisan as long as he was allowed to have a course of action and of thought unlike that of his party" (1:197, my emphasis). This peculiar definition of partisanship—membership in a group that nevertheless leaves its members free to exercise "manly independence"—encapsulates Trollope's message about professional autonomy and collectivity.

In a telling irony that hints at Trollope's disposition toward his subject, Mr. Arabin is exactly forty years old, the age specifically named by the *Jupiter* to be an appropriate age for the new dean. (Slope is thirty-six.) The *Jupiter*'s call for energy and ability in Church leaders is valid, Trollope indicates, even though the paper is hypocritical in the practice of them. The narrator approves of Arabin as a "studious, thoughtful, hard-working man," invulnerable alike to charges of faddism or of antiquation (2:270). The deanship and his marriage to a rich widow together constitute a material reward for decades of disinterested service during which he declined promotion in his "stoical rejection of this world's happiness" (1:196). His credentials of personal disinterest thus powerfully established, the narrator can comfortably award him material goods without compromising his professional service ethic. In Arabin Trollope presents a version of the professional ideal that fuses the residual with the emergent order to the deliberate exclusion of the dominant entrepreneurial ideal.

Harding, for his part, is a positive portrait of the residual order within the Church establishment. The traditionalism of his character is perhaps most evident in his relationship to the twelve superannuated paupers who live in the hospital, a relationship that is described as an ecclesiastical sort of aristocratic paternalism. The closing of *The Warden* clearly condemns the bedesmen, though Harding himself does not, for their legal agitation and the greed that motivated it. The bedesmen belatedly but unreservedly affirm that "[their] wants are adequately provided for, and [their] position could hardly be improved."[55] In other words, they learn the value and rightness of contentment with their lot, submission to the status quo, and grateful acceptance of the benevolent offices of their "master." The deaths of some of the men in the years following Harding's resignation are described in terms that blend the aristocratic and clerical functions of the warden:

> Six have died, with no kind friend to solace their last moments, with no wealthy neighbor to administer comforts and ease the stings of death. Mr. Harding, indeed, did not desert them; from him they had such consolation as a dying man may receive from his Christian pastor; but it was the occasional kindness of a stranger which ministered to them, and not the constant presence of a master, a neighbor, and a friend.[56]

Trollope is well aware of the residual nature of this formation, but his indulgence in this sort of nostalgia registers his belief that what is meritorious in the residual model must not be deprecated simply because it is traditional, in the manner of Slope's rubbish cart.

It is significant that the exemplar of the traditional order in *Barchester Towers* is the only one who sincerely believes in selection by merit even to his own disadvantage. When Mr. Harding states his resolve, to incredulous hearers, to reject the offer of the deanship, he pleads, "I do not find myself fit for new duties" (2:224). Dr. Grantly's response is telling: " 'New duties! what duties?' said the archdeacon, with unintended sarcasm" (2:224). As Dr. Grantly does his best to talk Mr. Harding out of his scruples,

> [Mr. Harding] would again and again allege that he was wholly unfitted to new duties. It was in vain that the archdeacon tried to insinuate, though he could not plainly declare, that there were no new duties to perform. . . . Mr. Harding seemed to have a foolish idea, not only that there were new duties to do, but that no one should accept the place who was not himself prepared to do them. (2:226)

In his recent experiences with the hospital, with Mr. Slope, and with the *Jupiter*, Mr. Harding has apparently accepted some of the moral authority of the entrepreneurial ideal—notably, the elements of it that coincide with professional ideals.

Notwithstanding Mr. Harding's morbid habit of self-reproach, the novel grants some legitimacy to his view. Harding's very announcement of the great news showcases his inappropriateness for such a leadership post. He can barely bring himself to tell the overbearing archdeacon the news, for his "modesty . . . almost prevented his speaking" (2:222). As Dr. and Mrs. Grantly celebrate with uncharacteristic exuberance (the archdeacon "walked around and around the room, twirling a copy of the *Jupiter* over his head, to show his extreme exultation" [2:222]), Mr. Harding literally cannot go on with his account. "It was all in vain that he strove to speak; nobody would listen to him. . . . At last Mr. Harding was allowed to go up-stairs and wash his hands, having, in fact, said very little of all that he had come . . . to say" (2:222–223). The scene is calculated to emphasize Mr. Harding's infantilization and impotence. One knows that "nobody would listen to him" as dean either. The novel endorses Harding's decision; the concluding paragraphs praise him because "[h]e does such duties as fall to his lot well and conscientiously, and is thankful that he has never been tempted to assume others for which he might be less fitted" (2:270). Again, Trollope's strategy of making Harding at once the embodiment of residual, almost aristocratic values and of the emergent professional ideal has the effect of legitimizing both ideals: the aristocratic ideal is made to partake of modern efficiency and ethical scruples, and the professional ideal is tinctured with time-honored dignity.

Equally important, however, is the fact that the novel presents Harding's preeminent performances of professional ideals as autonomous acts. Both his resignation of the wardenship in *The Warden* and his refusal of the deanship in *Barchester Towers* are vehemently opposed by Archdeacon Grantly, to whom Harding usually yields on all matters professional and personal. These decisions are also in defiance of his own material self-interest and therefore against the grain of professional norms—indeed, against what Trollope calls "the bent of human nature."[57] As mousy as Harding generally is, he refuses to be dissuaded from his resolve to put ideals above his loyalty to his professional hierarchy, embodied by the archdeacon, and above his own interests. Thus Harding's loyalty is seen to be first to the ethical principles of responsibility to the public—principles that ideally regulate his profession—and only secondly to the economic interests of the profession and of himself. In Harding, therefore, Trollope exalts the professional and his principled autonomy as constitutive of the public good.

In the case of Parliamentary Church reform in *The Warden*, Harding's autonomy simultaneously affirms the Benthamite rationality of fiscal responsibility and yet denies the necessity of intrusive oversight or accountability. Harding's resignation in the first novel therefore posits the high ethical standards of the clergy, rather than the shrill but hypocritical morality of the vulgar watchdog press, as the public's best assurance of good service from its clerical professionals. Similarly in *Barchester Towers*, Harding's decisive and autonomous act grants legitimacy to the principles that underlie the fulminations of Slope and the *Jupiter*: he comes to agree with them that Church institutions should be headed by men capable of active and effective leadership, as he came to agree with Bold that sinecures transgress upon the public's trust. In accepting this principle, and in acting on it to his own material detriment, Harding again testifies to the ability of the profession to conduct itself according to high ideals of professionalism. It is patently unnecessary to introduce Benthamite managerial methods into the Church in order to prevent abuses; it is unnecessary for a "new, busy, uncharitable, self-lauding" man like Slope to interfere to prevent Harding from being offered a position for which he is unsuited, since Harding himself will not accept such a position even when strongly pressured to do so.

In Trollope's formulation, then, individual autonomy enables the autonomy of the profession in general, and the autonomy of the profession strengthens the exercise of autonomy by the individual. Rather than working against each other, the two modes of autonomy actually reinforce each other. Trollope's narrative logic affirms that the exercise of autonomy by both the practitioner and the profession, far from endangering the public interest with its monopolistic and self-protective power, is instead the public's best guarantee of conscientious and capable service.

CHAPTER 3

PROFESSIONAL FRONTIERS
IN ELIZABETH GASKELL'S
MY LADY LUDLOW

These are the brainworkers, who, seeming to be idle, work, and are the cause of well-ordained work and happiness in others.

Ford Madox Brown (1865)

For both Benjamin Disraeli's professional politics and Anthony Trollope's clerical scene, professionalism is an exclusively male construct. Disraeli's heroines are principally conceived as the objects of the professional heroes' ardor, and Trollope's interfering women are conspicuously out of place in clerical affairs. As such, these examples reinforce the familiar paradigm of feminist critics who deplore professionalism's disempowerment of women. Julia Swindells, for example, sees Victorian professionalism as unequivocally dedicated to the exclusion and subordination of women. I will be arguing that this reductive picture fails to take account of the Victorians' capacity for self-critical reflection on professional ideals and professional realities. In their fiction, both Elizabeth Gaskell and George Eliot naturalized women's capacity for professional roles, and they did so not by refuting professional logic but by exploiting it. As we will see, this tactic was used by feminists in other areas as well, notably including those campaigning for women's access to the medical profession.

Gaskell's depictions of working middle-class women subtly and skillfully illustrate the reasonableness of women's professional work by recourse to the professional logic by which expertise trumps gender in the determination of the worthy professional. This is most evident in

My Lady Ludlow (1858), which, though set about 1811–1814, depicts the gradual transition of British society from a dominant aristocratic ideal to a dominant professional ideal. In this novel, the rise of conventionally male professional society is seamlessly integrated with corresponding, but peculiarly unrevolutionary, changes in women's relationship to specialized and expert labor. The fact that these changes are unrevolutionary, though quite significant, is an index of Gaskell's subtlety in normalizing middle-class women's work as of a piece with professionalizing trends and ideals normative to men.

A thoroughly professional author herself, Gaskell's fiction contains portraits of women in professional roles that are among the earliest in British fiction. Ruth's nursing in *Ruth* (1853) and Miss Matty's tea merchandising in *Cranford* (1853) are marginal occupations, given the traditional stigmas on both nursing and trade, but these depictions nevertheless show Gaskell's willingness to imagine middle-class women as financially self-supporting.[1] *The Life of Charlotte Brontë* (1857) was arguably the first major biography of a professional woman in England. Gaskell contemplated an ending for *Cousin Phillis* (1864) in which the classically educated Phillis, using skills learned from a former suitor who was a railroad manager, oversees the draining of a typhus-stricken village.[2] In *My Lady Ludlow*, the eccentric spinster Miss Galindo serves a memorable stint as a clerk. Both *Cousin Phillis* and *My Lady Ludlow* depict social constructs in which power is shifting away from land ownership toward specialized expertise, and both of them, crucially, make a space for women among the rising experts.

Moreover, Gaskell's republication of *My Lady Ludlow* in *Round the Sofa* (1859), in which she sets *My Lady Ludlow* and a few short stories within a new fictional frame, brings the professional transformation of society described in the novel into the reader's present. This frame, which is narrated by a young woman who hears and transcribes the text of *My Lady Ludlow* from an elderly friend, shows the contemporaneous application of the professional logic that unfolds in the main story. It makes clear that in this novel, the first significant fiction Gaskell wrote after finishing *The Life of Charlotte Brontë*, the relationship of women to esoteric and remunerative labor, particularly authorship, is very much on Gaskell's mind.

The novel's gently nostalgic depiction of the waning of aristocratic power is self-evident and frequently remarked upon,[3] but what has not been adequately recognized is the shape of the specific class structure that comes to replace the aristocracy, and the relationship of that class structure to both the gender and class orthodoxies of Gaskell's time. I argue that the novel represents a shift from traditional aristocratic hegemony to that of a professional meritocracy, while at the same time challenging the assumption of middle-class male exclusivism. The aristocratic ideal of Lady Ludlow, according to which birth is absolute and essential, gives way to the meritocratic and inclusive professional ideal of the vicar Mr. Gray and the land agent Captain James. According to Gaskell's formulation of this ideal, prejudices against women, the working class, and those of illegitimate birth are discredited and dismissed. Thus Gaskell's text demonstrates the potential for inclusiveness in the professional ideal, which she represents as open even to groups formerly marginalized by gender and birth status.

   To provide some context for this reading, this chapter will begin by referring briefly to Victorian reformers' use of the professional value of meritocracy to challenge male exclusivity in the medical profession. Turning then to the novel, I will first analyze Lady Ludlow and her changing relationships with professionals in order to illuminate the role that professional logic plays in the social transformations of the novel. Then I will use the characters of Miss Galindo and Harry Gregson, a laboring boy, to examine more closely the interplay of work, class, and gender that gives this account of professional hegemony its particularly progressive turn. Although my interest in this chapter is primarily with the gender inclusivity of Gaskell's representation of the professional order, the workings of Gaskell's meritocratic logic with respect to class and birth status are also relevant for the ways they reinforce the treatment of gender politics and work. Finally, I will explore the parallels between the frame story of *Round the Sofa* and the main story in order to explicate the book's embedded commentary about women's progress in the professional economy.

I

Although many just criticisms of the elitist tendencies of professionalism have been lodged, these criticisms often fail to account for the countervailing tendency of professional idealism. Swindells, in *Victorian Writing and Working Women*, argues that "[n]ineteenth-century sexual ideology . . . inscribes the incompatibility of women and a professional career."[4] As a result, Swindells concludes that women novelists such as Eliot and Gaskell cannot fully inhabit both discursive domains of "professional" and "woman." Rather, they are said to achieve their quasi-professional status only by reinforcing rather than disrupting the chauvinist assumptions upon which the professional apparatus was constructed.

However, on the subject of gender as on the other subjects under examination in this study, the professional project is too diverse and contested to be reduced to narratives of oppression such as that given by Swindells. Amanda Anderson's view of women's relationship to another intellectual practice, that of critical distance, is apropos here: "[I]t would be misleading to suggest that women are simply excluded from those forms of detachment seen as intellectually or morally heroic in the culture."[5] Recent studies of women's economic activity in the period bear out a more complex picture. Joan Perkin's *Victorian Women*, M. Jeanne Peterson's *Family, Love, and Work in the Lives of Victorian Gentlewomen*, and especially Eleanor Gordon and Gwyneth Nair, *Public Lives: Women, Family, and Society in Victorian Britain* all challenge the usual picture of the domestic female with reference to the managerial and professional aspects of women's unpaid work in schools, charity works, and even their husbands' professions or businesses. The involvement of Victorian women in fields of publishing, medicine, and the Civil Service has also been the subject of recent research.[6]

The picture of professionalism I have been sketching makes clear that professional ideals posed challenges to professionalism itself, engendering a culture of self-critique within the professional domain even early in its history. This is certainly the case for the ideal of meritocracy. According to the conventional narrative, after being effectively utilized to empower the middle-class male against a "do-nothing" aristocracy, merit became a convenient fiction for continuing to exclude the women and laborers who did not have access to the educational and cultural advantages that confer merit (or the signs taken for merit). However, even Harold Perkin, who is among the most trenchant critics of professionalism's exclusionary self-interestedness, concedes that the meritocracy essential for a professional society to function sets a necessary limit to a class- and gender-based monopoly of professional status. As he puts it in his bird's-eye survey of global professional economies, "[E]verywhere in professional society human capital still has to be earned, and it cannot be harnessed without some concession to merit wherever it can be found. . . . [F]or the same reason, all post-industrial societies have had to make concessions for able women."[7]

Even within the Victorian period there is evidence of a perceptible friction between the ideal of meritocracy, which helped bring professionals to power, and the desire of many of those professionals to close their own borders to outsiders. This friction is visible in the eagerness with which it was exploited by feminists, male and female. In the fight over women's access to medical education, for example, the proverbial appeal to "a free field and no favor" was regularly invoked.[8] The physician C. R. Drysdale maintained in 1870 that women's fitness for professions is well-established:

> Wherever women, in short, have a chance given them of arriving at any result, we find that, by means of their unflagging industry, their superior sobriety, their good conduct and mother wit, they can very often prove themselves even more than the equals of many of that sex which pretends to consider all human occupations except domestic ones as beyond their powers.[9]

Along the same line, Drysdale hopes that "in the end, the advice of whatever practitioner is the most eminent may be sought, independent of the consideration of the sex to which that practitioner may belong."[10] Drysdale thus transfers familiar appeals to class-neutral meritocracy into the realm of gender to validate women's becoming doctors.

When Sophia Jex-Blake and four female colleagues attempted to earn degrees in medicine from the University of Edinburgh, she used the university's antimeritocratic conduct as the keystone of her public protests against the university's opposition. In her account of their 1869–1872 battle for separate-but-equal matriculation status, Jex-Blake emphasizes that the women were permitted to enroll in the evident expectation that they would fail to master the content of the classes. After the first round of examinations, however, in which four of the five women took honors, "the results of the class examinations aroused in our opponents a conviction that the so-called experiment was not going to fail of itself, as they had confidently hoped, but that if it was to be suppressed at all, vigorous measures must be taken for that purpose."[11] Such measures were taken when some faculty members refused to teach the required separate classes for women, even when offered exorbitant fees. In another instance, a scholarship routinely awarded to the top four students in a class was denied to a woman who took the fourth place:

> as it had been distinctly ordained that we were to be subject to "all the regulations in force in the University as to examinations," it had *not* occurred to us as possible that the very name of Hope Scholar could be wrested from the successful candidate and given over her head to the fifth student on the list, who had the good fortune to be a man.
> But this was actually done.[12]

Throughout Jex-Blake's account, it is the faculty's refusal to reward merit evenhandedly that she exploits to rouse public indignation against the university.

This story contains plenty of evidence of Swindells's contention that "[t]he socio-political organization of institutions proceeds to consolidate that power in ways which are exclusive of women, and to deploy that power against women."[13] However, it also makes clear that in deploying their power against women the institutions were forced to commit naked transgressions against the ideals of the institutions themselves, and that these transgressions were ultimately self-defeating. The "vigorous measures" of the medical faculty of Edinburgh were so blatantly unjust as even to embarrass the *Lancet* and the *British Medical Journal*, in spite of their steady opposition to women doctors.[14] Though the University of Edinburgh School of Medicine did not open to women until 1894, the mid- to late-1870s saw the progressive dismantlement of all the *formal* barriers to women's access to the medical profession. These events attest that professional ideals had potential to erode male hegemony over the professions. The effort to normalize women's access to medicine vis-à-vis appeals to the ideal of meritocracy is echoed in *My Lady Ludlow*'s depiction of the meritocratic expansion of the professional class.

II

Much of the criticism on *My Lady Ludlow* has been devoted either to chastising the novel for its poor structure (most offensive is the long inset narrative decrying the excesses of the French Reign of Terror) or to rehabilitating it against such charges.[15] One of the more successful apologies for the novel's structure is the argument that Gaskell carefully juxtaposes the revolutionary social upheaval of France with the mild English evolution toward a sensible middle-class ideal, which replaces the dying aristocratic one.[16] What has not been fully appreciated is that the middle-class ideal that comes to hold sway in Hanbury is emphatically a professional ideal.[17] To understand the social transformations wrought by the professionals, it is first necessary to understand the aristocratic status quo, personified by Lady Ludlow, upon which they work. Reigning with unquestioned supremacy over Hanbury during the Regency, Lady Ludlow embodies the aristocratic ideal of paternalistic grandeur based on heredity. Certain that class is essence, Lady Ludlow seeks to save shabby genteel women such as Margaret from slipping to a station lower than that to which their birth and breeding entitle them; she is equally vigilant to prevent any low-born individuals from raising their social position. The poor must not be taught to read, she believes, because education will make them prone to challenge their social superiors. Those whose birth is not sanctioned by marriage are even less privileged: Margaret recalls, "My Lady Ludlow could not endure any mention of illegitimate children. It was a principle of hers that society ought to ignore them."[18] Lady Ludlow's fixation on class and birth, interestingly enough, translates into a singular disregard for mere wealth or poverty or even for gender, as we will see.

Lady Ludlow's aristocratic notions are represented by Margaret in a usually reverent tone that only occasionally approaches gentle satire. One such moment occurs when Lady Ludlow urges on Margaret that the ability to perceive certain scents is hereditary in the aristocracy. It may be significant that the smell she urges Margaret to perceive by way of proving Margaret's slight proportion of noble blood is the autumnal scent of decaying strawberry leaves. Lady Ludlow can pick out this fragrance on the evening breeze, but she is slow to realize the decay of the aristocracy itself, perhaps symbolized by the leaves that make up a ducal coronet.

For all that Lady Ludlow's notions occasionally border on the ridiculous, even in Margaret's eyes, Margaret ensures that the reader's picture of Lady Ludlow is one of almost unmitigated good. In her abundant charity to the needy, her perfect hospitality to high and low, and her unselfish dignity, Lady Ludlow earns and keeps the goodwill of all the inhabitants of her little village.[19] The common folk adore her for her hereditary associations combined with her gracious mien. Miss Galindo tells the countess, "Your ancestors have lived here time out of mind, and have owned the land on which their forefathers have lived ever since there were forefathers. You yourself were born amongst them, . . . and they've never known your ladyship do anything but what was kind and gentle" (154). Lady Ludlow maintains the spectacle of aristocratic grandeur and reserve somehow without hauteur; she sincerely regards that spectacle as the duty of her station, which she fulfills with personal humility. Margaret observes that "great as was my lady's liking and approval of respect, nay, even reverence, being paid to her as a person of quality—a sort of tribute to her Order, which she had no individual right to remit, or, indeed, not to exact— yet she, being personally simple, sincere, and holding herself in low esteem, could not endure anything like . . . servility" (253). Lady Ludlow represents, in short, the idealized premodern aristocracy, offered with only a shade of irony.

At the beginning of the novel, Lady Ludlow holds the status of patroness in relation to the professionals around her, particularly the vicar and the land agent. The old-fashioned gentleman-clergyman, Mr. Mountford, had been appointed because he "had won his lordship's [the late Lord Ludlow's] favor by his excellent horsemanship" (154), and the dominant interests of his life are those of the palate and the stable. Mr. Mountford is generous in aid to the poor but keeps his distance from them, with the result that, according to his successor, the inhabitants of Hanbury are as woefully ignorant of Christian teaching as they are of worldly instruction. Lady Ludlow does not scruple to command Mr. Mountford in the performance of his clerical duties, even to the point of ordering him from the pew to dispense with a Sunday sermon when she is not disposed to hear one. In traditional Hanbury, both countess and parson tacitly understand that the clergyman is at the service of—and takes all his cues from—his patroness.

Lady Ludlow's land steward Mr. Horner behaves toward his mistress in a similarly old-fashioned way. Mr. Horner, almost as old as Lady Ludlow and thoroughly imbued with a feudal view of class relations, regards himself essentially as an upper servant, whose task it is to carry out Lady Ludlow's orders about the estate. Lady Ludlow manages many of her own affairs about her land and her tenantry, usually basing her decisions on the "hereditary sense of right and wrong between landlord and tenant" (263), which is frequently at a variance with "mere worldly and business calculations" (248). Mr. Horner meekly swallows his objections to her unprofitable decisions. The result is that the land is badly mismanaged: crops are not rotated, fertilizer is not used, rents are not always collected, and the land produces well below capacity. Mr. Horner, however, was once a clerk to a London attorney, and he brings to Hanbury an early whiff of the professional ideal. Like Mr. Mountford's successor Mr. Gray, Mr. Horner deplores the ignorance of the estate workers, as we shall see.

Thus the opening picture of Hanbury is only superficially wholesome. The idyllic stability of the hereditary estate masks actual instability and weakness born of the poor use of resources, both human and real. The successors to Mr. Mountford and Mr. Horner bring to their tasks a professional ethos that collides with Lady Ludlow's sense of hereditary privilege. However, those collisions issue decisively in the good of the community, as the founding of a ragged school and the implementation of modern farming methods revitalize the sinking estate.

Unlike Disraeli, who alternately locates professional values inside and outside the aristocracy, Gaskell decisively places a professional ethos in the professional class, sharply distinguished from the aristocracy. Though Gaskell lingers nostalgically over the aristocracy's ideals, her hero is a professional who comes from outside the aristocracy and unselfconsciously usurps it, not by engaging in any kind of class struggle, but simply by doing his duty. Mr. Gray, the Evangelical vicar who succeeds Mr. Mountford, belongs to the new order of professional, zealous, and diligent clergy. He is committed to his religious duty to the exclusion of all considerations of rank. He singlemindedly, humbly, and courageously works toward the spiritual regeneration of the parishioners, especially the poor and even the extraparochial squatters. When Lady Ludlow tries to silence Mr. Gray's sermon on free literacy education via Sabbath schools, as she had routinely silenced Mr. Mountford's sermons in the past, he ignores her and preaches his sermon anyway. On another occasion the clergyman tells his lady that "he was bound to remember that he was under the bishop's authority, not under [Lady Ludlow's]" (181). In other words, Mr. Gray's professional hierarchy is preeminent over his social hierarchy.

Although Mr. Gray defers to Lady Ludlow on matters not touching his duty, he does not hesitate to incur her displeasure if necessary in following his professional judgment. Their first confrontation occurs when Mr. Gray pleads with Lady Ludlow to interfere in the wrongful imprisonment of an innocent man—a man, however, with a criminal record. Lady Ludlow refuses, using her characteristic assumptions of class essentialism to regard the gentlemen's agreement of the magistrates as more important than the actual guilt or innocence of the accused. She rebukes Mr. Gray: "I may wonder whether a young man of your age and position has any right to assume that he is a better judge than one with the experience which I have naturally gained at my time of life, and in the station I hold" (162). Mr. Gray's position is equally in character: "If I, madam, . . . am not to shrink from telling what I believe to be the truth to the poor and lowly, no more am I to hold my peace in the presence of the rich and titled" (162). In Mr. Gray's mind, the demands of clerical duty preempt considerations of age and status.

The most serious disagreement between the conscientious clergyman and the arch traditionalist, though, concerns the school Mr. Gray desires to found for the benefit of poor children. Lady Ludlow is convinced that teaching the lower orders to read and write is the first step toward a peasants' revolution. She repeats the classic formulation of the paternalistic aristocracy: education "unfits the lower orders for their duties, the duties to which they are called by God; of submission to those placed in authority over them" (245). Lady Ludlow sees a direct chain of causality from popular literacy to regicide.[20]

Both Mr. Gray and Mr. Horner resist in different ways and for different reasons Lady Ludlow's reactionary views on education. Dismayed at the spiritual degeneration of the laborers' children, Mr. Gray hopes that basic literacy education will train the children to higher thoughts and thereby facilitate their receptivity to spiritual instruction as well. For his part, Mr. Horner keenly regrets the waste of human resources under the current practice of keeping the estate workers ignorant. Earnestly and faithfully desirous of his lady's prosperity, Mr. Horner "wanted to make every man useful and active in this world, and to direct as much activity and usefulness as possible to the improvement of the Hanbury estates. . . . Mr. Horner . . . hoped for a day-school at some future time, to train up intelligent labourers for working on the estate" (176). Since this aim is impossible given Lady Ludlow's decided opposition, Mr. Horner contents himself with identifying the cleverest boy he can find among the local poor and teaching him to read, "with a view to making use of him as a kind of foreman in process of time" (176). That this boy is the son of the poacher Job Gregson indicates Mr. Horner's partial adherence to the meritocratic ideal.

As Mr. Mountford was replaced by a clergyman with a professional mentality, so Mr. Horner is replaced after his death with a steward who takes a professional approach to the management of the countess's estate. Captain James is chosen for the post because of a past connection with Lady Ludlow's dead son, who was once in the navy. When Mr. Smithson, the family solicitor, protests that a sailor cannot manage land, Lady Ludlow's perseverance testifies to her belief that family connections are more important than mere expertise.

From that inauspicious beginning, however, Captain James proves to be, like Mr. Gray, an adherent to a professional paradigm. He seeks specialized training, acts autonomously, and disregards traditional class boundaries. He intends to "set to in good earnest and study agriculture, and see how he could remedy the state of things" (279). Not content, like Lady Ludlow, to do things the way they have always been done, Captain James experiments ambitiously. In making his experimental reforms, he seeks advice from the neighboring (successful) farmer, who is, to Lady Ludlow's horror, a Baptist who purchased the estate with the proceeds of his successful bakery in Birmingham. Despite Lady Ludlow's delicate protests, Captain James "would judge in all things for himself. . . . [H]e spoke as if he were responsible for the good management of the whole and must, consequently, be allowed full liberty of action" (278). In short, Captain James operates like a professional: he expects autonomy and seeks expertise regardless of the respectability of the source. His marriage to Mr. Brooke's daughter completes Captain James's acceptance of the new professional class mobility. Lady Ludlow declares it "impossible" that Captain James should pay court to a Dissenting tradesman's daughter, but the young captain has no prejudices against the family's religious opinions or class background (281).

By the time Margaret Dawson prepares to leave Hanbury, a mere four years after her arrival, the professional ideals of Mr. Gray and Captain James have wrought a transformation in the village. The human resources of the parish are being utilized to good effect because of the weakening of the aristocratic rationality in the face of the rationality of expertise. As a result of the new schoolhouse, "the children were hushed up in school, and better behaved out of it, too" (289). As a result of the improvements in land management, "there were no more lounging young men to form a group at the cross roads, at a time of the day when young men ought to be at work" (289). Traditional class barriers are eroding, and expertise has come to be valued more than birth status. Captain James has married the Baptist baker's daughter, signaling the weakening of the traditional barriers between trade and land, Church of England and Dissent. Mr. Gray has married Bessy, the illegitimate daughter of a former lover of Miss Galindo, in another remarkable subversion of Lady Ludlow's social norms. Hanbury is still dominated by the countess's great house, and she is still supreme in the social scene. But her social tone must necessarily follow that taken by the professionals around her. She cannot refuse to countenance the Baptist baker's daughter or the illegitimate girl once they are married to the professionals whom she respects and on whom she depends. In receiving Mrs. James and Mrs. Gray, Lady Ludlow again "mak[es] the best of a bad job" as she did when she insisted that the girls at Mr. Gray's school learn spinning and knitting before they are taught to read (280). In the case of the social recognition of these hitherto unrecognizable persons, making the best of a bad job means turning her irresistible and inimitable social grace toward the welcome of even the gauche professional wives. In the account of a tea that closes Miss Galindo's final letter, Lady Ludlow shames her supercilious servants not only by accepting Mrs. Bessy Gray and the overawed wives of the nearby clergy, but also by covering up the breaches of etiquette of Mrs. Brooke, the wife of the Baptist baker from Birmingham.

In *My Lady Ludlow*, the replacement of aristocratic ideals with professional ideals is presented as the irresistible and natural outcome of usually mild conflict. Lady Ludlow is finally a gracious loser. When appeals to her age and position no longer command the same reflexive deference from the professionals around her that they did with an earlier generation of professionals, Lady Ludlow does exactly as she does when a dispute arises about the burial place of her last son: she "withdrew from the discussion, before it degenerated into an unseemly contest" (259). She retains her privileged social position, her undiminished grandeur, by giving up her benevolent autocracy and sharing the real power of the society with professionals who expect her to defer to their expertise rather than expecting to defer to her hereditary social position.

III

There is perhaps little remarkable about Gaskell's positive portrayal of rural England's transition from a landed or aristocratic social order to a professional one. What is remarkable, however, is the relative elasticity of the novel's professional constructs with regard to class and gender. In *My Lady Ludlow*, the shift toward professional social hegemony occurs simultaneously with the expansion of access to the increasingly powerful professional class. At the same time that Mr. Gray and Captain James are redefining the relationship of their professions to the aristocracy, the working class and women are redefining their relationships to the professional class. In the characters of Harry Gregson and Miss Galindo, Gaskell experiments with the boundaries of professional status. In a symmetrical narrative device, Gaskell subverts separately the class-based prejudices of the aristocrat and the gender-based prejudices of the old-fashioned professional, leaving the reader to connect the dots of an inclusive ethos of expertise exemplified in Mr. Gray.

Harry Gregson and Miss Galindo indirectly interact in the novel with respect to the position of clerkship: Mr. Horner intends to train Harry to be his clerk but is soon constrained to have Miss Galindo as clerk instead. In the last third of the century, clerkships became the means by which working-class men and middle-class women gained their first large-scale access to white-collar work. For working-class men, the putative meritocracy manifested by the competitive examination of the Civil Service motivated the ambitious and intelligent to "cram" in hopes of winning entrance on a respectable career. No such movement was visible in the 1810s, when this story is set, but clerkship would suggest an association with the aspiring lower middle class for Gaskell's 1858 *Household Words* audience. For middle-class women, the proliferation of the telegraph and the typewriter from the

1870s onward opened clerical careers for women in significant numbers. It thus appears that Gaskell is using her plot to suggest presciently how barriers to professional status can be undermined by competent members of traditionally marginalized groups.

In plotting the story so that Harry initially is trained as a clerk because his patron is ambitious for him to be a professional, Gaskell recreates the progress of a class of intelligent but low-born men into professional circles. Harry Gregson, with his "extraordinary capabilities," represents in the novel the meritocratic recruitment of members of the working class into the professional class (229). As the "brightest and sharpest" of the farm lads, Harry is specially chosen by Mr. Horner to learn the basic skills of reading, writing, and arithmetic (176). Mr. Horner admits to his lady that he wants to train Harry as his clerk, but Margaret suspects that Mr. Horner retains other, "almost unconscious" aspirations for his beloved assistant: "that Harry might be trained so as to be first his clerk, and next his assistant, and finally his successor in his stewardship to the Hanbury estates" (249). In other words, Mr. Horner intends to advance Harry through various stages of promotion until he attains a securely professional position. This project runs aground when Harry innocently reads an unsealed message from Mr. Horner to Lady Ludlow.

This transmission of literacy skills apart from the code of honor governing their use is precisely calculated to bring out all Lady Ludlow's horror at the dangers of indiscriminate education. Lady Ludlow declares that "the son of a poacher and vagabond," lacking what she calls the "instinct" of honor, is not capable of holding a position of trust (229–230). In Lady Ludlow's mind, trustworthiness, like every personal attribute, is hereditary and essential. No working-class boy, certainly not the son of a criminal, can acquire "instincts" necessary to trustworthiness; consequently, the powerful skills of literacy must be withheld from his ilk.

Lady Ludlow's assessment of Harry's essence proves to be the wrong one, of course. After crippling himself in a fall, Harry "will never be able to earn his livelihood in any active way" (254). He must either be a pauper on the parish or what our age might call a "mental worker"; thus, his literacy prevents the waste of his life. Having used his legacy from Mr. Horner to go to university, Harry becomes vicar of Hanbury following Mr. Gray's early death. Lady Ludlow's belief that low birth is a permanent bar to professional honor is thereby emphatically invalidated.

It is not Lady Ludlow, but Mr. Horner, who objects to the employment of Miss Galindo, a spinster who lives off the production of her genteel needlework. The bleak economic situation of the "surplus" unmarried woman—unable to earn money without compromising her middle-class position—is illustrated in Miss Galindo's very limited means of support. Her only marketable skills are her literacy and her needlework. At one point in youth she contemplated writing a novel, but following elaborate preparations, she found she had "nothing to say" (236). Failing that, Miss Galindo relies on her needle for sustenance. Since the direct sale of the productions of her needle would transgress against her gentility, she participates in an elaborate system by which the "ornamental" and "useful" productions of "ladies of little or no fortune" are sold indirectly and anonymously through a repository, created by a committee of wealthy ladies and managed by a "decayed gentlewoman" (231).

In spite of Lady Ludlow's opposition to "women usurping men's employments," Lady Ludlow makes no difficulty of employing Miss Galindo as Mr. Horner's clerk (236). In Lady Ludlow's eyes, Miss Galindo is qualified in a way Harry Gregson can never be: "Miss Galindo was by birth and breeding a lady of the strictest honour, and would, if possible, forget the substance of any letters that passed through her hands; at any rate, no one would ever hear of them again from her" (232). In other words, Miss Galindo's birth status obviates her gender in Lady Ludlow's eyes. This tendency has been seen before in Lady Ludlow. When she demands that the magistrate Mr. Lathom release Job Gregson on bail in defiance of the law disallowing bail for theft, she dismisses his objection cavalierly: "Bah! Who makes laws? Such as I, in the House of Lords—such as you, in the House of Commons" (166). By including herself among those who make laws in the House of Lords, she apparently unconsciously negates gender in her assertion of class authority.[21]

Whereas Lady Ludlow's class prejudices lead her to scorn Harry as a clerk while overlooking Miss Galindo's gender, Mr. Horner's gender prejudices make him antipathetic to Miss Galindo as a clerk. Miss Galindo is an eccentric; even Margaret says, "To tell the truth, I was rather afraid of Miss Galindo's tongue, for I never knew what she would say next" (239). As the village scold, Miss Galindo makes frequent visits to poor cottages; these visits are alternately missions of genuine mercy and investigations of private extravagances. She always keeps a servant who is really a charity case: her servants are blind, deaf, hunchbacked, or epileptic, and she takes care of them more than they do her.[22] Despite her eccentricity, Miss Galindo is a perfectly good clerk. Well aware of Mr. Horner's prejudice against using a female clerk, she tries to ease his discomfort by performing her job as well as a man: "I try to make him forget I'm a woman; I do everything as ship-shape as a masculine man-clerk" (241). When he continues non-plussed, she tries assuming male manners: "I have stuck my pen behind my ear; I have made him a bow instead of a curtsey; I have whistled . . . I have said 'Confound it!' and 'Zounds!' " (241). In spite of all her efforts, Mr. Horner cannot overlook her gender, with the result that, according to Miss Galindo, "I am not half the use I might be" (241). Mr. Horner's usual desire to maximize human resources for Lady Ludlow's benefit here runs aground on his gender prejudices.

Only after Mr. Horner's death is Miss Galindo known for the proficient she is. Miss Galindo knows that Mr. Smithson, the London solicitor, assumes that this unusual clerk is a whim of the countess's: "It was a form to be gone through to please my lady. . . . It was keeping a woman out of harm's way, at any rate, to let her fancy herself useful" (262). She gets the better of him, however, by her undeniable competence: "He believed that a woman could not write straight lines, and that she required a man to tell her that two and two made four. I was not above ruling my books, and I had Cocker a little more at my fingers' ends than he had" (262). Her competence extends not only to the content of her work but also her manner and bearing as a worker. As she tells Margaret, "[M]y greatest triumph was holding my tongue. He would have thought nothing of my books, or my sums, or my black silk gown, if I had spoken unasked. . . . I have been so curt, so abrupt, so abominably dull, that I'll answer for it he thinks me worthy to be a man" (262). Mr. Smithson's conventional elitism becomes the subject of ridicule as the reader shares with Margaret and Miss Galindo the last laugh on the grudgingly respectful solicitor.

Miss Galindo's power to control her speech is related, as is her "strictest honour," to her class background: "But, odd as Miss Galindo was in general, she could be as well-bred a lady as any one when she chose" (232).The narrator says again elsewhere, "But Miss Galindo was a both a lady and a spirited, sensible woman, and she could put aside her self-indulgence in eccentricity of speech and manner whenever she chose" (261). In other words, specifically because she is a "lady," Miss Galindo can pass as a professional man. At the same time, Miss Galindo's refusal of pay for her work illustrates the difficulty she experiences as a woman in participating in professional norms. Though her work is worthy of financial reward, she cannot bring herself to accept it, insisting that her primary motive of gratitude for Lady Ludlow's past kindness necessarily excludes pecuniary gain.

Gaskell's handling of the clerkship subplot finally undermines both gender and class prejudices. Harry Gregson, dismissed in disgrace from the apprenticeship of clerkship, grows up to be the parish vicar. Miss Galindo's outcome is less triumphant: she returns to her eccentric mode of life as village scold, supported only by her needlework, but not before vindicating herself before Mr. Smithson as a thoroughly good professional worker. Mr. Horner's and Mr. Smithson's suspicion of the female clerk is gently castigated as surely as Lady Ludlow's horror at the young vagabond clerk. Yet the working-class man's access to professional status is attained in the generation following Mr. Gray's reforms, while that of the woman is only prefigured.

The only character in the novel completely without prejudices, Mr. Gray, is finally its hero. Mr. Gray's unselfconscious acceptance of the professional ideal is bound up with his admirable religious and humanitarian zeal. In striving to advance the spiritual good of his parishioners, he also does them more material good than had been done in generations of aristocratic paternalism. These benefits to the villagers result directly from the passing of the paternalist order in favor of an implicit professional logic that empowers the workers by increasing their human capital. While the most important example of these benefits is Mr. Gray's hard-fought battle to get Lady Ludlow's approval for the school where the poor children are educated, Mr. Gray has other notable victories as well. Mr. Gray saves Harry's life by pulling him from the quarry where he had fallen. The vagabond poacher Job Gregson, softened and redeemed by Mr. Gray's love and care for his son, reforms into a model citizen and becomes gamekeeper under Captain James. Finally, Mr. Gray's lack of prejudice is seen in his hiring the illegitimate Bessy as schoolmistress, thereby admitting her to a sort of professional legitimacy.

In all these examples, Mr. Gray's generous and self-effacing labors enable and empower the productive labor of others, especially the most marginalized members of the society. The labor of these hitherto excluded workers then enables the productive labor of still others: Job Gregson oversees the building of the school, with his youngest ragamuffin son mixing the mortar; and Bessy teaches the girls of the village to sew and read, thereby equipping them for more genteel labor than they could otherwise have performed. The novel thus affirms that the efficient and productive use of human resources requires setting aside both class and gender prejudices, and that this process results in the common social good. The meritocratic logic valorized in Mr. Gray becomes the means to destabilize barriers against women's professional employment and against working-class social advancement.

This change is good for everyone, even Lady Ludlow, because the more complete use of the estate's human resources causes the standard of living and the prosperity of the estate to rise across the board.

A number of Marxist-influenced critics from Raymond Williams on have faulted the limitations of Gaskell's fundamentally bourgeois outlook on the working class.[23] A reading of *My Lady Ludlow*, for example, can easily emphasize the essential unity of interests between the novel's aristocrat and professionals: both the fading power of land and the rising hegemony of expertise collude to keep the working class in its subordinate position. While granting, of course, that Gaskell is no socialist, I nevertheless want to emphasize that Gaskell's particular slant on the bourgeoisie is relatively progressive. There is a meaningful difference, I argue, between maintaining the status quo by forbidding literacy education and (to use the least charitable reading of Gray's actions) maintaining the status quo by *providing* education. If nothing else, the inevitable if unintended consequence of providing education is to give the workers tools for class activism; indeed, this is exactly why Lady Ludlow initially forbids the founding of a school.

More than this passive effect, however, is involved in the professionals' advocacy for working-class education. *My Lady Ludlow* shows Gaskell hinting at the concept Harold Perkin refers to as the expandability of human capital: unlike the finite supply of land and industrial means of production, human capital can theoretically extend as far down the social scale as there are people to educate.[24] Gaskell makes Mr. Gray not only a paragon of conventional clerical benevolence (as in his rescue of Harry) but also a sort of one-man workforce development agency, as he enables others to acquire and demonstrate the human capital that raises their social position. (This is, in fact, Mr. Gray's most significant point of departure from his obvious model, Reverend Tryan from Eliot's "Janet's Repentance," which appeared the year before *My Lady Ludlow*.) As Ford Madox Brown put it in his panegyric on "brainworkers," represented in his 1865 painting *Work* by Thomas Carlyle and F. D. Maurice, Mr. Gray is not only a worker but also "the cause of well-ordained work and happiness in others."[25] As the professional generously reaches down the social scale and across gender lines to make more professionals, Gaskell represents professionalism as an agent for social progressivism.

IV

The potential for professionalism to open doors for women is broached but then tabled in *My Lady Ludlow* by Miss Galindo's capable but temporary and unremunerated performance in white-collar work. This plot element receives closure, however, in *Round the Sofa*. Shirley Foster has suggested that "the retrospective setting of 'My Lady Ludlow' tends to point the reader away from contemporary application of its unorthodoxy."[26] I contend, in contrast, that the Miss Greatorex plot, thin as it is, brings the social progress of Margaret Dawson's youth into the reader's present. Most critics have ignored the frame in *Round the Sofa*, regarding it as irrelevant to the text of *My Lady Ludlow*. When they have commented on it, they have usually treated it as a throwaway, a clumsy and mercenary effort to remarket a book that was overshadowed in *Household Words* by Dickens's publicizing his marriage difficulties.[27] Of course, Gaskell's undisguised financial motive in this republication, which Winifred Gérin documents, by no means excludes the possibility that Gaskell also used the opportunity of republication to say something in the frame that she wanted said. As I have claimed throughout this study, the professional position, which Gaskell inhabits, simultaneously admits of materialist and artistic aims for her productions.

The frame in *Round the Sofa* contains important echoes of the main story, which provide clues for the reader to perceive the contemporary continuity—and advancement—of the social transformations described in *My Lady Ludlow*. Miss Greatorex, the first-person narrator of the frame, benefits from an apprenticeship in writing that converts the amateur storytelling of her older friends into a professional and implicitly remunerative skill. Written two years after Gaskell completed *The Life of Charlotte Brontë*, the frame of *My Lady Ludlow* points toward a picture of the woman professional novelist, like Brontë and Gaskell herself. Miss Greatorex is away from her parents receiving medical treatment in Scotland from Mr. Dawson, the brother of Margaret Dawson, now a crippled old maid. When the doctor invites Miss Greatorex and her governess Miss Duncan to join him and his sister for their "at-home" evening weekly, Miss Greatorex is positioned to hear Mrs. Dawson's narration of her relations with Lady Ludlow. At the suggestion of her governess, Miss Greatorex transcribes the story in installments each Tuesday morning as a "good exercise . . . both in memory and composition" (292).[28] This transition from an oral to a written paradigm is reminiscent of Harry Gregson's acquisition of literacy skills, by which he effected his rise from laborer to parson. Similarly, Miss Greatorex's shift from the amateur, drawing-room narrations she hears to the book she writes encapsulates the difference between a Miss Galindo and a Mrs. Gaskell.

This frame implicitly poses questions about the difference the professionalization of society makes to women. How do the events and shifts related in *My Lady Ludlow* affect the position and opportunities for Miss Greatorex? The answer will be evident when we consider the parallels and the differences between the world of Margaret Dawson and that of Miss Greatorex. We should begin by noting that Miss Greatorex is a close analogue to the young Margaret Dawson. The young women's feelings, apprehensions, and impressions correspond almost exactly, and many physical details of their environments match up as well. Both girls are shy and overawed by the grandeur of the people they encounter while away from their families in late adolescence (139–140, 149). Both Hanbury Hall and the Dawsons' home are old-fashioned and grandly impressive (140, 149). Both homes are richly decorated with china jars filled with potpourri and have matching Indian wallpaper patterns (140, 171).[29] Mrs. Dawson and Lady Ludlow even resemble each other: both have beautiful smooth skin and wear white satin ribbons on their heads (140, 149). Both dine on a roll or biscuit and milk while serving their guests more elegant fare (140, 151). Like Margaret Dawson, Miss Greatorex is one of numerous children of parents who are "not rich" (137). Like both Margaret Dawson and Harry Gregson, she is physically infirm. Since a young invalid woman's chances of marriage were exceedingly slim, Miss Greatorex may well be required to earn a living eventually.

Yet the differences between the young women's situations are telling as well. Whereas the young Margaret enters a house filled with the riches and collections of aristocratic lineage, Miss Greatorex enters a house filled with artifacts of the wealth "Mr. Dawson had acquired . . . in his profession" (140). Whereas Margaret's activity at Lady Ludlow's house consists almost entirely of needlework, Miss Greatorex is expected to use her time in Scotland "to combine lessons with the excellent Edinburgh masters, with the medicines and exercises needed for my indisposition" (137). When Margaret is lamed at Hanbury, she is treated only by the local general practitioner and by Miss Medlicott's "homeopathic" remedies (158), not for lack of means but simply because no other options are considered. Miss Greatorex, however, is sent away to the best physician who can be found, an expert with a national reputation. These details show that Miss Greatorex inhabits a world in which the professional order—ushered in by the progressive Mr. Gray and Captain James—carries the day. In a sense, professionals are the new aristocrats, as Mr. and Mrs. Dawson have in a manner replaced Lord and Lady Ludlow to Miss Greatorex. The questions of Miss Greatorex's life, then, are whether the professional order will allow any room for her (as the aristocratic order did for Lady Ludlow), and whether the quasi-professional women of a previous generation will make any difference for her. Will Miss Galindo's pioneering incursion into the professions smooth Miss Greatorex's way to use her mental capacity to be productive in spite of her physical infirmity, as Harry Gregson had done a generation before? Will Lady Ludlow's assertion of gender-neutral competence blaze a trail Miss Greatorex can follow?

When Miss Duncan instructs Miss Greatorex to use no small portion of her school hours to write out Mrs. Dawson's story, there is a suggestion that Miss Greatorex is enjoying an apprenticeship in narrative writing. Her mistresses are not just Miss Duncan and Margaret Dawson, but also Lady Ludlow and Miss Galindo, who share the role of narrator with Margaret Dawson. Like Gaskell herself did, Miss Greatorex writes her tale in weekly "installments" the morning after she hears each portion of the tale. Given that Miss Duncan asks Miss Greatorex to write each week's installment as "a good exercise . . . both in memory and composition," it appears that Miss Greatorex is being trained in the writing of fiction (292). Following this exercise, it is unlikely that Miss Greatorex would ever replicate the experience of Miss Galindo when she attempted to write a novel: "[I]t ended in my having nothing to say, when I sat down to write" (167). In spite of her fine penmanship, Miss Galindo experienced a gap between literacy and literary production. This gap is puzzling given Miss Galindo's colorful life and her flair for anecdote, frequently on display before Margaret. What Miss Galindo lacked was the mental training, the training in memory, to turn her impromptu anecdotal flourish into coherent and extended narrative. This is exactly what Miss Greatorex acquires by her opportunity not only to hear but also to transcribe from memory the nested stories of Mrs. Dawson.

Unlike Miss Galindo, who received no guidance on how to make her way in the world as a single woman, Miss Greatorex is surrounded by women who facilitate her transition from an oral, amateur paradigm of storytelling to a literate and literary professional paradigm, like that which Gaskell herself put to good professional use. Felicia Bonaparte has observed, "What clerking is for Miss Galindo, writing was for Elizabeth Gaskell. The images in which she thinks of women working in her fiction are those in which she thinks of herself as the writer of her books."[30] This link between Miss Galindo's clerking and Mrs. Gaskell's writing is made visible by Miss Greatorex, who transfers the oral stories of her foremothers into a literary product. The result of Miss Greatorex's memory and composition skills is a marketable commodity: "[A]nd thus it came to pass that I have the manuscript of 'My Lady Ludlow' now lying by me" (292). Reading these words in a printed book, the reader imagines that the manuscript has since been transmuted into a volume that he or she has paid money to read.

My Lady Ludlow, therefore, does more than tell the story of Miss Galindo's creative and competent strategies for situating herself in an emergent social order dominated by professionals. Gaskell's plot, as I have shown, represents simultaneously a shift in power structures toward professionalism *and* an enlargement and reconfiguration of the professional class by means of meritocratic recruitment among women and the working class. Taken together with its frame, however, it also suggests a continued scenario of professional progress for women, one that carries forward into Gaskell's own time. The failed novelist becomes a clerk who is a pioneer for female white-collar workers; two generations later, the young middle-class woman is trained, by both aural and clerkly practices, in the marketable craft of storytelling. *My Lady Ludlow* ends, not with the death of the countess or even with the circle around Mrs. Dawson's sofa, but with the finished, marketable manuscript "now lying by" Miss Greatorex, whose "memory and composition" skills have been honed by its production (292). It ends, then, with the female writer poised to take the oral narratives of her female community and render them as literary products that not only challenge the hegemony of linear male narrative but also constitute her claim to professional status in her own right. *My Lady Ludlow* and *Round the Sofa* express an early validation of the female professional as well as a celebration of the potentialities of the professional ideal to benefit society.

The understated, unrevolutionary quality of the social change depicted in the novel makes it possible to miss the considerable claims Gaskell's text makes implicitly. Miss Greatorex's and Miss Galindo's mental labors hardly stir the surface of the narrative. This very quality, however, is an index of the strength of the argument Gaskell makes: women's performing as mental workers is an ordinary, unremarkable development, entirely of a piece with the societal transformation that is bringing professionals to replace aristocrats as hegemonic in the social domain.[31] Gaskell, in other words, seems to take it as a matter of course that meritocratic logic will prevail against elitist prejudice, and that the rise of professional ideology will naturally and inevitably result in the increased access of women and other marginalized groups to professional work. Her novel therefore accepts the assumptions Jex-Blake and other campaigners deployed to naturalize women's place in the medical profession.

The relationship of women to professional structures and ideals is a vital interest to Eliot as well. Eliot's more rigorous theorization of the issue in the 1860s and 1870s similarly foregrounds the application of professional ideology to women as well as men. Nevertheless, Eliot is also more critical of the nuances of the professional ideals themselves as they affect men and women. We will see in chapter 5 that Eliot complicates the similarity of professional and feminine ideals of self-sacrifice as she probes the limits of professional self-effacement and considers women's distinctive relationship to that ideal. First, however, chapter 4 will examine Eliot's handling of the problems as well as the potentialities of professional mentorship in *Romola*, and Eliot's conflicted relationship to her own professional authority.

CHAPTER 4

È VERO OR È FALSO? THE PASTOR AS MENTOR IN *ROMOLA*

> *But man or woman who publishes writings inevitably assumes the office of teacher or influencer of the public mind.*
>
> George Eliot, *Leaves From a Notebook*

> *I shrink from decided "deliverances" on momentous subjects, from the dread of coming to swear by my own "deliverances" and sinking into an insistent echo of myself. That is a horrible destiny—and one cannot help seeing that many of the most powerful men fall into it.*
>
> George Eliot to Frederick Harrison (1870)

If critical opinion of *Romola*'s artistry has greatly improved since Felicia Bonaparte deplored that the novel belongs to the half of George Eliot's oeuvre that her readers love to hate,[1] one thing that has not changed is the fact that *Romola* (1863), more than any of Eliot's other books, is famous for things said about it by the author. One such saying is her 1877 remark, "There is no book of mine about which I feel more thoroughly I could swear by every sentence as having been written with my best blood."[2] Eliot's unwavering preference for *Romola* out of all her fiction may have done something to fuel the welcome reconsideration of her "Italian story" in the last two decades. The second authorial comment that is inevitably quoted in studies of *Romola* is one reported by John Cross: "She told me she could put her finger on it as marking a well-defined transition in her life. In her own words, 'I began it a young woman,—I finished it an old woman.' "[3] Much the same thing happens to her heroine. A "maiden of seventeen or eighteen" when first introduced to the reader, Romola is by no means old by the time of the epilogue seventeen years later. In fact, she is still younger than Eliot when she began *Romola* on January 1, 1862, at the age of forty-two.[4] However, the description in the epilogue of Romola's physical features and her cast of mind make clear that youth in every sense is gone, even long gone, for her at thirty-four. The "well-defined transition" from young to old involves, for Romola as for Eliot, much more than the passing of years. It involves suffering in the grip of agonizing dilemmas that simultaneously demand and thwart resolution. In Romola's case between 1492 and 1498, maturation occurs by means of and in response to a series of relationships with male mentors. Out of these relationships Romola emerges as a mature woman, no longer needing a mentor and in fact capable of mentoring others. Eliot's comment about her own transition from young to old may have arisen from the sense that she was negotiating and understanding her troubled relationships with her mentors—and with her readers—in the process of writing the novel.

Eliot herself embodied contradictory roles as woman and public intellectual, both "requiring some one to lean upon" and serving as moral and spiritual guide to the reading public.[5] Eliot's complex relationships with her various male mentors—including Robert Evans, Isaac Evans, Charles Bray, Robert Herbert Brabrant, François D'Albert Durade, John Chapman, Herbert Spencer, and George Lewes—are beyond the scope of this study. Rather, I will first attend briefly to Eliot's disposition toward her own role as a mentor in the later years of her life; then I will more extensively examine her treatment of mentoring and pastorship in the novel that she said marked her transition from a young woman to an old woman. We will see that *Romola*'s focus on personal mentoring as an analogue for broader social pastorship foregrounds the problems that pertain to the transmission of professional ethics: how are professionals-in-training to be taught to use their human capital in proper ways and for proper ends? The failure of Bardo, Dino, and Tito to teach Romola how or why to use her expertise for the public good will be the subject of the third section below. The novel further engages the problem of the ethics of mentoring itself: what are the proper ethical restraints upon those who undertake to instruct trainees? Eliot's novelistic examination of Savonarola's errors falls under this heading. This reading will illuminate Eliot's ambivalence toward her own status as public sage and her efforts to contain the anxieties attendant on that status. Eliot's mid-career novel reflects the tension she perceived between the obligation of the professional, in this case the author, to guide the public, and the inappropriateness of "decided 'deliverances' on momentous subjects."

I

Some of Eliot's thoughts about her role as a mentor to the reading public are represented in her note or short essay on "Authorship." The 1870s essay, the first and longest selection in *Leaves from a Notebook*, collected and published by Charles Lewes in 1883, makes a number of interesting comments on the social obligations attending the literary profession. Eliot begins by deploring the lack of a guild-specific consensus about the ethical norms of the profession of authorship. In an extended metaphor, she compares authorship to calico manufacture only to emphasize that the ethical considerations for an author are far more complex.[6] In short, "the author's capital is his brain-power—power of invention, power of writing."[7] Yet while the calico manufacturer need not trouble himself with the ethics of the quantity and quality of the goods he produces, since the market will automatically adjust to correct any discrepancy, the author's work requires the author's own rigorous self-correction and self-censoring in order not to deteriorate the public taste and public morals. This is owing to the fact that "man or woman who publishes writings inevitably assumes the office of teacher or influencer of the public mind."[8] The specious claim that a given work is only for amusement is dismissed as disingenuous and pernicious: "[The author] can no more escape influencing the moral taste, and with it the action of the intelligence, than a setter of fashions in furniture and dress can fill the shops with his designs and leave the garniture of persons and houses unaffected by his industry."[9] The good author, one who "has this sign of the divine afflatus within him," must therefore determine not to "pursue authorship as a vocation with a trading determination to get rich by it. . . . An author who would keep a pure and noble conscience, and with that a developing instead of degenerating intellect and taste, must cast out of his aims the aim to be rich."[10]

The first broad point to be drawn from this essay is the relationship Eliot assumes between the possession of human capital and the attendant ethical responsibility to be concerned with the public good. The individual in possession of writing skill is adjured throughout this essay that to use such skill for vanity, for pecuniary benefit, or any end other than social reform is mercenary and immoral. In other words, she appeals to the professional ideal of special expertise in service of the public to characterize—and to dignify—the author's work.[11] In the case of the author, the public service that is required of the professional is the formation of "moral taste, and with it the action of the intelligence." The author, then, is a pastor, a mentor to a nation of readers, with a twist of Victorian moral earnestness.[12] Given the lofty expectations she put on authors, it is no wonder Eliot agonized over her ability to write worthily.

The second salient point, which follows from the first, is her insistence that literary attainments be regulated by a standard of conduct not pecuniary. The moral responsibilities of the author must be paramount over the desire to maximize income. This paradigm, familiar from the professional ideal, is here applied explicitly to authorship. Eliot anticipates that authors can make more money either by producing a greater quantity of reduced quality work or by writing in a popular vein without regard for the social effects of their work. Such authors are compared to a manufacturer of worthless trinkets colored with arsenic—wares not only frivolous but also poisoning. This is, in effect, the rationale at work in Eliot's publication decisions about *Romola*. She initially rejected the princely offering of £10, 000 for the novel because she felt she could not put the novel into the required sixteen serials without damaging her artistic intent, nor could she have the first parts ready in time for the *Cornhill*'s schedule. George Smith presumably hoped that his exorbitant offer would persuade her to rush her writing and "pad" her narrative, but Eliot was unmoved by the sum. Only when her artistic terms were satisfied by the agreement for twelve longer parts would she sell the manuscript for the reduced price of £7, 000, which was still more than she could have obtained from her previous publisher John Blackwood. She therefore observed the principle articulated in "Authorship": "It is in the highest sense lawful for [the author] to get as good a price as he honourably can for the best work he is capable of; but not for him to force or hurry his production . . . for the sake of bringing his income up to the fancy pitch."[13]

Eliot shows some lack of clarity on the subject of what should be done to rectify the state of affairs deplored in this essay, namely the incongruity between the actual practice of authors and the professional ideal. Usual sorts of institutional procedures for licensing and policing qualified professionals are not well adapted for the profession of letters. Eliot indicates that individual writers need to check their own ambitions with a healthy dose of diffidence, to which end she devotes her last paragraph to dressing down inferior writers. First she addresses the "ill-taught" writers, who require a stiff dose of "medicines of a spiritual sort [that] can be found good against mental emptiness and inflation." Next she more respectfully observes that the learned "can only be cured by the medicine of higher ideals in social duty."[14] This conclusion leads her into a paradox that she escapes by ending the essay rather abruptly. The medicine required by bad writers to learn diffident self-restraint is precisely that moral nurture that is taught by good authors. Yet good writers, who are diffident, have been given a very high standard of value—both morally and artistically—for their work to be worthy of inflicting on the public.

It is clear that Eliot felt this high standard acutely, and that she was often paralyzed by her sense of the enormity of the author's responsibility and her perceived inability to be equal to the author's august task. She wrote to Frederick Harrison, "I wonder whether you at all imagine the terrible pressure of disbelief in my own duty/right to speak to the public, which is apt with me to make all beginnings of work like a rowing against tide."[15] If the good writers are awed into silence by their right appreciation of the enormity of the task and their own inadequacy for it, then how will the bad writers and the society at large be reformed? Who will mentor the reading public if one's fitness for doing so is judged at least in part by one's hesitancy to do so? The conclusion to *Romola*, as we will see, similarly leaves this matter unsettled.

II

The mentoring relationships that comprise Romola's process of maturation have not yet been studied specifically in terms of professional models.[16] Doing so allows us to elaborate on the work of previous critics who have tended to see mentoring largely through the lens of sexuality. Patricia Menon's *Austin, Eliot, Charlotte Brontë and the Mentor-Lover* omits *Romola* from the novel-by-novel account of the figure of the mentor-lover, explaining that none of the mentors of the novel combine their role with a sexual relationship to Romola.[17] In this way she replicates the approach of Rosemarie Bodenheimer in *The Real Life of Mary Ann Evans*, who reads the mentoring relationships of *Daniel Deronda* in the context of Eliot's sexualized relationships with young men and women she mentored in her later years. Both Bodenheimer and Menon look to *Daniel Deronda*, written after Eliot's attainment of sibylline status, for the fictional expression of Eliot's felt tensions with respect to her mentor role, a valid reading that undoubtedly serves to illuminate aspects of that novel.[18] However, this reading problematically requires us to see Eliot in the figure of Deronda, negotiating submerged sexual tensions in his mentorship of Gwendolen as Eliot herself did in her relationships with Edith Simcox and John Cross. To make this attribution requires us to cross both gender and age, since Bodenheimer points out that part of the perplexity Eliot has about rendering Deronda as Gwendolen's mentor is that she is nearly the same age as he.[19] By far a better biographical analogue to Eliot's own mentoring experience is found in *Romola*, the novel she began as a young woman and finished as an old woman. Romola, like Eliot but unlike Deronda, is mentored herself before she mentors others.

More importantly, reading the mentoring relationships in terms of professionalism makes visible Eliot's engagement in a complex discussion of the legitimacy of disparate professional models. Tito Melema, Bardo de' Bardi, Fra Girolamo Savonarola, and Romola de' Bardi each possess a store of human capital gained through a long and arduous course of training, and each seeks to use that human capital to advance personal or political ends. The reader is invited to judge these professional characters on the basis of how they conceive of their social responsibilities for the use of their expertise. As a professional scholar, Tito is an unscrupulous mercenary, using his erudition and pleasant manners first to gain material reward and eventually to betray secrets to the highest bidder. Bardo's putatively disinterested pursuit of knowledge is nevertheless infused with his egoistic desire for recognition. Savonarola, whose vows of poverty and obedience should presumably safeguard him from worldly power seeking, uses his rhetoric and charisma to achieve altruistic ends in Florence. However, the power that accrues to him because of that charisma eventually proves corrupting and destructive. Each of these mentor-figures tries to inculcate his vision of social responsibility—or lack thereof—into Romola, but each fails more or less spectacularly. Romola eventually assumes the position of Eliot's valorized professional: the educated middle-class individual who combines the qualities of rectitude and self-knowledge that qualify her to provide the moral leadership—that is, the pastorship—for which the pragmatism of politics, the ivory tower of scholarship, and the pulpit of the Church have each proven themselves inadequate.[20] Thus Eliot uses the historical context of Renaissance Florence to critique the failings of professionalism in her own time and to imagine a solution that transcends those inadequate models.[21]

As this simple outline reflects, the transmission of expertise is eclipsed in the novel by the problems of the transmission of ethical norms, and particularly the *ethical* transmission of ethical norms. As one would expect from Eliot, and as the professional ideal itself makes necessary, mentoring is at least as much a moral project as an intellectual one. I will therefore be talking about mentoring chiefly in its moral dimension as the transmission of a system or sense of ethical obligations that pertain to the possession of professional expertise.

In *Romola*, the social upheaval of Renaissance Florence is figured as a crisis of literal pastorship in which churchmen, especially Savonarola, play major roles. Eliot's study of Savonarola's career leads her to probe the pitfalls of mentorship and pastorship both. In fact, mentorship and pastorship become analogues of each other: the need for a guide on the part of the social body generally is troped as the need for a guide on the part of the novice. Susan M. Bernardo maintains as much in pointing out that "Florence's need for a firm leader and Romola's search for meaning gradually emerge as analogous—both seek order, autonomy, and direction."[22] Thus in *Romola*, the mentoring of Romola by Bardo, Tito, and Savonarola particularizes the broader agenda of social pastorship put forward by each mentor-figure. Moreover, Romola's own eventual profession is Foucauldian pastorship, or, as Kimberly VanEsveld Adams puts it, "moral and social leadership."[23]

In this novel, the function of the pastor/mentor is chiefly hermeneutical.[24] The interpretation of political and personal events, of feelings, impressions, and even supernatural revelation is the special task of the professionals in *Romola*.[25] The pressing need for a pastor, a professional who can interpret the signs of the times, is indicated in the first chapter, when the worldly-wise skeptic Nello points out that the voices competing for the Florentines' spiritual and political allegiance are contradictory and mutually exclusive. The death of Lorenzo de' Medici has just become known, and the gathered curious Florentines are arguing about the meaning of supernatural portents reported by followers of Savonarola and others. The buffoon Goro readily agrees that a portent may be polysemous: "For when God above sends a sign, it's not to be supposed that he'd have only one meaning."[26] In spite of Nello's raillery at "believ[ing] that your miraculous bull means everything that any man in Florence likes it to mean," a follower of Savonarola decidedly affirms that interpretation is definitive and privileged: "[E]very revelation, whether by visions, dreams, portents, or the written word, has many meanings, which it is given to the illuminated only to unfold" (18). Nello's remark that follows then dryly points out that claims to illumination are themselves contested: "With San Domenico roaring *è vero* in one ear, and San Francisco screaming *è falso* in the other, what is a poor barber to do—unless he were illuminated?" (19). When multiple pastors claim to offer the reliable, illuminated interpretation, and when those interpretations are mutually exclusive, then the public requires illumination to know which of the supposedly illuminated pastors to adhere to. Presumably, even this illumination is also contestable, and so on *ad absurdum*. The question of who is qualified to render necessary judgments on interpretive questions will be pervasive in the novel. The need for a professional pastor to manage these conflicting ideologies—to find a humanist source of limited or contingent illumination, or "voice within"—assuredly resonates with nineteenth-century urgency in *Romola* (497).[27]

Just as resonant, however, is the novel's caution against dogmatic or overly certain claims to special expertise that presume to place the expert beyond public accountability. Dogmatism amounts to the perpetual denial of professional status to the novice, or the continued refusal to allow the autonomous exercise of judgment by the disciple. In this early conversation, the inappropriateness of dogmatic interpretations is established in concert with that of relativist interpretations. For the Florentines at the barbershop, the only alternatives available   seem to be religious dogmatism—according to which the nonilluminated obediently and unquestioningly follow the self-proclaimed illuminated—and nihilistic relativism—according to which any sign can mean anything that anyone wants it to mean. The problem of the novel is to theorize a pastorship that is competent to make interpretative assertions without devolving into dogmatism, a pastorship that recognizes the contingency of its own truth claims even as it makes them.[28]

As Pauline Nestor argues, such an epistemology is gendered feminine. In Nestor's reading, the novel posits a fundamental opposition between a masculine "world of partisanship and false simplicities" and a feminine alternative of "non-partisan openness and diffidence." Alone among the novel's central characters, Romola "knows neither the affliction—nor the protection—which comes from the certainty of polemicism." Rather, she has an "instinctive repugnance for the polemical and the divisive" that is grounded in her "capacity for doubt." Whereas masculine certainties are shown by the novel to be "destructive and dangerous," the social order is redeemed by the feminine "large and generous mind."[29] An important caveat is missing from Nestor's account, however. Romola's diffidence and doubt are surely in many ways preferable to the false certitude of polemicism, but they are not an unequivocal good. In fact Romola's indecision, as I will have occasion to note below, is unproductive and paralyzing at several key moments in the novel, whereas Savonarola's false certitude is in many ways productive for her and for the city. When Romola's impulse of fellow-feeling is contested, she becomes paralyzed with indecision and can only act, as it were, in a trance or haze, with her judgment suspended. It is her feminine qualities of "non-partisan openness and diffidence" that leave her vulnerable to manipulation by others who are anything but diffident. Thus Romola's feminine epistemology is not static or essential, as Nestor implies, but developing and contested. Romola needs to learn to trust her instinctive fellow-feeling and use it productively, rather than suspending it in the face of masculine polemicism.

The attainment of a model of pastorship without dogmatism, I will argue, is what makes the novel's conclusion coherent and hopeful rather than weakly disappointing. Romola eventually achieves the idealized and desired state of expertise without dogmatism, and her activities as mentor are oriented accordingly. The process by which she arrives at this state involves her painful experience with failed mentors, particularly Bardo and Savonarola. As the competing versions of professional ethics intersect her life, Romola repeatedly finds herself in Nello's position of being forced to choose between mutually exclusive claims to moral authority. Eliot ultimately shows that mentors must be self-aware of mixed motives, which is to say that no mentor can pretend to be, or imagine herself as, offering divine illumination, uncontestable truth, unchallengeable dogma. Rather, protection for professional neophytes and for the public is found in a brand of moral tutelage that is unapologetic in its assertions but open to correction and aware of personal bias.[30]

This study will next explicate the process by which Romola is tutored in the understanding of the moral ramifications of her special expertise, and how that process becomes complicated by events that require her to interpret the truth claims of her mentors. Then I will consider Romola's response to the failures she observes, arguing that in her surreal experience in the plague-stricken village and her later return to Florence she reverses the pastoral mistakes of Savonarola. Eliot's final statement about professional mentoring is therefore modest but affirmative: a responsible mentor can learn to instruct novices without succumbing to the fatal flaw of prideful dogmatism; however, Eliot suggests that this project can only succeed on a small and private (pastoral as opposed to bureaucratic) scale.

III

Romola's first mentor is of course her father Bardo de' Bardi, who has instilled in Romola the linguistic expertise of an accomplished classical scholar but has failed to school her in the morally appropriate use of that expertise for the benefit of society. Bardo's professional ethics are not without idealism: he regards scholarly expertise as a calling that justifies renunciation of self for the higher good of the advancement of knowledge. As such his moral philosophy emphasizes personal renunciation for the sake of filial and civic duty, and he likes to cast his scholarship as service to the public and to future generations. Bardo is immensely proud of his disinterestedness, signified by his independence from the patronage system or other means of material reward for his work. He boasts, "If even Florence only is to remember me, it can but be . . . because I forsook the vulgar pursuit of wealth in commerce that I might devote myself to collecting the precious remains of ancient art and wisdom, and leave them . . . for an everlasting possession to my fellow-citizens" (53).

Clearly, however, Bardo's vocation of scholarship is not as disinterested or serviceable as he would like to think. Having chosen to renounce worldly gain for the sake of lasting fame as a renown scholar, he is obsessed with the idea of his legacy. According to the narrator, Bardo's devotion to scholarship is inextricably mixed with his "love of pre-eminence, the old desire to leave a lasting track of his footsteps on the fast whirling earth" (46). The chief concern of his old age, ahead even of his duty to secure Romola's marriage, is his desire to ensure that his library is preserved intact so that "men should own themselves debtors to the Bardi library in Florence" (57). He is so jealous of guarding the ideas that he thinks will guarantee his lasting fame that he refuses to publish his work or to give other scholars access to it for fear that they will plagiarize him. Bardo is pitifully paralyzed between the desire to be recognized for his scholarly contributions and the desire to protect them from piracy. Clearly he does not think of his expertise as service to the wider public or even to the scholarly community, but rather as an avenue to self-aggrandizement.

Moreover, Bardo's indifference toward the social order has left him all but friendless. Absorbed in the study of the dead ideas of dead men in a dead language, he is utterly disconnected from the world beyond his own home and lacks all fellow-feeling. Unforgiving toward his absent son and brusque toward his devoted daughter, Bardo is estranged even from his family. Consequently, neither Dino nor Romola finds in Bardo's philosophy resources needed for an affective life. Emotionally disabled by his father's "vain philosophy," Dino seeks in eremitic asceticism an even more pathological revulsion from the social: "I must have no affection, no hope . . .; I must live with my fellow-beings only as human souls related to the eternal unseen" (159). This is not a reaction against but a further perversion of the upbringing he received.

In the case of Romola, her emotional stuntedness leaves her easy prey to the meretricious affections of Tito. Both her father and brother fail her as mentors: Bardo's ready acceptance of Tito's suit for Romola is motivated by his own hope of benefiting from Tito's scholarly assistance, and Dino's lack of normal fraternal regard prevents his warning Romola about Tito's abandonment of his adoptive father. Readily attracted to Tito's superficial merits, and starved for human affection, Romola attaches herself to Tito. His mentorship of her does not go far before she realizes and rejects his unscrupulousness, but for a time Tito performs the function for her that she will later rely on Savonarola to fulfill: that of interpreting or illuminating her questions and doubts. After their wedding, "[t]he new sensibilities and questions which [married life] had half awakened in her were quieted again by that subjection to her husband's mind which is felt by every wife who loves her husband with passionate devotedness and full reliance" (251).

Tito's character forms a close connection to the stereotypical critiques of professionals in Eliot's own day, types that Eliot exploited in "Janet's Repentance." Without the anchors of principle or duty, Tito uses his expertise solely for personal material gain, without regard for the consequences to others. He came to Florence because he had been told "Florence is the best market in Italy for such commodities as yours" (29).[31] In conversation with the barber Nello, Tito refers to his ability to sell his expertise as "capital," saying, "It seems to me . . . that you have taken away some of my capital with your razor—I mean a year or two of age, which might have won me more ready credit for my learning" (35). Tito, then, exemplifies the pure market rationality of commodified expertise deployed for maximum self-advancement. His scholarly profession becomes only a front for his treacherous espionage.

Tito's utilitarian philosophy has an anachronistic ring of Benthamism: he talks himself out of his duty to seek and redeem his enslaved adoptive father by reflecting, "What, looked at closely, was the end of all life, but to extract the utmost sum of pleasure? And was not his own blooming life a promise of incomparably more pleasure, not for himself only, but for others, than the withered wintry life of a man who was past the time of keen enjoyment?" (117). Cennini's naïve remark about Tito—"I like to see a young man work his way upward by merit"—is therefore best read as a parody of the professional ideal (398). Thus Eliot links morally bankrupt utilitarianism with materialistic egoism in her damning portrait of professional expertise without moral or altruistic bearings.

IV

Romola's first two mentors hold corrupted notions of the social obligations that attach to the possession of expertise, and her rejection of their efforts to transmit their ideals to her seems to be a function of her feminine instinct for personal connections. This instinct is fully realized in the intervention of her third mentor, Savonarola. Unlike Bardo and Tito, Savonarola sees his expertise (his rhetoric, prophecy, and charisma) as entailing incontrovertible ethical obligations. As a cenobitic monk, Savonarola understands the cause of God's kingdom to entail public service, and his civic career begins by organizing relief work. His apparent altruism engenders the charisma and popularity that in turn make him highly effective in motivating others. Savonarola's ethic of public service is therefore sincere and productive; however, it will prove ultimately to be misguided as a result of the dogmatism with which he wields his expert authority.

Our analysis of Savonarola requires first that we ascertain the nature of his pastorship of the city of Florence. We will see that in some ways he satisfies for the Florentines the felt need of Victorians, as described by Lauren M. E. Goodlad, for a pastorship that is "rational but unbureaucratic, omnipresent but personal, authoritative but liberatory, efficient but English."[32] We will further see that his mentorship of Romola particularizes the general pattern he has taken toward Florence as a whole. It will then become clear that in the last part of the novel Eliot portrays Romola as an analogue of Savonarola. Not only does she learn from him the sacred duty of rebellion and then ironically use it to rebel against him, but she also mimics the pattern of his pastorship when she attends to the plague-stricken village. It is in more ways than one that "the great problem of [Romola's] life . . . essentially coincides with a chief problem in Savonarola's."[33] Finally Romola's mentorship of Lillo particularizes the moral achievement she has attained and that Savonarola failed to attain. That is to say, Romola's "religious discipleship" to Savonarola eventuates in her becoming his equivalent and finally surpassing him (567).

Eliot records that Savonarola had entered the cloister at the age of twenty-three; his prophetic visions and public social reform work did not commence until some years later (199).[34] He was still on the rise in 1492, when the imaginary spirit of Eliot's Proem noted that he "denounced with a rare boldness the worldliness and vicious habits of the clergy, and insisted on the duty of Christian men . . . not to spend their wealth in outward pomp even in the churches, when their fellow-citizens were suffering from want and sickness" (8). The Frate's preaching is multifarious, and in it Eliot finds something to praise as well as to condemn. An early analysis of Savonarola's preaching exhibits this ambivalence. Along with the "false certitude which gave his sermons the interest of a political bulletin" and his "imperious need of ascendancy," Savonarola has for Eliot also "that active sympathy, that clear-sighted demand for the subjection of selfish interests to the general good, which he had in common with the greatest of mankind" (237). Eliot particularly favors his impulse toward active charity, the same thing that drew her to Evangelicalism in her adolescence. In his incessant call to all Florentines to subordinate their personal interests to the common weal, Eliot seems to voice her own moral conviction. Savonarola's staunch rebukes of hypocrisy and clerical misconduct are likewise appealing. Yet this greatness of soul and mind is seemingly unavoidably joined to a "need of personal predominance" that leads him toward increasingly shrill and defensive rhetoric and increasingly outrageous visions required to satisfy the popular appetite for the spectacular (237). As opposition to him hardens, so does his dogmatism in maintaining his position. Eliot's analysis continues: "[H]aving once held that audience in his mastery, it was necessary to his nature—it was necessary for their welfare—that he should *keep* the mastery" (238, emphasis in original). Here Eliot's free indirect discourse signals the Frate's gravest error: his failure to recognize how his zeal for the welfare of the public mingled with fervor for his own ascendancy until the latter replaced the former.[35]

As the Spirit of the Proem recalls, the elimination of vanities is originally oriented specifically toward poor relief. Under Savonarola's spell, "the women even took off their ornaments, and delivered them up to be sold for the benefit of the needy" (8). During times of civic economic crisis, Savonarola urged that even Church valuables be melted down and given to the poor as alms.[36] During the campaign of moral reform that followed the expulsion of the Medici, "the dominant note of Savonarola's reforming message was Christian charity, understood as the tangible expression of love for one's neighbor. . . . As he never tired of repeating, true Christian living, on which the blessings of Florence were stipulated, could not prosper in a city in which large numbers of people were degraded and brutalized by poverty."[37] The early band of organized Piagnoni particularly devoted themselves to the care of Florence's destitute and ill. By taking control of the city's hospitals and other relief institutions, and especially by instituting a civic lending agency so that the poor did not have to resort to usurers, those Florentines inspired by Savonarola's Christian social vision worked energetically to alleviate the suffering of both native-born and indigent poor.[38] As Eliot records, during the famine of 1496 Savonarola insisted that the city's scant provisions be shared equally with the many impoverished refugees who came to the city (373). All in all, the social vision of Savonarola and his followers was one of cooperative and sacrificial effort for the benefit—moral but also material—of all people.[39]

It is precisely this vision that Savonarola so effectively infuses into Romola during their roadside confrontation. He rebukes her desire to determine her own course of life without reference to the solemn obligations of a citizen and a wife. He instructs her that she is not at liberty to escape the duties to which she is born and that she has willingly contracted. He further commands her to feel the "glow of a common life with the lost multitude for whom that offering was made" (364). Thus Savonarola explicitly or implicitly indicts both of Romola's previous mentors. This "glow of a common life" is what Romola missed under the tutelage of Bardo, whom Savonarola characterizes as one of "those who sit on a hill aloof, and look down on the life of their fellow-men" (363). Moreover, his adjuration to her to honor her commitments to others stings her with "the suggestion . . . of a possible affinity between her own conduct and Tito's" (362). Though Fra Girolamo knows nothing of Tito's behavior, Romola realizes that her impulse to flee a burdensome responsibility formed under the influence of this second mentor.

Savonarola is successful in his persuasion of Romola for the same reasons he is successful with the Florentine populace generally: his personal charisma, almost mesmeric in its effect, and his apparent altruism. Romola "felt it impossible again to question his authority" once she has fallen under the spell of his "gaze in which simple human fellowship expressed itself as a strongly-felt bond" (361). Crucially, "the source of the impression his glance produced on Romola was the sense it conveyed to her of interest in her and care for her *apart from any personal feeling*" (361, my emphasis). That is, Savonarola compels the submission of others because of his dramatic personal disinterestedness, or radical self-effacement. Savonarola's frequent appeals to martyrdom in his sermons are an extreme, even perverse, manifestation of this same phenomenon. Because he was supposedly dead to the world, his stance on worldly concerns could be considered reliable. He alone among Florentines of stature could present himself as nonpartisan, disinterested, and ultimately devoted only to otherworldly aims. That this was not true Eliot has already indicated in her analysis of the sermon we examined above. In fact, in Eliot's reading, Savonarola's will to power is deeply involved in his program of reform and even in his impulse to glorious martyrdom.

It is also important to note that Savonarola's mentorship of Romola begins with his resolution of an ethical dilemma she had been unable to resolve. As she prepared to depart Florence the previous night, the narrator describes her stream of consciousness in terms of her inability to mediate the competing voices within her head, a state of mind that evokes Nello's remark about the competing truth claims of the Dominicans and Franciscans. The narrator summarizes her state of mind thus:

> No radiant angel came across the gloom with a clear message for her. In those times, as now, there were human beings who never saw angels or heard perfectly clear messages. Such truth as came to them was brought confusedly in the voices and deeds of men not at all like the seraphs of unfailing wing and piercing vision—men who believed falsities as well as truths, and did the wrong as well as the right. (329)

The narrator emphasizes the lack of what Nello called "illumination" as Romola sits in the darkness, without a "radiant angel" or a "clear message." In the absence of illumination, one can only rely on flawed human judgment when faced with competing truth claims. Romola desperately needs a mentor to adjudicate this crisis; however, as the narrator warns, no mentor is infallibly illuminated, and truth only comes mediated through individuals who are "not at all like the seraphs."

The mentorship Savonarola provides is therefore potentially as dangerous as it is necessary. Nevertheless, his "arresting voice" puts a stop not only to her flight but also to her interpretive dilemma. When they meet on the road the next morning, his call to duty and renunciation "had come to her as if they were an *interpretation* of that revulsion from self-satisfied ease, and of that new fellowship with suffering, which had already been awakened in her" (366, my emphasis). Savonarola's role is precisely that of interpreting Romola's conflicted impulses, much like the way Romola's "subjection to her husband's mind" had earlier "quieted" the "anxieties of her married life" (251). The "arrest" of Romola's interpretive melee therefore has both a positive and a negative connotation. Savonarola puts an end to Romola's crisis by telling her what is right and wrong in her own deadlocked mind; thus he "arrests" her whirling, indecisive thoughts. However, he can do so only by "arresting" or taking captive her critical faculties, thus taking over the role that Tito had briefly taken over from Bardo.

As Savonarola's pastorship of Florence is particularized in his mentorship of Romola, the positive and negative aspects of that wider social phenomenon are reproduced in her individually.[40] Though she remains unenthusiastic about many Piagnoni practices, Romola fully endorses the charitable work. Inspired by his vision of social amelioration, in which the strong sacrificially serve the weak, Romola gives up most of her own food to the poor during the famine, nurses plague victims at the hospital, and houses indigents in her courtyard. Accosted by a group of hungry men who threaten to take the bread she carries to the sick, she shames them into a collective "moral rebuke" (378). These activities demonstrate that "she had submitted her mind to [Savonarola's . . .], because in this way she had found an immediate satisfaction of moral needs which all the previous culture and experience of her life had left hungering" (389). Under Savonarola's mentorship Romola embraces the humanist ethical sense to which she is intuitively drawn, but that her previous mentors utterly failed to cultivate.

However, Savonarola's mentorship has two devastating shortcomings. The first is that, as we have seen, he confuses his self-interest with his service of others, an error into which Romola falls as well. Romola's enjoyment of the status her charity brings is palpable in the picture Eliot paints of her movements in the city. Greeted respectfully by Florence's most sober citizens, she serenely accepts their regard as she goes about her work. When she promises food to the refugees in her courtyard, " 'Bless you, madonna! bless you!' said the faint chorus, in much the same tone as that in which they had a few minutes before praised and thanked the unseen Madonna" (388). The title of this chapter, "The Visible Madonna," makes clear that Romola is being collapsed into the Virgin Mary in the minds of the Florentines. For her part, "Romola cared a great deal for that music. She had no innate taste for tending the sick and clothing the ragged" (388). There is, then, an egoistic strain to her social service of which she is unaware. The deference she is accorded—by Piagnoni of all ranks, by the overzealous bands of boys collecting vanities, and by the indigents she provides for—makes up a considerable portion of her tolerance for the distasteful elements of her work. As is the case with Savonarola, her apparent altruism engenders for her cultural capital, the possession of which is gratifying—even intoxicating—to her. The errors as well as the virtues of the mentor are replicated in the novice.

The other significant detrimental aspect of Savonarola's mentorship of both Florence and of Romola is the subtle progression by which charismatic inspiration shades into coercion. Partly because of the enthusiastic application of his teachings by overzealous followers, and partly because of the extremes of rhetoric to which Savonarola is given in the pulpit, his moral reform of the city takes on an increasingly militant character. The gangs of boys issue imperious demands, sprinkled with quotations from Savonarola's sermons, for "vanities" to be given to them to burn or give to charity (440). When Romola is not at hand to remind them that Savonarola "would have such things given up freely," the boys bully the passersby with an impunity that derives in part from their supposedly spiritual mission (436). However great Eliot's sympathies with Piagnoni practical charity, she can have no warm regard for such coercive tactics, especially when they are sanctified by religious aims.

The coercion exercised by these boys is a reflection of the willingness of Savonarola to utilize heavy-handed political tactics to achieve his reformist aims.[41] When Savonarola fails to speak against a Piagnone woman's vision calling for the murder of Romola's godfather Bernardo del Nero, Romola realizes that political expediency has brought Savonarola to compromise truth and principle. Romola's rejected plea that Savonarola insist that the right of appeal be granted to Bernardo exposes the hypocrisy inherent in Savonarola's refusal to act—Savonarola would prefer that justice be denied in this case because the death of the conspirators is politically expedient for him. In other words, he accepts the use of violent injustice to further his political ends. As she finds herself in angry opposition to him, Romola is explicitly acting on the basis of what she has learned from him about the sacred duty of rebellion against corrupt authority. She tells her erstwhile mentor, "I submitted . . . because I saw the light. *Now* I cannot see it. Father, you yourself declare that there comes a moment when the soul must have no guide but the voice within it" (497). Savonarola's assertion—"The cause of my party *is* the cause of God's kingdom"—effectively confirms Romola's worst suspicions of his insidious self-deception (497, emphasis in original). She sees that Savonarola's purported disinterest is inextricably bound up in personal ambition, and that Savonarola is not only unaware of this fact but incapable, at least in his present state, of being made aware of it. His credibility as an interpreter of events and an illuminator of supernatural revelation—in short, his pastorship—is therefore invalidated, and Romola now has no source of illumination besides herself.

V

The problem that Eliot has posed at this point in the novel is how an ethically responsible mentorship can be realized. How can the need of the populace for moral reform be met without the coercion of the simple, the use of heavy-handed politics, and the suspension of justice? How can the need of the individual for interpretive counsel be met without stifling dogmatism, without the arrest of the individual conscience to unthinking conformity? In other words, how can the positive effects of mentorship be achieved without the negative effects? Eliot's meticulous portrait of Savonarola's deficiencies has already suggested that the solution lies in the responsibility of the mentor to be self-aware and self-critical of his or her mixed motives. This solution is explored in the novel's final installment.

Romola's sojourn in the valley is a telescoped version of Savonarola's experience in Florence.[42] She arrives on a scene of death and desolation: the sound have fled for their own safety while the sick are left to die and lie unburied. Her fearlessness and indefatigability in her acts of mercy quickly shame the healthy to tend to the sick. Inspired by her example, the villagers overcome their self-protective panic and understand their essential relationship to other humans in need, both fellow-citizens and foreign indigents. In other words, she inspires them to the same social vision to which Savonarola inspired her personally and all of Florence generally. Her tremendous persuasive power over these frightened people, moreover, derives from her spiritual charisma. Whereas in Florence she was sometimes regarded as a Madonna figure, here she is briefly taken for an apparition of the Virgin, an impression that survives long enough to dispel the people's atomizing self-defensiveness. The priest's and the boy's momentary confusion about Romola's humanity recalls the first of Romola's own dark nights of the soul, when she "saw no radiant angel" but was nevertheless rescued by a great but flawed man. Now she is mistaken for the radiant angel. Soon the priest and the boy realize she is indeed mortal, but "their minds were filled instead with the more effective sense that she was a human being whom God had sent over the sea to command them" (565). In other words, they regard her as a prophet, whose commands carry divine imprimatur, precisely as Savonarola's followers regard him. Following her precept and example, the village is restored to both physical and social health and fecundity. The moral reform of the villagers brings material prosperity and social communion. When the village has recovered and Romola is able to rest, they honor "the Blessed Lady" with daily votive offerings of "their best . . . honey, fresh cakes, eggs, and polenta" (566).

Romola's abbreviated version of Savonarola's story has a fantasy ending rather than his tragic ending. In this primitive world away from political intrigue, the simple message of fellow-feeling, as taught by a charismatic and altruistic pastor, converts the atomized heathen and builds a healthy community. The crucial difference, however, can be seen in the use Romola makes of her charismatic power. Unlike Savonarola, who accumulated personal power with the misguided aim of putting it to righteous use, Romola adds nothing to her original message of loving one's neighbor as oneself. She has no grandiose projects; she makes no use, selfishly or otherwise, of the virtually unlimited power she has over these people who all but worship her. When she determines that her work is done and her strength has returned, she simply walks away.

Romola's decision to return to Florence is reached as torturously as her previous decisions to leave her native city. As in those cases, she wavers between two or more interpretations of her situation, but in this case there is no mentor to turn to and no arrest from without. Finally she resolves to return on the basis of the epiphany that she shares in the "maimed" condition of "life [that] has lost its perfection" (568). She asks, "What if Fra Girolamo had been wrong? What if the life of Florence was a web of inconsistencies? Was she, then, something higher, that she should shake the dust from off her feet, and say, 'This world is not good enough for me'? If she had been really higher, she would not so easily have lost all her trust" (568). In other words, she recognizes that she is not transcendent but human and fallible. She does not equivocate about her interpretive insight—she knows Savonarola was wrong—but neither does she claim an infallible source for that certainty; rather, she recognizes herself as one who also can be wrong.

On Romola's return to Florence this realization works itself out in various ways, the first of which is management of her finances. Although she is heiress to a large sum of money that Tito has saved, she gives the whole amount, except the value of her father's property, to the government (a means of disposal that is appropriately secular and public-spirited). Just as she renounced the privilege her charisma gave her in the village, Romola renounces the opportunity to be "blessed madonna" to the poor of Florence.

Romola's second major action on her return to Florence is to search out Tessa and her children, Lillo and Ninna, to provide for them as they have now become destitute and helpless following Tito's death. Significantly, Romola "never for a moment told herself that it was heroism or exalted charity in her to seek out these beings; she needed something that she was bound specially to care for; she yearned to clasp the children and to make them love her" (572). Romola is well aware that public opinion, like Monna Brigida, would regard it a noble and selfless act to embrace her dead husband's mistress and illegitimate children. Romola, however, views her motives without self-deception. Rigorously critical of her own motives, she refuses popular gratulation for her actions and firmly retains the ability to acknowledge frankly the unadorned truth of how her self-interest is implicated even in her actions that appear to be most altruistic.[43]

These actions and attitudes signify Romola's readiness to perform the decisive hermeneutics of Savonarola's confession, and by extension, of his life and calling, a role Eliot grants her in the concluding chapters.[44] All of Florence is agitated by the essential question of the Frate's veracity in his prophetic visions, and once again voices scream *è vero* and *è falso* from opposite corners of the city. Romola's task, in which she is guided only by the "voice within," is to read a pirated edition of an unfriendly account of a confession extracted under torture and determine the truth of Savonarola's life, work, and motives. The possibilities for misinterpretation are numerous. Nevertheless, Romola ponders the information available to her, paying attention to nuances of style, noting inconsistencies, and always reading through her remembered experience of Savonarola in both his private and public roles. The central question is whether or not his claims to divinely revealed prophecies were genuine or fabricated. His confession of deceit is dismissed as coerced; but his broken state, utterly devoid of self-glorifying rhetoric, convinces Romola and the narrator that his martyrdom is genuine because it is unsought.[45] Romola decides that Savonarola is at last aware of his inability to distinguish his own love of prominence with God's design. Romola perceives that Savonarola's agonizing fall had brought him to the realization that Romola had only recently arrived at herself in the valley: namely, to see himself as part of fallible humanity.

To corroborate Romola's conclusion, the narrator (perhaps intrusively) offers further evidence from Savonarola's prison writings, which Romola could not have yet seen. These meditations on Psalm 51 and 31, which became the most popular of all his writings for several subsequent centuries, contain no note of self-defense or self-exaltation.[46] They are rather penitential: Savonarola confesses his sins of vainglory and pride and beseeches God's gratuitous mercy. Eliot loosely translates from Latin one passage out of his *In te, Domine, speravi* that emphasizes Savonarola's awareness of his fallible participation in the fallen world in terms that evoke his experience as mentor/pastor to Romola and to Florence. The persona of Sadness says to Savonarola, "God placed thee in the midst of the people as if thou hadst been one of the excellent. In this way thou hast taught others, and hast failed to learn thyself" (580). This selection by Eliot encapsulates her assessment of Savonarola throughout the book: by thinking himself "one of the excellent," superior to ordinary people and engaged in extraordinary deeds, Savonarola fell into the folly of self-exaltation, losing the wisdom of humility. He taught others, of whom Romola is exemplary, but failed to learn himself about the limits of the mentor's or pastor's authority.

At the time of Savonarola's execution in May 1498, Romola, who was "seventeen or eighteen" at the novel's beginning in spring 1492, may be imagined to be twenty-three years old (48). She is the same age as Savonarola when he took orders (211) and Tito when he arrived in Florence (113). She has arrived at the age, then, at which professional careers begin, when novitiates become practitioners, when the ethical principles that will determine the character of the professional life to come are decided upon. By means of the events compressed into these concluding chapters, Eliot underscores Romola's readiness to assume the role of mentor by making compelling interpretations of public and private affairs without devolving into dogmatism or coercion. Her feminine order of value, which privileges the common middle ground of humanity as opposed to masculine rigidity of views, positions her to thrive where her powerful male mentors failed.[47] The epilogue, set eleven years later, shows this very practice underway.

As the matriarch of the domestic circle including Brigida, Tessa, Lillo, and Ninna, Romola is seen particularly in her role as Lillo's mentor. In his early childhood Lillo has been shown to be morally wayward: he runs away from home, kicks his nurse to avoid being dressed, and bullies his baby sister. Even now he resists Romola's teaching, being more interested in a passing fly than in his study of Petrarch's "Spiritu gentil." To avoid his homework, Lillo raises the question of his future profession: "Mamma Romola, what am I to be?" In answering, Romola shifts the conversation not to possible careers but to moral choices, affirming that "the highest happiness" is that which "goes along with being a great man, by having wide thoughts, and much feeling for the rest of the world, as well as ourselves" (587).[48] Lillo remains unimpressed until she briefly describes Tito's gradual descent into baseness, an account that causes Lillo to "look up at her with awed wonder" (588). Clearly there is yet much work to be done in the project of Lillo's moral formation, but the hope is raised that Romola's tutelage, bolstered with compelling positive and negative examples, will prove effective. What Lillo is "to be" as a result of his education is not only a trained expert, but a professional with a social conscience.

Finally, Romola and Lillo observe the approach of visitors who are to join them for the ceremony honoring Savonarola's death. Among the small band of "worshippers" at Savonarola's "altar" are the pragmatist Nello and the skeptic Piero, and Lillo remarks on that incongruity. Romola responds, "There are many good people who did not love Fra Girolamo. Perhaps I should never have learned to love him if he had not helped me when I was in great need" (588). This speculation, the last line of the novel, underscores Romola's awareness of the contingency of all interpretive truth claims.[49] Romola acknowledges the influence of personal prejudices in judgments of all sorts. She is preeminently qualified to judge Savonarola's life, works, and death, as well as the nature of goodness in general, precisely because she is aware of her biases and of the possibility of other valid interpretations.

Not only does she have this astute consciousness of contingency in human affairs, but she is careful to transmit this awareness to Lillo and thereby to try to preserve him from dogmatism either as a disciple or pastor, novice or mentor. That Lillo could use this very reasoning to resist her teachings about moral greatness is a real possibility that the novel raises, however subtly. If Savonarola cannot be definitively known to be a great man, does that not leave open to question all the ideals of greatness that Romola has been expounding? More broadly, is not relativistic nihilism the logical conclusion of the rejection of dogmatism? Romola's decision to teach Lillo both ethical principles and the necessary contingency of all pronouncements therefore constitutes a remarkable moral victory. Romola is seen to be confident enough in the truth of principles she teaches that she need not enforce them by dogmatic absolutism. She judges it sufficiently compelling to assert the truth claims she believes and her reasons for believing them. To resort to dogmatism, to stifle Lillo's and others' freedom to reach different interpretations from her own, would be to reproduce the error that led to Savonarola's destruction.

I therefore find myself in disagreement with the many readers who see Romola's domestic life at the novel's end as a disappointing betrayal of her remarkable professional potential.[50] In fact Romola's moral and professional achievement surpasses that of all of her mentors, including Savonarola, for whom Eliot has real though qualified admiration. Given the novel's preoccupation with the imperative and pitfalls of mentoring, Romola's status as valorized mentor at the novel's end is not a self-suppression of the female to her absent "fathers," but rather the most important and most challenging professional service imaginable.

There is another sense, however, in which Eliot's resolution remains incomplete: Romola's choice of the domestic sphere rather than the public for the exercise of her pastorship suggests the impossibility of conscientious *public* service. I have said that Romola's refusal of the public roles offered to her constitutes a moral victory, a laudable resistance to the temptations of power. In another sense, however, it is regrettable that such a choice should be deemed necessary. Perhaps, as Kimberly VanEsveld Adams has maintained, Eliot's commitment to historical veracity disallowed her to depict a publicly active woman.[51] Nevertheless, Romola's self-conscious retreat into the domestic suggests that civic politics are somehow incompatible with the practice of a nondogmatic mentorship. If this is so, if the able pastors must necessarily recuse themselves from public roles to remain true to their developed ethical sense, who will then assume the functions of public leadership?

This dilemma is not unlike that explicated in reference to the essay "Authorship," in which the authors capable of writing so as to cure social ills are arguably the least likely to publish their writing. Not only are the diffident slow to assert their "moral taste" in the marketplace, they are also, like Romola, vulnerable to being silenced or over-whelmed by the less scrupulous. As a sage herself, Eliot evidently found it difficult to strike her own balance between dogmatism and diffident silence. On the one hand, as Bodenheimer's helpful analysis of Eliot's epistolary mentoring relationships shows, Eliot thought of her novel writing and her proposed autobiography as exercises in moral improvement of the younger reader.[52] To effect the moral improvement Eliot strongly desired to bring about in others, one must write and publish with a proper understanding of one's role as "teacher or influencer of the public mind." On the other hand, this impulse to moral mentoring receives a constant check from the self-censoring avoidance of dogmatism. Eliot expressed her own diffidence in a letter to Frederick Harrison in 1870: "I shrink from decided 'deliverances' on momentous subjects, from the dread of coming to swear by my own 'deliverances' and sinking into an insistent echo of myself. That is a horrible destiny—and one cannot help seeing that many of the most powerful men fall into it,"[53] Savonarola assuredly among them.

Clearly, in *Romola*, as in "Authorship," Eliot is self-conscious of the challenges as well as the potentialities of the pastorship offered by professionals to novices and to the public. A note of self-critique can be heard in both texts: in "Authorship" the author castigates other professional authors who are insufficiently conscientious, and in *Romola* Eliot similarly illustrates that mentors cannot be too careful in how they transmit their expertise and values. Though Eliot endorses the professional ideal, using it to dignify the occupation of novel writing, she also holds it, and her own practice of it, under the microscope of moral examination.

It is not incidental that George Lewes referred to Eliot as "Madonna" in letters to members of their so-called spiritual family of her admirers and advice seekers.[54] Indeed, the balance between dogmatism and reticence seems to me to be precisely what Eliot worked out so painstakingly in her portrayal of Romola, the visible Madonna. When Eliot tells the young son of one of her most ardent admirers to "be handsome in all ways—chiefly in that best way of *doing* handsomely," it is hard not to hear this as an echo of Romola's instruction to Lillo.[55] Yet Romola's problem of the eschewing of public roles haunts Eliot too. As Bodenheimer demonstrates, Eliot's very refusals to play the sage tend to turn clumsily into sage-like pronouncements.[56] Eliot's position as a sage to the reading public and a mentor or "spiritual mother" to a few admirers may have given her an oracular status that was too close to Savonarola's for her comfort.

It remains for Eliot's final novel to attempt to delineate a model of professionalism that need not eschew public roles altogether in the interest of keeping oneself morally upright. Such will be the subject of the next chapter.

CHAPTER 5

"ONE FUNCTION IN PARTICULAR": SPECIALIZATION AND THE SERVICE ETHIC IN "JANET'S REPENTANCE" AND *DANIEL DERONDA*

Indeed he builds his goodness up
So high, it topples down to the other side
And makes a sort of badness.

Aurora Leigh, III: 492–494

In an illuminating study, Nancy Henry contextualizes the recent high volume of criticism on *Daniel Deronda* with respect to the postcolonial critique of the novel's supposed complicity with "imperialist ideology."[1] Henry concludes that the classic position of Edward Said, that *Daniel Deronda* (1876) participates in British imperialistic designs on Palestine in a manner criminally negligent of Palestinian Arabs,[2] is "a seriously distorted representation of the text, authorizing irresponsible and anachronistic readings," not least because "imperialist ideology" as such had only begun to emerge late in George Eliot's life.[3] Instead, Henry finds that *The Impressions of Theophrastus Such* "complicates Said's claims about nineteenth-century Orientalism because it represents a critical counter-discourse to the dominant norm, just as *Deronda* incorporates a critically self-conscious attitude toward the myth of empty land."[4] At the same time that imperialism was emerging as an ideology, Eliot's work subjected that proto-ideology to close critical examination.

I begin with this mention of Henry's thesis not only because readings of *Deronda* that spin off of Said's have been very influential recently but also because my contention about the author's engagement with professionalism is similar in shape, if not in content, to Henry's. Far from simply accepting the professional ideal uncritically, *Romola, Daniel Deronda*, and Eliot's other works problematize it, self-consciously examining its internal contradictions and striving toward a conceptual resolution of its dilemmas. The professional ideal for Eliot is no unconscious ideology, no mere sublimation of material interest as Harold Perkin and others would have it, but a matter for rigorous scrutiny from within an idealist worldview.

This chapter focuses on Eliot's treatment of problems that inhere in the service ethic that is a defining characteristic of the professions. Specifically, it explores Eliot's handling of the limits of the service ethic, which, when taken to extremes in a moral language given to absolutist formulations, can eventuate in self-destruction. Eliot identifies this problem as early as "Janet's Repentance," but only resolves it satisfactorily in her last completed novel. This resolution, as we will see, depends upon the modern professional formulation of specialization. Deronda's decision to "specialize" in political and philanthropic work on behalf of European Jews prevents his diffuse and altruistic sympathy from resulting in his own annihilation, as it does for Tryan in "Janet's Repentance."

I

According to Daniel Duman, the service ideal of professionalism was a reconfiguration of the traditional gentlemanly ideal in terms appropriate to the industrial age. By means of the service ideal, professionals retained their privileged social status as superior to trade even after the professions' traditional ties to the aristocracy (once virtually their only clients) eroded. Duman also shows that the professional service ideal proved to be enormously persuasive; by the twentieth century it was a commonplace of public opinion and the orthodoxy of the social sciences.[5] In spite of—or perhaps because of—its influence, the service ethic is probably the aspect of the professional ideal most frequently targeted for demystification. Theorists of professionalism such as Harold Perkin, Magali Sarfatti Larson, Penelope J. Corfield, and Burton J. Bledstein nearly universally assume that the service ethic of professionals and professional groups was effectively a self-interested ploy to gain prestige, to increase demand in the long term, and to justify monopolistic control of the market. In this influential narrative, the smokescreen of public service functioned, and was intended to function, to augment the hegemonic power of professionals. As Jennifer Ruth has recently and valuably shown in *Novel Professions*, this modern "discovery" of interestedness lurking in professional disinterest is misguided: the dialectic of interest and disinterest in professional life was actively queried, not disavowed or disguised, by Victorians themselves.

I am attracted to Eliot's fiction for my study of this matter because of Eliot's astute ability to deconstruct not only professionals' claims to probity—as, for example, Tryan's critics do in "Janet's Repentance"—but also to deconstruct the very deconstruction of those claims—in that she shows those critics to be wrong. In other words, she handily manages to turn the suspicious reading back on itself. She anticipates Bruce Robbins's view of professionalism in *Secular Vocations: Intellectuals, Professionalism, and Culture*, to which I will return.

If we understand professionalism not as a selling out to interested careerism but rather as a ground for negotiating an ongoing characteristic tension between self-interest and public service, we realize that not only the limits of egoism but also the limits of altruism are contested by the professional ideal. The service ethic is a check on irresponsible egoism in one's use of expertise, but it potentially gives rise to the reverse problem of extreme self-neglect. The revered Oxford moralist T. H. Green expressed the ground of this problem when he said, "Interest in the problem of social deliverance . . . forbids a surrender to enjoyments which are not incidental to that work of deliverance."[6] Those who took this sort of rhetoric seriously, and Stefan Collini's *Public Moralists* shows that there were many such, faced the necessity of determining the degree of material reward that was appropriate for them to accept without compromising their position as altruists.

This concern was obliquely raised in my previous chapter, in which I observed that Romola's eventual moral achievement is to realize and promulgate that "we can only have the highest happiness . . . by having wide thoughts, and much feeling *for the rest of the world, as well as ourselves*."[7] Her affirmation reflects the lesson she has learned from her experiences with her mentors, namely, that moral greatness is not the total suppression of the ego but the recognition that egoism and altruism are implicated in each other. The supposed self-annihilation staged in Savonarola's grandiose invocations of martyrdom, in Eliot's observation, actually worked to gratify his ego rather than subdue it. In contrast, Romola's explicit awareness that her desire for a family formed part of her decision to provide for Tessa and her children represents a valorized sort of self-consciousness that saves her from self-deceptive and self-aggrandizing egoism.

Dorothea Barrett has rightly said that "the one central and recurring problem of the Eliot canon" is "seeking a solution to egoism . . . without falling in to masochistic self-sacrifice."[8] While it is typical to describe Eliot's ethical project in terms of her privileging of altruism and remediation of egoism,[9] some critics have realized that her moral ideals are more complicated.[10] Notably, Patricia Menon addresses the extent to which "the virtues of selflessness and submission constitute an abdication of moral responsibility rather than the foundation of all virtue" in *Daniel Deronda*.[11] Of course, selflessness and submission mean different things for Victorian women from what they mean for Victorian men, so Eliot's treatments of the limits of disinterestedness also must be probed for what they say about the relationship of gender to self-effacement. Since self-sacrifice is both a professional and a feminine virtue, the female (or feminized) professional encounters the problem of extreme disinterest in an intensified way.

In her first and last works of fiction, in the characters of Edgar Tryan and Daniel Deronda, Eliot attends specifically to this more perplexing problem of unilateral self-denial.[12] These two characters, both of whom are admirable for their repudiation of egoism and their highly developed capacity for fellow-feeling, nevertheless face a real danger of self-annihilation because of these very characteristics. Like that of Elizabeth Barrett Browning's overzealous philanthropist Romney Leigh, the goodness of Tryan and Deronda "topples down to the other side/And makes a sort of badness."[13] The latter of the two, however, escapes the deleterious effects of excessive disinterest by developing a form of a specialist mentality. The "wide thoughts" of Romola's ethos are qualified by the "one function in particular" that Deronda finally learns to adopt.[14] A modern and specialized construct of professionalism, distanced but not divorced from Tryan's ascetic vocation, therefore supplies the imaginative solution for Eliot's ongoing struggle to balance the personal needs of an individual with his or her duty to serve society.

This balance, expressed in different language, remains part of professional culture today, as Robbins shows in *Secular Vocations*. Robbins critiques Franco Moretti's reading of *Daniel Deronda* in *The Way of the World* as an exemplary failure of the novel of vocation. Moretti finds fault with *Daniel Deronda* because Deronda achieves his vocation by specialization, which Moretti regards as a selling out of his "higher" universalist ideals.[15] Robbins's rebuttal of Moretti's reading of the novel implies that he sees a possibility that Deronda manages to inhabit a Janus-like position in which public service and self-fulfillment are united. Although Robbins successfully argues that specialization is not necessarily a sign of regress, he never explicitly addresses how specialization becomes productive in the novel.[16]

This chapter will examine the role that an idiosyncratic form of professional specialization plays in the resolution of Deronda's internal conflict between interest and disinterest. As I will argue, reading Deronda and his relationship with Gwendolen through the lens of professionalism offers an explanation of one of the more perplexing aspects of Deronda's character: Deronda's overdeveloped sympathy is related to his inability to specialize. The problematic amorphous quality of Deronda's character can only be resolved by a narrative process that disciplines him in the needed development of self-interest that particularizes his sympathy. Moreover, the trope of professionalism works in the novel to synthesize the "Jewish" narrative of Deronda's vocational self-fulfillment and the "English" narrative of Gwendolen's ethical development. The novel's two principal characters mirror each other in their growth toward ethical maturity: Deronda's problem of excessive disinterest involves him in a vocational morass, which he escapes by means of the crisis of specialization Gwendolen forces upon him. For her part, Gwendolen's problem of excessive self-interest requires that she move toward ethical maturity by means of Deronda's therapeutic intervention. Gwendolen's moral education therefore follows the usual pattern from egoism to enlightened self-effacement, but the moral education Deronda undergoes is reversed: from disproportionate self-forgetfulness to an appropriate level of self-interest.

II

In "Janet's Repentance," the third of the novellas that comprise *Scenes of Clerical Life* (1857), Eliot figures professional men as mercenary and selfish, a stultifying and immoral force in provincial Milby. Eliot locates the heroic opposition to professionalism in the Reverend Edgar Tryan, an Evangelical curate vociferously persecuted by Milby's professionals but beloved by its laborers, women, and retirees. The sign of Tryan's difference from the other professionals in town, including other clerical professionals, is his asceticism, which places him beyond the reach of material reward for his service to others. In making Tryan's ascetic vocation a solution to materialistic and self-interested professionalism, however, Eliot engenders another set of problems about the extremity of his self-denial. Tryan's obsessive adherence to a spartan way of life, extending even to unwarranted acts of renunciation, leads before long to his own death of consumption.

Such an extreme response to the evils of professionalism is hardly tenable, but a more balanced or healthy response is rendered moot by Tryan's early death. The Christian paradox prevails in "Janet's Repentance": Tryan can only save his soul by renouncing the world; he can save his life only by losing it. Moral perfection, in the form of altruism unmitigated with egoism, contains its own martyrdom.

I begin the discussion of "Janet's Repentance" by pointing out Eliot's self-conscious awareness of the potential for the discourse of ideality to serve egoistic ends. Eliot shows in "Janet's Repentance" an ability and disposition not only to read the claims of professionalism suspiciously, as so many did,[17] but also to read suspiciously the reflexive suspicious reading of those claims. When Tryan has recruited several friends to brave a potentially violent mob by walking with him to church, the narrator remarks sardonically, "Some of his more timid friends thought this conduct rather defiant than wise, and reflecting that a mob has great talents for impromptu, . . . were beginning to question their consciences very closely as to whether it was not a duty they owed to their families to stay at home on Sunday evening."[18] Collini has noted that under the culture of altruism, "morality was understood very much in a system of obligations in which . . . 'only an obligation could beat an obligation,' and in which, consequently, there was a tendency to extend the category of 'duty' as widely as possible."[19] As Eliot shows, the most pious of Victorians could be led into more or less self-aware efforts to rationalize their egoistic desires and fears as "duties" of one kind or another. Eliot's narrator here performs the effortless hermeneutical move that sees through their sophistry and dismisses their claims to disinterestedness.

It is as easy for Eliot to join in the general chorus of satire against self-serving professionals as it is to expose the false piety that renders selfishness as duty. However, Eliot does not stop with the exposure of cant, but rather goes on to explore idealist alternatives to it. The alternative to the purely market rationality she satirizes in the professions is available in the religious rationality of Tryan's vocation, and the suspicious reading that Milby's professionals reflexively put on his actions is not allowed to stand. However, Tryan's vocation raises still more moral quandaries as he reaches the limits of disinterest. Eliot wants to valorize Tryan's disinterested service, yet his excess of selflessness leads him into self-annihilating asceticism that she cannot countenance but does not clearly censure.[20]

For Eliot asceticism is both the solution to the egoism endemic to the professions and the problem engendered by excessive disinterest. Throughout "Janet's Repentance," Eliot remains keenly alive to the possibility of the cynical interpretation of ascetic gestures. However, she is determined to look deeper into asceticism than the dismissive suspicious reading offered by Tryan's opponents and the shallow adulation proffered by his friends.[21] Eliot knows that egoism and sublimation always exist in a dialectic.[22] Rather than a novel "polarized between didactic extremes of egoism and altruism," as Mary Wilson Carpenter's imagined reader sees *Daniel Deronda*, both *Daniel Deronda* and the much earlier "Janet's Repentance" reflect their author's preoccupation with questions of the interpenetration of egoism and altruism, particularly realized in the construct of professionalism.[23]

Alan Mintz's study *George Eliot and the Novel of Vocation* registers the dialectical tension between self-indulgence and self-denial that, he says, lies at the heart of the notion of vocation. Mintz makes this astute observation about Eliot's work:

> The refurbished idea of vocation allowed her to bypass the congealed conception of character in contemporary fiction, which most often explained personality in terms of such binary categories as egotism/compassion and mind/feeling, and to approach a more dialectical model of the personality. In the experience of vocation, selfish ambitions for personal distinction and selfless aspirations toward general amelioration are parts of a single matrix of desire.[24]

That is, the vocational or professional figure in Eliot's fiction experiences impulses, motivations, and desires in which altruism and egoism are mixed and often indistinguishable. The desire for power or prominence often blends imperceptibly with the desire to serve the larger society, as Eliot's meticulous portrait of Savonarola shows. Mintz's book takes *Middlemarch* and *Daniel Deronda* as its primary examples for understanding this phenomenon. Unfortunately Mintz's preference for the later fiction leads him to dismiss Eliot's earlier work as having only "oblique" reference to the theme of vocation.[25] However, I find that the tensions among altruism, egoism, and vocation are preeminent concerns as early as "Janet's Repentance," as Tryan's contentious engagement with the professional norms of Milby occasions examination of the limits of self-effacement within the novella's critique of professionals' self-gratification.

As David Carroll has shown, Milby's professional figures embody and originate the selfishness and materialism that account for the moral degeneracy of its citizens. In Milby, "[a]ll the professions, those vital organs of the community, . . . have become rigidified and self-perpetuating systems, utilising their own esoteric codes and rituals for the purpose of retaining power and making money."[26] The doctors and lawyers of the town prey upon their clientele, whose function is to pay the fees that maintain the professionals in a comfortable standard of living. The doctors are known to "discover the most unexpected virtues in a patient seized with a promising illness," because "[t]he doctor's estimate, even of a confiding patient, was apt to rise and fall with the entries in the day-book" (180). They avidly protect their material interests under the guise of public service. When a new doctor attempts to set up a practice in town, the two established physicians unite "in the determination to drive away the obnoxious and too probably unqualified intruder" (179). Qualifications are of course not the issue, as the doctors' own superstitious methods make clear, but the question of qualification provides the putative moral grounds for their entirely self-interested resistance.

The lawyers of the town, particularly Tryan's chief antagonist Dempster, are known and even reverenced for their moral laxity. The more upstanding lawyer Mr. Landor "had a very meagre business in comparison" to Dempster (177). The narrator relates that "the clients were proud of their lawyers' unscrupulousness, as the patrons of the fancy are proud of their champion's 'condition.' It was not, to be sure, the thing for ordinary life, but it was the thing to bet on in a lawyer" (177). Even the clergyman Mr. Crewe participates in the decadent professional culture. He has hoarded his salary (by withholding charity and depriving his household) in order to acquire a modest competency, and his notable lack of anything like an above-average moral standard accounts for much of his popularity among his parishioners. In short, all the professionals of Milby admirably perform their negative caricatures by selfishly exploiting their offices for personal benefit. The doctors and the clergy are as unconcerned about the people's actual physical and spiritual needs as the lawyers are disregardful of justice.

Tryan's threat to this social order, particularly to the professionals, is easily apprehended. In resistance to the mercenary professional culture, Tryan determinedly practices the asceticism that puts him out of the reach of material reward, thereby separating professional conduct from remuneration. By living "among heaps of dirty cottages" (188), eating coarse and badly prepared food, going on foot at all hours and in all weathers wherever he is asked to go, and giving the excess of his small income to charity cases, Tryan assures the public that he is not working for his own benefit but for the benefit of others. He is even determined not to benefit sexually from his charisma: though the ardent Evangelical women of the town have all fallen in love with him and vie for his attention, they eventually have to concede that Tryan is too otherworldly for their charms.

By means of these radical steps, so counter to the culture of Milby, Tryan tacitly exposes the professions as self-promoting and defines himself in opposition to them. By his self-denying conduct and altruistic public service, he teaches the people to expect their professionals to serve rather than to exploit. The professionals, led by the lawyer Dempster, can only respond by attempting to bring Tryan down to their level by slanderously accusing him of masking his actual mercenary professionalism behind a pretense of altruism: "[H]e goes about praying with old women, and singing with charity children; but what has he really got his eye on all the while? A domineering ambitious Jesuit, gentlemen; all he wants is to get his foot far enough into the parish to step into Crewe's shoes when the old gentleman dies" (172). Unable to explain Tryan's unaccountable behavior in any other way, they assume his ascetic actions are a subtler (and therefore more insidious) strategy of self-interest: "The Evangelical curate's selfishness was clearly of too bad a kind to exhibit itself after the ordinary manner of a sound, respectable selfishness. 'He wants to get the reputation of a saint,' said one; 'He's eaten up with spiritual pride,' said another; 'He's got his eye on some fine living, and wants to creep up the bishop's sleeve,' said a third" (230). As these passages make clear, the professionals' resistance is motivated by a desire to neutralize the threat that Tryan's antimaterialism poses to their comfortable position as joint exploiters of the town's poorer citizens. The narrator concedes that while his enemies were ready with erroneous interpretations of Tryan's behavior, "his friends found difficult to explain to themselves" why Tryan was "bent on wearing himself out" (258). The result, however, is not in doubt: Tryan wins the staunch loyalty and affection of the nonprofessionals— women, workers, and retirees—who recognize him as an ally.

Janet's repentance is brought about by the personal charisma that accrues to Tryan because of his ascetic habits: his obvious physical suffering bars her from continuing to demonize him as her husband does. For all its charismatic advantages, however, Tryan's way of life is not sustainable. In Tryan's convalescence, Janet's affection leads him to a repentance of his own from his sins of self-destructiveness and emotional isolation—the extreme and unaccountable manifestations of asceticism: "He was conscious that he did not wish for prolonged life solely that he might do God's work. . . . he was conscious of a new yearning for those pure human joys which he had voluntarily and determinedly banished from his life" (298).[27] In other words, Tryan repents of his self-destructive renunciations.

Having brought her hero to a more normal apprehension of his freedom to enjoy moderate pleasures, Eliot has little choice but to let him die. If Tryan married Janet and settled into ordinary bourgeois life, he would then be indistinguishable from the rest of Milby's professionals. For him to give up his asceticism (to renounce his renunciation) would mean to allow himself to benefit materially from his work, which would spell the end of his charismatic power among nonprofessionals. The scenario of a rehabilitated Tryan reconciling material reward with altruistic service is one that Eliot cannot yet imagine or represent.

As Eliot strives for a moral resolution of the dilemma of disinterest, she handily exposes the deficiencies at both ends of the continuum. Through Tryan's spectacularly ascetic vocation, Eliot censures the mercenary materialism of Milby's self-interested professionals. Tryan's utterly selfless alternative is not a tenable one either, as Eliot somewhat confusedly indicates by making his death by consumption a direct result of his excessive self-mortifications. Eliot is unable at this stage to represent a sound middle ground where a moral and compassionate individual can serve humanity without destroying himself. To save his soul—that is, to be morally irreproachable—Tryan must renounce the world even to the point of losing his life. Eliot's solution to Tryan's problem is essentially a Christian one: as several critics have noted, his death implies his translation into the well-deserved glory of a martyr, memorialized in Janet's subsequent life. However congenial this denouement may have been to the story's original readers, it could not be satisfactory to the agnostic Eliot, and we can be sure that when she returns to this issue in her later work the outcome will be different.

III

In *Daniel Deronda*, Eliot recreates the basic outlines of the "Janet's Repentance" plot, albeit on a much grander scale. The morally adrift heroine is appropriated by two mentors: first, her hedonist husband (who later dies) and second, an altruistic, charismatic moral exemplar.[28] Like Tryan, Deronda pushes the limits of disinterestedness in his ardent desire to fulfill his vocation and to resist base mercenary motives. Yet the professional constructs Eliot criticizes for lack of feeling and humanity now provide the only solution to the facile dilettantism of the moneyed classes. The central issue of *Daniel Deronda* is the realization of Deronda's vocational ambitions, and much of the novel is concerned with outlining his credentializing toward that end.

While several critics have explored the preparation for vocation that Deronda undergoes through Mirah and Mordecai,[29] the critical role that Gwendolen plays in preparing Deronda for his vocation has been largely underrated.[30] I maintain that it is through Gwendolen that the specialization comes about that saves Deronda from his vocational paralysis and finally resolves Tryan's dilemma.

Deronda's complex psychological problem involving his identity and subjectivity has perplexed many readers; I argue that this problem can be best understood in light of the vocational indecision it engenders and of the resolution Eliot will eventually proffer through the construct of professionalism. While Deronda's willing self-sacrifice for others is obviously a morally superior alternative to Gwendolen's and Grandcourt's (very different) modes of egoism, his unadulterated goodness lends him a quality of unreality. Deronda's consistent unselfishness is not the result of a successful struggle between his conscience and his desires but rather the simple result of his not having any sense of self out of which to construct self-interest. As I will show, this deficiency of subjectivity is connected to Deronda's uncertain parentage.

Naturally the lack of subjectivity poses a problem for the novelist. Deronda, lacking an ego, does not fit the traditional humanist models of psychology based on individual subjectivity, making him literally unrepresentable: Deronda is characterized by "a certain exquisite goodness, *which can never be written or even spoken.*"[31] As K. M. Newton observes, "[E]xtreme self-consciousness and his habitual suppression of personality make it seem that his feelings and sympathies do not centre on any self at all," and "his sense of self seems to disintegrate."[32] Tony Jackson shows that Deronda's highly developed and intuitive sympathy "amounts to the abandonment of a central, self-secured, what we would now call Cartesian, self. . . . George Eliot has put forward an image of egolessness."[33] Deronda's virtue of altruism arises from the necessity of his lack of ego. Deronda's spectacular goodness is not a well-intended but artistically deficient effort by Eliot to create an ideal hero to oppose to conventional Jewish stereotypes, but rather a complex representation of the problem of extreme altruism.

The critics who have recognized this problem have sometimes misread it due to their inclination to regard Deronda as static rather than dynamic. Leona Toker rightly disputes the critics who view Deronda's sympathies as "chameleon-like."[34] She argues instead that "Daniel consistently, though with consummate tact, resists the temptation of the loss of self in the merger with another."[35] However, the temptation of the loss of self is a real danger to Deronda early in the novel, and the resistance to it that Toker mentions must be developed in Deronda during the novel, as we shall see.

Daniel's boyhood altruism is explicitly connected to both his highly developed sympathy and his rejection of commercial values. At school, young Daniel's "acts of considerateness . . . struck his companions as moral eccentricity" (162). His mentors doubt his professional potential, for "how could a fellow push his way properly when he objected to swop for his own advantage, and . . . would rather be the calf than the butcher?" (162).[36] This vignette introduces the central vocational quandary of the novel, here rendered as a straightforward discrepancy between society's view of professionalism as a self-interested commercial undertaking and Deronda's altruistic impulse to sublimate his own desires for the sake of others. Like Tryan, Daniel refuses to enjoy the benefit of his expertise (in this case, the expertise of "swopping") and chooses to suffer rather than exploit.

The most obvious response to the commercial, capitalistic values given to professionalism by Daniel's teachers is to eschew professionalism entirely and instead pursue culture disinterestedly, as an amateur unconcerned with financial reward. This is in fact Deronda's position at the beginning of the novel. Clearly, though, amateur dilettantism is not a viable option for Eliot's hero, who, according to John Beer, is intended "to show in the midst of Victorian uncertainties what a commitment to a positive course of action might look like."[37] The course of the amateur dilettante had been discredited in *Middlemarch*'s Will Ladislaw, whose dilettantism is a mask for mediocrity and indecisiveness. In *Daniel Deronda*, this critique passes to Hans Meyrick, whose artistic ambitions keep him dependent on the support of his female relatives, themselves near poverty. In short, the uncommitted and unproductive individual is opposed to Eliot's ideal of energetic ameliorative public service: "that life of practically energetic sentiment" (337). Financial independence is for Eliot no excuse for unproductivity or mediocrity, as Herr Klesmer makes clear in his rebuke of the puerile musical education and taste of the upper classes. Deronda must somehow resist the selfish exploitation common to the professional classes, but he must find an alternative in professionalism itself, not in amateur dilettantism.

However, espousing the professional ideal is one thing, and selecting a specific profession to practice is something else entirely. Specialization remains a fraught issue for Deronda for two reasons: his vocational idealism, which leads him to condemn the careerism of the professional life, and his curious lack of self-interest, which arises from his indefinite identity. Both of these factors militate against his positive selection of any profession.

Deronda's vocational idealism leads him to clash with Sir Hugo, the novel's representative voice of the popular capitalistic notion of expertise as commodity, over the choice of a profession. Sir Hugo urges Deronda to go into politics, saying that the unpopularity of Deronda's opinions would make it all the easier for him to attract the attention that would get him elected. Sir Hugo wants Deronda to turn his martyr impulse into cultural capital. Deronda refuses, objecting to the compromises of integrity that are routinely required of politicians. Sir Hugo tells Deronda,

> The business of the country must be done. . . . And it never could be, my boy, if everybody looked at politics as if they were prophecy, and demanded an inspired vocation. . . . There's a bad style of humbug, but there is also a good style—one that oils the wheels and makes progress possible. . . . There's no action possible without a little acting. (354–355)

Sir Hugo defines politics in commercial terms ("the business of the country"), showing his conception that politics, like all the professions, has financial interest as its guiding principle. He emphasizes that the practical (read capitalistic) work of the world requires individual compromises of principle, and a person who cannot adjust his principle to accommodate such exigencies is "simply a three-cornered, impracticable fellow" (355). His offhand dismissal of "inspired vocation," one of Deronda's most treasured ideals, shows the gap between popular conceptions of the capitalistic professions and Deronda's (and Eliot's) quasi-religious notion of vocation.

Deronda, however, is actively looking for "an inspired vocation," and he does not accept that a profession dominated by humbug can be a noble one. Deronda replies, "I can't see any real public expediency that does not keep an ideal before it which makes a limit of deviation from the direct path" (355). To Deronda, practical compromise in the service of the public is oxymoronic, because only ideality can truly serve the public.[38] He goes on, "But if I were to step up for a public man I might mistake my own success for public expediency" (355). Deronda's awareness of the conflict of interest inherent in doing what is good for oneself in the name of public good leads him to eschew the political profession entirely. His overdeveloped capacity for reflection prevents his repeating Savonarola's tragic error of claiming divine sanction for his own partisanship, but it also prevents Deronda's accomplishing anything like Savonarola's prodigious social and political activism. The novel will need to develop an alternative to

Deronda's "radical refusal of all imperfection, and, with it, of all action," but without simply returning to Sir Hugo's fatuousness.[39]

Aside from the idealism that makes every profession seem a locus of disillusionment, Deronda faces a more fundamental obstacle to specializing in a profession: his lack of normal self-interest. Deronda's unselfishness is exacerbated and partly caused by his indefinite identity. He imagines that knowledge of his parents would bring with it an end to his vocational quandary, and indeed the novel will eventually prove him right. He feels his mysterious origin to be a hardship primarily because it cuts him off from the performance of renunciation that familial duty would require:

> The disclosure [of his parentage] might bring its pain, indeed the likelihood seemed to him to be all on that side; but . . . if it saved him from having to make an arbitrary selection where he felt no preponderance of desire? . . . Many of us complain that half our birthright is sharp duty; Deronda was more inclined to complain that he was robbed of this half. (437)

Deronda's very ease is his hardship; he is pained by his lack of pain.[40] Like Tryan, Deronda evinces the ascetic desire to renounce himself in order to perform his "sharp duty" for the good of others; unlike the curate, however, he cannot decide to whom he owes that duty, since he has "no preponderance of desire" (self-interest) or family ties. He desires a vocation of productive social service entailing renunciation on his part, but without a sense of self he is powerless to settle on one. Therefore, Deronda is passive, almost paralyzed, waiting for something external to happen that would determine his course of action. To borrow a phrase from Monica Cohen, Deronda is stymied by the "seemingly paradoxical ideal: the desired selfless career."[41]

Desiring to be of service to humanity, yet unable to select a specialized mode of doing so, Deronda has a brief career as an amateur philanthropist, an uneasy half-measure that allows him to avoid self-aggrandizing commercialism and still be serviceable. He cultivates the habit of acting on his sympathetic impulses to sacrifice himself on someone's—anyone's—behalf. In this he resembles Tryan, who actively sought opportunities to mortify his flesh while helping others as a way of atoning for his past sins. Deronda, for his part, embraces opportunities to sacrifice for others seemingly as a way of atoning for his idleness and unproductivity.

Yet his service to others occurs only in isolated cases when his affections are impulsively engaged on the side of some needy individual, as is the case with Mirah and Hans. He lacks an overall system to his sympathy because he lacks absolute affinity with any particular cause. As a result, his "many-sided sympathy . . . threatened to hinder any persistent course of action" (335). In his early manhood, "[a] too reflective and diffusive sympathy was in danger of paralyzing in him that indignation against wrong and that selectness of fellowship which are the conditions of moral force" (336). As an amateur philanthropist, unfocused and unspecialized (lacking "selectness of fellowship"), Deronda cannot turn his admirable sympathy into productive activity. In this state, Deronda "had not set about one function in particular with zeal and steadfastness"; he is in fact incapable of such specialization (337).[42]

The episode with Hans Meyrick at Cambridge is typical of the positive and negative aspects of Deronda's amateur philanthropy. Instead of studying for his own scholarship exam in mathematics, Deronda helps Hans (whose eyes are temporarily injured) to prepare for his exam in classics. Hans wins his scholarship, but Deronda fails. When Sir Hugo learns the reasons for Deronda's failure, he advises him, "[I]t is good to be unselfish and generous; but don't carry that too far. It will not do to give yourself to be melted down for the benefit of the tallow-trade" (168). Sir Hugo's metaphor suggests the dangers of Deronda's generosity and willingness to sacrifice: not only is he in danger of being diffused (melted) so as to lose his shape entirely and accomplish nothing, but he is also at risk of sacrificing himself for any inauspicious cause that presents itself to him as needy. Although Deronda is not at risk of destroying himself physically by want or exposure, as Tryan does, his lack of specialization puts him in danger of a more abstract form of self-annihilation—the destruction of his "moral force," his potential for active ameliorative service in the world.

A crucial element that is lacking in Deronda's relation with Hans is *suffering:* since Deronda lacks any "preponderance of desire," there is no internal tension between what he wants to do and what he ought to do. He does not suffer because he has no will of his own; the condition of the divided mind is unknown to him. Hans is right when he associates Deronda with a story of Bouddha's offering himself to be eaten by a starving tigress, for Deronda's sympathy for others is so much better realized than his self-interest that he does not have an adequate self-protective instinct. Although the idealistic Mirah calls the story "beautiful," the practical Amy Meyrick points out that "[i]t would be a bad pattern" if all virtuous people let themselves be consumed by hungry tigers (435)—a remark reminiscent both of Sir Hugo's warning and of Tryan's premature and avoidable demise.

Mirah valorizes Deronda's sacrificial impulse, saying that he "thought so much of others [he] hardly ever wanted anything for [him]self," an accurate characterization Deronda finds "exasperating" (434) in light of his rivalry with Hans for Mirah's affection. Deronda insists, "Even if it were true that I thought so much of others, it would not follow that I had no wants for myself" (434). Deronda's desire for Mirah— the first occasion of self-interest in him that opposes the will of another (in this case Hans)—is the crucial first step in the process of developing an ego that will enable Deronda to be professionally productive.[43]

Having found both commercialism and aimless, amateur philanthropy unsatisfactory, Deronda does finally receive a calling that matches the ideals of public service, personal renunciation, and professional specialization. Not only is the cause of Zionism a service to a downtrodden people, but it also will make use of Deronda's hitherto unproductive capital resources and require him to renounce his home and leisured life.[44] Significantly, Deronda's discovery of his parentage terminates his vocational indecision: it is during the conversation with Kalonymous, who tells Deronda about his ancestral past, that Deronda "found out the truth for himself" as regards his "vocation" (673–674). Kalonymous particularly contrasts Deronda to his grandfather Daniel Charisi in terms of resolve: Charisi had an "iron will" and hated indecision more than error (672). In light of what we have seen about Deronda's vocational ambivalence, clearly Kalonymous is right to "see none of that in [him]" (672).[45] Kalonymous's two parting questions therefore go to the heart of the pending decisions that cannot be postponed longer: "What is your vocation?" and "You will call yourself a Jew and profess the faith of your fathers?" (673). Deronda's pointed self-identification with Jewish ethnicity but not with Jewish religion delineates the nature of his secular vocation: political and philanthropic, not religious, service to the Jewish people.

Deronda's self-knowledge leads to the development of subjectivity that will finally enable his absolute commitment to a single cause. However, Deronda's problem of unbounded disinterestedness remains an obstacle to the necessary specialization that would transform his vocation into a profession. The Gwendolen plot therefore functions to teach or compel Deronda to add an element of specialization to his philanthropy and an element of self-protection to his service ethic. Like Tryan, Deronda is in some way converted by the very woman he converts. Unlike Tryan's deathbed conversion, Deronda's education in specialization is the beginning of his productive career, showing that Eliot has come to conceptualize the possibility of a secular vocation.

An adherent to the commercial model of the professions, Gwendolen spends roughly the first half of the book coming to terms with her own amateur status and the second half of the book as a "client" to Deronda's moral therapy.[46] As Deronda exhorts her in the broadening of her sympathy, he is painfully taught the necessity of specialization of sympathy: "Those who trust us educate us. And perhaps in that ideal consecration of Gwendolen's, some education was being prepared for Deronda" (401).

IV

Gwendolen's sudden poverty exposes her amateurism. When first confronted with the need to earn her livelihood, she resolves to turn her talents of music, acting, and beauty into cash. As Jennifer Cognard-Black has demonstrated, Gwendolen thinks of her status in terms of a professional system: her beauty is capital (a scarce resource), and she consciously develops it into a saleable commodity by setting and maintaining a high standard of expert polish in all her social encounters. However, Gwendolen is a "false professional," or one who relies upon the deceptions of "representational systems such as advertising" and who eschews the ideal of public good for a solipsistic benefit.[47] Gwendolen's professionalism is essentially prostitution, "and in the effort to reveal this perniciousness . . ., the novel effectively demonstrates that Gwendolen and the models of false professionalism she represents are finally commercial economies, even as they mime aesthetic ones."[48] Essentially, her error is the same as that of Sir Hugo: she thinks of the artistic vocation as a capitalistic undertaking, as he thought of the political vocation.

Eliot gives to Julius Klesmer the responsibility of teaching Gwendolen (and the reader) to repudiate this commercial model of false professionalism. Cognard-Black's discussion of the "true" professional, who belongs to the "aesthetic economy" rather than the "commercial economy," focuses on Klesmer. She emphasizes that true professionalism, which is indistinguishable from "art," is both learned and innate, simultaneously a cultivated skill or technique and a greatness of soul. She associates the technique with specialization and the greatness of soul with "comprehensive" knowledge.[49] However, Cognard-Black's readiness to excoriate specialization (a disposition we have seen before in Moretti) leads her to misread the novel's commentary about specialization. As she sees it, Eliot's false professionals are specialists, "[n]ecessarily narrow in training, [and] limited to the functionality of delivering a single sphere of under-standing" (107). However, as Klesmer himself makes clear, both tech-nique and greatness of soul are required of the true professional; analogously, both comprehensive *and* specialized knowledge must be present in the professional. Specialization is no more exclusive of com-prehensive knowledge than greatness of soul is exclusive of superior technique. Deronda's own specialization comes late in the novel, after his comprehensive education (Eton, Cambridge, and the Grand Tour) is already in place. Almost as if to forestall any doubt of the compre-hensiveness of his education, the narrator relates that at Cambridge, Deronda

> found the inward bent towards comprehension and thoroughness diverging more and more from the track marked out by the standards of examination: he felt a heightening discontent with the wearing futility and enfeebling strain of a demand for excessive retention and dexterity without any insight into the principles which form the vital connections of knowledge. (164)

Eliot seems anxious to distance her hero from any imputation of illiberality in his education; she preemptively exonerates him from the charge of the negative form of professional specialization Cognard-Black seems to have in view. However, the "reflective hesitation" that predisposed Deronda to prefer the study of "universal history" to specialized training is the same impulse to which the narrator attrib-utes his moral paralysis (164). It follows that a gentleman's compre-hensive education is the necessary but not sufficient basis for the mental training of the "true professional." In Eliot's conception, then, a "true professional" can no more do without specialization than the "true artist" can make greatness of soul suffice without tech-nical superiority in his medium.

Gwendolen's status as a false professional or amateur confronts her with her impotence: she cannot turn her imagined proficiencies into the capital that would give her control of her circumstances. When Gwendolen's marriage to Grandcourt results in disempowering her still further, the focus of her inner world shifts from trying to control her circumstances to trying to regulate her own conflicted impulses. Deronda's advice to the beseeching young wife is a prescription of ascetic sympathy, the subordination of selfish gratifications to outside affections: "Try to care about something in this vast world besides the gratification of small selfish desires" (416). Ironically, Deronda's extreme adherence to this same code is a source of his moral paralysis; in advising Gwendolen, Deronda is beginning to stumble upon the limitations of his own ethical philosophy.

Gwendolen's continued psychological agony makes clear that she needs more from Deronda than this exhortation to disinterestedness. In a series of encounters, Deronda's "many-sided sympathy" is contrasted to Gwendolen's exclusively solipsistic thought; whereas Gwendolen cannot rise above her endless inward obsessions, Deronda's exalted moral standing renders him oddly obtuse to the torments of the soul that Gwendolen suffers. Gwendolen vaguely confesses why the injunction to disinterestedness is inadequate for her: she is aware of and afraid of her conflicted self. She tells Deronda, "When my blood is fired I can do daring things—take any leap; but that makes me frightened at myself. . . . But if feelings rose—there are some feelings—hatred and anger—how can I be good when they keep rising?" (422). It is this sensation of inner conflict that Deronda, who has never experienced any such thing, cannot understand.[50]

When Grandcourt forces Gwendolen to go yachting with him, thereby cutting her off from all outside concerns in which she was trying to cultivate an interest and subjecting her to the unrelieved torture of his company, the internal struggle between her competing desires for revenge and for a clean conscience becomes more acute. As she drifts in the oceanic wilderness, she struggles against inner demons as fierce as any that ever afflicted the Desert Fathers. The narrator describes how "a white-lipped, fierce-eyed temptation had made its demon-visit" (628), and later Gwendolen confesses to Deronda that on the yacht "I felt a hatred in me that was always working like an evil spirit" (642).[51]

Later, when she confesses all to Deronda after Grandcourt's drowning, she describes the condition of her own divided mind during this voyage: "*I was like two creatures* . . . I wanted to kill—it was as strong as thirst—and then directly—I felt beforehand I had done something dreadful, unalterable—that would make me like an evil spirit" (643–644, my emphasis). Then Gwendolen narrates that dubious climax in the sailboat, when the two overmastering but competing desires seesaw indecisively: "I did kill him in my thoughts. . . . But yet all the while I felt that I was getting more wicked. And . . . what you once said—about dreading to increase my wrong-doing and my remorse . . . it came back to me then—but yet with a despair—a feeling that it was no use—evil wishes were too strong" (647–648). Clearly her better and worse self are at war in her psyche; her desire for a clean conscience, untroubled by remorse, is opposed to her desire for revenge and freedom.

Faced with Gwendolen's spectacularly divided self, Deronda is asked to interpret her motives, actions, and guilt. He does so, in keeping with his now established habit of amateur philanthropy, but this time there is a critical difference. Throughout the conversation, Deronda is described as experiencing emotional and even physical pain. His face wears the "expression of a suffering which he was solemnly resolved to undergo" (643), and he speaks "mournfully" (642) and "groan[s]" (645). The same pattern continues in their further conversations in London. When Deronda promises to visit Gwendolen, "he look[s] miserable" (717), and at Offendene he is again described as sorrowful and mournful. This note of suffering in Deronda is a new development in their relationship; in their previous interactions Deronda was as unruffled as he was in helping Hans. This time, Deronda himself is experiencing the agony of dividedness: "She was bent on confession, and he dreaded hearing her confession. Against his better will, he shrank from the task that was laid on him: he wished, and yet rebuked the wish as cowardly, that she could bury her secrets in her own bosom" (642). Crucially, Deronda's "dread" is a function of the conflict between his "better will" and (presumably) his worse will, or his spontaneous selfish wish and the immediate self-censoring of that wish as cowardly. When Gwendolen, divining his discomfort, says regretfully, "I make you very unhappy," Deronda hesitates awkwardly before "gather[ing] resolution enough to say clearly, 'There is no question of being happy or unhappy. What I most desire at this moment is what will most help you' " (647). This new hesitation, so unlike his previous stoical disregard for personal happiness, betrays that Deronda has rather suddenly found that renouncing desire costs him an effort. In short, Deronda is for the first time torn between conflicting and mutually exclusive desires that clamor in him simultaneously.

In a brilliant phrase, Eliot characterizes this sensation as the "anguish of passionate pity [that] makes us ready to choose that we will know pleasure no more, and live only for the stricken and the afflicted" (646). Passionate pity impels him to altruistic service and absolute self-effacement, yet the anguish accompanying such an impulse simultaneously makes him aware of his egoistic resistance to giving up his own happiness. In mediating and interpreting Gwendolen's internal dividedness, Deronda experiences similar dividedness himself for the first time.

The source of that new resistance can be found by looking at what has changed for him since the last time Gwendolen or anyone else appealed to him for help. Given that the meetings with his mother have just concluded the same day as Grandcourt's drowning, Deronda's resistance seems to stem from his unwillingness to be distracted just as he discovers his vocation and has a reason to hope that Mirah will marry him. Now that he has an identity he can develop self-interest, and this new experience of suffering is Deronda's first occasion of having personal desires and needs that conflict with others' desires and needs.[52] Thus when Gwendolen's beseeching forces him to promise that he will take care of her, Deronda "felt as if he were putting his name to a blank paper that might be filled up terribly" (643). He dreads making indefinite promises to Gwendolen that are likely to get in the way of his fulfilling his Jewish vocation and marrying Mirah. Deronda's suffering in this role—the sign that a struggle takes place—indicates that he has begun to mediate his sympathy with self-interest, thus correcting his problem of diffuse, ineffectual fellow-feeling. Deronda is no longer willing to be melted down for the tallow trade or eaten by a tiger, because now he has found "one function in particular" worthy of his life's devotion. His knowledge of internal dividedness has come through Gwendolen, who not only confesses to him her own experience of temptation, but who also occasions a similar conflict in him.

In a sense it can be said that Deronda's moral dilemma begins as Gwendolen's ends. In his case, excessive self-sacrifice, not self-indulgence, is the demon that must be overcome. As Deronda returns to England, shares his discovery of his identity and vocation with Mirah and Mordecai, and is engaged to Mirah, he becomes aware of the necessity of putting an end to his relationship with Gwendolen. After two abortive attempts, Deronda travels to Offendene to make the disclosure, knowing and dreading that he must inflict pain on Gwendolen in order to fulfill his "inspired vocation" of service to his people and to the world though the establishment of a Jewish state.

This scene, in the penultimate chapter, has the force of a climax as it brings closure to the relationship that has dominated the book from the first page. The novel's two narratives converge as each principal character performs a reversal of habit, a reversal that has been brought about by their contact with each other. Deronda's first hint at his forthcoming disclosure leads Gwendolen to admit that she has always regarded him with a reproachable selfishness. When told of Deronda's Zionist ambition, Gwendolen experiences "for the first time being dislodged from her supremacy in her own world" as she realizes that Deronda has active and complex affairs in which she plays no part (748). However, after a hysterical moment, Gwendolen masters herself enough to resolve "I will try—try to live" and to think of

Deronda's good instead of her own (750). For his part, Deronda finds that he must act against his ingrained habit of taking the worst in himself to spare others pain. He experiences conflicting desires as his disinterest and self-interest clash: his laudable desire to accommodate and serve Gwendolen proves almost as strong as his mutually exclusive desire to marry Mirah and serve the Jewish people. The narrator says that "Deronda's anguish was intolerable" in this interview (749). Yet that suffering—that experience of internal dividedness—is what gives Deronda the professional character of a specialist by forcing him to make choices establishing the boundaries of his altruism and sympathy. In a symmetrical climax, therefore, Gwendolen arrives at a state of enlarged sympathy brought about by Deronda's moral example and exhortation, and Deronda behaves toward her with a pained selfishness that is actually ethically sound.

The struggle between one's private desires and one's responsibility to others is a familiar one to readers of Eliot, but Deronda's dilemma is unusual. His struggle is not between selfish desire and selfless ideals, and his internal conflict is not between flesh and spirit. Both helping Gwendolen and working for Zionism are selfless and, in a sense, spiritual undertakings. However, trying to do everything for others, or to be everything that others want him to be for them, must result in Deronda's paralysis and in the neglect of his unique vocation. Therefore at the crucial point Deronda's own personal interest, reinforced by his sense of calling, must determine the specialization that will enable him to be productive. His love for Mirah and his mystical affinity for Judaism, both of which harmoniously coincide with his solemn sense of ancestral duty, together constitute a rational and limited ego, which engenders enough self-interest to protect Deronda from the self-annihilation of Tryan.

Between her first and her last works of fiction, Eliot underwent something of a conversion of her own. Her early work renders professionalism as normatively mercenary and locates the opposition to professional culture in the radical asceticism of Tryan's religious vocation. In Milby, authentic public service can only exist in a religious dimension, as a strict repudiation of all material gratification for one's labor. Tryan's eventual conversion from his self-destructive course comes too late to save his life, allowing Eliot to escape the dilemma in an essentially Christian way. Tryan's only two choices—to gain the world or to save his soul—are mutually exclusive, and his heroism lies in his decision to save his soul by renouncing the world. In *Daniel Deronda*, Eliot imagines a secular resolution that allows professional activity to accompany genuine vocation. Deronda "saves his soul" through his conscientious performance of fellow-feeling, yet he also "gains the world" emblematically by his marriage and his fore-shadowed life as a Zionist politician and activist. The collapse of this binary is brought about by means of Deronda's education in special-ization, and it prefigures Robbins's theory of professionalism as a "secular vocation." Eliot never idealizes the professions—in Deronda's world they are still tainted with unscrupulous self-interest— but a possibility exists for a happy union of altruism and professional specialization in the educated and sympathetic individual. In *Daniel Deronda*, Eliot's altruistic hero learns to mediate the extreme of dis-interest through specialization, thereby attaining a secular vocation that leaves behind the asceticism of Tryan while still resisting an exclusively market-driven mentality of expert labor such as Milby's professionals and Sir Hugo espouse.

The course of Eliot's career is toward a union of altruism and professionalism such as Robbins proposes and defends. Leaving behind mutually exclusive categories of altruism and egoism, Eliot theorizes a capacious model of professionalism that involves self-protection as well as service, and individual fulfillment as well as sacri-ficial giving. Collini is right to use Eliot as a premier example of the culture of altruism; she believed in the power of the feelings, rightly educated through fiction, to motivate people to act unselfishly in per-forming their moral duties to one another. Yet my analysis also shows that Eliot's handling of the egoism/altruism dialectic exemplifies the "more complex intelligibility" that Collini suggests as an alternative to purely suspicious readings of the claims to a service ethos so frequently heard in nineteenth-century discussions of professionalization.[53] Eliot understood that egoism and altruism inflect each other and mingle inseparably in the ethical choices of professional life. Understanding this about Eliot gives insight into her unusually capacious theory of pro-fessionalism and helps explain her contribution to the conceptualization of the professional ideal as a secular vocation.

V

The gender dimension of Eliot's handling of the tensions of interest and disinterest in professionalism merits separate consideration. The contrasts in the symmetrical development of Deronda and Gwendolen—his movement toward specialization from his unproduc-tively diffuse sympathy and her movement out of solipsism into the awareness of her responsibility to the world outside herself—can be seen more plainly in the Alcharisi. In the character of Deronda's mother, the limitations on the moral good of self-effacement are clearly visible. Deronda's advice to Gwendolen of submission and regard for the wishes of others, however appropriate for that "spoiled child," would have been out of place for Leonora, whose early formation was oversaturated with demands for self-effacement. The Alcharisi embodies the worst case scenario of excessive disinterest: the woman who is socialized to privilege others' expectations of her to the point of utterly denying the self. However dangerous Deronda's excessive and diffuse sympathy is to his vocation, the perils of such sympathy would be far greater for a woman, socially and economically disempowered, who is without recourse against the "iron will" of a patriarch. Leonora's refusal of this role, and her consequent choice of a malleable husband who will not interfere with her artistic vocation after her father's death, does not incur Eliot's censure.[54]

In contrast, Gwendolen has been socialized to be almost pathologically selfish by her indulgent mother. For her, any external interest would be an improvement, and it is in this vein that Deronda adjures her to look beyond herself. The Alcharisi is psychologically injured by forced self-repression in childhood; Gwendolen is inversely psychologically injured by indulgence in childhood. Both of them are thus maimed as human beings, unable to make good relational choices balancing egoism and altruism, self and service. The Alcharisi's rejection of her child is really, as Anna K. Nardo shows, a rejection of her father and of the role her father forced on her. Simultaneously, her decision to forcibly "convert" Daniel into an English gentleman is a repetition of her father's imposition of a given identity on her.[55] As an adult the Alcharisi continues to be dominated by her father. In this light, the "enforced condition of moral autonomy," which Menon (critically) notes that Deronda gives Gwendolen by means of his abandonment, is perhaps the best thing that can be done for Gwendolen, who would otherwise willingly persist in subjection to Deronda.[56] The prolongation of Gwendolen's childlike condition with respect to Deronda is no more desirable than the prolongation of the Alcharisi's adolescent rebellion.

But whether Gwendolen, any more than the Alcharisi, may possibly attain to the moral maturity of Eliot's valorized professional—able to mediate egoism and altruism—is by no means certain. These two feminine foils, like the masculine foils of Grandcourt and Deronda, suggest that gender both does and does not play a definitive role in the cultivation of professional ideals. On the one hand it is clear that Eliot sees the dialectic of egoism and altruism to be a problem for both genders. Personality and early formation—nature and nurture—intersect with circumstances in ways influenced but not determined by gender to produce the adult moral specimen. However, it is only the feminized man—Tryan or Deronda—who finds himself in the position of excessive disinterest, and it is only under the professional discipline of specialization that the second of these feminized heroes achieves a healthy resolution of the dilemma of disinterest. Could a woman, without access to professional specialization, overcome the problem of disinterest as Deronda does? This question may be addressed obliquely in the character of Mirah, whose submission to Mordecai and Deronda at least approaches excessive self-effacement. Yet Mirah's artistic expertise gives her the opportunity that Gwendolen does not have to support herself, if meagerly, and thereby secure her independence from the oppressive patriarch. Moreover, Mirah's insistence, even in the face of Mordecai's correction, on interpreting the story of the Jewish maiden in a manner empowering to the woman (684), implies that Mirah's ego will not be easily swept aside even by an iron-willed patriarch.

Although Eliot is more analytical than Gaskell on the subject, the two novelists share a preoccupation with the question of how gender dynamics intersect with professional ideals. Both Gaskell and Eliot assume the normalcy of expert women's participation in mental or artistic labor. More notably, both of them problematize the professional ethic of service by experimenting with its extremes. Mr. Gray, an obvious derivation from Mr. Tryan, is neglectful of his own health and eventually dies of consumption. In both *My Lady Ludlow* and "Janet's Repentance," the price of pioneering an ethic of compassionate professional service is the life of the heroic practitioner. One can hardly imagine a professional character in Trollope or Disraeli, or for that matter in Dickens, who would pursue the demands of public service to the point of self-destruction, as Tryan does, or of whom it could be said, however jestingly, that he would allow himself to be eaten by a starving tigress.

This pattern suggests that the scrutiny of the limits of the service ethic in the professional ideal is a contribution of women professionals, who frequently bring to their professional roles expectations of self-effacement formed out of domestic ideology. Even today the notion persists that women professionals should be self-effacing and unconcerned with financial reward to a degree not expected of men.[57] Women's unique difficulties with professional ideology are also illustrated by the life of Octavia Hill. We will see in the next chapter that Hill's refusal of pay for philanthropic work, like Miss Galindo's refusal of pay from Lady Ludlow, is symptomatic of her difficulty reconciling the materialist and idealist rationalities both present in professional activity.

CHAPTER 6

"A Kind of Manager Not Hitherto Existing": Octavia Hill and the Professional Philanthropist

The great field for the contest between the head and the heart is the domain of political economy.

Edwin P. Whipple (1877)

Until recently, most academic and quasi-academic work on Octavia Hill (1838–1912) has evinced a distinct partisan bias. Her immense stature in her own time, her controversial positions, and the intense affection and loyalty borne toward her by a large number of friends and fellow-workers, determined that for at least two subsequent generations of housing and social workers, Hill was the iconic figure either to revere or revile. Consequently, even through most of the twentieth century, Hill was invoked with scorn by the left and with adulation by the right in debates over social housing and social work. Hill's persistent opposition to state-subsidized housing, her insistence on the primacy of the moral reform of the poor, her preference for small cottages over large blocks of tenements, and her rhetoric of paternalist squirarchy have earned her the opprobrium of socialists of every description.[1] These same characteristics made her a darling of conservatives calling for a retrenchment of the welfare state and a revitalization of private-sector responses to the housing need.[2]

Some recent work on Victorian philanthropy, building on the groundbreaking *Women and Philanthropy in Nineteenth-Century England* by F. K. Prochaska and "A Home from Home" by Anne Summers, has illuminated the complex relationships between philanthropy and the domains of domesticity, religion, governmentality, and professionalism. Dorice Williams Elliott, in *Angel out of the House: Philanthropy and Gender in Nineteenth-Century England*, shows that representations of women's philanthropic activity contributed to substantial changes in public opinion about women's nature and roles. Elliott analyzes opposition between professional men defensive of their special expertise and privilege and the muted but perceptible encroachments of female philanthropists such as Anna Jameson. Elizabeth Langland's *Nobody's Angels: Middle-Class Women and Domestic Ideology in Victorian Culture* emphasizes women's "domestic management" as a quasi-professional role, citing the Victorian construction of an affinity between a woman's own domestic management and district visiting. Langland sees visiting the poor as an expression of proto-managerial skill and status on the part of middle-class women. Lauren M. E. Goodlad, in "Character and Pastorship," demonstrates that the Charity Organisation Society's (COS) opposition to state-sponsored poor relief did not extend to a repudiation of bureaucracy per se. On the contrary, the COS, of which Hill was a prominent member, explicitly sought to systematize the provision of relief and embraced bureaucratic methods to make the distribution of relief more efficient. Their principal difference from the Fabians, as they understood it, was in their insistence on personal and affective interventions, the personal element being the critical factor in whether relief was morally deleterious or beneficent to the character of the recipients.[3]

Accordingly, we now have a richer and more accurate context in which to situate Hill. The acknowledgment that her work, in spite of some of its reactionary tendencies, did much to advance the professionalization of social work and employment for women gives us opportunity to consider the emergent professional valences of apparently traditional feminine roles. I find that Hill's commentary on her work and ideals yields a revealing portrait of the possibilities and ambivalences of the professional ideal. Although Hill rejected the label "professional" for her activities and those of her colleagues (a choice that in itself says much about her negotiation of professionalism), her actions and ideals evinced on every level a close relationship to the professional ideal of trained labor, meritocracy, and disinterested public service. It should not surprise us to find that the problems of the professional ideal, such as the problems we have been examining in the fiction, were Hill's problems as well.

Some affinities and some distinct incompatibilities will be apparent between Hill and the other figures of this study. Like Benjamin Disraeli, Hill believed that the solution to social ills would be found in individuated, nonstatist interpersonal relations across class lines. However, the granddaughter of Southwood Smith was very deliberate about how specific bureaucratic systems could increase the efficiency and effectiveness of the benevolent impulses of her middle- and upper-class volunteers. Like Anthony Trollope, Hill was committed to the autonomy of practitioners, but she struggled with the simultaneous need to standardize and systematize the action of the practitioners as a whole. Like George Eliot, Hill experienced the imperative of pastorship of the public along with the anxiety arising from diffidence. And like two of Eliot's feminized heroes, Hill felt so strongly and urgently the imperative of public service that she went to extremes of compulsive, sacrificial work. Like both Elizabeth Gaskell and Eliot, Hill worked to earn needed financial support for her household in spite of the common discourses that defined a middle-class woman as "leisured." However Hill's resolutions (or failures thereof) differ from those of these others, the point is that the tensions she experienced in daily life apparently impelled her to similar sorts of ideological work.

In short, the case of Hill presents the ideological contradictions of the professional ideal as they were embodied in a particular historical life. An examination of her life in these terms allows us to advance the contentions of Langland, Elliott, and Goodlad about Victorian philanthropic discourses by delineating with greater specificity the relationship of professional to philanthropic idealism. To talk about the professionalization of philanthropy is undoubtedly to describe the material mechanisms of training, credentializing, supervision, and pay that characterized the changes in philanthropic practice during the late Victorian period.[4] But just as important are the interactions and negotiations of the competing rationalities that comprised and legitimated the relevant material processes. In other words, to describe the professionalization of philanthropy is surely to indicate as well that the professional ideal became central to the rationality and the practice of philanthropists. As such we may expect that the internal contradictions and tensions of the professional ideal were experienced and negotiated by those who inhabited the hybrid space of the professional philanthropist. As we have seen in the novels, the felt tension between and within rationalities is evident in the mid-Victorian period, prior to the widespread organizational and structural changes that occurred in late-century philanthropy in response to the growing dominance of professional paradigms. That is, before philanthropy was recognizably professionalized in the material sense, the professional ideal informed the thinking of individuals such as Hill who laid the groundwork for the professionalization of philanthropy. Thus we find in Hill's essays and letters, mostly written in the 1860s and 1870s, a marked, and sometimes conscious, negotiation of the dilemmas of governmentality, mentoring, autonomy, public service, and gender.[5] Hill's handling of these problems will be examined in the sections that follow.

Elliott, following the basically materialist approach of Magali Sarfatti Larson and other theorists of professionalism, assumes that the fundamental difference between professionals and amateurs is that the former are paid, the latter not.[6] In Hill's case, however, it is manifest that the material sign of pay is not the only meaningful signifier of professional status. Rather, evidence of different levels of acceptance of the professional ideal alerts us to gradations of status between professional and amateur rather than a strict either-or binary. Therefore Hill, in accepting the professional logic of systematic training in special expertise but rejecting pay for her labor, inhabits a liminal position that is professional in terms of ideality but nonprofessional in terms of materiality.

These idealist investments are not surprising in one whose opinions were formed in close contact with F. D. Maurice and John Ruskin. Hill's family moved in Christian Socialist circles from her early adolescence; both she and her mother were employed by the Ladies' Guild beginning when Hill was fourteen. At around the same time, through her employment as secretary at the Working Men's College, Hill became acquainted with Ruskin, who later employed her as a copyist. Ruskin himself determinedly associated professional status not with occupation but with idealist markers. In "The Roots of Honor," Ruskin insists that the essence of professional status derives from the willingness of the practitioner to suffer personal loss in the performance of his professional duty; Ruskin extends this expectation, which he declares is normative in the learned professions, to the occupation of the merchant. Similarly, in "The Mystery of Life and Its Arts," the category of "artist" is said to cover all those engaged, whether as laborers or managers, in the works of feeding, clothing, and housing the population. By these uses of the terms "professional" and "artist," Ruskin not only privileges work that serves the public, but he also uses this idealism to collapse differences between traditional professionals, industrialists, and laborers. As we will see, Hill's approach to the problems of professionalism shows a clear debt to these idealist thinkers.

GOVERNMENTALITY

We saw in Disraeli a confusion of idealist and materialist rationalities in that the idealist social interventions he imagined as effective for reform could not be reconciled with the political machinery that formed his professional element. In Hill we find an unapologetic insistence on having it both ways: for her, materialist organizational structures are needed to enable and enhance the idealist work carried out by trained and serviceable individuals. Her deepest loyalties, however, are to the idealist rationality that overlaps, but is not coterminous with, the professional ideal.

When, in his review of *Hard Times*, Edwin P. Whipple described "political economy" as "the great field for the contest between the head and the heart," he was deriding the "sentimental" objections, such as those offered by Dickens, Carlyle, and Ruskin, to the "demonstrated laws of this science" of political economy, which he compared to the law of gravity. He acknowledged that the "gushing sentiments" were apt to be offended by the operation of the laws of political economy, but insisted that the only rational response to such laws is to learn to use them for the greater good, not to declare them untrue because they trouble the sentiments. Whipple's rigid politico-economic dogma therefore sees itself as functioning only in the arena of (implicitly masculine) science, which is contrasted to the (implicitly feminine) emotional domain of philanthropy. Philanthropists, for their part, are those "accustomed . . . to subordinate scientific truth to amiable impulses."[7]

It was precisely this mutual exclusion of science and benevolence, or head and heart, which Hill rejected. On the question of "whether investigation, organisation, deliberate and experienced decision . . . are, or are not, compatible with gentle and kindly relief; whether charity can be fully of the heart, if it is also of the head"[8] her answer, in this speech and elsewhere, was always and unequivocally yes: "for you cannot give up either." Given that Hill's ideological commitments do not allow her to exclude either domain, her only possible course is to synthesize them. To Hill, systematization and bureaucratization were just as indispensable as benevolent impulses in the work of philanthropy. In this way, Hill echoes Alfred Marshall's formulation of "cool heads but warm hearts, willing to give at least some of their best powers to grappling with the social suffering around them."[9]

Hill's critics, citing her frequent insistence that alms had a detrimental pauperizing effect on their recipients, have sometimes tended to take her as a textbook political economist. Her close association with the Charity Organisation Society, a group committed to many politico-economic principles on the subject of the regulation of charity, has strengthened this impression. It is not difficult to assemble evidence of Hill's politico-economic leanings. Complaints about "foolish gifts" and "irregular alms" pepper her addresses and articles.[10] Hill accepted the Smilesian dictum that "the highest . . . philanthropy consist[s] not so much in altering laws and modifying institutions as in helping and stimulating men to elevate and improve themselves by their own free and independent individual action."[11] She endorsed the necessity of a deterrent system of indoor relief as a means to rehabilitate the undeserving poor. Additionally, there is her conviction, not unlike Whipple's, that market forces are potent and inexorable. Hence one of the greatest services the middle class can offer the poor is to teach them to abide by the laws of financial obligation: "There is, firstly, the simple fulfillment of a landlady's bounden duties, and uniform demand of the fulfillment of those of the tenants. We have felt ourselves bound by laws which must be obeyed."[12] The poor tenant and the middle-class manager alike are bound by economic and moral laws (the boundary between these domains is indistinct), the defiance of which only harms both.

Finally, we note Hill's penchant for Benthamite institutional structures, such as complex centralizing systems for the investigation of appeals and the distribution of relief. Hill endorsed and even developed elaborate bureaucracies for the organization of relief work in a clear evocation of the style of her revered grandfather, Southwood Smith, a close colleague of Edwin Chadwick who served energetically on Chadwick's doomed national board of health. The driving notion of the COS was to centralize and standardize the distribution of relief funds; private charitable agencies and public Poor Law guardians were supposed to consult the "experts" of the COS district committee to evaluate the legitimacy of each appeal for relief. The detailed system Hill created for the functioning of a local COS district committee, with its secretary (herself) in charge of funneling information between a large network of volunteer district visitors/caseworkers and the committee charged with investigating and responding to requests for aid, was virtually impossibly elaborate. It only worked as intended for a short time; it was not reproducible outside her Marylebone district. All the same, it shows that her instinct for Benthamite managerial strategies was well-established.

However, these materialist values must be seen through the lens of her more fundamental idealist commitment. Materialist actions were always to be judged by idealist standards and arranged for idealist ends. Hence she could say, "I do not feel that in urging any of you to consider the right settlement of a question of temporal relief, I am asking you to devote yourselves to a task which is otherwise than holy."[13] She embraced the "laws" of political economy not for their own sake, but for their moral pedagogical potency. Her continual question about alms is not their effect on the national economy but rather "what is the effect on [the working man's] *character* of these irregular doles?"[14] Similarly, her managerial systems always had as their end the enablement of pastorship. A typical statement is found in "The Work of Volunteers in the Organisation of Charity":

> [A] great and growing conviction is abroad that our charitable efforts need concentrating, systematising, and uniting. There are many signs that this conviction is bearing practical fruit. . . . But now a new danger seems to be arising; a danger lest, rushing from one extreme to the other, we should leave to committees, with their systems of rules, the whole work of charity, and deprive this great organising movement of all aid from what I may call the personal element.[15]

It is clear from Hill's work that "concentrating" and "systematising" are only virtues to the extent that they increase the efficacy of the personal work of individual pastors. As ends in themselves they have little or no value. Hence she wrote in 1875, "[V]olunteers must rally round the Charity Organisation Society, and prevent it from becoming a dry, and because dry, an ineffectual machinery for enquiring about people."[16] Hill's approval of the COS was effusive, but it was also conditional:

> I think the operations of the Charity Organisation Society have been wholly beneficial so far, but that it will have to secure more extended personal influence between rich and poor if it is to be permanently successful. . . . The society can never be a vital, loving, living force; it can never wake up enthusiasm, nor gently lead wanderers, nor stir by unexpected mercy, nor strengthen by repeated words of guidance.[17]

The COS's permanent success is contingent upon its "secur[ing] more extended personal influence between rich and poor" because only individuals, not committees, can be effective pastors. To the extent that the COS facilitates and enables morally instructive intercourse among individuals of different classes, it is good, but Hill is emphatic that in itself it cannot perform any of the pastoral functions upon which real social reform depends.

There are other ways in which Hill's idealism put her in opposition to Benthamite materialism. The private-enterprise solution to the slum housing crisis, so-called five-per-cent philanthropy, can hardly be comprehended under a doctrine of pure self-interest.[18] The anthropology of *homo economicus* was equally alien to her, given that she averred that the material condition of the poor would improve only with their moral betterment. In addition, the doctrine of felicitous calculation did not sit well with her more humble epistemology: "I think we should not weigh results. Our measures of them are often very false . . . even as good people measure."[19] Hill is critical of quantitative measures; she dwells on the inadequacy of "our reformers who trust to inspection for all education, our would-be philanthropists or newspaper correspondents who visit once a court or block, and think they have *seen* it, even our painstaking statisticians who catalogue what can be catalogued." Rather, decisions about solving the housing problem must be left to people who have intimate, long-term interaction with the poor.

It is this commitment to idealist rationality that makes intelligible Hill's rejection of state involvement in spite of her affinity for centralization and bureaucracy. Because the state is by definition devoid of the idealist infusion provided by volunteers, it is incapable of delivering on the "personal element" that vitalizes all managerial systems, that makes machinery a means rather than an end.[20] All of her other objections to subsidies—that they are inefficient and expensive, that they tax the "steady" poor to subsidize the shiftless, that electoral politics will compromise the ability of the publicly employed landlords to enforce rent payment or collect arrears—circle back to this point about their effect on the character of the working class.[21] Hill's objections to large housing blocks as opposed to cottages are in the same vein: the "massing together of herds of untrained people" without any contact with superior classes can only lead to the further degeneration of future generations.[22] The state cannot provide the individuated pastorship that is needed, and therefore its usurpation of the pastoral efforts of private landlords is ultimately destructive.

The union between head and heart—or materiality and ideality, or science and sympathy—was not easy to achieve, yet it was Hill's constant, reiterated goal. For example, in "Trained Workers for the Poor," first published in 1893 in *The Nineteenth Century*, she wrote, "The problem . . . is how to unite the fresh, spontaneous, individual sympathy with the quiet, grave, sustained, and instructed spirit of the trained worker; it is, in fact, how to gain the wisdom, and increase, not lose, the love."[23] Again, in "The Work of Volunteers in the Organisation of Charity," she wrote,

> The problem to be solved, then, is how to collect our volunteers into a harmonious whole—the action of each being free, yet systematized; . . . how, in fact, to secure all the personal intercourse and friendliness, all the real sympathy, all the graciousness of individual effort, without losing the advantage of having relief voted . . . according to definite principles.[24]

Hill's 1876 essay "District Visiting" lays out the problem specifically in terms of personnel. She dwells on the inadequacy for effective philanthropic work of both local clergy, whom she casts as having some training but no time to look into particular cases, and district visitors, who have time and sympathy but lack the necessary knowledge of "wise principles." The problem she elucidates, then, is that "[t]hese two classes, gentle doers and wise thinkers, stand far apart, yet, if they could be brought into close communication, both would gain much; the people for whom they are both labouring would gain much more."[25] Hill's solution to this dilemma is notable: she posits the COS secretary as the link between the visitors and the guardians or others responsible for giving relief. Thus her solution is to create a professional role with the function of keeping the head and the heart in close, productive communication. This secretary is a professional in both idealistic and materialistic terms: she receives specialized training, even if most of her training is on-the-job; she is actuated by a desire to serve the poor; and "next to ready sympathy, method will be of all things most necessary to her."[26] Although Hill characteristically refused to be paid as COS secretary, she regarded pay for secretaries as normative.[27] Hill even imagines an informal association of secretaries: "We might meet, too, we secretaries, now and again, to talk over important questions and strengthen one another."[28] Head and heart are equally indispensable in the project of effective moral and material amelioration of the poor, and their admittedly problematic reconciliation is to be achieved by the mediation of an ideal professional.

AUTONOMY

The autonomy of the worker was very important to Hill, at least in theory, but she imperfectly negotiated the tensions it generated for her both as a subordinate and later as a manager. Her commitment to the autonomy of others can be seen well before her housing work started. While away on holiday in 1859 she wrote to her mother, "Tell Minnie [Hill's sister Emily] that, although I gave her directions about what she was to do, she is not to think that I mean to bind her to do these things if circumstances alter. She is to use her own judgment."[29] Both the desirability and the difficulty of implementing autonomy in an organization are manifest early in Hill's working life, and autonomy continued to present problems to her throughout her life.

Her work for Ruskin exhibited some contradiction with regard to autonomy. Although she praised him for the autonomy he granted her, she clearly did not feel free in her work for him. Soon after she entered Ruskin's employ as a copyist trainee, she rapturously reported, "Of all the ways of working I think Ruskin's alone right. He does not say or think of paying you for work done. He says, 'You have power, you must be given the means to use it; don't trouble yourself any more about how you are to live. I have been given means, take some of them, live, set your mind at ease.' "[30] Despite this reported freehold paradigm on Ruskin's part, around the same time Hill, anticipating a day's work at Ruskin's home, wrote, "I often wish I were quite free and could work at what I liked. . . . It requires a strong heart to go on working, without anyone caring whether you are longing to do anything else."[31] Clearly here she is disenchanted with work Ruskin assigned without regard for her preferences. Hill was quite slavish about following his directions. On one occasion she wrote to ask for directions, saying that "[s]he would not venture to set up her ideas of what is best or most necessary above her master's."[32]

Hill struggled with autonomy with her other mentor as well. Her 1859 letter to Maurice, whose advice she asked about the appropriateness of pleasure-excursions on Sunday, reflects a conflicted sense of the duty to form her own opinions and the duty to be guided by those wiser than herself:

> Sometimes I act for a little while on my own convictions, and am very happy, till the recollection of how wrong I was, and how sure I was about other things which you have taught me, principally by advising my giving up a course of action and adopting another, or some partial failure, make me think I am arrogant and self-willed; and yet when I take the other course I am oppressed with a sense of neglected duties, fear of my own honesty, and confusion about how far I ought to trust people, and you specially. This produces inconsistency in action; tho', on the whole, I adopt the latter course for the questions relating principally to the College; I feel my position there implies very complete obedience.[33]

Her troubled soul-searching is not simply about the Sunday excursions but about her standing with Maurice and the duty of freedom of conscience. Her dilemma resembles that of Arabin, who was led to decide that freedom of conscience is an inescapable obligation and that implicit obedience implies a defaulting on a sacred duty. In a convoluted sentence that manifests her confusion, she poses the question of whether obedience against one's conscience is a duty or a dereliction of duty, the very question Romola had to answer for herself. Unable to settle this fraught issue, Hill deflects her concern to her function as secretary at the Working Men's College. She finds surer ground in her role as employee to Maurice. However, even this role generated private, barely acknowledged resistance from Hill. Two years earlier, when she began teaching women's classes at the College, she wrote to Mary Harris, "I am getting on very well at the College now I have the teaching. It is very difficult for me to work with zeal and not be supreme."[34] Clearly there is a latent resentment, like that expressed when she wished she "could be quite free" from Ruskin's direction, at jobs that do not allow her to exercise autonomy. This resentment is set against her impulse to chastise her desire for self-determination.

Perhaps such personal experiences informed Hill's ideological commitment to granting autonomy to those she mentored, whether those were poor tenants or fellow-workers. Hill underscored in many ways her belief that "[i]t is a principle of modern life in free countries that we are not directed from above, as a tool, but have to think out what is best to do, each in his own office."[35] Theoretically the responsibility and prerogative of thinking for oneself applied equally to poor and rich. In addressing potential donors and volunteers, Hill emphasized the importance of not transgressing the tenants' autonomy. She wrote, "It is essential to remember that each man has his own view of his life, and must be free to fulfill it. . . . Our work is rather to bring him to the point of considering, and to the spirit of judging rightly, than to consider or judge for him."[36] However, one wonders whether the rent-paying tenant who was threatened with eviction if he did not send his children to school felt that he was being allowed to judge for himself.[37] Another protestation of noninterference is more revealing: Hill imagines herself telling her tenants, "I would not set my own conviction, however strong, against your judgment of right; but when you are doing what I know your own conscience condemns, I . . . will enforce right."[38] In fact Hill's policy of noncoercion in the lives of her tenants depended upon an implicit contract of deferential cooperation on the part of those tenants,[39] much like Ruskin's assurances of freedom to Hill depended on her actual compliance with his tacit as well as spoken expectations.

This same tension pertained as well to Hill's relations with her fellow-workers. Hill considered that blind adherence to principles, however wise and well-considered those principles were, was as pernicious as a lack of correct principles to begin with. This philosophy particularly applies to housing management, in which the landlady's intimacy with the people and circumstances under her pastorship is precisely the grounds to which Hill trusts for her to make appropriate decisions. She told a group of housing workers, "[T]he decision whom to keep and whom to send away must depend on hopes, beliefs, and perceptions one could not prove true to a committee."[40] Rather, personal judgment must be utilized in the application of general principles: "I can say, for example, 'It is our plan to keep some repairs as employment for men out of work'; but it needs the true instinct to apply this plan beneficially: the time to give the work, its kind, its amount, above all the mode of offering it, have to be felt out fresh on each fresh occasion, and the circumstances and characters vary so that each case is new."[41]

Though she was ideologically committed to the independent functioning of trained practitioners, in her later role as supervisor of a large and complex organization Hill encountered the opposing need of standardizing the "product" by exerting control over the actions of the workers. As her organization grew, so did the number of workers for whose actions she was accountable. Hill's work shifted from that of a manager of houses to that of the manager of managers of houses, and this shift brought her face to face with the limitations of her sanguine belief that perfect systematization and perfect autonomy could be had simultaneously. Obviously the management of all but a handful of these properties had to be delegated, but Hill generally met with each manager every week to inspect account books and discuss problems. As Hill's biographer Gillian Darley relates,

> There was a constant tension in Octavia's work between her wish to let the projects become autonomous and also to keep the necessary control upon the venture as a whole. . . . Octavia's delight in the detail and the personal approach was hard to reconcile with her desire to establish an approach that would be widely applicable.[42]

One can almost hear the sigh of resignation when she conceded in 1875, "I am sure it is best for them that I should stand aside and let the local or appointed workers make some good thing of the work without my meddling."[43] Her decision not to move to the new Women's University Settlement reflects the same desire: "Is it not right that [this new work] should develop in accordance with the aspirations of a younger generation? Will not this very limitation of not living there keep my rather over-powering presence just far enough away to foster native growth?"[44] Yet these acts of conscious self-restraint testify to the persistence of the impulse to dominate the work of others.

In theory, Hill resolved the tension between autonomy and systematization by recourse to training. Any well-trained worker would judge rightly how to apply principles to particular circumstances. When longtime friend Emma Cons took over the management of Barrett's Court, the first set of houses Hill could not oversee personally, she operated with complete autonomy. However, in some respects Cons, like Hill toward Maurice, chose obedience to Hill's program over her own preferences. Hill wrote that Cons would regard Cons's own perfectly kept accounts as "quite thrown away labour. . . . She would do a thing of the kind any day to spoil me, but she would think me quite mad to care, all the time."[45] Such behavior is apparently what Hill expected of all her "trained workers," but this expectation may have caused dissatisfaction for some colleagues.[46]

All this shows that in spite of her genuine commitment to autonomy, it was difficult for Hill to suspend her pastoral role and allow others—whether tenants or colleagues—to take their own course. Hill's difficulties demonstrate that for Victorians conscientious about duty, autonomy could cut both ways. Moral agency, the keystone of the Victorian ethos of character, was paradoxically opposed to the ideologies of deference that called for the voluntary, dutiful subordination of one's own judgments to those of one's superiors. Taken to its logical conclusion, this deference would nullify the goal of "independence" of the working class avowed by middle-class pastors across the whole political spectrum.

MENTORING

Hill believed throughout her life that the only real and meaningful reform of individuals or societies was that which was effected by intensive personal intervention. It is easy to dismiss her frequent talk of "friendship" with her poor tenants as so much condescending mystification, as Dickens shows in Sir Joseph Bowley, his satirical portrait of paternalistic philanthropy in *The Chimes*. Nevertheless, Hill sought and cultivated personal relationships with her tenants in the sincere belief that such relationships alone enable real improvement in the material no less than the moral condition of the poor. She wrote, "Human intercourse in God's own mercy seems appointed to be the influence strongest of all for moulding character."[47] In addition to her projects to rehabilitate the poor by means of pastoral intervention, her many public campaigns—for housing improvements, preservation of open spaces, and urban beautification, to name a few—constituted an unapologetic effort to shame or cajole her own class into the responsible use of its resources. Furthermore, she believed that the training of new workers could only occur effectively in the context of an extended apprenticeship under an experienced worker. In her mentorship of the poor, of her own class, and of fellow-workers, she exhibited some of the tension between confidence and diffidence that characterized Eliot's reaction to her own status as mentor.

The mentorship of Maurice and Ruskin was transformative for Hill, and throughout her life she understood their investment in her in terms of a sacred trust. "But if one has Maurice and Ruskin in one's youth," she wrote to her friend Mary Harris in 1869, "one ought surely to share the light they gave."[48] Hill passionately wanted to "share the light" by improving the appalling living conditions of the very poor; but as we have seen, she just as firmly believed that real improvement was predicated on moral reform effected by personal contact. To her credit, moral reform for Hill never meant Pardiggle-esque sermonizing or tract distribution. In fact, Hill's primary method of mentoring was not district visiting at all, as has been widely but erroneously assumed. While Hill did write and speak about district visiting, her principal and most characteristic effort was rental management. Tenement management resembled visiting in some salient ways; but the distinction was a crucial one for Hill, who wrote that "the control of the house itself, judiciously used, gives power for good much greater than that possessed by the ordinary district visitor."[49] This innovation, the use of rent collection as a platform for mid-Victorian-style social work, is Hill's chief conceptual and practical contribution to the world of Victorian philanthropy. In a time when most slum rent collectors were untrained and decidedly "unpastoral" working-class men and women, Hill conceived of "a kind of manager not hitherto existing."[50] This new manager was a hybrid figure—professionally trained but serving as a volunteer—whose hard-nosed business practices were joined with pastoral intentions and energies.

Instead of merely wringing her hands at the overcrowding, dilapidation, and poor sanitation observed in the homes she visited, the landlady had the power to remedy these problems. The "clear contractual relationship" between rent collector and tenant significantly mitigated the intrusiveness of traditional visiting.[51] More importantly, whereas the Pardiggle approach involved condescending patronage that, in Hill's view, militated against the "friendly" intercourse between classes upon which moral reform depends, the more "natural" and business-like relations between tenant and manager were more amenable to friendship. As George K. Behlmer has observed, "It is reasonable to assume that the receipt of visiting charity was often a negotiated process in which the poor . . . were willing to perform rituals of deference as the price for material aid."[52] Seth Koven documents this phenomenon, quoting working-class Londoners who self-consciously played upon the sentiments of visitors and others who were passed over for aid because of their refusal to do so.[53] Hill's landlady, by contrast, could sidestep these problematic rituals.

Hill's intentionally cultivated relationships with each family created opportunities for her to advise them about work, education, and health issues as they arose. She wrote that her tenants were "not merely counted, but known, man, woman, and child."[54] In short, the position of the landlady became the starting point for direct, interpersonal pastorship of individual tenants. Even Beatrice Potter (later Webb), in many ways critical of the Octavia Hill method, considered that rent collecting was an unexceptional avenue of social service, not to mention of training in social work:

> Unlike philanthropic visiting under the parochial clergy, or detective visiting under a COS committee, one was not watching instances of failure in the way of adaptation to this world or the next. . . . From the outset the tenants regarded us, not as visitors of superior social status, still less as investigators, but as part of the normal machinery of their lives.[55]

However, the scale of such work is severely limited, notwithstanding Hill's phenomenal energy. She conceded that the tenants of Barrett's Court, her third group of houses, "are not individual men and women to me" as were the tenants in her first two courts.[56] With a view to expanding the scale of her work, Hill undertook another sort of pastorship: the education of the holders of capital and property in their responsibility to manage their holdings conscientiously. Hill urged other landlords or potential landlords either to become effective pastors or to employ landladies of her ilk to serve as pastors over the dwellers in their tenements. Hill's early essays, including

"Cottage Property in London" (1866), "Four Years' Management of a London Court" (1869), and "Landlords and Tenants in London" (1871) make this appeal explicitly. She writes in the last of these,

> Firstly, I would call upon those who may possess cottage property in large towns, to consider the immense power they thus hold in their hands. . . . When they have to delegate it to others, let them take care to whom they commit it. . . . And I would ask those who do *not* hold such property to consider whether they might not, by possessing themselves of some, confer lasting benefits on their poorer neighbors?[57]

Such pleas to the social conscience of the moneyed classes were part of a larger program of pastorship of the public that also included urging them to refrain from harmful almsgiving. Many of Hill's public addresses, later published, urge that the well-intentioned rich utilize their philanthropic resources with "wisdom": "Give, by all means, abundantly, liberally, regularly, individually, with all enthusiasm, by all manner of means, but oh, give wisely too."[58] Wisdom in Hill's parlance is best read not as stinginess but as deliberate attention to the aims, actual effect, and adequacy of the gift.

Hill believed in such wisdom strongly enough to make what Eliot might disapprovingly call "decided 'deliverances' " on the subject. On the whole Hill shrank less than Eliot from the explicit mentorship of the reading public. Indeed, Hill was unnerved by Eliot's subtler efforts at the moral reformation of her readers. After reading "The Spanish Gypsy," she wrote to a friend, "To me the power of looking all round questions, and seeing how all view them, is not specially delightful, unless at the end there comes some deliberate or distinctive sense of reverence or sympathy with the most right."[59] Hill, on the other hand, though she professed to leave the freedom of final decision with her audience, remained determined to direct them toward a specific action or outcome: "I have, therefore, usually said, 'Look for yourself, but look with the sound of my voice ringing in your ears.' "[60] Clearly she hopes that the sound of her voice ringing in others' ears will lead them to see through her eyes as well.

Notwithstanding such determined asseverations, Hill also had a contradictory instinct toward diffidence. Darley observes that Hill's "absolute sureness of her own convictions and dominant personality [were] oddly at variance with her shyness and uncertainty."[61] Evidence of the latter is not wanting in her letters. Hill was always anxious about having a sibylline status, an aura of unquestionability. As early as her management of the child toy makers, she wrote of needing to "bring . . . to reason" the children's excessive regard for her: "an exaggerated admiration, an immovable belief that all I do is perfect, a dislike of anyone who even tells me to do anything which they see I do not wish to do."[62] Compellingly, Hill wrote to Mary Harris in 1874, as her reputation and influence were growing, "I do so often tremble lest I should spoil all by growing despotic or narrow-minded, or over-bearing, or selfish; such power as I have is a quite terrible responsibility; and so few people tell me where I am wrong."[63] This diffident side of her personality is less salient than her dogmatic side, but it shows that a real tension existed between her sense of a powerful imperative to instruct the public and an opposing sense of the danger of doing so. Maurice wrote to encourage her not to dismay at the "perils of success" but to retain humility and gratitude as a defense against those unspecified perils.[64] Late in life, when Hill was as sibylline in her circle as Eliot had been in hers, Hill seemed to regret the distance her status imposed between herself and younger colleagues.[65]

The moral instruction of the public took much more targeted and detailed form in the training provided to Hill's apprentices. Given Hill's convictions about personal relationships as the only effective context for "moulding character," it is not surprising that she depended totally on individual, time-intensive mentoring for the reproduction of trained workers. The remark in her 1881 annual report to donors, volunteers, and other friends is typical: "During my absence every one has been buying courts, and so few, comparatively, have been training workers. I have now taken one to train myself, and one of my best friends . . . is ready to train another, and I would at all times be glad to tell workers where they could serve a sort of apprenticeship."[66] Hill created what Darley calls "an effective cell system" by which a core of workers, personally trained by and accountable to Hill, undertook to train others.[67] Hill's description of this process in her 1872 article, "The Work of Volunteers in the Organisation of Charity," shows that every trainee was seen as a future practitioner and eventual trainer.[68]

In his brief treatment of Hill, Geoffrey Searle generalizes that "what political economists meant by a proper training was learning to exercise an iron control over one's emotions" so as not to give money away indiscriminately.[69] For Hill, however, training was considerably more complex, involving business and legal instruction with both a theoretical and practical orientation. She presupposed that candidates would bring with them the moral qualities needed for the work, qualities she believed were developed in domestic relationships,[70] but she insisted that new workers be provided with specialized instruction in the details of rental management as well as the ideological orientation needed for effective pastorship of the poor. She advised potential volunteers: "[W]e must recognize that there must be special training, and it is only the extreme boldness of the wholly ignorant which induces them to rush in, confident in their goodwill, with a temerity which it makes the more experienced tremble to see."[71]

Hill wrote in "Trained Workers for the Poor," "In the management of houses the duties are so responsible, and the knowledge needed so special, that I have always been obliged . . . to put those who offer help through a long and careful course of preparation."[72] Further, "if any of you think of extending this work you must set yourselves under a good leader and get a steady training in all branches of the business *as if you were learning a profession.*"[73] The "as if" in that remark indicates the pioneering nature of Hill's advocacy for trained social work as well as her ambivalence toward professionalism in general. Moreover, the normative mode of training is to "set [one]self under a good leader." The special skills, the ideological enculturation, and especially the delicate balance of toughness and benevolence Hill valued could only be transmitted personally, interactively, and over extended time.

However, as the scale of her work grew and she felt the urgency of training more workers at a quicker rate, a formal program took shape in the Women's University Settlement. This course included a reading list and attendance at lectures as well as extensive field experience under established workers.[74] Ideological principles—the value of self-sufficiency and the evil of state involvement—were of course included. Hill's insistence on a one- or two-year unpaid training regimen for new workers essentially limited her pool of trainees to the upper middle class and above. To mitigate this effect, she appealed to donors to fund scholarships that would "set a standard of necessary preparation which may go far to save our poor . . ., as well as having started willing and good women on a useful professional career."[75] In 1900, Hill hoped that the training program of her organization would generate more workers than her own organization could absorb, so that these could be employed by private owners. In fact they were soon to be employed by the state.[76]

SERVICE ETHIC AND WOMEN PROFESSIONALS

Like that of Tryan and Deronda, Hill's goodness became a sort of badness in that her acute sensibility of the demands of the service ethic led her to push herself not only to overwork but even, in her words, to moral deterioration. When expressing concern about the possibility that her constant labor "among the crowd of small cares and worries . . . may make me small and mean," she determines, "I suppose one would unhesitatingly choose self-deterioration for the sake of raising others. I suppose such experience throws light on the words, 'He who will lose his life shall save it.' "[77] The repeated "supposes" in these sentences indicate the tentative nature of the radical ideal she asserts. In fact she struggled throughout her life, particularly in her youth, with the question of how much work and rest were appropriate in her vocation, and to what extent the self could and should be sacrificed for the sake of others. As we have seen in previous chapters, this professional ethic of service and self-sacrifice is particularly fraught for women. Because of the close relationship between the service ethic and its limitations and the connection between feminine and professional ideals, I will discuss Hill's response to both together in this section.

Hill thoroughly subscribed to the Victorian "culture of altruism."[78] The Christian vocational ideal of service to others was for her an imperative duty. She did not think of this service ethic as a professional phenomenon; rather, she viewed professionalization in the material sense, the acceptance of payment for service, as antithetical to the true nature of service itself. However, her ethos of service exemplifies an extreme form of the vocational ethic that was supposed to set professional labor off from commercial labor. As such, her views on the material aspects of professionalization exhibit the tensions of a particular historical phenomenon in the disaggregation of vocational and professional work: a moment in which the categories of training and expertise became differentiated from untrained voluntary labor undertaken as a social duty on the one hand and from expert paid labor on the other. The figures of the residual Lady Bountiful, the dominant volunteer district visitor, and the emergent state-funded social scientist not only brushed shoulders in London's slums, but also blurred into each other in the lived experience of philanthropists and poor Londoners alike. For Hill, it went without saying that "the kind of manager not hitherto existing" was a middle-class woman. In a representative comment in a letter to fellow-workers, she wrote of the work of her agency, "Ladies must do it, for it is detailed work; ladies must do it, for it is household work; it needs, moreover, persistent patience, gentleness, hope."[79] Hill used this domestic ideology to secure a place for herself and her trainees in the housing management market. However, as we will see, she did not see this effort as a project to gain remunerative employment for women, except perhaps incidentally; instead, she expected her colleagues to work for the poor out of the disinterested desire to do good to others.

Hill's potent service ethic actuated her phenomenal energy. Her need to support herself and others of her family, exacerbated by her refusal to accept payment for her work among the poor, together impelled her to compulsive work, austere living, and an antipathy for rest. Unlike most of her volunteers, Hill did not have other financial support, so she supported herself by remunerative employment that she maintained alongside her philanthropic work. Until 1874, when an anonymous group of friends collected enough money to provide her with an annuity, she earned her living from various taxing and time-consuming employments, including copying for Ruskin and teaching drawing at various venues. Besides her housing management and training, her extensive correspondence with donors and workers, and her involvement with various charitable committees, she acted as housekeeper for her own home, including her sisters' school. In addition to bearing the lion's share of the family's financial support for many years, she voluntarily undertook to pay off her father's considerable debts from his last bankruptcy. Having assumed financial responsibility for the family, she denied herself pleasures and comforts in order to secure them for her mother and sisters.

Although Hill wrote about philanthropic volunteers, "if they are to preserve their vigour they must not be overworked,"[80] she blithely ignored this principle as regards herself. In her case overwork caused a series of illnesses and breakdowns that periodically devastated her and forced her to take long restful vacations. In comparing her attitudes about work and rest, duty and leisure with those of Maurice and Ruskin, both of whom tried to influence her to moderate her work habits, we observe that for Hill as for Eliot gender is a significant factor in shaping her compulsion to serviceable work.

Ruskin remonstrated with Hill about her overdeveloped sense of duty to others and even to work. Early in her employment he told her that the quality of her art would suffer if she did not close herself off from the petty demands of others on her time. He wrote, "But you oughtn't to have much of that advising and lamenting. It is quite adverse to all good work. I know that well. Whensoever I want to do anything decently well, I must shut doors or go to the hills. Convents were glorious things after all, weren't they?" Hill was not convinced that withdrawal is a morally responsible option. In reply she rejected the hills as a possibility for her: "[A]s God has placed me in London, He means to teach me that He has a work for me to do here, and not among the hills, which He has not shown to me."[81] As for "advising," her response—that "the wrong is in me, and not in it, if it interferes with my work"—was inevitable for her. She could not conceive of shutting out "duty" in the form of people's petty importunate needs, even for the sake of work or art.

Later it appears that Ruskin learned to turn Hill's ideals against her own extremes. For example, he told her that preserving her health was a duty she owed him as her employer. In a letter to a friend, Hill quotes Ruskin as telling her, "Mind there is one thing you can do to grieve me, and that is to hurt your health." Ruskin seems to use her work ethic—her determination to give him good value for the salary he pays her—to persuade her to "rest as much as ever you want," including while on his payroll.[82] When she consulted him about volunteering to nurse cholera victims, he adjured her "not to come back [to London] to crush yourself with cholera-nursing. It would be wholly absurd and therefore wholly wrong. . . . I fear for the strong helpful instinct—*please don't*." The moral language used here may indicate that Ruskin has learned how to appeal to Hill's scruples to mitigate the potentially destructive effects of her "strong helpful instinct." He further declared to her that she must not risk her health because "we have no business either of us to risk cutting off all our plans [about the houses]."[83]

Maurice, for his part, understood and shared Hill's attitudes about the imperative of duty, and from an earlier date used this understanding to influence Hill's behavior. When lectured by a friend "on the way I am ruining my health, but especially about Sunday work," Hill responded "that to leave off working was a privilege, to continue a duty—that I dared not claim any time as my own; that I had sometimes felt as if I had earned a time to rest or enjoy leisure; and then had been convinced that all time was God's and to be used for Him." Unable to persuade Hill otherwise, Miss Sterling referred the matter to Maurice, whose advice to Hill took the form of correcting her theology:

> He thought rest was as much a part of God's order as work was; that we have no right to put ourselves out of that order, as if we were above it. He told me that the division of things into duties and privileges was an arbitrary one; . . . every privilege involves a duty; our highest privilege is to perform our duty; rest is as much a duty as work; it is very self-willed to try to do without it; it is really hopeless to try to exist, if one is for ever giving out, and never receiving.[84]

Although Hill was unpersuaded, she did follow his advice to curtail some of her activities. Perhaps the best expression of her conflicted disposition toward leisure is found in a pithy, undated fragment: "We are bound to use all power of enjoyment as much as we can, provided no duty is left undone."[85] Duty always comes first, and after that there is another *bounden* duty to enjoy oneself, whether one likes it or not.

Rather than finding a way out from the destructiveness of excessive disinterest through specialization, as Eliot has Deronda do, Hill imagined the rescue of volunteers through diversification. She maintained that "work among the poor is, in short, better done by those who do less of it, or rather, who gain strength and brightness in other ways." On the contrary, she anticipated that full-time workers among the poor would weaken or burn out: "those who, leaving domestic life, are ready to sacrifice all in the cause of the poor" deserve "reverence," but, she implies, are ultimately less effective because they cannot be as "strong, happy, and sympathetic" as those with varied outside interests and relationships.[86] To "sacrifice all" for others is ultimately self-defeating, she seems to acknowledge. Her difficulty applying this principle to herself has already been noted.

This look at Hill's difficulty finding the appropriate limits of service to others, and the responses to it by her mentors, suggests a fundamental convergence between Eliot and Hill on the subject of the gender difference of the service ethic. Whereas a measure of withdrawal from others' needs, or a periodic respite from "duty," was normative to both Maurice and Ruskin (though justified differently by each), any such resolution was hard-won for Hill. Even Maurice, every bit as serious a moralist as Hill, held that service to others must be moderated by restorative leisure. Like Tryan, Hill rejects this reasoning, but unlike him, she changes her behavior in obedience to Maurice's advice. For his part, Ruskin's commonsense assumption that one has to shut out others to do "anything decently well" is rejected by Hill; and indeed, according to Nancy Boyd, it was Hill's inability to "put herself first" that led Ruskin to give up on her as a professional artist.[87] In short, the issue of the necessary or appropriate limits to the service ethic is once again a much more fraught problem for a woman than for men, even men who shared her convictions very nearly.

Perhaps the most spectacular manifestation of Hill's highly wrought service ethic is her persistent refusal to accept payment for any of her philanthropic work, whether for organizations, committees, or housing ventures. I have observed that Hill's innovation to philanthropy was her use of capitalistic means and norms to bring about the intercourse between classes that engenders material and moral reform. Yet in spite of having propagated this method of philanthropy, Hill found herself unable to participate fully in its implied logic. Though she maintained that the development of self-respect on the part of the poor depended on their knowing that they fully paid their own unsubsidized way, she refused to accept the payments thus dutifully rendered for her labor as tenement manager. From her first experiments managing for Ruskin she set aside a sum to pay the rent collector in order to prove that the house could generate enough revenue to operate on a commercial footing; however, she declined to pocket this money on the houses she managed. Although she believed that the best way to help the poor was by utilizing capitalistic tools to produce moral reform, she could not receive the inevitable capitalistic benefit from that activity. She seems to have tolerated the materialistic logic of her own pursuits only as long as she could retain her status outside of it. Much like Eliot's Tryan, Hill felt that the moral aims of her work required her to set herself beyond the reach of material reward for her serviceable labor. Like Gaskell's Miss Galindo, Hill believed that to accept money for her work would constitute an abandonment of the properly primary motive (whether gratitude or compassion) for the work.

Hill's insistence on doing her philanthropic work on a volunteer basis involved her in some peculiar mystifications. When she first assumed responsibility for the houses Ruskin purchased for her, Hill offered to resign as his copyist since she would have very limited time to continue painting. He assured her, " '[The salary] is yours now, as long as you want it, for you are doing some of the work which I ought to do.' "[88] In other words, the salary from Ruskin had become a subsidy, a payment for "nominal work" that allowed her to pretend to volunteer her time to the houses.[89] Essentially, she accepted a salary directly from Ruskin for managing his houses while refusing to accept the salary generated out of the houses themselves. The long-standing relationship between them, and the fact that Hill apparently intended to keep up some painting after assuming responsibility for the houses, undoubtedly made this mystification easier to swallow. However, the arrangement lasted only a year, and it is possible that her discomfort with this disguised subsidy contributed to her decision to resign the salary in 1865.

Looking at the reasons for Hill's refusal of pay for philanthropic work leads us to see her unexamined tension between materialist and idealist rationalities. Hill felt that the refusal of an income from her management labor was necessary to preserve her status as a disinterested friend of the tenants, a status on which her whole theory of moral reform was based. To receive money for her work would reduce her relations with her tenants to the "cash-nexus" so derided by Carlyle and Ruskin, and so deplored by Hill when she observed it in other landlords.[90] It was necessary to Hill's ideology of paternalism that she not profit by her work, even though it was necessary to her ideology of self-help that her work generate profit. Hill accepted the material rationality as far as the functioning of the houses, but not as far as the earned reward for her own expertise. She was unable to permit the economic rationality, by which trained individuals are compensated at a rate reflecting the cost of that training and the cultural capital that their expertise enables them to command, to coexist with her Christian ethic of service. The fact that her "service" had an avowedly capitalistic basis may have made that reconciliation even harder to achieve.

The collision of rationalities seen in her refusal to accept money for slum management is also seen in her ambivalence toward professionalism as applied to philanthropy. In spite of her pioneering advocacy for professionally trained female workers, Hill was ambivalent about the professional standing of her activities and those of her fellow-workers. She believed that trained women, whether paid or not, could be a positive presence in the "useful professional career" of rental management.[91] For those who had no other means of support, she did not object to their working on a salaried basis. Emma Cons, who, like Hill, had to earn her own livelihood, lived on the properties she managed and earned her living as a manager. Indeed, Hill saw housing work as an opportunity for women who needed financial support to contribute to the public good and maintain themselves at the same time. She wanted her workers to "feel that when they draw their salary and take it back to help their own home, they have earned it by work which was really wanted."[92] Here is a clear expression of the conceptualization of professionalism as a Janus-faced model uniting the provision of one's livelihood with a vocational ideal of service.

However, at other moments she expressed a distrust of paid work for the poor, or at least a belief that such work, being less altruistic, is morally inferior to volunteer work. The chief protection against self-interestedness in social work, as she saw it, was that it be carried out by volunteers. The egoism she saw as inherent to all remunerative employment would necessarily compromise the worker's nobility, the very quality upon which Hill relied for the gradual transformation of the poor. She told a group of students that "paid work for the poor is no nobler, or more self-sacrificing than any other paid work."[93] At times Hill regarded the paid worker with a tone of reluctant resignation to undesirable necessity: "As the board of guardians . . . has its paid clerk; as the good Charity Committee has its paid secretary; as the choir has its choir-master; so most groups of volunteers have, and must have, their paid worker."[94] Hill assumed that professionalization would introduce an element of self-interest into the work, which would be destructive of its altruistic aims. She wrote in another essay that "professed" workers would "quickly begin to hug our system and perhaps want to perpetuate it even to the extent of making work for it."[95]

In short, Hill's hybrid "kind of manager not hitherto existing" involved an ideological dilemma that she only temporarily escaped by recourse to domestic ideology. She wanted her workers to meet professional standards while retaining amateur status. This was possible for mid-century women in a way it was not later in the century as work for middle-class women became more normative. By setting a high standard for training and time, as she did for her managers (especially later in the formalized training program of the Women's University Settlement), she made it inevitable that payment of managers would be expected and required. In some instances she found herself prepared to embrace that reality. But in other instances, and certainly in her own case, her habitual attraction to residual modes of class relations caused her to regard paid labor for the poor with aversion, even while she pioneered professional and entrepreneurial methods of such labor. Hill's new kind of manager, the bureaucratic pastor, was the liminal and short-lived type that enabled the transition from Lady Bountiful to the state-employed social worker.

The limitations of that type expose the contradictions of her syncretic strategy of maintaining idealist and materialist ideologies cheek-by-jowl in her own thinking. The logic of the heart and that of the head are in contest after all, at least in certain respects, and Hill's effort to synthesize them—or to harmonize them, as she would probably say—is finally imperfect. Nevertheless, Hill's statements and attitudes on the subjects examined here bespeak a conceptualization of the professional ideal that evinces precisely the uneven and contested process of disaggregation that impacted professionalism with respect to materialist and idealist discourses.

EPILOGUE

In all of the figures and texts examined here, professional practice and professional institutions have been seen as loci of the tension between idealist and materialist rationalities. Whether those tensions are imaginatively resolved or clumsily patched up, they have always been present in such a way as to attract attention to the necessary cultural work of understanding professionalism in terms of its conflicting allegiances.

In Benjamin Disraeli's Young England trilogy, Disraeli's ardent insistence on idealist solutions to the nation's social problems is never convincingly aligned to the materialist ways and means that his politicians only gesture toward. While giving his valorized politicians a clearly professional ethos, Disraeli nevertheless mystifies their application of materialist apparatus to their specific governmental tasks. Anthony Trollope invokes professional ideals of autonomy and integrity to demonstrate that the best professional service is provided by the autonomous practitioner, whose autonomous actions reinforce rather than subvert the autonomy of the profession as a whole. In Trollope's early Barcetshire novels, the emergent professional ideal is shown as related to aspects of the dominant Benthamite ideals while nevertheless offering a trenchant critique of the unreflecting application of the same. In Elizabeth Gaskell's *My Lady Ludlow*, the ideal of meritocracy becomes the basis for an understated expansion of the boundaries of the professional class to include women as well as the illegitimately born and even the working class. Gaskell extends the application of professional norms to women and shows the suitableness of giving women professional opportunities. For George Eliot, arguably the most theoretical and self-consciously idealist of these figures, idealism in professional practice redeems professionalism from its mercenary tendencies. She does not flinch from the problems thereby engendered, showing the pitfalls of extreme disinterest as well as its opposites. Eventually Eliot makes specialization the solution to excessive disinterest, using one ideal to delimit another. Finally, Octavia Hill strove throughout life to harness materialist means to achieve idealist ends. She succeeded at this endeavor to a considerable extent, literally transforming the living spaces of thousands of London's underprivileged citizens with her combination of physical and personal reform. Even she, however, never escaped the contradictions of market and nonmarket logic that her activities in both domains brought to the fore.

Through their depictions of professional life, the Victorians show us what the negotiation of idealist and materialist rationalities looks like, what dilemmas it entails, and some possible limited solutions. They show us, in short, that professionalism is not merely a matter of intellectual workers' position in the division of labor but also a complex culture in itself, and that it has been so since the outset of modern professionalism. Analysis of the professional class, past as well as present, must therefore take account of more than the evolving material conditions of professional position; professionalism must be understood dialectically as part of a thick culture of self-critical practices and priorities with potential to transform it.

Two portraits of the state of the professions today, one from the left and one from the right, illustrate the resources for—and limitations on—contemporary professional self-concepts. Harold Perkin, in *The Third Revolution: Professional Elites in the Modern World*, scrutinizes the global processes and effects of professionalism in the leading developed nations. Perkin's trenchant analysis shows, ultimately, that the modern elites have exhibited the same culpability as the previous feudal and industrial elites in channeling a disproportionate amount of the wealth created by professional expertise to themselves, even at the expense of lower-level professionals. In fact, professional elites are more culpable than their predecessors because human capital, unlike capital in land or in the industrial means of production, is highly expandable, allowing the benefits of wealth creation to permeate much further down the social scale than was previously imaginable. In most cases, though, and especially in the United States and the United Kingdom, this has not occurred. Instead, powerful politicians, CEOs, and boards have adopted a radical individualist view that rationalizes their own acquisitiveness as productive of the common good. Perkin shows, for example, that the so-called free market is in fact rigged to the advantage of key players whose political muscle enables them to legalize measures that extract surplus value to an inordinate degree. This process enriches CEOs and directors while shortchanging employees, customers, and other stakeholders. This "over-exploitation," Perkin believes, has the potential to fatally destabilize British and American societies, just as the over-exploitation practiced by earlier elites brought about the demise of feudalism and industrialism.[1]

Perkins' portrait of irresponsibly selfish elites is challenged by David Brooks, whose version rather emphasizes that most professionals have idealist investments that are mostly submerged and inarticulate. The penchant of Victorian professionals to hybridize their materialist and idealist impulses is not unlike the syncretism of American professional elites today as described by David Brooks in *Bobos in Paradise*. His formulation of "bourgeois bohemians" (Bobos, for short) is an attempt to explore—or explode—the means by which contemporary elites seek to reconcile the rationality of material success with that of idealist values such as community, public service, and environmental protection. Bobos seem generally to achieve this reconciliation more or less in the same way Octavia Hill did: by insisting it must be done and then implementing aspects of both without thinking through the contradictions thereby entailed.

Brooks's picture of American society, in which many if not most professions retain undertheorized idealist impulses, is surely more accurate than Perkins' picture, in which heartless, indeed criminal rapacity is the only consideration regarded by elite professionals. For both Perkin and Brooks, however, the elites are unable or unwilling to reflect on the fact of their own privileged status or the implications thereof. Perkin's elites have eyes only for their material self-interest, while Brooks' better-intentioned elites lack a moral vocabulary to articulate their responsibility to society. Brooks observes in *On Paradise Drive* that meritocracy, while superior to hereditary aristocracy in important ways, nevertheless has its own unexplored pitfalls: "The best members of the WASP aristocracy knew that privilege corrodes virtue in certain ways. They worked up a moral language to fight that. We have only the dimmest notion of how the achievement ethos corrodes virtue in certain other ways. And we have not yet begun to come up with a way to counter it."[2]

In saying such things, however, both Perkin and Brooks fail to account for their own position as *critical* professional/cultural elites. They implicitly insist, as countless other professional critics of professionalism have insisted, on the uniqueness of their ability or inclination to defrock professionalism. But of course critiques of professionalism have long since become more orthodox than oppositional; Bruce Robbins has shown that the professional jeremiad is more a chorus than a lone prophetic voice. Or as Jonathan Freedman has wryly observed, "The critique of professionalism is one of the most respectable means of making one's way in the academic profession itself."[3] What the existence of this chorus suggests is consonant with the argument of this study: professional culture has always embedded self-critical reflection. Figures such as Brooks and Perkin are not so much speaking against the grain of professional culture as with it, or at least with a strain of reflection on professional ideology that has been viable since its formation.

Such a view of professionalism can be seen as grounds for a guarded optimism about professional culture. Clearly there is much work to do to establish the professional ideal of a level playing field where gender, race, and socioeconomic status are no obstacles to merit; to secure the autonomy of practitioners from bureaucratic management neglectful of human needs; and to enculturate elites in the "enlightened self-interest" Perkin calls for which sees the wider social good as constitutive of, not counter to, the material goods of the corporate bottom line.[4] This study suggests that there are resources within the professional culture as well as outside it to achieve the sort of reflexivity that can enable such work.

The specialist culture we live in today is irreversible. No revolution or social reconstruction will obviate the need for legions of specialized experts in today's global society. It behooves us, therefore, to look for solutions to professional misconduct from within professional culture itself, rather than imagining a solution that would somehow stand outside the past century and half or so of increasing dependency on expert labor. It is necessary to find a tone, as Bruce Robbins says, for acknowledging professionalism's frequent complicity with exploitative capitalism without shortchanging its potential to advance progressive ends.[5] Such a tone would create a space for us, as self-critical professionals, to cultivate that potential by developing personal and institutional responses to the failures of our professions to meet their own ideals. Responses could involve a better balance of liberal arts courses in predominantly technocratic pre-professional programs; these courses could be designed to educate students in more global, holistic, and even empathetic ways of seeing work in their chosen profession in terms of its social impact. In the shorter term, conscientious members of professions could, as so many already do, use the structures available within their associations to gather attention and momentum for issues of social justice within the profession itself and in the social spheres impacted by the profession. In many if not most professions, it will be possible to find exemplary figures in the profession's history whose dual commitment to the excellence of the profession and to social justice can be invoked and built upon.

Efforts like these are facilitated if not enabled by the prior adoption of a tone that allows for the full recognition of both materialist and idealist investments in professional activity. *The Professional Ideal in the Victorian Novel* shows that recognition of this dual allegiance was not only more intuitive to our professional forebears of the Victorian period than it is to us, but also more theorized by them than we have tended to recognize. Their full-blooded engagement with these issues highlights the richly dialectical discourse of Victorian professional culture.

NOTES

INTRODUCTION: COOL HEADS
AND WARM HEARTS

1. A. Marshall, *Memorials of Alfred Marshall*, 174.
2. Ibid., 155–156.
3. Ibid., 323–346.
4. Ibid., 324.
5. On the progress of the professional project in the Victorian period, see Burton J. Bledstein, *Culture of Professionalism*; Penelope J. Corfield, *Power and the Professions in Britain 1700–1850*; T. R. Gourvish, "Rise of the Professions"; T. W. Heyck, *Transformation of Intellectual Life in Victorian England*; Magali Sarfatti Larson, *Rise of Professionalism*; Harold Perkin, *Origins of Modern English Society* and *Rise of Professional Society*; W. J. Reader, *Professional Men*; and Geoffrey Searle, *Morality and the Market in Victorian Britain*. On the professionalization of authorship, see Clare Pettitt, *Patent Inventions*.
6. Most recently, Jennifer Ruth's *Novel Professions* argues that "the novel attempted to 'theorize' the professional, trying to do what nonfiction failed to do" (4). Jennifer Cognard-Black's illuminating study on *Narrative in the Professional Age* looks to the final third of the century for articulations of professional self-construction in women writers. Her analysis of the public and private writing of three women writers in the 1870s and after explores their negotiation of professional tropes to create a space for a feminine professional ideal based on aesthetics, which she terms "strong femininity" (14). John Kucich, in *Power of Lies*, has considered relations between professionals and the antibourgeois in Anthony Trollope and Wilkie Collins. Bruce Robbins's well-known work on *Bleak House* ("Telescopic Philanthropy") and Lauren M. E. Goodlad's recent work on Dickens in *Victorian Literature* have contributed to our understanding of professional issues in Victorian fiction, as has Monica Cohen's *Professional Domesticity in the Victorian Novel*. Nicholas Dames, in "Trollope and the Career," examines professional issues in Trollope's Palliser novels. Robert Butterworth, "Professional Adrift," and Antonia Losano, "Professionalization of the Woman Artist," have done the same for Anne Brontë's fiction. See also

Laura Fasick, *Professional Men and Domesticity in the Mid-Victorian Novel.*

7. Duman, "Creation and Diffusion of a Professional Ideology," 120. See also Rosemary O'Day, "Clerical Renaissance," which argues that the professional ideals that altered the clergy in mid-century were not reactions to developments in the secular professions. Rather, the Victorian clergy's recourse to early modern paradigms of clerical function more likely provided the model followed by the secular professions.

8. Duman says that "the developing professional ideal . . . was promoted by writers who were by and large drawn from the professional classes" ("Creation and Diffusion of a Professional Ideology," 127). Duman draws on Austen, Trollope, and Dickens, the last of whom he sees as an unequivocal critic of professionalism.

9. H. Perkin, *Origins of Modern English Society*, 219.

10. But see Goodlad's more nuanced account of the highly contested implementation of the New Poor Law, a contest in which professional and aristocratic biases also played a major role in moderating the law's Benthamite apparatus (*Victorian Literature*, esp. 32–36).

11. H. Perkin, *Origins of Modern English Society*, 252.

12. Ibid.

13. Ibid., 258.

14. Ibid., 428.

15. Ibid., 321.

16. H. Perkin, *Rise of Professional Society*, 6.

17. Larson, *Rise of Professionalism*, xviii.

18. Ibid., esp. 57–63.

19. Bledstein, *Culture of Professionalism*, 107–108.

20. B. Ehrenreich and J. Ehrenreich, "Professional-Managerial Class," 10.

21. See B. Ehrenreich's interview, "Professional-Managerial Class Revisited," esp. 178–180.

22. Haber, *Quest for Authority and Honor*, ix.

23. O'Day, "Clerical Renaissance," 186.

24. Haber, *Quest for Authority and Honor*, ix.

25. Collini, *Public Moralists*, 85.

26. Robbins, *Secular Vocations*, 15, 7, 55.

27. Ibid., 80

28. Ibid., 15, 20, 32.

29. See Weber, *Protestant Ethic and the Spirit of Capitalism*, 70, 72, 176–177, and 180.

30. This idea is most prominently argued in Goodlad, "Middle Class."

31. Goodlad, *Victorian Literature*, 22. Goodlad continues, "By *worldviews* I refer to sets of beliefs that, for all their preponderance, were fluctuating and contested (rather than statically dominant), and more palpable and plain than underlying epistemological questions (however inextricable from them)" (22, emphasis in original). On the

relationship between idealism and materialism, see also Pettitt, *Patent Inventions*, esp. 8 and 12. Pettitt describes the "irreconcilable tensions" between the "stereotypes" of the author-as-romantic creator and the author-as-middle-class professional. My view differs from Pettitt's in that I see the professional type itself as exemplifying the coexistence of the romantic and materialistic rationalities.

32. Goodlad, *Victorian Literature*, 22–23.

33. Ibid., 37.

34. Ibid., 22.

35. Ibid., 18. In stating this argument, Goodlad cites critiques of Foucault offered by Edward Said ("Foucault"); Christopher Norris (" 'What Is Enlightenment?' "); Anderson ("Temptations"); and Christopher Lane *(Burdens of Intimacy)*. Norris tellingly notes the incapacity of genealogical methodology to handle "substantive ethical or socio-political questions" (qtd. in *Victorian Literterture*, 18).

36. Miller, *Novel and the Police*, 115.

37. Ruth, *Novel Professions*, 22.

38. Ibid., 112–114.

39. Ibid., 16.

40. H. Perkin, *Origins of Modern English Society*, 268–269.

41. Priti Joshi, for example, evinces this assumption in "Edwin Chadwick's Self-Fashioning." Joshi's detailed and sympathetic treatment of Chadwick's project of constructing and justifying himself as a professional in his *Sanitary Report* regards Chadwick's professional ambitions of scientific expertise as indistinct from his bureaucratic impulses and "entrepreneurial spirit" (366).

42. Freedman, *Professions of Taste*, 52.

43. Searle, *Morality and the Market in Victorian Britain*, 105.

44. The concept of disaggregation and competing rationalities I borrow from Poovey, *Making a Social Body*, esp. 5–15. Institutions in emergent domains always betray on some level their relative autonomy: that is, they operate according to their own rationality yet, in contradictory ways, remain subject to the rationalities of the residual domains out of which they disaggregated.

45. Duman, "Creation and Diffusion of a Professional Ideology," 114.

46. Goodlad, *Victorian Literature*, 21.

47. A notable exception is Henrika Kuklick's "Professional Status and the Moral Order." Kuklick acknowledges "clear disparities between professionals' claims and the realities of social life," but she nevertheless persuasively documents that "the professional creed of a century ago was not merely the self-serving ideology of a would-be elite" (128, 137). Although her study pertains to fin de siècle social scientists in America, Kuklick's reconsideration of the claims of altruism reinforces my own similar consideration of the ideality that formed an important part of professional consciousness in Victorian Britain.

48. Anderson, "Victorian Studies," 197.
49. Trollope, *Barchester Towers*, 2:259.
50. This study, unlike some influential accounts of middle-class formation, does not find gender to be *the* salient category. Leonore Davidoff and Catherine Hall in *Family Fortunes*, and Nancy Armstrong in *Desire and Domestic Fiction*, to give two examples, maintain that the gender binary fundamentally constituted the English bourgeoisie. Armstrong's Foucauldian thesis further argues that the novel performs the cultural work of naturalizing state surveillance as domestic management. However, in "Middle Class," Goodlad argues that the Foucauldian treatment of gender subjectivity and surveillance over-simplifies British subject formation into the categories of male and female. Specifically, she shows that in some cases the categories of expertise, competency, and autonomy are more important social categories than gender, and that the former categories as well as the latter bear a definitive relationship to domesticity (152–157).
51. Escaping the anachronistic binary of "sameness" and "difference" feminism, Caine instead focuses on the complex relationship between Victorian feminism and various idealist strains of domestic ideology, as well as the equally ambivalent relationship between Victorian feminism and liberalism.
52. I have in mind accounts such as Julia Swindells's *Victorian Writing and Working Women* and, to a lesser extent, Anne Witz's *Professions and Patriarchy*.

Chapter 1   Brains More Precious than Blood, or the Professional Logic of the Young England Trilogy

1. Monypenny and Buckle, *Life of Benjamin Disraeli*, 1:28–29. Disraeli wrote that he did, however, hear lectures on Plato.
2. Smith, *Disraeli: A Brief Life*, 62.
3. Disraeli, *Vindication*, 66.
4. H. Perkin, *Origins of Modern English Society*, 237–252.
5. For example, Morris Edmund Speare, in *Political Novel*, writes about an uncomplicated notion of "a rejuvenated aristocracy," following Carlylean ideas of the heroic, in Disraeli's novels (170). Michael Flavin, in *Benjamin Disraeli*, similarly assumes that Disraeli's allegiances were thoroughly aristocratic in every significant way. Rosemarie Bodenheimer, in *Politics of Story*, is aware of the hybridity I find in Disraeli's idealized professional/aristocratic figures: "Disraeli has to have it both ways. The genealogical satires assert that the fake aristocrats can be measured against some 'real' genealogy that traces an unbroken line back to a legitimate origin. At the same time Disraeli must allow for an aristocracy of talent

coming from nowhere, in order to justify his own claim to renew English politics" (173).

6. R. Blake, *Disraeli*, 70.
7. Disraeli, *Vindication*, 153.
8. Ibid., 140.
9. Disraeli, *Coningsby*, 401.
10. H. Perkin, *Origins of Modern English Society*, 261.
11. Harrold and Templeman, *English Prose*, xlix.
12. Disraeli, *Coningsby*, 149. Subsequent page references to this text will be given in parentheses.
13. John Holloway, in *The Victorian Sage*, takes this passage as evidence that "the aristocracy which Disraeli admires is one of quality, not lineage," and identifies the same ethos in *Sybil* (96).
14. Disraeli, *Sybil*, 65–66. Subsequent page references to this text will be given in parentheses.
15. Patrick Brantlinger first pointed out that the idea of England as two nations is proved to Sybil to be a "dangerous illusion," and that the "diversity of the class system is a refutation of 'the two nations theory' " ("Tory Radicalism," 16–17; and *Spirit of Reform*, 102–103). Many other critics have followed this line, noticing that Morley's ideas are thoroughly discredited by his dishonorable and even criminal behavior. According to Robert O'Kell's reading, for example, Morley's "utilitarian frame of mind" and "materialist conception of human nature" render him untrustworthy and distance him absolutely from Disraeli's own values ("Two Nations, or One?" 226), a view that coincides with that of Daniel Schwartz (*Disraeli's Fiction*, 120–121). The novel therefore ultimately insists that although England appears to be divided into two nations, the interests of rich and poor are, when rightly understood, coterminus. Gary Handwerk, "Beyond Sybil's Veil," gets closer to an adequately-nuanced account of Morley's role in the book by observing that Disraeli focuses his attention on the failure of communication between the two nations, not the income disparity that fosters that failure. Parama Roy, in "*Sybil*," sees a contradiction in Disraeli's treatment of this issue: "the 'two nations' formula, first broached in all seriousness by Morley, and later exposed as simplistic, is finally reaffirmed by the trajectory of the plot" (69).
16. Disraeli, *Vindication*, 10–16.
17. R. A. Levine, *Benjamin Disraeli*, 67.
18. This view was probably first advanced by Monckton Milnes in his 1847 review of the trilogy (R. Blake, *Disraeli*, 206). See also Thom Braun, *Disraeli the Novelist*, 101; and Daniel Bivona, "Disraeli's Political Trilogy," 316–317.
19. Williams, *Culture and Society*, 100.
20. Sampson, "*Sybil*, or the Two Monarchs."
21. O'Kell, "Two Nations, or One?" 216.

22. Yeazell, "Why Political Novels Have Heroines," 132.

23. Schwartz, *Disraeli's Fiction*, 124.

24. Bodenheimer, *Politics of Story*, 173.

25. Ulrich, *Signs of Their Times*, 136.

26. Bodenheimer, *Politics of Story*, 173.

27. Gallagher, *Industrial Reformation*, 212.

28. Ibid., 215.

29. Bodenheimer, in *Politics of Story*, argues that the novel exhibits a pattern of elaborating the past and future while skipping over the present (186–187).

30. Braun's objection, in *Disraeli the Novelist*, that this impulse to violence is unconvincingly imposed on Gerard for reasons of narrative expediency, is easily overcome by looking at Gerard as a representative of the aristocratic ideal.

31. See Kristina Deffenbacher, "Designing Progress," for analysis of the Puginesque social meanings of architecture as explored in Disraeli's fiction.

32. See Alice Chandler's study of Disraeli's medievalism in *Dream of Order*, in which she finds marked affinities between the social philosophy of William Cobbett and Disraeli (179).

33. To a limited extent the working-class ideal corresponds with the aristocratic: "the rights of labor [are] as sacred as those of property," as Egremont boldly tells his Parliamentary colleagues (291). But he no less boldly tells Sybil that the people can never be trusted with political power (276).

34. On Disraeli's attitude toward the commercial middle class, see Smith, *Disraeli: A Brief Life*, 69–70.

35. With respect to the passages of revisionist Tory history in the novel, Susan Zlotnick, *Women, Writing, and Industrial Revolution*, sees Disraeli in Hatton, the exegete of the past who capitalizes on his unique ability to discern authenticity as well as to manufacture the appearance of authenticity. Bodenheimer, in *Politics of Story*, argues that Morley is Disraeli the politician and Hatton is Disraeli the novelist, with "talent coming from nowhere," who "reveres the past but uses it to create the fictions of the present" (185). She notes that the illegal activities of Morley and Hatton allow Egremont to benefit from historical discontinuities without soiling his own hands. Handwerk similarly emphasizes that Morley and Hatton are ultimately and ironically "responsible for the political promise at the end of the novel, for [the] restoration of legitimacy and sympathetic openness to the British politics" ("Beyond Sybil's Veil," 338).

36. See Albert Pionke, "Combining the Two Nations," for the historical sources of this scene. This oath is verbatim from the 1838 Report on Select Committee on Combinations, except for the second phrase, in which three of the Parliamentary words are found. Disraeli therefore

seems to have revised the oath to emphasize an imaginative connection between trade unions and Parliament.

37. Smith's comment is that "the social problem is not resolved but eluded by abruptly elevating a few of the Many as a sort of payment on account," specifically Sybil, Dandy Mick, and Devilsdust (*Disraeli: A Brief Life*, 73).

38. R. Blake, *Disraeli*, 214. See also Todd M. Endelman, " 'Hebrew to the End,' " esp. 126–127; and Frietzsche, *Disraeli's Religion*.

39. Race figured prominently in the first two books of the trilogy as well, but in *Tancred* it becomes the central and almost exclusive determiner of value. See the discussion of race as the unifying theme in the trilogy in R. A. Levine, *Benjamin Disraeli*. See also Brantlinger, *Rule of Darkness*, 149–157. Rolf Lessenich, "Synagogue, Church, and Young England," shows that the trilogy argues for the need of England to apprentice itself to the superior Semitic race. Also of interest is Bernard Glassman, *Benjamin Disraeli*, which examines Disraeli's "fabricated" Jewishness, fabricated both by Disraeli himself and others.

40. See Brantlinger, "Disraeli and Orientalism," for a thorough analysis of Disraeli's self-conscious racial "self-fashioning." See also Smith, *Disraeli: A Brief Life*, for a reading of the novels that emphasizes Disraeli's strategies of self-definition (esp. 64–69, 92–93).

41. Disraeli, *Tancred*, 62. Subsequent page references to this text will be given in parentheses.

42. For an unironic presentation of this sentiment, see 99–101.

43. Qtd. in Monypenny and Buckle, *Life of Benjamin Disraeli*, 3:49.

44. Brantlinger, *Rule of Darkness*, 157.

45. Said, *Orientalism*, 169.

46. Disraeli, *Coningsby*, 420.

47. Lord Eskdale is given this epithet frequently. See, for example, 27, 80, and 107.

48. Flavin, *Benjamin Disraeli*, 134.

49. Brantlinger, "Nations and Novels," 267.

50. Monypenny and Buckle, *Life of Benjamin Disraeli*, 3:55.

Chapter 2   "Manly Independence": Autonomy in *The Warden* and *Barchester Towers*

1. See Nicholas Dames, "Trollope and the Career," for a reading of the Palliser novels in terms of political and imperial career. See also Elsie B. Michie, "Buying Brains," on economy and human capital in *The Last Chronicle of Barset*. Christopher Harvie, in *Centre of Things*, is the only critic I have found who discusses the early Barsetshire novels in even slightly political terms (87–88), although Joseph Ellis Baker goes so far as to say, without examining the implications of the statement,

that "Trollope's Church . . . is a bureau of state" (*Novel and the Oxford Movement*, 141).

2. See Baker, *Novel and the Oxford Movement*, 140; and Andrew Drummond, *Churches in English Fiction*. As will be apparent from the following, I cannot agree with Drummond that "ecclesiastical issues" go unexamined in the novels (80).

3. Trollope, *Barchester Towers*, 1:46.

4. For a survey of critiques of Trollope's political novels as insufficiently political, see John Halperin, *Trollope and Politics*, 5.

5. Trollope, *Barchester Towers*, 2:259.

6. See Bertha Keveson Hertz, "Trollope's Racial Bias against Disraeli." See also Michael Ragussis, *Figures of Conversion*, for a detailed reading of the disgust and virtual paranoia in Trollope's Jewish novels (234–260). Trollope and Disraeli were of course competitors in the formation of the political novel, and the qualitative comparison seems irresistible to many who write about either figure. In early studies of the political novel, Disraeli received high accolades, while Trollope's political novels were denigrated as vastly inferior to Disraeli's. See, for example, Morris Edmund Speare, *Political Novel*; and H. A. L. Fisher, "Political Novel" (excerpted in R. W. Stewart, *Disraeli's Novels Reviewed*, 67–71). Disraeli's biographer Robert Blake predictably agrees with the disparagement of Trollope's political novels in comparison with those of Disraeli (*Disraeli*, 217). Halperin, in contrast, writes in *Trollope and Politics*, "Unlike Disraeli, Trollope was a novelist, not a pamphleteer" (5). For some other parallels, see Harvie, *Centre of Things*, 84.

7. Trollope, *New Zealander*, 13. It will be apparent why I regard Halperin's comment that "[t]his is certainly plain enough," as short-sighted (*Trollope and Politics*, 14).

8. Trollope, *New Zealander*, 13. Trollope goes on to say that the enjoyment of hereditary status is contingent upon the performance of duty: "The aristocracy of pleasure only is quickly becoming sufficiently unaristocratic . . . . [B]e their titles what they may, they are ceasing to be in any way the rulers of the people" (17).

9. Durey, *Trollope and the Church*, 106.

10. Divergent readings of the novels' implicit morality, particularly the tensions involved in the application of abstract principles to concrete situations, can be found in Ruth apRoberts, *Moral Trollope*; James Kincaid, "Anthony Trollope"; Shirley Robin Letwin, *Gentleman in Trollope*; and Jane Nardin, *Trollope and Victorian Moral Philosophy*. See also Ilana Blumberg, " 'Unnatural Self-Sacrifice,' " which analyzes how Trollope escapes a rigid binary of praiseworthy self-sacrifice and blameworthy personal benefit.

11. Bledstein, *Culture of Professionalism*, 92.

12. One definition of a profession is an occupation in which the cognitive activity of the practitioner is relatively high in indeterminacy and

relatively low in technicality. See Magali Sarfatti Larson, *Rise of Professionalism*, 41, for a discussion of this definition posed by H. Jamous and B. Peliolle. Technicality refers to knowledge that can be rendered as rules, and indetermination refers to knowledge that resists rule making.

13. Thomson, *Choice of a Profession*, 5.

14. "Church as a Profession," 751.

15. Thomson, *Choice of a Profession*, 41. This disciplined system of public school education, however, is distinguished from the "semi-military" French *gymnase*, in which boys are "[p]ushed, crammed, overtaught, overworked, drilled, and disciplined," yet are left "quite unable to teach themselves anything" and "entirely without self-guidance and self-control" (43). Thomson ranks this system as even less appropriate for professionals-in-training than a permissive home education or private seminary.

16. See, for example, Harold Perkin, *Rise of Professional Society*, 20; Bledstein, *Culture of Professionalism*, 85–86; and K. Theodore Hoppen, *Mid-Victorian Generation*, 40–41.

17. See Larson, *Rise of Professionalism*, 54.

18. Dicey, "Legal Etiquette," 177, note 1.

19. For example, in Larson's view, the profession corporately requires individual sacrifices of professionals, such as providing reduced-rate services to the poor, in order to uphold the fiction of a service ethic, which would then help the individual practitioner and the profession in general in the long run by creating a market that has to be maintained at state expense (*Rise of Professionalism*, 58–59).

20. See, for example, Dicey, "Legal Etiquette," 176.

21. Freidson, *Profession of Medicine*, 370.

22. Larson, *Rise of Professionalism*, 40–41.

23. Trollope, *Warden*, 203–204.

24. Ibid., 190.

25. Trollope, *Barchester Towers*, 2:50. Subsequent references to this text will be given in parentheses.

26. Terry, *Trollope*, 51.

27. Victoria Glendinning says that Trollope's "lack of servility" and "marked insubordination" posed problems for him in the London Post Office (*Trollope*, 110). See also N. John Hall, *Trollope: A Biography*, 81–85. Of course many factors were involved in Trollope's improved prospects in Ireland, but increased autonomy may well have been one of them.

28. Trollope, "Civil Service as a Profession," 11.

29. Ibid., 23–24. See also Trollope, "Civil Service as a Profession," which formed chapter 12 in the first edition of *The Three Clerks*.

30. Trollope, "Civil Service as a Profession," 5.

31. In 1860, Trollope testified before a Parliamentary committee against the Trevelyan-Northcote competitive examination reforms. See R. H. Super, *Trollope and the Post Office*, 33, 52.

32. Trollope's 1858 novel *The Three Clerks* contains his clearest fictional statement of these opinions. The torturous exams caricatured in that novel of course do not evaluate the skills or knowledge connected to the position at stake, but that is not the worst of their evils. The unscrupulous but charming Alaric Tudor succeeds, chiefly because he is the examiner's favorite, and senior and more worthy candidates are denied the opportunity of advancement and forced to regard him as their superior. Trollope indicates that the absurdly-administered examination process all but guarantees that the worst man will get the promotion rather than the best. Moreover, the examination contributes to enmity between colleagues and strains office relations. See Cathy Shuman's analysis of *The Three Clerks* in *Pedagogical Economies* and Jennifer Ruth's in *Novel Professions*.

33. My views largely accord with those of John Kucich, who describes the novels "not as a study of old-fashioned aristocratic culture but as an example of its appropriation by the middle class" (*Power of Lies*, 54). Kucich avers that "[f]rom roughly 1855 to 1865, Palmerston's appointments transformed the clergy's desire for independence from the state to the more pathetic goal of independence from its own bishops" (52–53). I am more interested than Kucich in distinguishing the entrepreneurial and professional strains in the "middle-class ideology" that displaces "upper-class life and institutions" in the novels and in analyzing the tensions those competing strains generate (51).

34. Goodlad, *Victorian Literature*, 137.

35. H. Perkin, *Origins of Modern English Society*, 362. See also Rosemary O'Day, "Clerical Renaissance." O'Day argues convincingly that what I am calling the professionalization of the clergy in the nineteenth century was not a reaction to the emerging paradigms of secular professions, but rather the intensification of long-standing ideals within the clerical profession. O'Day's argument may not be fully compatible with H. Perkin's view of the professionalization of the clergy, but it is compatible with my reading of Trollope. I will show that Trollope's resolution to the problem of autonomy in the clerical profession is realized in the discovery that the traditional ideals of the clergy are actually its most professional resources.

36. H. Perkin, *Origins of Modern English Society*, 255.

37. Chadwick, *Victorian Church*, 126.

38. Thompson, *Bureaucracy and Church Reform*, 68–70.

39. See Chadwick, *Victorian Church*, 126–130; and G. I. T. Machin, *Politics and the Churches*, 50–51. For a more detailed account, see Olive Brose, *Church and Parliament*, 120–177. A more anecdotal version of these events appears in Desmond Bowen, *Idea of the Victorian Church*, 3–40.

40. Machin, *Politics and the Churches*, 53–71.

41. Qtd. in Bowen, *Idea of the Victorian Church*, 38.

42. Bowen in fact indicates a direct causal relationship between Wilberforce's managerial strategy and his relative success in deflecting lay control of the Church: "This liberty was granted because the labours of prelates like Blomfield and Wilberforce persuaded statesmen like Peel and Russell that the long slumber of the Church was over, that a new sense of mission had arrived" (Ibid., 38).

43. Trollope, *Warden*, 21.

44. Ibid., 22.

45. Trollope, *Four Lectures*, 11; and Trollope, *Autobiography*, 78.

46. Trollope, *Warden*, 121. It is certainly true, as Dames has written, that the world of *The Warden*, in comparison to that of the Palliser novels, is characterized by stable factions inhabited by stable personalities ("Trollope and the Career," 265–266). However, Harding's action shows that the factions are not absolutely stable; Harding's own exercise of autonomy in resistance to his faction is what shows him to be morally sound.

47. Not so the university reforms, which, passed in 1854 and 1856, still sting Barchester sensibilities.

48. H. Perkin, *Origins of Modern English Society*, 287. "Religion apart, nothing could have been more puritanical than the education of John Stuart Mill, and if labouring in one's vocation, seriousness of mind, the exclusion of all but intellectual pleasures, the consciousness of being of the elect, compulsive preaching to potential converts, and coercion of the stubbornly unenlightened, are marks of the puritan, the Benthamites were puritans to a man" (287). See also Thompson's description of the affinity between Evangelicalism and Benthamism in *Bureaucracy and Church Reform*, 15–18.

49. Trollope, *Warden*, 124.

50. Trollope betrays some uneasiness concerning the shift in Dr. Grantly's characterization, prefacing his "revision" of Grantly's character with the comment, "And here we can hardly fail to draw a comparison between the archdeacon and your new private chaplain; and despite the manifold faults of the former, one can hardly fail to make it much to his advantage" (1:230).

51. In "The Civil Service as a Profession," Trollope observed that overbearing supervisors are usually also servile to those above them: "[O]ne meanness will accompany the other. When I see that Smith wants to make a machine of Jones, I know that Smith is a machine ready to the hands of Brown" (16).

52. Again, "The Civil Service as a Profession" sheds light on Trollope's reasoning behind this incident. "It may be imagined that there is partiality of selection, but it is not imagined that men are selected without reference to their competence. The selector may judge badly, and may possibly have allowed himself to be influenced by his likings; but he no longer dares to throw all judgment to the winds. The clamor would be too great" (17).

53. See Nardin, *He Knew She Was Right.*

54. Trollope, *Warden*, 102.

55. Ibid., 273. While I agree with Blumberg's analysis in " 'Unnatural Self-Sacrifice' " of the unity of interests between Harding and the bedesmen, I cannot assent to her conclusion that Harding's resignation is morally ambivalent, not to say blameworthy. Blumberg holds that his resignation, rather than being a personal sacrifice on Harding's part, actually sacrifices the well-being of the bedesmen to Harding's overly fastidious conscience (538). However, the "harmony" enjoyed by the bedesmen and their warden is broken not by his resignation, but by their litigation; his remaining in his post could not have restored it.

56. Trollope, *Warden*, 280.

57. Trollope, *Autobiography*, 76.

CHAPTER 3   PROFESSIONAL FRONTIERS IN ELIZABETH GASKELL'S *MY LADY LUDLOW*

1. Gaskell was a friend of the Nightingale family and was well aware of Florence's paradigm-shifting efforts to professionalize nursing, in part by idealizing it. Gaskell's daughter Meta appears to have considered nursing as a possible career, and Gaskell encouraged her to seek proper training for it. See Gaskell, *Letters*, Letter 217, p. 320. See Kristine Swenson's study of the relationship of Gaskell's fiction to the Nightingale nursing campaign in *Medical Women and Victorian Fiction.*

2. Gaskell outlined this ending to her publisher, George Smith, in a letter of December 1863. She clearly preferred this ending to the rapid conclusion that was published, saying, "I think it will be a pity to cut it short," and "I shall be sorry [to end it abruptly] for it is, at present, such a complete fragment" (*Further Letters*, 259–260).

3. Edgar Wright, "*My Lady Ludlow*," observes that Gaskell "reveal[s] by illustration how the transition to changed social attitudes is achieved over a period of time, while recollection and explanation extend the time presented" (37). Angus Easson, in *Elizabeth Gaskell*, offers a conventional assessment of the novel's "clash between the old aristocratic ways of Lady Ludlow and the new evangelicalism of the clergyman Mr. Gray" (214). Jenny Uglow, in *Habit of Stories*, argues that within the novel's span "[w]e recognize a fundamental change—in [Lady Ludlow] and in the society. Nothing, and everything, has happened" (470).

4. Swindells, *Victorian Writing and Working Women*, 19. For similarly negative readings of professionalism and women, see Gail L. Savage, "Wrongful Confinement," and Elsie B. Michie, *Outside the Pale*. The

discussion of Gaskell in the latter work shows the limitations of mapping a male/female binary onto a commercial/domestic binary, when the experience of the actors described obviously spanned both sides. A characteristic example is the slip between page 2, where we find that "in the nineteenth century to become a professional writer was to enter a territory implicitly defined as masculine," and page 94, where we are told that "the terrain of professional writing may have been seen as generally feminized." My approach instead emphasizes, with Hilary Schor, the "tension between these visions of what the Victorian novelist was to be; how she was to write; how she could read and be read by those around her" (*Scheherezade in the Marketplace*, 5).

5. Anderson, *Powers of Distance*, 35.

6. The recent spate of books on women in the publishing and periodical fields includes Hilary Fraser, Stephanie Green, and Judith Johnston, *Gender and the Victorian Periodical*; Alexis Easley, *First-Person Anonymous*; and Barbara Onslow, *Women of the Press in Nineteenth-Century Britain*. On women's entrance to medicine, see Alison Bashford, *Purity and Pollution*; Catriona Blake, *Charge of the Parasols*; and Beatrice Levin, *Women and Medicine*. The story of women's efforts to secure equal pay and equal access to all grades of the Civil Service is told in Hilda Martindale, *Women Servants of the State 1870–1938*; and in Barbara Bagilhole, *Women, Work, and Equal Opportunity*. Women's progress in the legal profession is covered in Christine Alice Corcos, *Portia Goes to Parliament*. Notable studies historicizing women's admission to the Anglican clergy include Sean Gill, *Women and the Church of England*; and Brain Heeney, *Women's Movement in the Church of England*. See also Bronwyn Rivers, *Women at Work in the Victorian Novel*. For a rare attempt at synthesis across the professions, which remains inadequate in many ways, see Nellie Alden Franz, *English Women Enter the Professions*. See also Karen Michalson, *Victorian Fantasy Literature*, which makes the argument in passing that women first made significant inroads into professions in the colonies, where gender roles became a casualty of the increased pressure for survival and the general shortage of labor (177–185). For American women's responses to professional ideology, see Fransceca Sawaya, *Modern Women, Modern Work*.

7. H. Perkin, *Third Revolution*, 180.

8. See, for example, Sophia Jex-Blake, *Medical Women*, 135; and C. R. Drysdale, "Medicine as a Profession for Women," 4.

9. Drysdale, "Medicine as a Profession for Women," 5–6.

10. Ibid., 18.

11. Ibid., 94.

12. Jex-Blake, *Medical Women*, 93, emphasis in original.

13. Swindells, *Victorian Writing and Working Women*, 21.

14. C. Blake, *Charge of the Parasols*, 141; and Swenson, *Medical Women and Victorian Fiction*, 88.

15. John Sharps, in *Mrs. Gaskell's Observation and Invention*, is very critical of what he perceives to be the structural flaws and disorganization of the novel: "The chief and most obvious structural fault is the long digression, told by Lady Ludlow for the flimsiest of reasons, which occupies nearly a third of the work. This tale within a tale . . . has every appearance of having been included solely to draw out the weekly numbers" (276). Arthur Pollard, in *Mrs. Gaskell*, similarly complained of the novel's haphazard structure: "*My Lady Ludlow* would not suffer for the excision of the whole of the Créquy incident in revolutionary Paris" (178).

16. See E. Wright, "*My Lady Ludlow*"; and Elizabeth Leaver, "What Will This World Come to?" Christine Krueger, " 'Female Paternalist' as Historian," offers a feminist defense of the novel's unusual structure, finding that the text's representation of a "female paternalist" uses heterogeneous narrators and narratives to "examine the narratives' varied genealogies and to multiply the forms of resistance to hegemonic historical discourse" (166). See also Krueger's expanded argument about Gaskell's social discourse in *Reader's Repentance*, 157–233. Other feminist readings of *My Lady Ludlow* are offered by Ruth McDowell Cook, "Women's Work"; Shirley Foster, *Elizabeth Gaskell: A Literary Life*; and Aina Rubenius, *Woman Question*. My own reading will suggest a thematic intention for the nested narratives that comprise the book; namely, I will show that the stories told by Lady Ludlow and Miss Galindo, and later renarrated by Margaret Dawson to Miss Greatorex, comprise a pre-professional variety of female storytelling that informs Miss Greatorex's presumed arrival at professional status. Thus while the de Créquy narrative is not an explicit part of my argument, I do see its inclusion as germane to Gaskell's commentary on women and professionalism.

17. For example, in her introduction Charlotte Mitchell cites "the shift of power from the landed to the manufacturing interest" (xx), in spite of the fact that manufacturing interests are rarely and obliquely referred to in the novel.

18. Gaskell, *Round the Sofa*, 277. Subsequent references to this text will be given parenthetically.

19. See Terence Wright's discussion of the "gracious accommodating love which my lady stands for" (*Elizabeth Gaskell "We Are Not Angels*," 124).

20. One overeducated young girl is dismissed with the injunction to "beware of French principles, which had led the French to cut off their king's and queen's heads" (152).

21. This attitude is explained by the fact that she has been a longtime widow, and more so by the fact that she was her father's only child and he consequently "had given her a training which was thought unusual in those days" (262).

22. Probably because of this eccentricity Miss Galindo has been dismissed by some critics as an unsavory portrait of a working woman that "almost betrays the cause as it is so much of a caricature to rob the subject of much of its seriousness" (P. Beer, *Reader, I Married Him*, 170). Most critics have been more laudatory of Miss Galindo. Notably, Cook, "Women's Work," emphasizes the nurturing ethic that pervades Miss Galindo's work and the sturdy autonomy that gives her the power to resist not only the male work culture but also the failing aristocratic code of Lady Ludlow. In a similar vein, Foster has said that Miss Galindo and Lady Ludlow both model autonomous work: "With both these women, Gaskell shows us that she has faith, albeit cautious faith, in the capacities of female independence" (*Victorian Women*, 166). Miss Galindo "seems a proto-feminist in a world which she largely accepts because she does not see it as restricting" (Foster, *Elizabeth Gaskell: A Literary Life*, 91). Among those sharing this more optimistic assessment of Miss Galindo are T. Wright, *Elizabeth Gaskell "We Are Not Angels,"* 123; Françoise Basch, *Relative Creatures*, 179–180; Rubenius, *Woman Question*, 126–128; and Uglow, *Habit of Stories*, 471–472. Krueger, " 'Female Paternalist' as Historian," privileges Miss Galindo's role as "the recording angel, the historian of everyday life" (179).

23. Williams, *Culture and Society*, 87–92. See also John Lucas, *Literature of Change*, 1–33; and Melissa Schaub, "Sympathy and Discipline in *Mary Barton*," 15–20.

24. H. Perkin, *Third Revolution*, xii–xiii.

25. Brown, *Exhibition of* Work, qtd. in Kenneth Bendiner, *Art of Ford Madox Brown*, 152.

26. Foster, *Victorian Women's Fiction*, 166.

27. See E. Wright, "*My Lady Ludlow*," 29–30; Winifred Gérin, *Elizabeth Gaskell: A Biography*, 206. Although Mitchell makes a case for the appropriateness of reading the text and frame as important to each other, she does not draw any specific conclusions about how they illuminate each other. Krueger, " 'Female Paternalist' as Historian," takes the frame seriously as part of Gaskell's project "to show how women might use and discard a variety of literary forms to represent their experience, and write their histories" (171). She notes one similarity between Margaret Dawson and Miss Greatorex: both experience an infirmity which "figures forth the simultaneously abnormal and privileged position of the female author and her intimate relationships with her audience of sororal sufferers" (172).

28. Foster, in *Elizabeth Gaskell: A Literary Life*, argues that *My Lady Ludlow* "not only resists the formal shaping of history as 'story' but also seems to represent a feminine mode of writing, expressing a Kristevan female cyclical temporality" (90). Similarly, Krueger finds that the narrative form in *My Lady Ludlow* "suggest[s] the diversity of

female desire and practice in the production of historical narrative" (" 'Female Paternalist' as Historian," 180).

29. The similarity in the wallpaper pattern is pointed out by Sharps, *Mrs. Gaskell's Observation and Invention*, 311.
30. Bonaparte, *Gypsy-Bachelor*, 222.
31. See Josie Billington's observation that "Gaskell's was a form of vision so bravely subtle as to have positively risked the danger of being underrated" ("Watching a Writer Write," 225).

Chapter 4   È Vero or È Falso? The Pastor as Mentor in *Romola*

1. Bonaparte, *Triptych and the Cross*, observes, "Never, of course, did Eliot disappoint us as utterly as she did in *Romola*, the book that contemporary reviewers greeted, as George Henry Lewes reports, 'with a universal howl of discontent,' and that, in the hundred years since, escaped our censure only when it secured our neglect" (1). See, for example, Joan Bennett's firm conclusion that "the book is . . . a failure" (*George Eliot*, 140).
2. Eliot, *George Eliot Letters*, 6:335–336.
3. Cross, *George Eliot's Life*, 2:352.
4. Haight, *George Eliot: A Biography*, 351.
5. Ibid., 51. The phrase is taken from George Combe's phrenological assessment of George Eliot's head in 1844.
6. See Catherine Gallagher's commentary on "Authorship" in "George Eliot and *Daniel Deronda*." Gallagher notes Eliot's distinction between a writer, whose private productions are not properly a "social activity," and an author, who is paid for his or her work, and concludes, " 'social' here means, first of all, economic" (45). But Eliot's principal distinction is not between authors as paid producers of text and unpaid ones, but rather between producers of text who do their work with a social conscience and those who do it out of baser motives. The category of "social activity" for Eliot is more ethical than it is economic: "Let it be taken as admitted that all legitimate social activity must be beneficial to others besides the agent" ("Authorship," 357).
7. Eliot, "Authorship," 356.
8. Ibid., 358.
9. Ibid.
10. Ibid., 359.
11. To see how Eliot's sentiments fit into a broader context of the professionalization and dignification of authorship, see the discussion of Eliot and of "Authorship" in Clare Pettitt's *Patent Inventions*.
12. See this book's introduction (10–11) for an explanation of pastorship.
13. Eliot, "Authorship," 359.
14. Ibid., 362.

15. Eliot, *George Eliot Letters*, 6:387.

16. Bardo, Tito, and Savonarola are usually taken as representatives of competing worldviews counterpoised in Renaissance Florence: classical stoicism, hedonism, and medieval Catholicism. The novel can thus be read as an epic survey of Western civilization (symbolized in Romola) at a historical crossroads. See Bonaparte, *Triptych and the Cross*, 34–72; and Joseph Wiesenfarth, *George Eliot's Mythmaking*, 146–169, for classic formulations of this position.

17. But see Anna Nardo's contentions that "[t]he encounter between Savonarola and Romola outside the Florentine walls is the most erotic scene in the novel" and that "[t]he energy that redirects Romola's ardent love from father and husband to service to Florence is sublimated sexuality" (*George Eliot's Dialogue with John Milton*, 76).

18. See Bodenheimer, *Real Life of Mary Ann Evans*, 257–265; and Menon, *Austin, Eliot, Charlotte Brontë and the Mentor-Lover*, 178–187.

19. Bodenheimer, *Real Life of Mary Ann Evans*, 258.

20. Caroline Levine, in "The Prophetic Fallacy," is right to describe Romola's epistemological development as a movement toward autonomous empirical judgment, verified by personal experience, and away from received conventions, but Levine underrates the importance of Romola's mentors' contributions to this shift (136–137). These mentors serve not just as figures of authority for her to reject but rather as influences significantly forming her resources for interpreting the lived experience out of which she draws her conclusions.

21. Tom Winnifrith, in "Renaissance and Risorgimento in *Romola*," discusses the particular historical connections between Romola's Florence and Eliot's England, as well as the perceptions of such connections by Eliot's contemporary reviewers.

22. Bernardo, "From Romola to *Romola*," 89.

23. Adams, *Our Lady of Victorian Feminism*, 70. Susan M. Greenstein's article, "Question of Vocation" explores the novel's preoccupation with vocational issues. While Greenstein's study makes valuable connections between Romola's vocational anxieties and the transitional significance of the novel in Eliot's career, I take exception to her conclusion that Romola's dilemmas receive an unearned, magical resolution which falls short of a real vocation such as Dorothea achieves vicariously through Ladislaw.

24. The association of authority and hermeneutics in the novel is widely granted. For example, Caroline Levine and Mark Turner's introduction to *From Author to Text* makes mention of the novel's contest over "interpretive authority" (8).

25. Bonaparte observes as much by saying that Romola's benefit from her classical education is not a scholarly career but the "clear critical

intelligence . . . that was, in Eliot's view, the highest gift of the ancients" (*Triptych and the Cross*, 42). Similarly, Mary Gosselink De Jong maintains that Romola's education "does enable her to question authority, to see through specious arguments" ("*Romola*—A *Bildungsroman* for Feminists?" 81).

26. Eliot, *Romola*, 18. Subsequent page references to this text will be given in parentheses.

27. See Karen Mann on the relationship between the intangible voice and the visible light in Eliot's representation of Savonarola as a pastor (*Language That Makes George Eliot's Fiction*, 77–83).

28. This is a curiously similar dynamic to that explored in the most recent collection of *Romola* criticism, *From Author to Text*, edited by Levine and Turner. In their introduction, the editors explicitly advocate "theoretical pluralism," which they describe as the use of distinct but overlapping and sometimes contradictory theoretical approaches to a single text. In their words, "Arguing for the simultaneity of critical arguments is not to suggest that all readings of a text are equally valid, for such an approach leads ultimately to an uncritical relativism. Rather, it is through attention to intersections and departures across critical approaches that political readings become dialectical, dynamic and generative rather than fixed and programmatic" (7). Further, "if the essays collected here convince the reader of the legitimacy and compatibility of these variations, fixing 'authority' authoritatively emerges as impossible. [In the critical readings assembled here], authority turns out to be not univocal, rigid and complete, but rather multiple and productive" (8).

29. Nestor, "Leaving Home," 336, 337, 338.

30. According to Alison Booth, the narrator enacts this very awareness of contingency, though in the historical rather than moral mode: "Eliot's narrator . . . does not insist on his own absolute authority. Indeed, he emphasizes changing perspectives and selective evidence, conceding the interpretive accidents of historiography without questioning the reality of a 'universal history' to which all historians refer" (*Greatness Engendered*, 179).

31. See Lesley Gordon, "Greek Scholarship," on the Florentine fascination with Greek scholarship.

32. Goodlad, *Victorian Literature*, 21.

33. Eliot, *George Eliot Letters*, 4:97.

34. Eliot is in fact slightly mistaken. Savonarola entered the monastery on April 24, 1475, a few months before his twenty-third birthday on September 21. See Pasquale Villari, *Life and Times of Girolamo Savonarola*, 16–17. Perhaps Eliot was thinking of his age when his novitiate ended and he took his Dominican vows, or perhaps she had an artistic reason for this unusual inaccuracy (see 117, below).

35. See Beryl Gray, "Power and Persuasion," for an analysis of the rhetoric of this sermon and its effect on its hearers, including Romola and

Baldassarre. See also Christine Krueger, *Reader's Repentance*, on Eliot's use of the inheritance of women's sermonic discourse. Krueger argues that Eliot makes Romola a "preaching icon," or nondiscursive evangelist, in order to "construct a model of female evangelism that is meant to surpass the historical limitations of preaching" (265).

36. Ridolfi, *Life of Girolamo Savonarola*, 91, 114; and Villari, *Life and Times of Girolamo Savonarola*, 259–260.

37. Polizzotto, *Elect Nation*, 30.

38. Ibid., 32–36. This is notwithstanding the fact that at least some of the impetus behind the elimination of usury was anti-Semitic.

39. I do not intend to diminish Eliot's admiration of some of Savonarola's moral reforms by thus emphasizing his material charity. The two are, in fact, indistinguishable. The material relief of the poor and the reform of the well-to-do toward the practice of charity are two sides of the same project.

40. Barbara Hardy, in *Novels of George Eliot*, refers to Savonarola as "an ambivalent moral quantity, at one time reinforcing Romola's altruism, at another running parallel to Tito" (118). Recognition of Eliot's ambivalence toward Savonarola's influence over Florence and Romola is the only way to do justice to Eliot's complex treatment of the character. Mann argues that the "real effect he has had on Romola individually and on various Florentine citizens collectively" consoles the reader in the face of his devastating fall (*Language That Makes George Eliot's Fiction*, 82–83). Deirdre David pointedly disagrees, seeing Savonarola's influence over Romola as disciplinary and therefore negative (*Intellectual Women and Victorian Patriarchy*, 253, note 14). I maintain that Eliot is fully conscious of both beneficial and detrimental outcomes of Savonarola's activities, and that such ambivalence is fundamental to her representation of Savonarola and of the problem of mentoring this chapter examines.

41. William Myers, in *Teaching of George Eliot*, points out that, by involving himself in political affairs, Savonarola repeats the same papal practices against which he inveighed and eventually rebelled (62–63).

42. Adams, in *Our Lady of Victorian Feminism*, hints at a relationship between Romola's experience in the valley and Savonarola's experience in Florence, though she emphasizes rather the positive and distinctly feminist difference of Romola's "style of leadership" (175).

43. Booth, in *Greatness Engendered*, sees this textual moment as evidence that Romola has thoroughly "abandoned self-interest in a grand cause" (193). Conversely, but also mistakenly, Victor Neufeldt, in "Madonna and the Gypsy," regards it as evidence of Romola's incomplete renunciation, which he imagines that Eliot disapproved (45). On the contrary, I see it as evidence that Romola understands that self-interest cannot be annihilated, and that earnest attempts to do so can only result in either Dino's pathological condition or Savonarola's self-deception. Rather, after seeing the spectacular errors of both Dino and Savonarola, Romola comes to realize that self-interest and

altruism must be frankly acknowledged as implicated in each other, an understanding that Eliot approves.

44. David Carroll, in *Conflict of Interpretations*, points out that this exercise is analogous to the gospel hermeneutics of German Higher Criticism, in which Eliot participated as a translator (197). See also Nardo, *George Eliot's Dialogue with John Milton*, for a description of Romola's hermeneutic process (81).

45. See Carroll, "George Eliot Martyrologist," for a discussion of Eliot's representation of Savonarola's martyrdom as a response to other Victorian martyr fiction.

46. See John Patrick Donnelly's introduction to his Latin-English edition of Savonarola's prison meditations, especially pages 20–23.

47. As Krueger puts it somewhat differently, "Romola succeeds where Savonarola failed because she never assumes the prophetic voice, the voice asserting absolute authority over its audience and a unique rather than universal vision" (*Reader's Repentance*, 284).

48. Romola's final phrase lends support to my argument that total suppression of egoism is not called for, but rather a balance of egoism and altruism. See Dorothea Barrett, *Vocation and Desire*, esp. 83–84.

49. Mary Wilson Carpenter, *George Eliot and the Landscape of Time*, emphasizes the indeterminacy of Romola's and the novel's reading of Savonarola, who becomes for Carpenter "an example of the ambiguity of prophesy and the unreliability of prophets" (102).

50. A few noteworthy examples will suffice. According to Margaret Homans, *Bearing the Word*, the epilogue shows Romola's self-effacement of the feminine, her complicity in her exclusion from the world of history and scholarship (197). While I agree with Homans that most of the novel relates Romola's successive devotion to a male authority, I disagree that this submission persists unchanged at the book's end. David, *Intellectual Women and Victorian Patriarchy*, similarly indicts Eliot's "active, necessary compliance with the patriarchal culture" (179). In David's reading of the epilogue, what is salient is the devoted female worship of the male authority who "redirected her wish for 'instructed' independence into acceptance of benevolent subjugation" (*Intellectual Women and Victorian Patriarchy*, 195). Booth, in *Greatness Engendered*, grants Romola's moral superiority at the novel's end, but finds it a hollow pretence: "The futility of women's rebellion lends them an appearance of selfless obedience, of moral superiority, though like men they may desire preeminence" (194).

51. Adams, *Our Lady of Victorian Feminism*, 174, 180.

52. Bodenheimer, *Real Life of Mary Ann Evans*, 236–240.

53. Eliot, *George Eliot Letters*, 5:76.

54. Bodenheimer, *Real Life of Mary Ann Evans*, 243. See, for example, Eliot, *George Eliot Letters*, 6:121,157, 169, 322, 389; 9:188.

55. Eliot, *George Eliot Letters*, 6:71, emphasis in original.

56. Bodenheimer, *Real Life of Mary Ann Evans*, 240–241.

CHAPTER 5 "ONE FUNCTION IN PARTICULAR": SPECIALIZATION AND THE SERVICE ETHIC IN "JANET'S REPENTANCE" AND *DANIEL DERONDA*

1. Henry, *George Eliot and the British Empire*, esp. 109–127.
2. See especially Said, "Zionism from the Standpoint of Its Victims."
3. Henry, *George Eliot and the British Empire*, 114. Henry goes on to show that the imperialistic aspects of Zionism were by no means clear in 1876. Among those readings following Said's lead, Henry mentions Bruce Robbins, "Forum"; Susan Meyer, *Imperialism at Home*; and Deirdre David, *Fictions of Resolution*. Examples of readings of *Daniel Deronda* influenced by Said include Reina Lewis, *Gendering Orientalism*; Katherine Bailey Linehan, "Mixed Politics"; and Carolyn Lesjak, "Labours of a Modern Storyteller."
4. Henry, *George Eliot and the British Empire*, 121.
5. Duman, "Creation and Diffusion of a Professional Ideology." A brief but clear analysis of the service ethic of professions is available in Robert MacIver, "Professional Groups and Cultural Norms."
6. Qtd. in Collini, *Public Moralists*, 83. Collini further comments, "[I]t was because these assumptions were so widespread that his philosophy enjoyed the success it did" (83).
7. Eliot, *Romola*, 547, my emphasis.
8. Barrett, *Vocation and Desire*, 83–84. The tension Barrett describes had roots in Mary Anne Evans's adolescent Evangelical fervor, when she eschewed pleasure in order to devote herself to Bible study, introspection, and works of charity. For detailed analysis of Mary Anne Evans's early enthusiastic pursuit of self-denial and its connection to Evangelicalism, see Frederick R. Karl, *George Eliot*, 31–47; and Rosemarie Bodenheimer, *Real Life of Mary Ann Evans*, 57–84. See Helena Granlund, *Paradox of Self-Love*, for a review of previous critical studies examining the relationship of Eliot's ethics to those of Christianity. For insight into the connections between Eliot's moral philosophy and the idealistic altruism of Feuerbach and Comte, see the analysis provided in William Myers's introduction to *The Teaching of George Eliot*. But see also Peter Charles Hodgson, *Mystery Beneath the Real*, for a critique of Myers's and others' reductive treatments of Eliot's relationship to Feuerbach and Comte.
9. Jeanie Thomas, in *Reading* Middlemarch, calls this view "practically universal" (7). John Halperin, in *Egoism and Self-Discovery*, offers a typical reading of Eliot's ethics: "[T]he moral process in her novels is from egoism through despair to objectivity" (125). K. M. Newton, in *George Eliot: Romantic Humanist*, deals at length with the tension between egoism and sublimation in defense of his thesis that Eliot's Romanticism is of an organicist rather than egoistic strain. Newton

shows how Eliot's admirable characters or "positive egos" experience a struggle between self-gratification and social ideals, and they eventually succeed in sublimating their egos to those ideals. Granlund's *The Paradox of Self-Love* similarly explores Eliot's treatment of the essentially Christian paradox that "the choice of self [as the highest good] leads to the destruction of self, whereas the choice of non-self leads to the fulfillment of self" (2). While these critics accurately describe the prevalent pattern in Eliot's fiction, they miss the complex ways that Eliot questions the absolute good of self-denial in her most altruistic characters, Tryan and Deronda.

10. Barrett is one of these, as mentioned above. M. C. Henberg, "George Eliot's Moral Realism," identifies, but does not analyze, this problem in Eliot's ethical philosophy. Noting that "altruism has its natural limits," he cites Dinah Morris as exemplifying the "more subtle failing" of "excessive selflessness" (31–32). He theorizes "an acceptable egoism" that neither denigrates nor exalts the self and thereby makes true sympathy possible (31). A careful exploration of that phenomenon and how it might be represented, however, is not Henberg's purpose. Other critics have addressed Eliot's problematizing of sympathy, a concept related to but not coterminous with altruism as I use the term. Bodenheimer, in *Real Life of Mary Ann Evans*, argues that Eliot deconstructs sympathy, and with it the realist novel, in *Daniel Deronda* (259–265). Lisabeth During, in "Concept of Dread," explores the sense in which "sympathy acts as an incentive to egoism, rather than as its corrective" (77). Thomas, in *Reading Middlemarch*, provides a good reading of the "complexity, limitation, compromise" of sympathy in *Middlemarch* (9). The treatment of sympathy in Heather Armstrong, *Character and Ethical Development*, emphasizes Eliot's awareness of the potential misuse of sympathy as an instrument of power and appropriation. Leona Toker, "Vocation and Sympathy in *Daniel Deronda*," builds on these readings to find that in that novel "the danger of excessive sympathy to its donor is emphasized at least as strongly as its positive effects on its recipient" (569).

11. Menon, *Austin, Eliot, Charlotte Brontë and the Mentor-Lover*, 136.

12. For an interesting reading of this same problem in Anthony Trollope's fiction, see Ilana Blumberg, " 'Unnatural Self-Sacrifice.' "

13. Barrett Browning, *Aurora Leigh*, III:492–494.

14. Eliot, *Romola*, 547; and Eliot, *Daniel Deronda*, 337.

15. Moretti, *Way of the World*, 227.

16. See also Robbins's "Death and Vocation." His brief reading of *Daniel Deronda* in this article makes note of Deronda's specialization, which he refers to as the "exclusion" of the Alcharisi, of Gwendolen, and of Palestinians (44). Robbins adds, "With more space, I might certainly present Deronda as the anticipation of a certain professional hero" (45).

17. See Corfield, *Power and the Professions in Britain 1700–1850*, 200–201.

18. Eliot, "Janet's Repentance," 248–249. Subsequent page references to this text will be given in parentheses.

19. Collini, *Public Moralists*, 63.

20. Thomas Noble, in *George Eliot's* Scenes of Clerical Life, discusses the connection between Tryan's self-denial and Eliot's doctrine of fellow-feeling, but he misses the way in which the community's (and the reader's) suspicion of Tryan's motives works in the text to complicate the issue of Tryan's heroism. Katherine M. Sorenson, in "*Daniel Deronda* and George Eliot's Ministers," briefly addresses Tryan's self-denial in the context of the historical phenomenon of the Methodist ministers on which Tryan is patterned, but she too ignores the paradox of Tryan's self-destructiveness.

21. U. C. Knoepflmacher, in *George Eliot's Early Novels*, sees this dual rejection as a "mixture of satire and hagiography" (82). The novella is hagiographic insofar as it rejects the cyncism of Tryan's enemies and satirical insofar as it rejects the adulation of his friends. Elisabeth Jay, in *The Religion of the Heart*, notes that Eliot is trying to do two contradictory things with Tryan: on the one hand to "suggest that Evangelicalism was consistent with a good education and gentlemanly manners," and on the other to portray what Eliot called "the real drama of Evangelicalism" (229–230). The former aim requires an ideal hero, the latter a complexly flawed human character. Jay finds that the result is a "pasteboard character" (230). I maintain that the lack of realist psychology in the characterization of Tryan is not so much an artistic failure as an index of the complexity of Eliot's portrayal of the problems that inhere in professionalism's claims to disinterest.

22. See Geoffrey Galt Harpham, *Ascetic Imperative in Culture and Criticism*, esp. 45–46.

23. Carpenter, "Apocalypse of the Old Testament," 56.

24. Mintz, *George Eliot and the Novel of Vocation*, 20.

25. Ibid., 61.

26. Carroll, *Conflict of Interpretations*, 60.

27. See also Laura Fasick, *Professional Men and Domesticity in the Mid-Victorian Novel*, which argues that the sublimated sexuality of Tryan and Janet's relationship bespeaks Eliot's conception that men's professional success is tied to their domestic success.

28. These and other parallels are elaborated by Sorenson, "*Daniel Deronda* and George Eliot's Ministers." Sorenson's helpful analysis of Deronda as following the type of the Methodist minister identifies many similarities between the personalities and priorities of Deronda and Tryan as religious figures. My approach takes in both the continuity and discontinuity between them as professional figures. See also Oliver Lovesey, *Clerical Character in George Eliot's Fiction*.

29. See, for example, Newton, *George Eliot: Romantic Humanist*, 193–197; Amanda Anderson, "George Eliot," 47–52; Carroll,

Conflict of Interpretations, 287–294; and Tony Jackson, "George Eliot's 'New Evangel,' " 238–246. Jackson sees Mordecai as the force that saves Deronda from his amorphous excessive sympathy, or as the one who pulls Deronda into the "framework" of egoism in order to save him for realism (238). In helping Mordecai, however, Deronda is in much the same position he is in when helping Hans or even Gwendolen: there is no strong conflict with Mordecai that would force Deronda to choose between Mordecai and some other person or desire. Hence I maintain that the conflict Gwendolen occasions in Deronda, described below, is more definitive of his ego than is Mordecai's influence.

30. See, for example, Menon, *Austin, Eliot, Charlotte Brontë and the Mentor-Lover*: "[I]t is difficult to discover what Daniel learns from his experience with Gwendolen that is of any benefit in the life he is to lead" (172). Newton, in *George Eliot: Romantic Humanist*, grants that Gwendolen has a meaningful role in Deronda's education, but he attributes it to the limited observation that "in recognizing another's need for a larger aim in life and in his efforts to make this clear to her, Deronda discovers a deeper emotional awareness of his own similar need" (197). Without disputing this basic claim, I contend that Gwendolen's role is more complicated than Newton allows. Bodenheimer, in *Real Life of Mary Ann Evans*, does give attention to the education Gwendolen gives Deronda: in Bodenheimer's reading, Deronda learns the personal and painful cost of being a mentor, something that Eliot also learned in the 1870s.

31. Eliot, *Daniel Deronda*, 163, my emphasis. Subsequent references to this text will be given in parentheses.

32. Newton, *George Eliot: Romantic Humanist*, 189–190. This difficulty is widely acknowledged and variously explained. For Newton, the problem is that Eliot is less interested in exploring Deronda's psychological problem than in solving it. Carroll, *Conflict of Interpretations*, sees Deronda as more a "hypothesis" than a self, in that "Deronda is seeking to be born into the world without the originary facts upon which to base a world-view" (285–286). For Moretti, *Way of the World*, the problem is that Deronda is not a man at all but a "functionary of abstract beliefs" (227). Anderson, in *Powers of Distance*, sees Deronda's predicament as an "allegory" about "the instabilities of modern cosmopolitan life," instabilities resulting from the tension between excessive and insufficient partiality (121). Another explanation is available in the theory of narratology put forward by Harpham in *Ascetic Imperative in Culture and Criticism*. Arguing that hagiography is the paradigmatic form of narrative, Harpham finds that the internal struggle of the hero against temptation, or between desire and denial, is the basis of narrative. Deronda does not experience such a struggle, and therefore cannot be a fully realized character, until Gwendolen's own internal battle

with temptation, discussed below, becomes the occasion for a similar struggle in him.

33. Jackson, "George Eliot's 'New Evangel,' " 236. For Jackson, the consequence of this image is the self-destruction of realism, for egolessness is incompatible with the "nature of the self that her writing has all along presumed" (231).

34. The phrase is from Susan Ostrov Weisser, "Gwendolen's Hidden Wound," 6. David Marshall, in *The Figure of Theatre*, similarly finds that Deronda "seems ready to take another for a larger self, enclosing his self in another" (224).

35. Toker, "Vocation and Sympathy in *Daniel Deronda*," 573, note 6.

36. Granlund, in *Paradox of Self-Love*, sees this narratorial background as evidence for Deronda's being a pure "higher egoist," a position of unqualified good (114). My position is that Eliot is using Deronda to explore how the good of self-disregard becomes qualified at its extremes and to probe the double paradox: not only that selflessness leads paradoxically to self-fulfillment, but also that unmitigated selflessness leads to self-destruction.

37. J. Beer, *Providence and Love*, 204.

38. See Felicia Bonaparte, "*Daniel Deronda*," for a discussion of the interaction of materiality and ideality in the novel.

39. Robbins, *Feeling Global*, 4.

40. The paradoxical nature of Deronda's curiously dispassionate suffering may explain why, as Louise Penner observes, "Daniel's psychic distress before the revelation of his parentage has gone relatively unnoticed in the novel's criticism" (" 'Unmapped Country,' " 89). I contend that the sign of that psychic distress is the frustration of his vocational ambition by his inability to specialize.

41. Cohen, *Professional Domesticity in the Victorian Novel*, 131.

42. See Anderson, *Powers of Distance*, for a discussion of Deronda's "cultivated partiality" (121–124). Anderson reads Deronda as an exemplar of a species of Judaism that engages in dialogic and reflective encounter with multiple traditions; this is precisely the opposite of the legalistic and monologic tradition that oppressed Leonora.

43. Cohen, in *Professional Domesticity in the Victorian Novel*, elaborates how domestic plotlines, which often seem to be in competition with vocational plotlines for the ultimate loyalty of the hero, are better understood as allies of vocational fulfillment. My analysis similarly finds that Deronda's desire for Mirah, far from distracting him from his vocation, actually helps him achieve the specialization required to achieve his vocation.

44. Henry, in *George Eliot and the British Empire*, is right to point out that "Deronda's idea of helping the Jews who were already living in various Eastern countries is vague, and as much philanthropic as nationalistic" (117).

45. However advantageous this "iron will" may be for the furthering of social and political objectives, it takes a severe toll on dissident females, as the Alcharisi's reminiscences of Charisi make clear. She too uses the phrase "iron will" to describe him (589). Deronda's difference from his grandfather is therefore a positive value from the standpoint of how he is likely to treat his wife and daughters.

46. See Carole Stone, "George Eliot's *Daniel Deronda*," for a reading of the novel as a Freudian case history of Gwendolen's hysterical symptoms with Deronda in the therapist role.

47. Cognard-Black, *Narrative in the Professional Age*, 100–101.

48. Ibid., 101. Cognard-Black goes on to show that the aesthetic economy ironically depends upon the reception of the commercial economy for its existence. Gwendolen turns out to be the ideal reader, the market that receives the socially beneficial interventions of the aesthetic professional, and without which the aesthetic professional could not exist. So ultimately "George Eliot's own treatment of Gwendolen Harleth . . . reveals *Deronda*'s reliance on the very systems the book discredits, namely advertising, consumer culture, and the false professionalization of nineteenth-century authorship" (116).

49. Ibid., 107. See also the discussion in David, *Fictions of Resolution*, of Klesmer's theory of creative genius, a theory David finds contradictory (188–189).

50. Menon, in *Austin, Eliot, Charlotte Brontë and the Mentor-Lover*, rightly observes that Gwendolen's problems are opaque to Deronda (173, 176). They do not remain so, however, as I will show. I therefore disagree with her conclusion that Deronda is culpably impotent as a mentor. Deronda's advice is basically sound (granting Eliot's terms); Gwendolen's inability to apply it, because of her psychic dividedness, can hardly be blamed on Deronda. Analogous to the Jewish law in St. Paul's description (Romans 3), Deronda makes Gwendolen aware of her moral shortcomings, but his function is not to remove them. Significantly, St. Paul's word for the function of the law is "tutor" or mentor (Galatians 3:24–25). Deronda is a "priest" (401), not a savior (but see Saleel Nurbhai and K. M. Newton's contention that Deronda is a messianic figure [*George Eliot, Judaism and the Novels*, 171–180]). Menon's outrage at Deronda's abandonment of Gwendolen is similarly misplaced. The "enforced autonomy" Gwendolen is given is surely preferable to Savonarola's ongoing denial of autonomy to Romola; in fact, this forced curtailment of Gwendolen's desired submission ought to mitigate the distaste with which Menon regards Gwendolen's "progress" toward childlike submission (175).

51. The explicitly hagiographic description of this conflict again suggests the applicability of Harpham's narratology of ascesis. Gwendolen's struggle between desire and denial is needed to involve Deronda in

such a struggle in order that he can become intelligible as a narrative character.

52. The fact that Deronda's discovery of his Jewishness accompanies the development of self-interest would seem to chime with Marx's equation of Judaism with "huckstering," that is, capitalistic self-interest, and with European anti-Semitic stereotypes generally. See Marx, "On the Jewish Question," 48. This fact may form part of the narrative logic that leads Meyer to assert that the novel is fundamentally anti-Semitic, a conclusion she bases in part on the rapacity exhibited by the "vulgar" Jewish characters ("Safely to Their Own Borders," 745). However, it is worth noting that Sir Hugo, in his own way, is as prone as Ezra Cohen to determine all difficult questions in terms of his own monetary interest. "I find the rule of the pocket the best guide," Sir Hugo says (388). Deronda's nascent self-interest is actually in opposition to a market rationality that prevails in English drawing rooms as much as in Jewish pawnshops (see David, *Fictions of Resolution*, 162–163). This point is made clearer when we reflect that even the implied contrast between Daniel, the schoolboy who refuses to "swop for his own advantage," and Jacob Cohen, who aggressively negotiates a "shwop" of knives with Deronda, attributes nothing worse to Jacob than that degree of self-interest that is considered normative by Eton schoolboys and their masters as well.

53. Collini, *Public Moralists*, 79–80, 85.

54. See Kathleen Blake, *Love and the Woman Question in Victorian Literature*, for a discussion of the tension between love and art in character of the Alcharisi.

55. Nardo, *George Eliot's Dialogue with John Milton*, 232–234.

56. Menon, *Austin, Eliot, Charlotte Bronte and the Mentor-Lover*, 175.

57. See Linda Babcock and Sara Laschever, *Women Don't Ask*.

CHAPTER 6   "A KIND OF MANAGER NOT HITHERTO EXISTING": OCTAVIA HILL AND THE PROFESSIONAL PHILANTHROPIST

1. See, for example, Anthony S. Wohl's chapter on Hill, titled "Benevolent Despotism," in *The Eternal Slum*. See Marion Brion, *Women in the Housing Service*, for a summary of reactions to Hill prior to 1995. Brion argues that partisan politics and misogyny are at the root of much of the often acerbic and emotive criticism of Hill (14–22). Jane Lewis's chapter on Hill in *Women and Social Action* provides a balanced account of the views that make Hill unpopular today and the mitigating effect of her genuine and energetic concern for individuals in need. Since then, notable studies have included Diana Maltz, "Beauty at Home or Not?"; and George K. Behlmer,

"Character Building," which includes an account of the relationship between COS paradigms and social casework.

2. An early example is found in the conservative *British Social Work in the Nineteenth Century* by A. F. Young and E. T. Ashton. More recent examples include Robert Whelan, *Octavia Hill and the Social Housing Debate*; James L. Payne, *Befriending Leader*; and George W. Liebmann, *Six Lost Leaders*. It is to such as these that we owe the only modern reprints of Hill's work; unfortunately the small collections of Hill's essays edited by Whelan and Payne emphasize the political agendas of their editors in such a way as to obscure much of Hill's complexity. In this chapter and in the bibliography, these editions of Hill's essays are referred to by the editors' names, in that the titles and contents of the collections are very much reflective of the editors' priorities. For similar reasons, and in keeping with convention, Hill's letters are cited by the names of their editors. The first collection of her letters was edited by her brother-in-law Charles Edmund Maurice, and the second by Hill's sister and C. E. Maurice's wife, Emily Southwood Maurice.

3. Goodlad, "Character and Pastorship," 243–246.

4. In addition to Prochaska and Summers, see Roy Lubove, *Professional Altruist*, on professionalized social work in the United States, and Young and Ashton, *British Social Work in the Nineteenth Century*, on its development in Britain.

5. I will include a few references to Hill's later public and private writing as well, a decision justified by the fact that her opinions remained largely consistent throughout her life. In fact, when her later writings are read in the light of her earlier work they seem far more intelligible. Though she lived well into the Edwardian period, she continued to think along the lines normative in her mid-Victorian youth.

6. Elliott, *Angel out of the House*, esp. 127–130.

7. Whipple, "Dickens's *Hard Times*," 353.

8. Hill, *Our Common Land*, 64.

9. A. Marshall, *Memorials of Alfred Marshall*, 174. See my discussion on 1–2.

10. See, for example, Hill, *Our Common Land*, 54–56, 59, and 61–62.

11. Smiles, *Self-Help*, 19.

12. Hill, *Homes of the London Poor*, 23.

13. Hill, *Our Common Land*, 43.

14. Ibid., 53, my emphasis. See Behlmer, "Character Building," on the centrality of character to the COS.

15. Hill, *Homes of the London Poor*, 54–55.

16. Whelan, *Octavia Hill and the Social Housing Debate*, 82.

17. Hill, *Homes of the London Poor*, 67.

18. Like the Peabody Trust and the Society for Improving the Condition of the Labouring Classes, Hill targeted five percent as the appropriate return on the owners' investment in a house. Unscrupulous slum

landlords could profit by as much as twelve to fifteen percent. See John Nelson Tarn, *Five Per Cent Philanthropy*, 34–35.

19. E. S. Maurice, *Octavia Hill: Early Ideals*, 218.
20. Goodlad, in "Character and Pastorship," shows that the COS's critique of the Fabians in the late nineteenth century centered on the state's purported "incapab[ility] either of understanding or relating to the family and the personal questions of character that sustain it" (244).
21. The essays and letters included in Whelan's volume *Octavia Hill and the Social Housing Debate* emphasize these themes. See esp. 94–113.
22. Whelan, *Octavia Hill and the Social Housing Debate*, 109.
23. Hill, "Trained Workers for the Poor," 368.
24. Hill, *Homes of the London Poor*, 56.
25. Hill, *Our Common Land*, 27–28.
26. Ibid., 33.
27. See Hill, "Trained Workers for the Poor," 372; and Hill, *Homes of the London Poor*, 59.
28. Hill, *Our Common Land*, 41.
29. C. E. Maurice, *Life of Octavia Hill*, 137.
30. E. Maurice, *Octavia Hill: Early Ideals*, 121.
31. C. E. Maurice, *Life of Octavia Hill*, 39.
32. Ibid., 104.
33. Ibid., 154.
34. E. S. Maurice, *Octavia Hill: Early Ideals*, 43.
35. Qtd. in Bell, *Octavia Hill: A Biography*, 122.
36. Hill, *Homes of the London Poor*, 37.
37. Ibid., 21
38. Ibid., 27.
39. Seth Koven, *Slumming*, describes a similar phenomenon in the Oxford House Settlement. The settlers espoused democratic governance of institutions by their working-class members, yet continued to exert effective control of the men's club, sometimes against the will of the local working men (see especially 276–281).
40. Whelan, *Octavia Hill and the Social Housing Debate*, 119.
41. Hill, *Homes of the London Poor*, 42.
42. Darley, *Octavia Hill*, 150.
43. Qtd. in Ibid., 149.
44. Qtd. in Boyd, *Josephine Butler, Octavia Hill, Florence Nightingale*, 134.
45. C. E. Maurice, *Life of Octavia Hill*, 295.
46. Darley, *Octavia Hill*, 320.
47. Payne, *Befriending Leader*, 87.
48. E. S. Maurice, *Octavia Hill: Early Ideals*, 103.
49. Qtd. in Darley, *Octavia Hill*, 146. In another context, Hill wrote, "But visitors would be incomparably more useful if they would train themselves to undertake the management of houses . . . . It may be

more difficult work: it will be much more thorough." Whelan, *Octavia Hill and the Social Housing Debate*, 103.

50. Qtd. in Darley, *Octavia Hill*, 277.
51. Behlmer, *Friends of the Family*, 41.
52. Ibid., 40.
53. Koven, *Slumming*, 194.
54. Hill, *Homes of the London Poor*, 34.
55. Webb, *My Apprenticeship*, 252.
56. Qtd. in Darley, *Octavia Hill*, 143.
57. Hill, *Homes of the London Poor*, 52.
58. Hill, *Our Common Land*, 48.
59. C. E. Maurice, *Life of Octavia Hill*, 246.
60. Hill, *Our Common Land*, 88–89.
61. Darley, *Octavia Hill*, 34.
62. C. E. Maurice, *Life of Octavia Hill*, 69.
63. Ibid., 310.
64. E. S. Maurice, *Octavia Hill: Early Ideals*, 105–106.
65. Darley, *Octavia Hill*, 320.
66. Whelan, *Octavia Hill and the Social Housing Debate*, 84. At times the offers of money to purchase houses outstripped the supply of prepared workers to manage the houses, in which case Hill declined the money until she had a suitable manager available. Ibid., 125, 150, 277.
67. Darley, *Octavia Hill*, 276.
68. Hill, *Homes of the London Poor*, 65.
69. Searle, *Morality and the Market*, 188.
70. See Hill, *Our Common Land*, 6.
71. Hill, "Trained Workers for the Poor," 368.
72. Ibid., 370–371.
73. Qtd. in Darley, *Octavia Hill*, 276, my emphasis.
74. This program became the School of Sociology in 1903 and then in 1912 joined with the London School of Economics to form the Department of Social Science and Administration. See Kathleen Woodroofe, *From Charity to Social Work*, 54.
75. Hill, "Trained Workers for the Poor," 374.
76. Within a generation or so, these publicly employed women managers had given way to male employees. See Brion, *Women in the Housing Service*, on the fate of women housing managers in the decades following Hill's death.
77. E. S. Maurice, *Octavia Hill: Early Ideals*, 93.
78. I borrow this phrase from Stefan Collini, *Public Moralists*.
79. Whelan, *Octavia Hill and the Social Housing Debate*, 86.
80. Hill, *Homes of the London Poor*, 67.
81. E. S. Maurice, *Octavia Hill: Early Ideals*, 123–24.
82. Ibid., 156.
83. Ibid., 169, emphasis in original.
84. Ibid., 95–96.

85. Ibid., 215.
86. Hill, *Homes of the London Poor*, 66.
87. Boyd, *Josephine Butler, Octavia Hill, Florence Nightingale*, 102.
88. E. S. Maurice, *Octavia Hill: Early Ideals*, 163. It is typical of Ruskin's attitude toward his protégé in the later years of her employment with him that he would urge her to follow her instincts for social work and continue to receive a salary from him. He seems to have realized well before she did that she was better suited for (and more interested in) social work, and he apparently regarded it as his responsibility to nourish and enable her talent with people just as he initially planned to do her artistic talent. The enigmatic speech she reports on this occasion, that the salary was intended "to enable her partly to do, and partly not to do, the work," is comprehensible in light of Hill's belief that the best workers among the poor were those with other responsibilities and interests (163). Ruskin may have meant that the regular supply of money would enable her to do the work among the poor, and also that a sense of obligation to do some painting for him would keep her from being wholly engrossed in that work.
89. Ibid., 163.
90. See, for example, Hill, *Homes of the London Poor*, 20. Carlyle's critique is most famously expressed in *Past and Present*; Ruskin's in *Unto This Last*.
91. Hill, "Trained Workers for the Poor," 374.
92. Ibid.
93. Qtd. in Darley, *Octavia Hill*, 277.
94. Hill, "Trained Workers for the Poor," 372.
95. Hill, *Our Common Land*, 27.

EPILOGUE

1. H. Perkin, *Third Revolution*, 187.
2. Brooks, *On Paradise Drive*, 179.
3. Freedman, *Professions of Taste*, 57.
4. H. Perkin, *Third Revolution*, 200.
5. Robbins, "Village of the Liberal Managerial Class."

BIBLIOGRAPHY

Adams, Kimberly VanEsveld. *Our Lady of Victorian Feminism: The Madonna in the Work of Anna Jameson, Margaret Fuller, and George Eliot*. Athens, OH: Ohio University Press, 2001.

Anderson, Amanda. "George Eliot and the Jewish Question." *Yale Journal of Criticism* 10 (1997): 39–61.

———. *The Powers of Distance: Cosmopolitanism and the Cultivation of Detachment*. Princeton: Princeton University Press, 2001.

———. "The Temptations of Aggrandized Agency: Feminist Histories and the Horizon of Modernity." *Victorian Studies* 43.1 (2000): 43–63.

———. "Victorian Studies and the Two Modernities." *Victorian Studies* 47.2 (Winter 2005): 195–203.

apRoberts, Ruth. *The Moral Trollope*. Athens, OH: Ohio University Press, 1971.

Armstrong, Heather. *Character and Ethical Development in Three Novels of George Eliot: Middlemarch, Romola, Daniel Deronda*. Studies in British Literature, vol. 61. Lewiston, NY: Edwin Mellen Press, 2001.

Armstrong, Nancy. *Desire and Domestic Fiction: A Political History of the Novel*. Oxford: Oxford University Press, 1987.

Babcock, Linda, and Sara Laschever. *Women Don't Ask: Negotiation and the Gender Divide*. Princeton: Princeton University Press, 2003.

Bagilhole, Barbara. *Women, Work, and Equal Opportunity: Underachievement in the Civil Service*. Brookfield, VT: Ashgate, 1994.

Baker, Joseph Ellis. *The Novel and the Oxford Movement*. Princeton Studies in English No. 8. Princeton: Princeton University Press, 1932.

Barrett, Dorothea. *Vocation and Desire: George Eliot's Heroines*. London: Routledge, 1989.

Barrett Browning, Elizabeth. *Aurora Leigh*. 1856. Ed. Margaret Reynolds. Athens, OH: Ohio University Press, 1992.

Basch, Françoise. *Relative Creatures: Victorian Women in Society and the Novel*. New York: Schocken Books, 1974.

Bashford, Alison. *Purity and Pollution: Gender, Embodiment, and Victorian Medicine*. New York: Palgrave Macmillan, 1998.

Beer, John. *Providence and Love: Studies in Wordsworth, Channing, Myers, George Eliot, and Ruskin*. Oxford: Oxford University Press, 1998.

Beer, Patricia. *Reader, I Married Him: A Study of the Women Characters of Jane Austen, Charlotte Brontë, Elizabeth Gaskell and George Eliot*. London: Macmillan Press, 1974.

Behlmer, George K. "Character Building and the English Family: Continuities in Social Casework, ca. 1870–1930." In *Singular Continuities: Tradition, Nostalgia, and Identity in Modern British Culture*, ed. George K. Behlmer and Fred M. Leventhal, 58–74. Stanford: Stanford University Press, 2000.

———. *Friends of the Family: The English Home and Its Guardians*. Stanford: Stanford University Press, 1998.

Bell, E. Moberly. *Octavia Hill: A Biography*. London: Constable & Co., 1942.

Bennett, Joan. *George Eliot: Her Life and Her Art*. Cambridge: Cambridge University Press, 1954.

Bendiner, Kenneth. *The Art of Ford Madox Brown*. University Park, PA: Pennsylvania State University Press, 1998.

Bernardo, Susan. "From Romola to *Romola*: The Complex Act of Naming." In *From Author to Text: Re-reading George Eliot's Romola*, ed. Caroline Levine and Mark W. Turner, 89–102. Aldershot: Ashgate, 1998.

Billington, Josie. "Watching a Writer Write: Manuscript Revisions in Mrs. Gaskell's *Wives and Daughters* and Why They Matter." In *Real Voices on Reading*, ed. Philip Davis, 224–235. New York: St. Martin's, 1997.

Bivona, Daniel. "Disraeli's Political Trilogy and the Antinomic Structure of Imperial Desire." *Novel* 22 (1989): 305–325.

Blake, Catriona. *The Charge of the Parasols: Women's Entry to the Medical Profession in Britain*. London: Women's Press, 1990.

Blake, Kathleen. *Love and the Woman Question in Victorian Literature: The Art of Self-Postponement*. Sussex: Harvester Press, 1983.

Blake, Robert. *Disraeli*. New York: St. Martin's, 1967.

Bledstein, Burton J. *The Culture of Professionalism: The Middle Class and the Development of Higher Education in America*. New York: W. W. Norton, 1976.

Blumberg, Ilana. " 'Unnatural Self-Sacrifice': Trollope and the Ethic of Mutual Benefit." *Nineteenth-Century Literature* 58.4 (2004): 506–546.

Bodenheimer, Rosemarie. *The Politics of Story in Victorian Social Fiction*. Ithaca, NY: Cornell University Press, 1988.

———. *The Real Life of Mary Ann Evans: George Eliot, Her Letters and Fiction*. Ithaca, NY: Cornell University Press, 1994.

Bonaparte, Felicia. "*Daniel Deronda*: Theology in a Secular Age." *Religion and Literature* 25 (1993): 17–44.

———. *The Gypsy-Bachelor of Manchester: The Life of Mrs. Gaskell's Demon*. Charlottesville: University Press of Virginia, 1992.

———. *The Triptych and the Cross: The Central Myths of George Eliot's Poetic Imagination*. New York: New York University Press, 1979.

Booth, Alison. *Greatness Engendered: George Eliot and Virginia Woolf*. Ithaca, NY: Cornell University Press, 1992.

Bowen, Desmond. *The Idea of the Victorian Church: A Study of the Church of England 1833–1889*. Montreal: McGill University Press, 1968.

Boyd, Nancy. *Josephine Butler, Octavia Hill, Florence Nightingale: Three Victorian Women Who Changed Their World*. London: Macmillan Press, 1982.

Brantlinger, Patrick. "Disraeli and Orientalism." In *The Self-Fashioning of Disraeli, 1818–1851*, ed. Charles Richmond and Paul Smith, 90–105. Cambridge: Cambridge University Press, 1998.

———. "Nations and Novels: Disraeli, George Eliot, and Orientalism." *Victorian Studies* 35 (Spring 1992): 255–275.

———. *Rule of Darkness: British Literature and Imperialism*, 1830–1914. Ithaca, NY: Cornell University Press, 1988.

———. *The Spirit of Reform: British Literature and Politics, 1832–1867*. Cambridge, MA: Harvard University Press, 1977.

———. "Tory Radicalism and 'The Two Nations' in Disraeli's *Sybil*." *Victorian Newsletter* 41 (1972): 13–17.

Braun, Thom. *Disraeli the Novelist*. London: George Allen & Unwin, 1981.

Brion, Marion. *Women in the Housing Service*. London: Routledge, 1995.

Brooks, David. *Bobos in Paradise: The New Upper Class and How They Got There*. New York: Simon & Schuster, 2000.

———. *On Paradise Drive: How We Live Now (And Always Have) in the Future Tense*. New York: Simon & Schuster, 2004.

Brose, Olive. *Church and Parliament: The Reshaping of the Church of England 1828–1860*. Stanford: Stanford University Press, 1959.

Butterworth, Robert. "The Professional Adrift in the Victorian Novel (1): *Agnes Grey*." *Victorian Newsletter* 104 (Fall 2003): 13–17.

Caine, Barbara. *Victorian Feminists*. Oxford: Oxford University Press, 1992.

Carlyle, Thomas. *Past and Present*. 1843. Ed. Richard Altick. New York: New York University Press, 1977.

Carpenter, Mary Wilson. "The Apocalypse of the Old Testament: *Daniel Deronda* and the Interpretation of Interpretation." *PMLA* 99.1 (1984): 56–71.

———. *George Eliot and the Landscape of Time: Narrative Form and Protestant Apocalyptic History*. Chapel Hill: University of North Carolina Press, 1986.

Carroll, David. *George Eliot and the Conflict of Interpretations: A Reading of the Novels*. Cambridge: University Press of Cambridge, 1992.

———. "George Eliot Martyrologist: The Case of Savonarola." In *From Author to Text: Re-reading George Eliot's Romola*, ed. Caroline Levine and Mark W. Turner, 105–121. Aldershot: Ashgate, 1998.

Chadwick, Owen. *The Victorian Church: Part One*. New York: Oxford University Press, 1966.

Chandler, Alice. *A Dream of Order: The Medieval Ideal in Nineteenth-Century English Literature*. Lincoln: University of Nebraska Press, 1970.

"The Church as a Profession." *Cornhill Magazine* 9 (June 1864): 750–760.

Cognard-Black, Jennifer. *Narrative in the Professional Age: Transatlantic Readings of Harriet Beecher Stowe, George Eliot, and Elizabeth Stuart Phelps*. New York: Routledge, 2004.

Cohen, Monica. *Professional Domesticity in the Victorian Novel: Women, Work, and Home*. Cambridge: Cambridge University Press, 1998.

Collini, Stefan. *Public Moralists: Political Thought and Intellectual Life in Britain 1850–1930*. Oxford: Clarendon, 1991.

Cook, Ruth McDowell. "Women's Work as Paradigm for Autonomy in Gaskell's *My Lady Ludlow*." *Gaskell Society Journal* 11 (1997): 68–76.

Corcos, Christine Alice. "Portia Goes to Parliament: Women and Their Admission to Membership in the English Legal Profession." *Denver University Law Review* 75.2 (1998): 307–417.

Corfield, Penelope J. *Power and the Professions in Britain 1700–1850*. London: Routledge, 1995.

Cross, John W. *George Eliot's Life as Related in Her Letters and Journals*. 3 vols. New York: Harper & Brothers, 1885.

Dames, Nicholas. "Trollope and the Career: Vocational Trajectories and the Management of Ambition." *Victorian Studies* 45 (2003): 247–278.

Darley, Gillian. *Octavia Hill*. London: Constable & Co., 1990.

David, Deirdre. *Fictions of Resolution in Three Victorian Novels: North and South, Our Mutual Friend, Daniel Deronda*. New York: Columbia University Press, 1981.

———. *Intellectual Women and Victorian Patriarchy: Harriet Martineau, Elizabeth Barrett Browning, George Eliot*. Ithaca, NY: Cornell University Press, 1987.

Davidoff, Leonore, and Caroline Hall. *Family Fortunes: Men and Women of the English Middle Class, 1780–1850*. Chicago: University of Chicago Press, 1987.

Deffenbacher, Kristina. "Designing Progress: The Architecture of Social Consciousness in Disraeli's 'Young England' Novels." *Victorian Review* 24 (1998): 95–104.

De Jong, Mary Gosselink. "*Romola*—A *Bildungsroman* for Feminists?" *South Atlantic Review* 49 (1984): 75–90.

Dicey, Alfred V. "Legal Etiquette." *Fortnightly Review*, 1867 n.s. 2: 177–180.

Dickens, Charles. *Bleak House*. 1852. Ed. Norman Page. Harmondsworth: Penguin, 1985.

———. *A Charles Dickens Christmas: A Christmas Carol; The Chimes; The Cricket on the Hearth*. New York: Oxford University Press, 1976.

Disraeli, Benjamin. *Coningsby, or the New Generation*. 1844. Ed. Sheila M. Smith. The World's Classics. Oxford: Oxford University Press, 1982.

———. *Sybil, or The Two Nations*. 1845. Ed. Sheila M. Smith. Oxford World's Classics. Oxford: Oxford University Press, 1998.

———. *Tancred, or the New Crusade*. 1847. London: Longmans, 1907.

———. *Vindication of the English Constitution in a Letter to a Noble and Learned Lord*. London: Saunders and Otley, 1835. Republished by Gregg International Publishers Limited, Westmead, 1869.

Donnelly, John Patrick, S.J., ed. and trans. Introduction to *Prison Meditations on Psalms 51 and 31*, by Girolamo Savonarola, O. P. Milwaukee: Marquette University Press, 1994, 11–23.

Drummond, Andrew. *The Churches in English Fiction*. Leicester: Edgar Backus, 1950.

Drysdale, C. R. "Medicine as a Profession for Women." London: Edward J. Francis, 1870.

Duman, Daniel. "The Creation and Diffusion of a Professional Ideology in Nineteenth Century England." *Sociological Review* 27 (1979): 113–138.

Durey, Jill Felicity. *Trollope and the Church of England.* New York: Palgrave Macmillan, 2003.

During, Lisabeth. "The Concept of Dread: Sympathy and Ethics in *Daniel Deronda.*" In *Renegotiating Ethics in Literature, Philosophy, and Theory,* ed. Jane Adamson, Richard Freadman, and David Parker, 65–83. Cambridge: Cambridge University Press, 1998.

Easley, Alexis. *First-Person Anonymous: Women Writers and Victorian Print Media, 1830–1870.* Aldershot: Ashgate, 2004.

Easson, Angus. *Elizabeth Gaskell.* London: Routledge, 1979.

Ehrenreich, Barbara. "The Professional-Managerial Class Revisited." In *Intellectuals: Aesthetics, Politics, Academics,* ed. Bruce Robbins, 173–185. Minneapolis: University of Minnesota Press, 1990.

Ehrenreich, Barbara, and John Ehrenreich. "The Professional-Managerial Class." In *Between Labor and Capital,* ed. Pat Walker, 5–45. Boston: South End Press, 1979.

Eliot, George. "Authorship." *Essays and Leaves from a Notebook.* 2nd ed. Edinburgh: Blackwood & Sons, 1884, 353–362.

———. *Daniel Deronda.* 1876. Ed. Graham Handley. Oxford: Clarendon, 1984.

———. *The George Eliot Letters.* Ed. Gordon S. Haight. 9 vols. New Haven: Yale University Press, 1954–1978.

———. "Janet's Repentance." *Scenes of Clerical Life.* 1857. Ed. Thomas Noble. Oxford: Clarendon, 1985.

———. *Middlemarch.* 1872. Ed. David Carroll. Oxford: Clarendon, 1986.

———. *Romola.* 1863. Ed. Andrew Brown. Oxford: Oxford University Press, 1994.

Elliott, Dorice Williams. *Angel out of the House: Philanthropy and Gender in Nineteenth-Century England.* Charlottesville: University Press of Virginia, 2002.

Endelman, Todd M. " 'A Hebrew to the End': The Emergence of Disraeli's Jewishness." In *The Self-Fashioning of Disraeli, 1818–1851,* ed. Charles Richmond and Paul Smith, 106–130. Cambridge: Cambridge University Press, 1998.

Flavin, Michael. *Benjamin Disraeli: The Novel as Political Discourse.* Portland, OR: Sussex Academic Press, 2005.

Fasick, Laura. *Professional Men and Domesticity in the Mid-Victorian Novel.* Studies in British Literature, vol. 73. Lewiston, NY: Edwin Mellon Press, 2003.

Foster, Shirley. *Elizabeth Gaskell: A Literary Life.* New York: Palgrave Macmillan, 2002.

———. *Victorian Women's Fiction: Marriage, Freedom, and the Individual.* Totowa, NJ: Barnes & Noble Books, 1985.

Foucault, Michel. *Discipline and Punish: The Birth of the Prison.* Trans. Alan Sheridan. New York: Vintage, 1977.

Franz, Nellie Alden. *English Women Enter the Professions.* Cincinnati: Privately printed for the author, 1965.

Fraser, Hilary, Stephanie Green, and Judith Johnston. *Gender and the Victorian Periodical.* Cambridge: Cambridge University Press, 2003.

Freedman, Jonathan. *Professions of Taste: Henry James, British Aestheticism and Commodity Culture.* Stanford: Stanford University Press, 1990.

Freidson, Eliot. *The Profession of Medicine.* New York: Dodd, Mead, & Co., 1970.

Frietzsche, Arthur H. *Disraeli's Religion: The Treatment of Religion in Disraeli's Novels.* Monograph Series, vol. 9, no. 1. Logan: Utah State University Press, 1961.

Gallagher, Catherine. "George Eliot and *Daniel Deronda*: The Prostitute and the Jewish Question." In *Sex, Politics and Science in the Nineteenth-Century Novel,* ed. Ruth Bernard Yeazell, 39–62. Baltimore: Johns Hopkins University Press, 1986.

———. *The Industrial Reformation of English Fiction: Social Discourse and Narrative Form 1832–1867.* Chicago: University of Chicago Press, 1985.

Gaskell, Elizabeth. *Cousin Phillis and Other Tales.* 1864. Ed. Angus Easson. Oxford World's Classics. Oxford: Oxford University Press, 1982.

———. *Cranford.* 1853. Ed. Elizabeth Porges Watson. Oxford World's Classics. Oxford: Oxford University Press, 1998.

———. *Further Letters of Mrs. Gaskell.* Ed. John Chapple and Alan Shelston. Manchester: Manchester University Press, 2000.

———. *The Letters of Mrs. Gaskell.* Ed. J. A. V. Chapple and Arthur Pollard. Manchester: Manchester University Press, 1966.

———. *The Life of Charlotte Brontë.* 1857. Ed. Angus Easson. New York: Oxford University Press, 1996.

———. *North and South.* Ed. Angus Easson. Oxford World's Classics. Oxford: Oxford University Press, 1998.

———. *Round the Sofa.* 1859. Ed. and intro. Charlotte Mitchell. In *The Works of Elizabeth Gaskell,* vol. 3: Novellas and Shorter Fiction II. London: Pickering and Chatto, 2005.

———. *Ruth.* 1853. Ed. Angus Easson. London: Penguin, 1997.

Gérin, Winifred. *Elizabeth Gaskell: A Biography.* Clarendon: Oxford University Press, 1976.

Gill, Sean. *Women and the Church of England: From the Eighteenth Century to the Present.* London: Society for Promoting Christian Knowledge, 1994.

Glassman, Bernard. *Benjamin Disraeli: The Fabricated Jew in Myth and Memory. Studies in Judaism.* Lanham, MD: University Press of America, 2003.

Glendinning, Victoria. *Trollope.* London: Hutchinson, 1992.

Goodlad, Lauren M. E. "Character and Pastorship in Two British 'Sociological' Traditions: Organized Charity, Fabian Socialism, and the Invention of New Liberalism." In *Disciplinarity at the Fin de Siecle,* ed. Amanda Anderson and Joseph Valente, 235–260. Princeton: Princeton University Press, 2002.

———. " 'A Middle Class Cut into Two': Historiography and Victorian National Character." *English Literary History* 67 (2000): 143–178.

———. *Victorian Literature and the Victorian State: Character and Governance in a Liberal Society*. Baltimore: Johns Hopkins University Press, 2003.

Gordon, Eleanor, and Gwyneth Nair. *Public Lives: Women, Family, and Society in Victorian Britain*. New Haven: Yale University Press, 2003.

Gordon, Lesley. "Greek Scholarship and Renaissance Florence in George Eliot's *Romola*." In *George Eliot and Europe*, ed. John Rignall, 179–189. Aldershot: Ashgate, 1997.

Gourvish, T. R. "The Rise of the Professions." In *Later Victorian Britain 1867–1900*, ed. T. R. Gourvish and Alan O'Day, 13–35. New York: St. Martin's, 1988.

Granlund, Helena. *The Paradox of Self-Love: Christian Elements in George Eliot's Treatment of Egoism*. Stockholm, Sweden: Almqvist & Wiskell International, 1994.

Gray, Beryl. "Power and Persuasion: Voices of Influence in *Romola*." In *From Author to Text: Re-Reading George Eliot's* Romola, ed. Caroline Levine and Mark W. Turner, 123–134. Aldershot: Ashgate, 1998.

Greenstein, Susan M. "A Question of Vocation: From *Romola* to *Middlemarch*." *Nineteenth-Century Fiction* 35 (1981): 487–505.

Haber, Samuel. *The Quest for Authority and Honor in the American Professions, 1750–1900*. Chicago: University of Chicago Press, 1991.

Haight, Gordon. *George Eliot: A Biography*. New York: Oxford University Press, 1968.

Hall, N. John. *Trollope: A Biography*. Oxford: Oxford University Press, 1993.

Halperin, John. *Egoism and Self-Discovery in the Victorian Novel: Stories in the Ordeal of Knowledge in the Nineteenth Century*. New York: Burt Franklin, 1974.

———. *Trollope and Politics: A Study of the Pallisers and Others*. London: Harper and Row, 1977.

Handwerk, Gary. "Beyond Sybil's Veil: Disraeli's Mix of Ideological Messages." *Modern Language Quarterly* 49 (1988): 321–341.

Hardy, Barbara. *The Novels of George Eliot: A Study in Form*. London: Athlone Press, University of London, 1959.

Harpham, Geoffrey Galt. *The Ascetic Imperative in Culture and Criticism*. Chicago: University of Chicago Press, 1987.

Harrold, Charles F., and William D. Templeman. *English Prose of the Victorian Era*. New York: Oxford University Press, 1954.

Harvie, Christopher. *The Centre of Things: Political Fiction in Britain from Disraeli to the Present*. London: Unwin Hyman, 1991.

Heeney, Brain. *The Women's Movement in the Church of England, 1850–1930*. Oxford: Clarendon, 1988.

Henberg, M. C. "George Eliot's Moral Realism." *Philosophy and Literature* 3 (1979): 20–38.

Henry, Nancy. *George Eliot and the British Empire*. Cambridge: Cambridge University Press, 2002.

Hertz, Bertha Keveson. "Trollope's Racial Bias against Disraeli." *Midwest Quarterly* 22 (1981) 374–391.

Heyck, T. W. *The Transformation of Intellectual Life in Victorian England*. Chicago: Lyceum, 1982.

Hill, Octavia. *Homes of the London Poor*. 2nd ed. London: Macmillan & Co., 1883. Republished by Frank Cass & Co., London, 1970.

———. *Our Common Land and Other Short Essays*. London: Macmillan & Co., 1887.

———. "Trained Workers for the Poor." Reprinted in *The Voice of Toil: Nineteenth-Century British Writings about Work*, ed. David Bradshaw and Suzanne Ozment, 368–374. Athens, OH: Ohio University Press, 2000.

Hodgson, Peter. *The Mystery Beneath the Real: Theology in the Fiction of George Eliot*. Minneapolis: Fortress Press, 2000.

Holloway, John. *The Victorian Sage: Studies in Argument*. London: Macmillan & Co., 1953.

Homans, Margaret. *Bearing the Word: Language and Female Experience in Nineteenth-Century Women's Writing*. Chicago: University of Chicago Press, 1986.

Hoppen, K. Theodore. *The Mid-Victorian Generation, 1846–1886*. Oxford: Clarendon, 1998.

Jackson, Tony. "George Eliot's 'New Evangel': *Daniel Deronda* and the Ends of Realism." *Genre* 25 (1992): 229–248.

Jamous, Haroun, and B. Peloille. "Changes in the French University-Hospital System." In *Professions and Professionalization*, ed. J. A. Jackson, 111–152. Cambridge: Cambridge University Press, 1970.

Jay, Elisabeth. *The Religion of the Heart: Anglican Evangelicalism and the Nineteenth-Century Novel*. Oxford: Clarendon, 1979.

Jex-Blake, Sophia. *Medical Women: Two Essays*. Edinburgh: Oliphant and Co., 1872.

Joshi, Priti. "Edwin Chadwick's Self-Fashioning: Professionalism, Masculinity, and the Victorian Poor." *Victorian Literature and Culture* 32.2 (2004): 353–370.

Karl, Frederick R. *George Eliot: The Voice of a Century. A Biography*. New York: W. W. Norton, 1995.

Kincaid, James. "Anthony Trollope and the Unmannerly Novel." In *Reading and Writing Women's Lives: A Study of the Novel of Manners*, ed. Bege Bowers and Barbara Brothers, 87–104. Ann Arbor: UMI Research Press, 1990.

Knoepflmacher, U. C. *George Eliot's Early Novels: The Limits of Realism*. Berkeley: University of California Press, 1968.

Koven, Seth. *Slumming: Sexual and Social Politics in Victorian London*. Princeton: Princeton University Press, 2004.

Krueger, Christine. "The 'Female Paternalist' as Historian: Elizabeth Gaskell's *My Lady Ludlow*." In *Rewriting the Victorians: Theory, History and the Politics of Gender*, ed. Linda Shires, 166–183. New York: Routledge, 1992.

———. *The Reader's Repentance: Women Preachers, Women Writers, and Nineteenth-Century Social Discourse*. Chicago: University of Chicago Press, 1992.

Kucich, John. *The Power of Lies: Transgression in Victorian Fiction*. Ithaca, NY: Cornell University Press, 1994.

Kuklick, Henrika. "Professional Status and the Moral Order." In *Disciplinarity at the Fin de Siecle*, ed. Amanda Anderson and Joseph Valente, 126–152. Princeton: Princeton University Press, 2002.

Lane, Christopher. *The Burdens of Intimacy: Psychoanalysis and Victorian Masculinity*. Chicago: University of Chicago Press, 1999.

Langland, Elizabeth. *Nobody's Angels: Middle-Class Women and Domestic Ideology in Victorian Culture*. Ithaca, NY: Cornell University Press, 1995.

Larson, Magali Sarfatti. *The Rise of Professionalism: A Sociological Analysis*. Berkeley: University of California Press, 1977.

Leaver, Elizabeth. "What Will This World Come To?: Old Ways and Education in Elizabeth Gaskell's *My Lady Ludlow*." *Gaskell Society Journal* 10 (1996): 53–64.

Lesjak, Carolyn. "Labours of a Modern Storyteller: George Eliot and the Cultural Project of 'Nationhood.'" In *Victorian Identities: Social and Cultural Formations in Nineteenth-Century Literature*, ed. Ruth Robbins and Julian Wolfreys, 25–42. New York: St. Martin's, 1996.

Lessenich, Rolf. "Synagogue, Church, and Young England: The Jewish Contribution to British Civilization in Benjamin Disraeli's Trilogy." In *Jewish Life and Suffering as Mirrored in English and American Literature*, ed. Franz Link, 33–46. Paderborn: F. Schoningh, 1987.

Letwin, Shirley Robin. *The Gentleman in Trollope: Individuality and Moral Conduct*. Cambridge, MA: Harvard University Press, 1982.

Levin, Beatrice. *Women in Medicine*. Lanham, MD: Scarecrow Press, 2002.

Levine, Caroline. "The Prophetic Fallacy: Realism, Foreshadowing and Narrative Knowledge in *Romola*." In *From Author to Text: Re-Reading George Eliot's Romola*, ed. Caroline Levine and Mark W. Turner, 135–163. Aldershot: Ashgate, 1998.

Levine, Caroline, and Mark W. Turner. "Introduction." In *From Author to Text: Re-reading George Eliot's Romola*, ed. Caroline Levine and Mark W. Turner. Aldershot: Ashgate, 1998.

Levine, Richard A. *Benjamin Disraeli*. New York: Twayne Publishers, 1968.

Lewis, Jane. *Women and Social Action in Victorian and Edwardian England*. Stanford: Stanford University Press, 1991.

Lewis, Reina. *Gendering Orientalism: Race, Femininity and Representation*. New York: Routledge, 1996.

Liebmann, George W. *Six Lost Leaders: Prophets of a Civil Society*. Lanham, MD: Lexington Books, 2001.

Linehan, Katherine Bailey. "Mixed Politics: The Critique of Imperialism in *Daniel Deronda*." *Texas Studies in Literature and Language* 34.3 (1992): 323–346.

Losano, Antonia. "The Professionalization of the Woman Artist in Anne Brontë's *The Tenant of Wildfell Hall*." *Nineteenth-Century Literature* 58.1 (2003): 1–41.

Lovesey, Oliver. *The Clerical Character in George Eliot's Fiction*. English Literary Studies Monograph Series. Victoria, BC: University of Victoria, 1991.

Lubove, Roy. *The Professional Altruist: The Emergence of Social Work as a Career 1880–1930*. Cambridge, MA: Harvard University Press, 1965.

Lucas, John. *The Literature of Change: Studies in the Nineteenth-Century Provincial Novel*. Sussex: Harvester Press, 1977.

Machin, G. I. T. *Politics and the Churches in Great Britain 1832 to 1868*. Oxford: Clarendon, 1977.

MacIver, Robert. "Professional Groups and Cultural Norms." *Professionalization*. Ed. Howard Vollmer and Donald Mills. Englewood Cliffs, NJ: Prentice Hall, 1966. Reprinted from "The Social Significance of Professional Ethics." *The Annals of the American Academy of Political and Social Science* 297 (January 1955): 118–124.

Maltz, Diana. "Beauty at Home or Not? Octavia Hill and the Aesthetics of Tenement Reform." In *Homes and Homelessness in the Victorian Imagination*, ed. Murray Baumgarten and H. M. Daleski, 187–211. New York: AMS Press, 1998.

Mann, Karen. *The Language That Makes George Eliot's Fiction*. Baltimore: Johns Hopkins University Press, 1983.

Marshall, Alfred. *The Memorials of Alfred Marshall*. Ed. A. C. Pigou. New York: Kelley & Millman, 1956.

Marshall, David. *The Figure of Theatre: Shaftesbury, Defoe, Adam Smith, and George Eliot*. New York: Columbia University Press, 1986.

Martindale, Hilda. *Women Servants of the State 1870–1938: A History of Women in the Civil Service*. London: Allen & Unwin, 1938.

Marx, Karl. "On the Jewish Question." In *The Marx-Engels Reader*, ed. Robert Tucker. 2nd ed. New York: W. W. Norton, 1978.

Maurice, Charles Edmund, ed. *Life of Octavia Hill As Told in her Letters*. London: Macmillan & Co., 1914.

Maurice, Emily Southwood. *Octavia Hill: Early Ideals*. London: George Allen & Unwin, 1928.

Menon, Patricia. *Austin, Eliot, Charlotte Brontë and the Mentor-Lover*. London: Palgrave Macmillan, 2003.

Meyer, Susan. *Imperialism at Home*. Ithaca, NY: Cornell University Press, 1996.

———. " 'Safely to Their Own Borders': Proto-Zionism, Feminism, and Nationalism in *Daniel Deronda*." *ELH* 60 (1993): 733–758.

Michalson, Karen. *Victorian Fantasy Literature: Literary Battles with Church and Empire*. Studies in British Literature, vol. 10. Lewiston, NY: Edwin Mellon Press, 1990.

Michie, Elsie B. "Buying Brains: Trollope, Oliphant, and Vulgar Victorian Commerce." *Victorian Studies* 44 (2001): 77–97.

———. *Outside the Pale: Cultural Exclusion, Gender Difference, and the Victorian Woman Writer.* Ithaca, NY: Cornell University Press, 1993.

Miller, D. A. *The Novel and the Police.* Berkeley: University of California Press, 1988.

Mintz, Alan. *George Eliot and the Novel of Vocation.* Cambridge, MA: Harvard University Press, 1978.

Mitchell, Charlotte. Introduction to Novellas and Shorter Fiction II, vol. 3 of *The Works of Elizabeth Gaskell.* London: Pickering and Chatto, 2005.

Monypenny, William Flavelle, and George Earle Buckle. *The Life of Benjamin Disraeli Earl of Beaconsfield.* 6 vols. New York: Macmillan, 1914.

Moretti, Franco. *The Way of the World: The* Bildungsroman *in European Culture.* Trans. Albert Sbragia. London: Verso, 1987.

Myers, William. *The Teaching of George Eliot.* Leicester: Leicester University Press, 1984.

Nardin, Jane. *He Knew She Was Right: The Independent Woman in the Novels of Anthony Trollope.* Carbondale, IL: Southern Illinois University Press, 1989.

———. *Trollope and Victorian Moral Philosophy.* Athens, OH: Ohio University Press, 1996.

Nardo, Anna K. *George Eliot's Dialogue with John Milton.* Columbia, MO: University of Missouri Press, 2003.

Nestor, Pauline. "Leaving Home: George Eliot and *Romola.*" *Women's Writing* 10.2 (2003): 329–342.

Neufeldt, Victor A. "The Madonna and the Gypsy." *Studies in the Novel* 15 (1983): 44–54.

Newton, K. M. *George Eliot: Romantic Humanist: A Study of the Philosophical Structure of Her Novels.* Hong Kong: Macmillan Press, 1981.

Noble, Thomas. *George Eliot's* Scenes of Clerical Life. New Haven: Yale University Press, 1965.

Norris, Christopher. " 'What is Enlightenment?' Kant According to Foucault." In *Reconstructing Foucault: Essays in the Wake of the 80s,* ed. Ricardo Miguel-Alfonso and Silvia Caporale-Bizzini, 53–138. Amsterdam: Rodopi, 1994.

Nurbhai, Saleel and K. M. Newton. *George Eliot, Judaism and the Novels: Jewish Myths and Mysticism.* New York: Palgrave Macmillan, 2002.

O'Day, Rosemary. "The Clerical Renaissance in Victorian England and Wales." In *Religion in Victorian Britain,* vol. 1, ed. Gerald Parsons, 184–212. Manchester: Manchester University Press, 1988.

O'Kell, Robert. "Two Nations, or One? Disraeli's Allegorical Romance." *Victorian Studies* 30 (1987): 211–234.

Onslow, Barbara. *Women of the Press in Nineteenth-Century Britian.* New York: Palgrave Macmillan, 2000.

Payne, James L., ed. *The Befriending Leader: Social Assistance Without Dependency: Essays by Octavia Hill.* Sandpoint, ID: Lytton Publishing Co., 1997.

Penner, Louise. " 'Unmapped Country': Uncovering Hidden Wounds in *Daniel Deronda*." *Victorian Literature and Culture* (2002): 77–97.

Perkin, Harold. *Origins of Modern English Society*. London: Routledge, 1969.

———. *The Rise of Professional Society: England Since 1880*. London: Routledge, 1989.

———. *The Third Revolution: Professional Elites in the Modern World*. London: Routledge, 1996.

Perkin, Joan. *Victorian Women*. New York: New York University Press, 1993.

Peterson, M. Jeanne. *Family, Love, and Work in the Lives of Victorian Gentlewomen*. Bloomington: Indiana University Press, 1989.

Pettitt, Clare. *Patent Inventions—Intellectual Property and the Victorian Novel*. Oxford: Oxford University Press, 2004.

Pionke, Albert. "Combining the Two Nations: Trade Unions as Secret Societies 1837–1845." *Victorian Newsletter* 97 (2000): 1–14.

Plato. *Republic*. Trans. G. M. A. Grube, rev. trans. C. D. C. Reeve. In *Plato: Complete Works*. Ed. John M. Cooper. Indianapolis: Hackett Publishing Company, 1997.

Polizzotto, Lorenzo. *The Elect Nation: The Savonarolan Movement in Florence 1494–1545*. Oxford: Clarendon, 1994.

Pollard, Arthur. *Mrs. Gaskell: Novelist and Biographer*. Cambridge, MA: Harvard University Press, 1966.

Poovey, Mary. *Making a Social Body: English Cultural Formation, 1830–1864*. Chicago: University of Chicago Press, 1995.

———. *Uneven Developments: The Ideological Work of Gender in Mid-Victorian England*. Chicago: University of Chicago Press, 1988.

Prochaska, F. K. *Women and Philanthropy in Nineteenth-Century England*. Oxford: Clarendon, 1980.

Ragussis, Michael. *Figures of Conversion: "The Jewish Question" and English National Identity*. Durham: Duke University Press, 1995.

Reader, W. J. *Professional Men: The Rise of the Professional Classes in Nineteenth-Century England*. New York: Basic Books, 1966.

Ridolfi, Roberto. *The Life of Girolamo Savonarola*. Trans. Cecil Grayson. Westport, CN: Greenwood Press, 1959.

Rivers, Bronwyn. *Women at Work in the Victorian Novel: The Question of Middle Class Women's Employment*. Lewiston, NY: Edwin Mellon Press, 2005.

Robbins, Bruce. "Death and Vocation: Narrativizing Narrative Theory." *PMLA* 107.1 (1992): 38–50.

———. *Feeling Global: Internationalism in Distress*. New York: New York University Press, 1999.

———. "Forum." *PMLA* 108:3 (1993): 541–542.

———. *Secular Vocations: Intellectuals, Professionalism, and Culture*. London: Verso, 1993.

———. "Telescopic Philanthropy: Professionalism and Responsibility in *Bleak House*." In *Nation and Narration*, ed. Homi Bhabha, 213–230. London: Routledge, 1990.

————. "The Village of the Liberal Managerial Class." In *Cosmopolitan Geographies: New Locations in Literature and Culture*, ed. Vinay Dharwadker, 15–32. New York: Routledge, 2001.

Roy, Parama. "*Sybil*: The Two Nations and the Manorial Ideal." *Victorians Institute Journal* 17 (1989): 63–75.

Rubenius, Aina. *The Woman Question in Mrs. Gaskell's Life and Works*. The English Institute in the University of Upsala: Essays and Studies on English Language and Literature. Upsala: Almqvist & Wiksells Boktryckeri Ab, 1950.

Ruskin, John. "The Mystery of Life and Its Arts." 1868. In *The Works of John Ruskin*, ed. E. T. Cook and Alexander Wedderburn, Vol. 18, 145–187. London: George Allen & Unwin, 1905.

————. "Roots of Honor." *Unto This Last and Other Writings*. 1860. New York: Penguin, 1985.

Ruth, Jennifer. *Novel Professions: Interested Disinterest and the Making of the Professional in the Victorian Novel*. Victorian Critical Interventions. Columbus: Ohio State University Press, 2006.

Said, Edward. "Foucault and the Imagination of Power." In *Foucault: A Critical Reader*, ed. David Couzens Hoy, 149–155. Oxford: Blackwell, 1986.

————. *Orientalism*. New York: Pantheon Books, 1978.

————. "Zionism from the Standpoint of its Victims." In *Dangerous Liaisons: Gender, Nation, and Postcolonial Perspectives*, ed. Anne McClintock, Aamir Mufti, and Ella Shohat, 15–38. Minneapolis: University of Minnesota Press, 1997.

Sampson, Jennifer. "*Sybil*, or the Two Monarchs." *Studies in Philology* 95 (1998): 97–119.

Savage, Gail L. "Wrongful Confinement: The Betrayal of Women by Men, Medicine, and Law." In *Victorian Scandals: Representations of Gender and Class*, ed. Kristine Ottesen Garrigan, 43–68. Athens, OH: Ohio University Press, 1992.

Savonarola, Girolamo, O. P. *Prison Meditations on Psalms 51 and 31*. Ed. and trans. John Patrick Donnelly, S. J. Milwaukee: Marquette University Press, 1994.

Sawaya, Francesca. *Modern Women, Modern Work: Domesticity, Professionalism, and American Writing, 1890–1950*. Rethinking the Americas. Philadelphia: University of Pennsylvania Press, 2004.

Schaub, Melissa "Sympathy and Discipline in *Mary Barton*." *Victorian Newsletter* 106 (2004): 15–20.

Schor, Hilary M. *Scheherezade in the Marketplace: Elizabeth Gaskell and the Victorian Novel*. Oxford: Oxford University Press, 1992.

Schwartz, Daniel. "Art and Argument in Disraeli's *Sybil*." *Journal of Narrative Theory* 4 (1974): 19–31.

————. *Disraeli's Fiction*. London: Macmillan, 1979.

Searle, Geoffrey. *Morality and the Market in Victorian Britain*. Oxford: Clarendon, 1998.

Sharps, John. *Mrs. Gaskell's Observation and Invention: A Study of Her Non-Biographic Works.* Fontwell, Sussex: Linden Press, 1970.

Shuman, Cathy. *Pedagogical Economies: The Examination and the Victorian Literary Man.* Stanford: Stanford University Press, 2000.

Smiles, Samuel. *Self-Help: With Illustrations of Character, Conduct, and Perseverence.* Nashville, TN: M. E. Church, 1912.

Smith, Paul. *Disraeli: A Brief Life.* Cambridge: Cambridge University Press, 1996.

Sorenson, Katherine M. "*Daniel Deronda* and George Eliot's Ministers." *Victorians Institute Journal* 19 (1991): 89–110.

Speare, Morris Edmund. *The Political Novel: Its Development in England and in America.* New York: Oxford University Press, 1924.

Stewart, R. W., ed. *Disraeli's Novels Reviewed, 1826–1968.* Metuchen, NJ: Scarecrow Press, 1975.

Stone, Carole. "George Eliot's *Daniel Deronda*: The Case-History of Gwendolen H." *Nineteenth-Century Studies* 7 (1993): 57–67.

Summers, Anne. "A Home from Home—Women's Philanthropic Work in the Nineteenth Century." In *Fit Work for Women,* ed. Sandra Burman, 33–63. New York: St. Martin's, 1979.

Super, R. H. *Trollope and the Post Office.* Ann Arbor: University of Michigan Press, 1981.

Swenson, Kristine. *Medical Women and Victorian Fiction.* Columbia, MO: University of Missouri Press, 2005.

Swindells, Julia. *Victorian Writing and Working Women: The Other Side of Silence.* Minneapolis: University of Minnesota Press, 1985.

Tarn, John Nelson. *Five Per Cent Philanthropy: An Account of Housing in Urban Areas Between 1840 and 1914.* Cambridge: Cambridge University Press, 1973.

Terry, R. C. *Trollope: Interviews and Recollections.* New York: St. Martin's, 1987.

Thomas, Jeanie. *Reading* Middlemarch: *Reclaiming the Middle Distance.* Ann Arbor: UMI Research Press, 1987.

Thompson, Kenneth A. *Bureaucracy and Church Reform: The Organizational Response of the Church of England to Social Change 1800–1965.* Clarendon: Oxford University Press, 1970.

Thomson, H. Byerley. *The Choice of a Profession: A Concise Account and Comparative Review of the English Professions.* London: Chapman and Hall, 1857.

Toker, Leona. "Vocation and Sympathy in *Daniel Deronda*: The Self and the Larger Whole." *Victorian Literature and Culture* 32.2 (2004): 565–574.

Trollope, Anthony. *Autobiography.* 1883. New York: Houghton Mifflin, 1918.

———. *Barchester Towers.* 1857. Ed. Michael Sadleir and Frederick Page. Oxford World's Classics. Oxford: Oxford University Press, 1996.

———. "The Civil Service as a Profession." 1861. *Four Lectures.* Ed. Morris Parrish. London: Constable & Co., 1938.

————. *The Last Chronicle of Barset.* 1867. Ed. Stephen Gill. Oxford World's Classics. Oxford: Oxford University Press, 1989.

————. *The New Zealander.* Ed. N. John Hall. Oxford: Clarendon Press, 1972.

————. *The Three Clerks.* 1858. London: Oxford University Press, 1929.

————. *The Warden.* 1855. Ed. David Skilton. The World's Classics. Oxford: Oxford University Press, 1980.

Uglow, Jenny. *Elizabeth Gaskell: A Habit of Stories.* New York: Farrar Straus Giroux, 1993.

Ulrich, John M. *Signs of Their Times: History, Labor, and the Body in Cobbett, Carlyle, and Disraeli.* Athens, OH: Ohio University Press, 2002.

Villari, Pasquale. *Life and Times of Girolamo Savonarola.* Trans. Linda Villari. 10th ed. London: T. Fisher Unwin, 1909.

Webb, Beatrice. *My Apprenticeship.* London: Longman, 1926.

Weber, Max. *The Protestant Ethic and the Spirit of Capitalism.* Trans. Talcott Parsons. New York: Charles Scribner's Sons, 1958.

Weintraub, Stanley. *Disraeli: A Biography.* New York: Truman Talley Books/Dutton, 1993.

Weisser, Susan Ostrov. "Gwendolen's Hidden Wound: Sexual Possibilities and Impossibilities in *Daniel Deronda.*" *Modern Language Studies* 20.3 (1990): 3–13.

Whelan, Robert, ed. *Octavia Hill and the Social Housing Debate: Essays and Letters by Octavia Hill.* London: The IEA Health and Welfare Unit. Rediscovered Riches No. 3. 1998.

Whipple, E. P. "Dickens's *Hard Times.*" *The Atlantic Monthly* 39 (March 1877): 353–58.

Wiesenfarth, Joseph. *George Eliot's Mythmaking.* Heidelberg: Carl Winter Universitätsverlag, 1977.

Williams, Raymond. *Culture and Society, 1780–1950.* New York: Columbia University Press, 1983.

Winnifrith, Tom. "Renaissance and Risorgimento in *Romola.*" In *George Eliot and Europe,* ed. John Rignall, 166–178. Aldershot: Ashgate, 1997.

Witz, Anne. *Professions and Patriarchy.* London: Routledge, 1992.

Wohl, Anthony S. *The Eternal Slum: Housing and Social Policy in Victorian London.* Montreal: McGill-Queen's University Press, 1977.

Woodroofe, Kathleen. *From Charity to Social Work in England and the United States.* Toronto: University of Toronto Press, 1962.

Wright, Edgar. "*My Lady Ludlow*: Forms of Social Change and Forms of Fiction." *Gaskell Society Journal* 3 (1989): 29–41.

Wright, Terence. *Elizabeth Gaskell "We are not angels": Realism, Gender, Values.* New York: St. Martin's, 1995.

Yeazell, Ruth Bernard. "Why Political Novels Have Heroines: *Sybil, Mary Barton,* and *Felix Holt.*" *Novel* 18.2 (1985): 126–144.

Young, A. F., and E. T. Ashton. *British Social Work in the Nineteenth Century.* London: Routledge, 1956.

Zlotnick, Susan. *Women, Writing, and Industrial Revolution.* Baltimore: Johns Hopkins University Press, 1998.

INDEX